The Realms of
Ancient Series

SCION *of the* FOX

S.M. BEIKO

SCION

OF THE

FOX

THE REALMS OF ANCIENT

ECW

Published by ECW Press
665 Gerrard Street East, Toronto, ON M4M 1Y2
416-694-3348 / info@ecwpress.com

This is a work of fiction. Names, characters, places, and incidents either are the product of the author's imagination or are used fictitiously, and any resemblance to actual persons, living or dead, business establishments, events, or locales is entirely coincidental.

Editor for the press: Jen Hale
Cover design: Erik Mohr
Interior illustration: S.M. Beiko
Author photo: Teri Hoffard Photography
Type: Rachel Ironstone

Library and Archives Canada
Cataloguing in Publication

Beiko, Samantha, author
Scion of the Fox / S.M. Beiko.
(The realms of ancient ; book 1)
Issued also in electronic formats.
ISBN 978-1-77041-357-3 (hardcover)
ISBN 978-1-77305-070-6 (PDF)
ISBN 978-1-77305-071-3 (EPUB)
I. Title.
PS8603.E428444S25 2017
jC813'.6   C2017-902409-4
C2017-902988-6

The publication of *Scion of the Fox* has been generously supported by the Manitoba Arts Council, by the Canada Council for the Arts, which last year invested $153 million to bring the arts to Canadians throughout the country, and by the Government of Canada through the Canada Book Fund. *Nous remercions le Conseil des arts du Canada de son soutien. L'an dernier, le Conseil a investi 153 millions de dollars pour mettre de l'art dans la vie des Canadiennes et des Canadiens de tout le pays. Ce livre est financé en partie par le gouvernement du Canada.* We also acknowledge the support of the Ontario Arts Council (OAC), an agency of the Government of Ontario, which last year funded 1,737 individual artists and 1,095 organizations in 223 communities across Ontario for a total of $52.1 million, and the contribution of the Government of Ontario through the Ontario Book Publishing Tax Credit and the Ontario Media Development Corporation.

Printed and bound in Canada by Friesens
5   4   3   2   1

To any young person who has ever felt powerless.
There is only one of you in this entire world.
That is your superpower.
You brighten the world by being in it.

It was snowing — no real shocker in February. Plows and salt trucks couldn't keep up, the snow disposal sites and the boulevards piling high. These were the Martian conditions we were used to in Winnipeg. No one batted an eye.

I rode my bike through the bad weather. It made me feel independent, stronger than I really was. People call winter cyclists crazy for good reason. I stood in the seat, tires gripping the fresh powder over the train tracks on Wellington Crescent. But I didn't see her in time, and I lost control, twisted, and flew over my handlebars, joining her prone body in the road.

I couldn't move, face to face with blank eyes and icy flesh. The girl was dead, yeah, but well preserved, the weather doing double duty as a morgue cooler. The frost had kept her pretty face safe, made her look carved out of ice and porcelain.

Stumbling to my feet, I struggled to move my numb hands. She'd made a snow angel before she died, wings scuffed around her broken arms, crooked legs frozen mid-dance. Her mouth was open in a hollow scream.

This was the first dead body I'd ever seen. I hadn't even seen my parents' bodies after the accident, so it felt as though this one belonged to me. Her hair was red. Her knees were knobby. And her eye had been gouged out — we could almost pass for sisters. Even though it was a horrible thing to see — like looking into a death mirror — I knew this body was meant for me to find.

I didn't scream. I didn't do anything. I should have, because *reacting in the slightest way* would've eked me out as "a stable human." But let's face it — I was too far gone for that.

Before any cars could pull over to see what the lone girl by the train tracks was staring at, before the police and the ambulance and the news trucks could appear to wrap the girl in a cocoon of speculation and black plastic — before they found out it was my fault — all I could do was grab my bike and ride away until my legs were stone, trying not to think of all the things that were coming for me in broad daylight, or how my brain buzzed with two words: *You're next.*

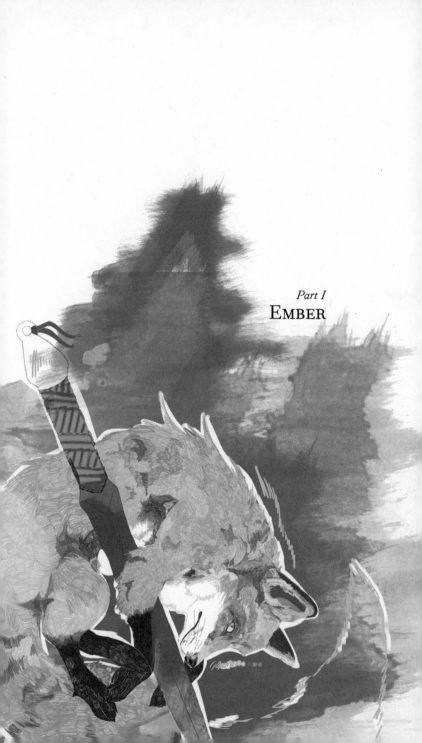

Part I
EMBER

The STONE FOX

Oh she's so glamorous, she's so cool, long legs that go to heaven and lips that tell me to get outta town. Pretty lady that won't give me the time of day — she's a stoooone FOX!

That song. The song my dad used to sing at my mom on the good and the bad days. It's my only memory of my parents. I was too young when they died, became an orphan before any other memories could stick. But this one did.

My dad singing intentionally off-key, chasing Mom around the kitchen until she gave up being mad at him for whatever unspeakable thing hung between them, and then they'd kiss and make it better. I'd squeal and demand to be picked up, to be a part of their fun, and we'd hold each other until I fussed to be put down again. I felt their love like a fire. They loved me. I know they did. Even if it didn't last.

My mother was a compact creature. Very hard to crack. Sometimes she would lock herself in my dad's little greenhouse and go quiet for days. She would let only me in (though I don't remember my father ever trying to get through to her), and I'd give her peanut-butter-and-banana sandwiches that my sloppy preschool hands had made, hoping it would make her remember she had to love us. It was as hot as a sauna in there, even in winter, the warmth rolling off her in angry waves. I would find her in the back by the stuff Dad called *belladonna*, and she would be staring out through the glass, fixated on our big yard as if imprisoned.

She spoke like someone else was standing over her, and she'd say something like, "A darling little stone menagerie, with the power to kill and create." Was it a fairy tale she was telling me? Was she even speaking to me at all?

I never asked. I should have.

Instead, I would put down the sandwich and jump to see over the table of plants and out at the little statue garden. Still in her trance, and without looking away, my mother would lift me as if I were a pebble in the palm of her hand.

Then I would wind my fingers in her seemingly infinite hair. "The fox is the prettiest, Mommy, the prettiest like you."

She sighed and squeezed me so tight it hurt, but I didn't ask her to stop.

Out in the garden, there was a pair of stone deer leaping. A stone owl midflight. A stone seal diving through a stone wave, a stone rabbit bolting, and, yes, a stone fox. It sat amongst them but apart from them, still and staring and quiet. The set had been a present from my grandma, my mother's mother. There was no special occasion, but a truck had backed into our yard one day with men hired to move the statues into it.

I frolicked and cartwheeled that summer, feeling like it

was Christmas in July. But my mother just stood there, still as a warrior waiting for the next onslaught.

Take it back, she'd scream over the phone to someone I never knew. *I don't want it anywhere near this family.* My dad would try to calm her, but she'd only grow angrier. *She's telling me to just accept it. To let it happen for the greater good. I won't! I won't let them take her!*

We'll find another way.

I wish I'd been old enough to ask. I wish they could have trusted me with their secrets.

The statues had been my grandmother's and now they were ours. I never met my grandmother, or if I did, I don't remember what she looked like. She went far, far away before I was born. Mom never talked about her, but I could tell she thought about her often; mouth set in a hard line, beryl eyes crystallized. She stared at the statues. She hated them. And was maybe afraid of them, too.

Once, I climbed up onto the deer, gripping its ears or antlers and pretending I was riding it. Like we were flying through a forest being chased by whatever evil thing pursues kids and ultimately fails to catch them. I saw my mother and scrambled off. I wasn't allowed near them. I thought I was in trouble.

But she only folded her arms. She had accepted something I didn't understand, and instead of disciplining me, she wondered aloud if I'd asked the deer permission to ride them. I felt suddenly guilty, as if the statues were real. I didn't say anything. But she said that if I asked for something with true and honest intention, I'd always get what I needed. Then she left me alone.

I should have *asked*.

I didn't ride the deer after that. When I looked at the statues closely, eternally jumping or flying or sprinting, I realized they were all running away from something. Except the fox. It gave off warmth. Sometimes when I sat very still, I could hear it whispering stories to me, tales of things I'd never understand.

Kid stuff. Imaginary friend complex.

Back in the greenhouse, my mother would stare into the dark whirlpool in her head that I couldn't see, saying nothing for a long time. But she wouldn't move from that spot. For hours, for ages. But I'd keep by her, until I fell asleep. I'd wake up in my bed the next day, like it was all a dream.

And sometime later, I'd hear Mom and Dad downstairs, Dad singing the stone fox song to Mom until she gave in to his kisses. And we'd all be happy again. I don't remember the last time I heard the song. Just the absence of it.

My mother was twenty-eight when she died. Dad's friend Audrey from his gardening club was looking after me in her sweet-smelling bungalow when she got the call. My parents had driven out to Assiniboine Park; my father could work wonders with plants, and the city consulted him when designing the elaborate English Gardens that tourists and locals fell all over.

When I was old enough to understand, I'd heard it went like this:

Their little Volvo plowed right through the fencing along the bike path, careening headlong into the river. They dredged the car from the water, but they could not find my mother's body. My father's washed up like a discarded shopping cart on a bank near the Alexander docks. My mother evaded local crime scene investigators until they eventually gave up — *Must have washed all the way to the States*, they said. I thought maybe she had gone off on an adventure, like the heroes of my stories, and that she'd left us behind to protect us. *An accident*, they'd officially said. *Maybe intentional*, others whispered. We'd never know.

But nothing could be so easy. The dead never rest when they've left too many secrets behind. I only learned that after the moths.

The SIGIL *of the* MOTH QUEEN

Five days before the dead body in the snow, and fourteen years after Ravenna and Aaron Harken inhaled a lungful of the Assiniboine, I sat in the back of English class, trying really, *really* hard not to rub my left eye. The best solution I'd come up with after all these years was to claw at the eye patch I wore over it, faking relief. I had a bunch of eye patches actually, and I took pride in decorating them. The plan was to wear my disability like a badge, to show people I didn't care.

But after adjusting the patch in the mirror every morning before school, I'd inevitably cover it with my messy auburn hair. It took less energy to hide it than own it. My left eye had had this lingering infection thing since I was small. I'd apparently started rubbing it sometime after my parents' deaths and couldn't stop. The psychologists branded this a coping mechanism and shrugged it off.

And it got worse. A "chronic weeping infection," caused

by what could've been an autoimmune disorder. All I could do was use drops and antibiotics, keep it covered, and hope I'd grow out of it. Stress made it worse. And I was always stressed. Vicious cycle.

I tried to stay positive. I was always trying really, *really* hard at that. But tapping on the patch wasn't doing a damn thing, so I dug my pen into the well-worn groove on my desktop, wishing it was my eye, wishing I could just grind it out and trade it for a bionic one that shot lasers and gave me some social cred.

I felt a hand on my arm and looked up. Phae's placid, deep-brown face was in mine, and she was shaking her head. Smiling, she told me to take a deep breath and sit back. So I shut my good eye and my evil eye, and sighed deeply. It worked for a few seconds. *Breathe*, a wise dwarf once said. *That's the key*.

Thankfully, it was the end of the day. The bell went off and everyone stuffed their bags desperately, afraid that if they didn't move fast enough they wouldn't be allowed to leave. I tucked my well-worn copy of *Wuthering Heights* into my bag.

". . . and it wouldn't be so bad if you weren't on edge all the time. Stress is a killer," Phae was saying. Phae was always trying to help. "Why don't we try yoga again in my studio? I promise it gets better after the first time."

I was feeling generous, so I did the math for her. "C'mon, Phae. Me plus contortionist calisthenics minus one eye equals doom." I shouldered my bag. "Don't worry about me. I've just got the usual stuff on my mind."

I didn't elaborate. Usual stuff could mean anything. Usual teenager stuff — grades, periods, boyfriends (or lack of interest in them), body anxieties, family drama, trying to fit in at school — yep, all boxes checked. Then there were the extras. Double dead parents. Freaky new house. Gunky eyeball . . .

Everyone was rushing for the door, including the few peers Mrs. Mills asked me to help with essay composition. I felt like she was punishing me for being a good student, because these particular kids didn't give a crap about English or the provincial exams coming up next term. Which meant they gave *less* of a crap about me, if that was possible.

If you haven't gotten it already, I wasn't exactly a social butterfly, or up to confrontation, so when I called out to John Hardwick and the rest of his cronies about their practice essays, they threw glances over their shoulders, sneering and slapping each other on the backs. Ugh, whatever. Let 'em fail. They'd still end up CEOs.

Phae came to my side, smiling and shrugging as she steered me towards our lockers.

Tutoring my peers, caring about school, keeping to myself. I'd been making it seem like I had it all together, that I had plans and goals, because I didn't want tragedy to always define me. Besides, grades, private teenage thoughts, fleeting attempts at friendships — these were the things normal people cared about, right? I felt like each one got me closer to the status quo that everyone around me took for granted, and mercifully farther away from the pang of having little direction in life except *forward*.

But right now, I wanted to live. I wanted my biggest concerns to be getting into university, having some semblance of privacy, or worrying about what kind of leftovers I could heat up after ten p.m. without my aunt knowing. I wanted it all badly enough to put the eye patch on every day, to tutor lazy idiots on their shitty papers, and steer any cruelty or pity, intended or otherwise, into the immense vortex caused by my convincing and well-practised Brave Face. And so far it was working, except when a few impulses slipped through the cracks.

My eye twitched and I reached for it.

Phae slapped my hand away from my face, full stop.

I winced. "Hey, we trying physical abuse now, guru?"

I felt Phae squirting my palms with hand sanitizer. "I think abuse is my only remaining option. This place is a germ factory, and you're shoving your fingers *into your infected eye?*"

Oh, Phaedrapramit Das. Calming manatee and life coach since grade three. She'd marked me as her best friend almost immediately, asking blunt but kind questions about my eye and if I needed someone to talk to, on account of my dead parents and all, since, according to all the books she'd read, orphans were the ones who had it roughest. I think she mostly stuck by me because I was helpless with some things, even though I tried hard (and failed) to look capable.

I flexed my now-sanitized hands, squeezing them into fists. "It feels really bad today. I don't know." I lifted the patch. "I know this is gross, but, can you . . . ?"

Phae was on the med-school track, and no injury had ever phased her. But I noticed a tremor at the edge of her mouth when she frowned. "That bad, huh?"

She leaned in for a closer look. "It looks worse than usual, that's for sure." She ushered me up to my cheap plastic locker mirror. "That lump there is very large and red. Can't you feel it under your eye?"

The truth was, I couldn't. And seeing it in the mirror was such a shock that I had to look away before I started prodding it. It looked like something from a hospital horror BuzzFeed article. I slapped the patch down and my hair over it.

"No, it just . . . it feels irritated, that's all. There's been swelling like that before, though, so . . ." I didn't mention the headache creeping on. Seeing that lump really freaked me out.

"Go to the emergency, Roan. Seriously."

I waved her off. "Look, it's the end of the day. If it's worse in the morning, I'll skip first period and go to a walk-in clinic."

Phae fussed all the way into the winter air and to the bike racks, and I promised I'd text her a play-by-play of my mutating opto-tumour if it made her feel any better. As I ran my bike up to the road and started pedalling, I was already strategizing how I'd manoeuvre around Deedee and Arnas. Phae was bad enough (in a good way), but my aunt and uncle were tougher to get around. Well, Arnas wasn't too bad, since he had always been as assertive as a two-by-four, but where he lacked, Deedee made up in spades . . . in a loving, hypochondriac way.

Arnas was my father's brother, and Deidre, his wife. They weren't technically married, but they had been together for as long as the "conventional" parents of my classmates. Deidre was doting and always concerned (all the doctors' and psych visits had been her idea) and always busy. She said that sitting still was something she could do when she was dead. I admired her tenacity, but it had been a long day, and I didn't need someone else going, *Oh hey, what's wrong? Here are a hundred suggestions — fuss, preen — let me get you something*. Good intentions and all, but the last thing I wanted was another helicopter hovering over my life. And a lump now? God, it hadn't been *that* bad before. Maybe I could check WebMD when I got home. What I'd find there would probably be worse than Deedee, though.

I pulled up to the house and stared up at it before parking my bike. Being here felt like crash-landing on an alien planet.

This house wasn't mine, and in the year since we'd moved in, it still didn't feel like home. And this house wasn't Deidre's or Arnas's, either; it belonged to my grandmother, the one who had given us the stone menagerie. When my parents died, my aunt and uncle moved in with me in the house I grew up in — a white little Wolseley two-storey, ivy growing up the front, greenhouse in the back — to keep my life as uninterrupted as possible, tragedy notwithstanding. I spent a lot of time in that greenhouse after it all happened, trying to tend the plants that my father could will out of the dirt with a promise. They all died, of course. Neither Arnas nor Deidre had any interest or passion for plants. They turned the greenhouse into a shed, but it didn't stop me from going in there, digging my hands into the earth, and missing my mother.

We stayed there up until last year, when the lawyer's letter came. I hadn't seen or heard from my grandmother since we got the statues. After that, she seemed to just melt back into the absence I was accustomed to, travelling all over the world for "work," the nebulous excuse I was always fed when I asked about her. She was just as compact as my mother, except so unreachable as to exist in some other dimension. She would sometimes send me postcards with pictures of exotic places. She only sent them to me, and that made me feel like I was a part of her strange adventures. That's what I told myself, anyway.

Then the postcards stopped. And the lawyer's letter came.

I took my bike around the side of the enormous house and to the backyard, where I locked it to the black wrought-iron fence hemming in the property. On my way to the door, I paused at the stone menagerie. Deidre had it moved here with us. I thought, at first, that it was a gesture to make me feel better, but it was one of the many weird "stipulations" we had to fulfill to stay here.

The stone fox stared at me from between the legs of its companions. An untouched layer of snow frosted each statue except the fox's, and for a second I swore its eyes flickered at me, almost hot as they met mine. My bad eye tingled harder than it had all day, and my hand shot up to it.

"There you are!"

I whipped around, more than startled. "Gee-*ʒus*, Dee, can you quit it with the ninja stealth?" I clutched my heart, trying to laugh off the fact that it was slapping around my rib cage like a trapped bird.

Deidre rolled her eyes under the black fringe of her perfect bob. "Teenagers only get jumpy when they're up to something." She held the back door open, smile twitching. The inquisition was coming.

On my way in, I threw one last look behind me at the stone fox. Its stone eyes were settled in its stone head. I was already forgetting what I thought I'd seen.

And Deidre was already on the fuss-track. "I saw you pawing your eye out there, missy." She poured herself a steaming mug of coffee and, without giving it a second to cool off, she'd downed the contents.

I just wanted to beat a hasty retreat to my room for some peace and quiet. I tried to sidestep her impending investigation. "Uh. Yeah, it's just a bit itchy, that's all. The usual. Just going to put my drops in . . ."

"Are you sure you don't want me to look at it?" Deedee had already ditched her mug and reached for me.

"No, no," I said, trying to desperately ignore how my eye felt like it was going to burst out of my skull and scuttle across the granite floor. *Awkward*. "C'mon, Deedee, can't we talk about *you* for once? Where's Arnas?"

Deidre swooped into my path like Bela Lugosi before I could dodge her up the stairs and head to my room. I was losing at exercising tact here, leaving me with the only option of faking a hormonal tantrum just to escape.

But Deedee was suddenly distracted, glancing up the stairs and back at me, instantly forgetting about my eye. "Look, I wanted to talk to you about . . . well, you know. The other resident."

I peered past the shoulder of Deidre's grey blazer, eyes searching for the room that hovered above our lives on the third floor. "You mean the host."

Crash. We both froze, and suddenly Arnas's head poked into the hall, glomming his wet eyes onto Deidre. "You'd better get up there, that's about the third time today."

Deidre was already taking the stairs two at a time. "Thanks for the heads up," she grumbled, and curious enough to ignore the heartbeat in my eye socket, I followed her.

We flew past the room that Arnas had taken as his study. I caught a glimpse of him in passing; he shrugged uselessly, looked at the carpet, and shut the door — his usual reaction to anything he wanted to avoid (read: reality).

Uncle Arnas . . . not much to say about him. He was a ropey guy, features long and narrow like a scarecrow's. And he always looked somewhat troubled, guilty. Maybe that's just the way his face was made, but he'd been more distant lately — if that were possible. He may be my father's only brother — his fraternal twin, actually — but aside from having shared the same womb, I'd never known two people to be so different. From what fading snippets I remembered of my dad, he was so full of life. Arnas barely spoke but to complain, or to relate a new bit of paranoia, or to cluck about his sciatica. He was a freelance editor, so he retreated into work and left Deidre to handle anything difficult that went on in our house. He was pretty much an extra in the play of his life.

I don't know how Deidre dealt with him, off in his weird world and totally vacant from this one. And things between them lately had been terribly tense, but no one seemed willing to talk about why. He barely looked at me anymore.

When I got to the hallway on the third floor, Deidre was talking in a low voice to one of the nurses who had been consoling a much younger nurse in tears and holding her hands out, palms up. They were red and blistered, ice packs pressed into them. The source of the crash had been a ceramic basin, now in pieces coming loose of the bedsheet the basin had been wrapped in.

I gave them all a wide berth, but I could hear the cogent nurse telling Deidre what happened: "She just said she was bathing her and the water suddenly got very hot. So hot she burned herself. It's just that this is the third or fourth incident, you understand. And well, naturally, the lot of us aren't really sure what's going on."

Deidre's classic forehead knot made a cameo as she tried to push back her disbelief. "I really don't get it, we had someone come in to service the boiler and check the heating system the last time. He said nothing was wrong, and it's the middle of *winter . . .*"

I checked to make sure Deidre was fully engrossed with the nurses. I heard the words *strange voices* and *sorry* and *this might not work out for us* as I slipped inside the master bedroom.

There were wide, beautiful windows overlooking the street and the Assiniboine River on one side of the room, but they were half shuttered to the sunlight as it faded over the west. This room, like so many of the closed-up, unused rooms throughout the house, was filled with beautiful furniture, all mismatched and from varied countries and eras. My grandmother had eclectic taste, and the spoils of her life had accumulated in this massive, lonely house. My hands danced over her vanity, the kind of table and mirror in which a vaudeville starlet would fawn over herself, staring past silver-gilt hair brushes and pearls and a bundle of age-yellowed letters tied with twine.

I wish I'd known more about her. Wish she had taken me with her on her mysterious globe-trekking adventures. All I knew about her was enclosed in a handful of postcards, locked in barely-sentence-long observations about cities I had never heard of and climates filled with spices.

It was even worse, seeing her on the bed in the centre of the room, looking even smaller than she had the last time I'd been in here, like the bed was absorbing her into the sheets.

Cecelia. Her name gave away a kind of glamour — not just the Hollywood type of glamour, but capital-G Morgan le Fay faerie-realm kind. She was at least sixty-five, but her face didn't really look it, except for the slackened features and pale skin that came with a deep coma. She'd lived a full life and had a few lines to prove it, true. But her flesh cleaved to her bones protectively, and even now, on her literal death-bed, she was beautiful.

And I stared at her now just to hope. Hope that maybe I'd escape my awkward seventeen-year-old phase and grow into such a face as the one on that bed. It also gave me comfort that here lay my last connection to my mother's family, and that — even though I would be soon — at this moment I wasn't alone.

There really hadn't been much warning. I hadn't heard from her in years. Arnas referenced some vague falling-out that Cecelia had with my parents, that she had her issues and it *wasn't a shock* that she'd lost touch. It was a while before Arnas thought to bring that up, though, and that was well after the letter.

Cecelia had collapsed at the airport in Toronto on a return trip from Greenland, brought down by a sudden seizure that had rendered her a rag doll in less than a second. She hadn't been alone on the trip, thankfully, and after that she was admitted to hospital. *Aneurysm*, they said. Her travel companion tapped her lawyer for whatever arrangements Cecelia had made for her personal care. And her wishes would baffle a genie:

Return me to Winnipeg despite whatever state I'm in.

Alert my next of kin that they are to take residence in my home for the duration of my hospice care.

Do not remove my life support until I have expired of my own accord.

This last one had been the most confusing of all. She had been in this coma for the past six months, an unfamiliar wax figure with a thousand secrets behind closed eyes.

So here she was, hooked up to a ventilator, fed all the liquid food groups via tubes, the waste products carried away into sterile little bags by yet more tubes. She had the charitable forethought to be mysteriously wealthy in order to pay for the personal health care staff *ad infinitum*, but why she had to drag us into it was beyond me. Maybe she just wanted to be surrounded by family at the end?

A nice thought. Except that I was her only relative left, and if she'd had no love for my dad, she'd have even less for Arnas. So while I sometimes came into her room to sit next to her, I never ended up saying much, like they do in the movies, thinking it'll help. Too many futile questions — questions about my mother, about Cecelia herself, and most of all, why she didn't feel the need to bring me closer to her when I was young and things were hardest. And now, without a clue as to why, she expected us to drop everything and hang around in her dusty house of rare objects until she croaked?

All of this would clatter around inside me until I would get so mad, knowing she was right there but out of my reach, that I'd have to stay away from her cloying room for a while. She had parts of me locked inside her that I needed but I'd never have access to.

But I stood there this time, at her bedside, chewing my nails and trying not to punch my eye or screw my fist into it. I felt like I needed to be here today when the nurses were burning themselves on possessed basins and hearing voices and complaining about the heat of the room. It felt comfortable to me in here, but who knows. There'd been a pretty quick turnaround on the in-home nursing staff lately. Arnas muttered something about *foreigners* and their deep-seated *cultural paranoias*.

"Psst."

I whipped my head to the doorway, chest pounding. Of course it was Deidre, beckoning me out. I looked back down at the shrinking woman in the grand bed, shook my head, and left.

❦

It was late. My eye hadn't improved, and I was getting worried. Worried to the point that I couldn't sleep, and I found myself padding down to the kitchen.

I cupped my hands under the cool tap water, bringing my eye down to meet it. It offered only a second's relief. I'd jokingly asked Deidre for an eyewash station in my room for my seventeenth birthday and, man, now I wish I'd been serious.

I dabbed my eye with a wet paper towel. I tried to ignore the lump, even though it felt bigger than before. The burning was something new, same with the swelling, and it was getting to the point where even sleep wouldn't make these symptoms, or the headache, go away. I caught my reflection in the kitchen window and scowled at it and the darkness beyond speckled by falling snow. *Sticking my head in a snowbank might actually be therapeutic*, I thought, before I focused out and saw the stone menagerie beyond the window.

I threw on my jacket and stuffed my thick legs into my boots, careful to unlatch the back door to avoid triggering the motion light. I popped my hood up and trudged into the yard, until I was standing in front of the stone animals, my breath a clouded curtain that dissolved to reveal shattered stone at my feet.

There was nothing much left of the fox. I knelt down and scooped up the remains of its pointed head, brushing the snow off its elegant snout, whiskers, and nose. There were pieces scattered everywhere, and they crumbled in my hand when I tried to pick them up and fit them back together. I don't know why, but tears sprung to my eyes. The rest of the animals were fine, which was odd, since they all had more vulnerable pieces — unfurled wings, swiping claws, outstretched flippers, delicate antlers. But the fox had been the most grounded, not to mention my favourite. It felt like another member of my family had just been smashed to pieces.

I got up, dejected. But something twinkled in the rubble. I bent down and picked up a glistening green stone I'd never seen before. I turned it over. Geology had never been my strong suit. When I switched hands, it suddenly became molten-hot, and I dropped it.

The motion light came on. I swiped away the tears and dropped my eye patch down, so Deidre or Arnas wouldn't see. But when I turned to look, there wasn't anyone there. No — there was *something*. My throat thickened and I froze. It was a huge, melting shadow, suspended in the air like a black tablecloth until I let out the breath I'd been holding and it took shape.

"What the —" Then something glimmered green in my periphery — the stone — and the shadow snapped around it like a fist, darting across the veranda and around the other side of the house.

Without thinking, I lurched around the old house, legs twisting under me in the knee-high snow dunes until I'd made it to the semiplowed sidewalks of Wellington Crescent. I bounced on the balls of my feet, checking one way then the other, and saw the shadow bounding west towards the bend in the Assiniboine River.

"Hey!" I shouted, my panting trailing fog down the street. My heart set the tempo in my bones, pounding along with my feet. It was an unfamiliar rhythm, since I didn't usually chase after hoodlums in the wee hours, but this was too severely personal to let go. As I ran under the St. James Bridge I asked myself if this was really happening or if the shadow was just a trick of my horrible eyeball.

I lost steam at a loop in the path, the one that suddenly became bush before ending at the intersection of Wellington and Academy. That part of the path wasn't lit, and I wasn't about to let myself get stuck in the snowy dark if my quarry pulled a knife or something worse. Hands on my hips, I bent, trying to catch my breath, swearing and mad and wondering why I'd expected to catch the creep, let alone what I'd do with them if I did.

I turned back towards the knot of trees, and peering out from the corner of the path was a fox.

Now, wild forest animals in this city weren't at all weird. I mean, as you got closer to Charleswood and the Assiniboine Forest, you'd find deer in almost everyone's front yards, or even as far out as Tuxedo, they might be devouring the expensive annuals one day and bringing their friends the next. And if you happened to have a cabin out in the Whiteshell, foxes were a given.

But this was the first time I'd seen a fox in the suburbs, and it was staring straight at me, curious and calculating. And looking way too *familiar* for me not to be weirded out.

"Hi," I breathed, not sure what else to do. Every time I saw a wild animal, I immediately (somewhat stupidly) wanted to get as close to it as possible. I didn't care if it could hurt me — in that moment, I wanted to have mystical animal-communicating powers, whatever the cost.

I got down to a crouch and edged closer, each half an inch a boon before the fox would inevitably take off into the trees. But I jumped back up when it actually *came towards me* in a pounce-stance. I grit my teeth. *Did foxes attack people? Did they carry significant diseases? My kingdom for Wikipedia.* The fox was suddenly at my feet, staring up at me with golden, clear eyes, and without breaking eye contact, it swept its enormous tail to the side, and sat down.

"Uh. Okay," I said to it.

The fox cocked its head.

"I don't have food," I shrugged, hands open. It blinked.

Someone in the neighbourhood had been feeding it, probably. I took a second to scan the street, the path, and the general area. I was totally alone, save for a couple of porch lights. I took a chance and offered my nearly numb, open palm. The fox got to its feet, sniffing. It looked up at me again as if to say, *Uh, it's empty, dude.*

I cleared my throat, quickly pocketing the hand and wondering how late it really was. My muscles were draining fast.

"Well," I said, shrugging and wishing I'd brought my camera phone with me, "I better head home, little guy." I backed away until the fox was a good few feet off, turned, and started jogging back to my grandmother's house.

I clenched and unclenched my hands, trying to keep the heat in them. All the anger I'd felt from my little brush with backyard vandalism and a totally failed citizen's arrest fell away into the snow underfoot. The night air had a surreal texture, and I wondered if the fox had really been there at all. People didn't normally encounter the flesh-and-blood versions of their busted garden statuary. Imagine being jumped by a gnarly gnome after dropping your ceramic one. Too bizarre, even for fanfiction.

I shook my head. What had I been chasing, anyway? I blinked and saw the glinting green in my mind's eye, the shadow that took it. The hot stone I'd dropped in the snow. Had there been some precious gem inside that statue all along, and the suburban vandal just got lucky?

Ugh. I clenched my teeth. Being out in the cold had distracted me from the pain in my head, but now it was boomeranging back with full force. I just wanted to get back to my warm bed.

A few houses down from home free, a chill separate from the night skittered up my neck. I stopped and looked over my shoulder. The fox was following a few paces behind me, head lowered, eyes like a guilty younger sibling trailing the elder.

I stared.

"I dunno what you think I've got," I sniffed, walking backwards so I could keep moving while keeping an eye on it. The fox padded after me until it was beside me, keeping pace. It was a real fox, all right, and I couldn't help but grin.

Then we reached the house. I sighed up at it, the only glow the kitchen light I'd left on. Thankfully, through the crack in the living room curtain, I couldn't see anyone moving around.

I felt a nudge at my ankle. The fox brushed around me and looked up at the house, tilting its head. It had stopped snowing for once, some of the cloud cover breaking up and letting the knife-gleaming moonlight through. Ice glittered in the fox's orange fur and white muzzle. It looked up at me, expectant.

"Uh. Okay. Well . . . you'd better head back to . . . whatever it is a fox lives in. A den? A foxhole? No wait, maybe that's a military thing . . . anyway . . . shoo?"

The fox huffed like I'd insulted it. Then it darted up to the house, hopping through the massive snowdrifts as though they weren't even there. This time it was me following the fox at a clip, until I stumbled back where I started, the motion light blinking on and throwing the pile of crumbled stone into relief. I sighed and took a quick look around. No fox, stone or otherwise.

I frowned at the remains. Should I clean this up? Deedee would just think I did it. Best to leave it . . . but I bent down and sorted through the rubble and snow. No big shiny. Maybe there hadn't been one. Maybe I'd been duped. It didn't matter now; real or not, the stone was gone.

I went in, kick-tapping clots of snow from my boots before throwing them on the rack. I felt a sudden rush of heat at my bare ankles before I closed and locked the door behind me, grateful for the house's warmth already bringing my flesh back to life.

Back in my room, my digital alarm clock's bloody letters shone one eighteen a.m., and I groaned. Tomorrow was gonna be rough.

I flicked the light on in my bathroom, the fan humming to life at the same time. I took my eye patch off and left it on the counter, running some more water and splashing it onto my face. I patted it dry and lowered the towel, leaning in, eye-first, towards the mirror. My stomach dropped.

What a sight, yeesh. I looked like I'd been kicked in the face by a horse with a score to settle. The lump just under my bottom eyelid had gone bruise-purple. I felt the panic creeping in and was instantly awake again, starting to think I should wake Deedee to take me to the hospital ASAP.

I pushed my messy hair back, steeled myself, and prodded at the lump. It was pretty much the size, shape, and hardness of a Tootsie Roll.

When my finger connected, I felt the lump shudder. Not my eye, not the swollen parts. The lump itself. I screwed both my eyes shut, because the vibration travelled over my entire face, and I wanted it to stop. When I dared open them again, I leaned closer to the mirror. The lump was shivering in time with my pulse. Undulating. Throbbing. And moving out.

The hyperventilating was sudden and scary. The bathroom light guttered; the fan screeched to a stop. But I didn't look away from the mirror, not for a second, not even as the lump migrated totally from one end of my eye to the other, and especially not when it started pushing out into the open.

The pain was a knife and I wheeze-screamed. I dug both hands into my eye as I stumbled back, tripping on the bath mat, and landing hard on the tile. Flailing, I threw my hands back up and pressed harder with each new wave of pain, as if the next thing to fall out of my skull would be the eyeball itself.

Then I felt nothing, and I could breathe again.

I tried to calm down, tried to call it a fluke attack, promised myself that I'd go wake Deedee up *right the eff now* if only it'd be over.

But I felt something wriggling in my hands. Shaking, I lowered them, and saw the bloody lump shuddering and rolling around.

Then it stopped, and unfurled pointed, triangular wings, flexing them as it spread its tiny black feet. It took flight for the flickering bathroom light bulb and fluttered gaily in its aura.

A moth. An extremely real, horrible moth covered in *my* blood, dancing around the light as if it hadn't just sprung out of my body. I crawled to the sink and got to my wobbly legs, holding tight to the basin. My muscles felt like they were liquefying, but I forced myself to stay standing and looked up at my reflection.

The swelling had gone down, and there was a Rorschach splatter of blood on my cheek, but I could still feel my heart beating in the socket. And I blinked, for the first time in a long time able to see out of my demon eye without swelling or a filmy caul preventing me.

But in the next moment I wanted my bad eye back, because suddenly the pupil grew enormous, the black bleeding into the white until it was a solid dark marble. My whole body tensed, ready to eject everything under my skin.

I fell backwards through the bathroom door and into my room then, my screams muffled by the stream of moths rushing out of my skull, maybe hundreds of them, maybe every moth in the universe, beating their wings out of my head and around me in a torrential, invertebrate hurricane. I writhed and rolled, my nerves marionette strings as I danced in the waves of wings that carried me up.

When the full litter of grey monsters had left their ocular womb, I finally lost my legs, drowning in wings. The moths lifted me bodily from the ground, pinning me to the ceiling, crawling over each other to get a piece. I struggled weakly, only managing to shake them from my face as the tornado continued whirling in the centre of my room, over my bed. Helpless, I watched the moths below come together in one throbbing shape, one body, and from it emerging their mother, their *queen*, black eyes devouring me, a hundred spindle hands reaching.

Then suddenly there was rush of orange and a riling snarl. The queen beat her wings and the attacker back. The fox dodged and landed on my bed, with me crashing in a crumpled heap to the floor as my captor-moths swirled to their mother's defense.

"A grave error to interfere in my dealings, fox," came a voice like burnt, crinkled paper. "This vessel has been marked, as always. She bears my sigil."

The fox stood its ground and barked, "A mark that signifies backroom dealings with a demon, Mother Death. I never thought I'd live to call the Moth Queen herself a fool for doing the bidding of a serpent."

I sat up, hand to my head. The fox had spoken, yes, with authority and anger. A female voice, too. Her hackles were up, lips peeled over yellowed canines, ears pinned back — even in the eye of the moth-storm, she held her ground. And mine.

The Moth Queen, or whatever she was, stood eight feet tall at least, her enormous head brushing the ceiling, cicada body doubling over the fox as though it would crush it in half. She had the arms of a woman, so many arms, and delicate needle fingers. Her wings gaped and flexed, the extent of them lost in the wings of her babies, beating around her like a shivering maelstrom.

It seemed as though the fox and the moth had forgotten about me, until one of those elegant, deadly hands shot out for my throat and pinned me to the wall without a glance.

The Moth Queen surveyed the fox, long face giving nothing away as her leaf-antennae twitched. "Death is no slave. And this is the bidding of the Families, not the Snake. I have been bound to do this thing to maintain the precious Narrative. You were there when the accord was made. You did nothing to stop it then."

The fox's snarl deepened. "You will release her."

"I will take her. As is the due to be paid. It was the mother who interfered with the work, and there will be blood for blood. This is the pact. Take up your grievance with the Owls — this one has had fourteen years to be spared. Feel grateful." I felt the hand squeeze tighter, felt the moths closing in again. Felt myself disappearing . . .

Then there was extreme heat coming from the bed. A fire, growing bigger. "I wonder," said the fox amidst the flames, "*can* Death burn?"

The flames flashed outwards, meteoric, and the fox grew with them, and somehow, in the guttering blaze, I saw what could have been a woman with a fox head, lashing out her nine tails into the torrent of moths, scattering them, attracting them. Killing them.

Had we been devoured by the fire? Had the entire house burned down? I couldn't tell. But I knew that I was just . . . elsewhere, all of a sudden. I could feel that I still had a body, but that it was less important than it had been a second ago. *God, so sleepy, just let me sleep.* I wanted to fall backwards into nothing, let my limbs migrate in different directions and scatter the remaining pieces. The less weight I had bearing down on my spirit, the freer I could be.

I was being held possessively by branch-like arms, many hands wrapping me in the loving embrace of a cocoon.

These hands would grant all my wishes. And all I wished for was sleep.

"You cannot take her," said the flaming fox-woman, creature, *thing*. She was nearby, because I could feel her heat.

"Firefox! Daughter of Deon! You know my purpose. I am Death, and Death is an impartial judge. I take this child so that the others may live. So that the wrath of Zabor will be slaked for the season. This was the deal that was made. You cannot reclaim this sacrifice." The Moth Queen dug her fingers into my flesh tighter as she wove.

The flames guttered slightly. A laugh. "For the will of a lesser demon, a snake hiding in a riverbed! You do not have to be a slave."

The Moth Queen seemed to take offense. "I will take the dead from this place until the end times, until the wheels stop turning. I will not stop, even when Sky and Earth come back together, even when this world ends and another begins. You all made this pact with me, while the eyes of Ancient were turned away, in your moment of weakness. It is not with me that the fault lies."

I felt myself being pushed into shadow, felt the darkness leaking into my bones, but the heat from the fire didn't fade.

"The River Snake will be driven out. Give the girl to me, and I will set it in motion."

The blackness submerged me. I was being pushed into the Moth Queen's body, becoming a part of it. I wanted to be a part of her darkness. By choice or by force.

But I felt the air shift as her wings flickered. Hesitation. "The Five Families did not unite before. Their ignorance will keep this game in play until they are all dead."

The fox barked flames. "The Families have grown weary of feeding their children to the beast. The girl is key to ending it."

A pause. A turning of the head. "The River Snake will know she has been denied her quarry. She will unleash her wrath in a deluge greater than the one before. Will you take responsibility for the thousands drowned, my arms full with the burden of their souls?"

I felt the cocoon separating, the threads singeing as the fire brushed against me.

"The Families have protected this world since the beginning. I will not see them punished because Ancient has fallen silent. We will take our salvation for ourselves, as we ought to have done years ago. And Death can be impartial again."

I was inside the fire, delicately handed over to the arms of it, pressed up to a furred mantle of flames, nine blazing tails spinning behind the fox-woman like a wheel. This place — whatever it was — started undoing itself, and the fear diminished along with it. Their voices followed me home.

"No matter what you do, Zabor will know. And in the spring, she will have a terrible waking. The Families will align only to see this girl die. You and I will see each other very soon, old fox."

"There is still snow on the ground," the fires whispered, "and soon I will go gladly into your arms, Mother Death, for I have been waiting a long time."

The FIVE FAMILIES

Awake. *Awake.* What a dream. I'd never experienced one that was so . . . real. *Maybe I ate something weird before bed*, I thought. My body rose and fell as my lungs inhaled oxygen in a healthy rhythm. Sunlight streamed through my window onto my bed, which I was firmly tucked into. I squinted. My alarm hadn't gone off yet, one pitiful saving grace. I had no idea where a dream like that could have come from — well, okay, maybe I needed to put down the *World of Warcraft* for a while. I couldn't remember where the seams of being out in the snow with a fox met with the dream of being eaten by moths shooting out of my eye.

My eye.

My hand flew to it, dabbing and poking to make sure the eye was there. And it was. And there was no pain, no swollen flesh, no moth-body lumps. And craziest of all, I could see clearly, both eyes wide open and facing the world.

I staggered out of bed, but I grabbed the headboard as my legs buckled. Waves of ache flooded my muscles, like I'd been hit by a truck. I hesitated and looked up, swallowing. *Hit by a truck, or dropped from the ceiling.* I shook my head, and I picked my way, jelly-legged, to the bathroom.

I flicked on the light, and there was my reflection, unfamiliar as it was. My thick hair was all over the place; nothing new. I pulled aside my bangs like a curtain on a mystery door.

My good eye was hazel, and it was the eye I'd seen the most of these past few years. My bad eye had been swollen, bloodshot, weeping, or covered for so long, that I'd almost forgotten about colouring. Still, I was a bit taken aback to see that my left eye was now bright amber. It was clear, though, and when I blinked the pupil shrank in the light. Aside from the colour, it looked normal. *I* looked normal. Sort of. For once.

There was something else orange in the mirror aside from this new eye, something in the room behind me and sitting on my bed. I whirled around and, still jelly-legged, fell over. The fox sat motionless on my duvet, tilting its head.

I dropped my disbelieving voice to a harsh whisper. "There's no way you can really be here."

It blinked those big yellow eyes, ears flicking. "If I'm not here, then why did you fall over?"

I paused, trying to control my face. "Yeah, yeah, smart." I started crawling over to my dresser, trying to take this in stride. "I didn't know foxes from the Red River Basin could talk back."

"Not many of them remember how," she said, watching me, "but I do."

"Peachy," I said, finding a comfortable spot in the corner to draw my knees up to my mouth and rake my quivering fingers through my hair. "Then maybe you wouldn't mind telling me why my body feels like it's just been pushed out through a really small drainpipe?"

The fox hopped from my bed and into the sunlight, taking a minute to nip at an itch on her shoulder and shake herself out before looking up at me again. "You were technically dead. It takes time for a body to bounce back from that."

I had been chewing my fingernail and, at that, pulled my thumb out of my teeth, eyes locked on the fox. *Dead*. She'd said it so casually, but I believed her, this real-life talking Disney forest creature. *Well, that'd do it*. I groaned, then buried my face in my knees. "You mean that wasn't a dream?"

"Mm. Sort of." The fox clicked her tongue. "But that doesn't mean it didn't happen."

This was getting annoying. "Ugh, I seriously cannot handle riddle-speak right now, okay? I think I deserve a straight answer."

My attitude took the fox aback slightly. I think she even frowned. "Or you could say *thank you*, you ungrateful pup."

I frowned as the surreal memories bobbed to the surface. "Oh," I said dumbly, remembering that it was a fox-turned-warrior-woman who had burned up the moths and pulled me out of the dark. Out of death. I swallowed the rising lump in my throat, looking away. "That was you, huh?" Her face didn't change. I sniffed. "Well. Thanks."

I studied my hands from behind my knees, following their creases and lines, not sure what to say or think. I took a hold of my wrist and felt my pulse there, a small surge, warm and familiar and forgiving. I remembered everything so clearly, the feeling of letting go, of letting everything slip away, and being all right with it. I wondered if that's how it was for everyone, if that's how it was for my parents. I hadn't meant to think of them just now, but . . . I rubbed away oncoming tears.

When I looked up again, the fox was standing on her hind legs, paws on my windowsill, ears twitching as she considered the neighbourhood below.

"Can I ask what you are?" I said, point-blank.

"I don't know," the fox tilted her head at a crow wheeling past the house. "*Can* you?"

Great. A hallucination well-versed in smartass. I slammed by head to knees. "Just . . . are you a god, or a demon, or a Pokémon, or what?"

She snorted. "I'm clearly a fox. You said so yourself."

"Well, pardon me for having no friggin' clue as to what's going on, Chatty McFurball. I just woke up from an *Alien*-worthy eyeball-bursting experience, complete with a monster mom that could be defeated only by your super pyrotechnics, all in my bedroom in a rambling house in the freaking *Prairies*. I'm just looking for some context, here."

"You're not very good at telling stories," the fox admonished, head whipping back to the window.

I sighed, legs flopping as I eased my head into the wall. "Do you have a name, at least?"

She dipped her head down, surveying me. She finally sat down near me. We stared each other down until her black lips curled back in an unmistakable smile. "Sil," she said finally. "My name is Sil. And your name is Roan. I am a fox. And I have come here for you."

"Great," I said, my next thought interrupted by Deidre's shrill voice.

"I hope you're at least dressed, Roan — it's twenty-to!"

I leapt to my feet, losing one of them to pins and needles but getting it back when I stumbled forward. "Oh man, just what I need." *How the hell was I going to bike to school like this?*

I tore through my drawers, flinging tops and undershirts at the fox named Sil as I struggled into my jeans.

"Where are you going?" she half barked, shaking her head free from an *Achievement Unlocked* T-shirt.

I pulled a plain long-sleeved tunic over my head and shoved my arms into a button-up shirt. "You know my name, you know where I live. I'm clearly not an adult. You'd think you'd know it's a weekday and that I have *school*."

Sil darted a frantic half-circle around my feet, trying to stall me. "School is the least of your troubles. There are dire things that need to be addressed."

I sidestepped her and lurched to the door. I steadied myself and took as much of a power-stance as possible, feeling like crumpling as I did. "Look. I've read enough epic-quest hero books that, in the unlikely event that I was tapped for some crazy mission like the one you and the giant butter-fly of death —"

"*Moth.*"

"— moth . . . were keen on discussing over my corpse, I promised myself I'd go for it, no questions asked. Throw in some talking animals, and why not? Orphaned teenager with an infuriating fox-familiar, seems a solid premise. But," and I counted off the obstacles on my fingers, "I've got provincial exam prep, a threadbare social life, and a diploma to get. It's a Friday. The quest can wait."

Sil huffed but kept silent. I snatched my hoodie from the hook on the back of the door, then checked my extremely dishevelled self in the mirror. Usually I'd be slightly bummed that I hadn't any fashion sense, or really any style to speak of. Today, I shrugged, because it could be worse. *I could be dead.*

I whirled on Sil with an afterthought. "Oh, and don't even *think* about leaving this room. Deidre leaves after I do, but Arnas is home all day. If he catches you nosing around, he'll be calling pest control in five seconds flat."

I held the door, about to slam it shut, but with a rush of red and heat, Sil forced the door wide open and out of my hand. It cracked on its hinges and seemed slightly singed as it bounced off the wall. I cringed, the fox staring up at me and into my soul.

"This isn't some penny dreadful, or some game your fragile human mind has conjured," her voice was thick and harsh in the back of her throat, a rising snarl. "And if you value the life I've stolen back for you, you will *not* tell me what to do."

She launched down the hall in a sonic flare, and I jumped back at the heat of her, her afterimage burned into my eyes. I jerked after her, unsure I should even give chase after a threat like that. But I figured she was still a wild animal and if she was caught in this house, we'd both be dead.

"*Wait!*" I shout-whispered, careening around the corner, down the stairs, and straight into the kitchen. Luckily Deidre had her back to me when I realized I could feel the air *whooshing* against my fresh eye, uncovered as it suddenly was. The sensation brought me up short and made me forget the chase. I clapped a hand over the new eye, unsure how Deidre would react. I didn't have time to think up a valid reason as to why my years-long affliction was suddenly cured, so I wrenched the fridge door open and hid my face as she turned from her smartphone to greet me.

"There you are, lazy bones! Didn't your alarm go off?"

I aimlessly shifted through the jars of pickles and cocktail onions. "Er. No, I guess I forgot to set it." *Yeah, too busy hanging in the spirit realm to do that, srs business.*

"Oh. Well . . ." I caught a glance of Deidre looking forlornly out the kitchen window and into the backyard. She cleared her throat. "Now, honey, I don't want you to be upset . . ."

I sifted through the cheeses, only half listening. *Man, we have a lot of cheese.* I weighed one in my palm. I couldn't keep this up for long.

"Roan, could you just *look* at me? I want you to come over here for a sec."

I knew she wanted to talk about the stone fox and try to console me, but I had bigger fish to fry than some busted up statuary from my childhood. "I, uh, one sec, I just need to find that leftover pasta salad so I can take it for lunch —"

"Why's the fridge door open?" said Arnas's pinched voice. Before I could stop him, he'd shut it, and we were face to face. My mouth clamped shut, and I balled my fists, holding off the urge to slap a palm over my left eye.

Arnas stared in disbelief. He hadn't looked hard at me in months, but now he saw me, stared directly into my golden eye, and his face drained of blood frantically trying to make it back to his heart. Suddenly I saw two Arnases: the one standing in front of me, and another one beyond it, overlapping him like a negative, a dark thing reaching around him and consuming him. *Betrayal. Shame.* These words emerged from nothing and rattled around my head. And something else; something small and swift and frightened. *A rabbit.* Huge ears and a twitching nose superimposed over his face.

I couldn't tell you what made me think of it, but it was there, and I suppressed a nervous laugh.

Deidre's voice made the world come carouselling back into focus, and I winced, a pain I'd never felt before entering my eye as my hand shot up to it.

"What's the matter? Roan, are you —" She spun me around and I let her. She covered her mouth. "Oh my — Roan, your . . . your eye!"

I glanced at Arnas, who was still frozen behind me, and I tried to get as far away from him as I could in the small space. "Yeah, I . . . I just woke up and rinsed it out, and — ta da?"

"But this is *incredible!*" Deidre crooned, snatching my chin and forcing my face into the light. I shook her off. "I don't think I've ever seen it this healthy looking! Oh honey, this is wonderful. How's your vision? I can't believe this! I'll make an appointment for a follow-up but . . . I'm just blown away."

"Yeah . . ." I said, scratching my cheek and trying to change the subject. I just wanted to get out of here. "What'd you want to show me, Deedee?"

"Oh." That thankfully brought her back down to Earth. "Well, I . . . I'm sorry, honey. The house alarm didn't go off, and I didn't hear anything last night, so I don't know what happened but —" She steered me to the kitchen window, pointing towards the ruined fox to let the scene speak for itself. All it did was make me nervous, because running around somewhere in this house was a live fox with a sharp tongue who could incinerate us all on a whim. A fox that had been born from the rubble of a statue I'd played with my entire life. A fox come for me with a quest in her teeth. *Or maybe that was just part of the dream . . .*

"Oh that's . . . that's too bad." I turned away quickly. "You're sure you didn't hear anything last night? Nothing?"

"Sorry, love." She shrugged. "I sleep like the dead."

Ugh, don't say that. "Did you hear anything *in* the house, though?" I pressed, remembering the guttering torrent of moths, the oaths of what could have been gods going head-to-head, and the fire . . .

"You don't think someone was trying to break in, do you?" She looked to Arnas for support but, as usual, he was leaving quickly with his coffee. I could've sworn he looked slightly traumatized.

I shook my head, pulling on my winter gear mechanically, legs getting their stamina back. I tried to reassure Deidre. "No, no. Maybe I was just . . . dreaming." *I wish.* I hoisted my bag onto my back, pulled up my face mask, and dropped my goggles down.

"Well, I'm sorry about the statue, Roan. I know what it means to you. We can talk about it later, if you want. I can also look into getting it fixed. Maybe we should get the alarm system checked. Hm. Oh, and I'll make that doctor's appointment!" Good ol' Deedee, already springing into action. Then she stepped back, appraising me. "You sure you don't want a ride? You look like you're going snowmobiling. On Hoth."

I shrugged. Four layers, long underwear, jeans, two pairs of socks, two hoods, face mask, touque, parka, gloves, ski goggles. This was my armour against the prairie subarctic. Though now, I admitted, I felt extremely warm, as though I could shed one or five layers and face minus forty naked.

"I could use the air," I said instead, my words muffled as I waved and tore out the door, grabbing my bike and heading for the roads. Luckily the plows had been out, and as I pedalled hard, I exhaled, setting myself free into the speed and the wind and the cold. I felt alive. And I suddenly understood that it was a terrible, fragile thing to feel.

❧

Arnas peers between the slats of his office blinds, watching his niece pedal up the road. He lets go with a snap, running a shaking hand over his mouth. He's still dizzy, but that's a symptom of the shock, so he eases into his desk chair, recording each creak of the leather and plastic to keep his mind from collapsing.

He thought it would be over by now. The last piece moved across the board, as it had been planned all these years. Unless — *unless* . . .

Bending his head forward, almost reverently, he pulls free the chain hanging around his neck, and with it, the key. His hands keep still long enough for him to unlock the desk drawer, slide it open, look down into it, and to enjoy the momentary relief that washes over him like a hit of nicotine.

Arnas's slender-fingered hand wraps around the object rolling at the bottom of the drawer. He pushes it to his chest as hard as he can, trying to absorb it into his body, trying to make himself feel anything radiating from it. He swears that it's still warm, that there is still power left in this tiny, remnant husk, but he doesn't hold out much hope that it could be his for long. He rocks back and forth and nearly chokes when his wife knocks at the door, asking him something he's already tuned out.

"I'm f-fine," he stammers at a half shriek, entire body coiled around his layered fists. Her footsteps retreat, defeated.

They've barely spoken a civil word in the last year, all because of the tension that has kept Arnas so tightly wound, gazing long around corners, holing himself up behind locked doors. He loves Deidre, he does. And he has loved her enough not to involve her in this, as much as he ever could. But this house was haunted with power and secrets and the reminder of his failures long before they moved in.

And the girl. His niece. Arnas folds himself inward a degree deeper, feeling his fists bruise his bones, an inchoate sob squeezing out through a tight mouth as the shame rises. He looked into her eyes this morning and knew that she had seen into parts of him that he would never name out loud. He knows he isn't ready to do what he'll be called to do. And the call would come very soon.

The relief of weeping allows him to take a breath, to unravel and sit back, even though his hands stay clasped. Like petals, his fingers bloom out, revealing the small, wrinkled thing, the last of his family's power. And he thinks, *Things would've been so much easier if she'd stayed dead.*

⤝⤞

Our exchange had started with me sidling up to an unassuming Phae, whispering loudly, "Can I talk to you?" though now it had boiled down to me batting her hands away from my newly minted eye.

"I just don't understand," Phae muttered, frowning. This was what usually constituted excitement for her, however left-brained restrained it was, so I let her have it.

"Neither do I!" I finally grabbed both her hands and held them at her sides. "Listen, I know your family is Hindu, so you've got a sort of window into . . . the ancient spiritual, I guess. But yeah, it's just that . . . I think I had some kind of, um, *experience*, last night, and I'm not really sure what to do about it. Not even really sure if it's 'spiritual' — more like 'supernatural.'"

Phae just stared as I worked through this. A group of passing boys sniggered and jeered "Get a room!" at us, since I'd locked Phae in an intimate pose. Instead of letting go, I whipped my head around, snarling and hoping my new eye could shoot fire.

"How about I get *you* a room and call it *your grave?*" I barked.

Faces falling, the boys retreated to their lockers, mumbling something about being a Cyclops lesbian — as if *that* was the worst thing in the world to be. Besides, the Cyclops part was an obsolete insult now.

I finally let go of Phae. "Well *that* escalated quickly," she said, almost reverently. "Must've been some *spiritual experience* you had."

I did usually ignore verbal abuse, but today of all days I wasn't about to endure it. I slouched against the bank of lockers, rubbing my forehead. "You have no idea." She clicked her locker shut, appraising me with a new level of concern that I didn't think possible.

But I looked up at her with my mismatched eyes, and figured, *Why not, she's my best friend (only friend?), and I've told her everything already and she still sticks by me, so why stop now?*

I swallowed. "Phae, I think I died last night."

Her shoulders lifted and she sighed. "Oh boy."

By the time we'd climbed up from the basement and were hustling to our first class, caught in the undertow of hundreds of students, I'd spilled it all. The eyeball-borne moth tornado, the huge queen they served (who was basically Death itself), a talking fox that had followed me home and had turned out to be an enormous fire-engulfed spirit guide, and now a golden eye that was seeing Thumper in the face of the uncle I barely knew.

"And the fox — Sil, she said her name was — she's still running around loose in the house. If Deedee or Arnas find her ripping up the trash, I am so dead. Not to mention what'll happen if she decides to go all pyro again and burn down my grandmother's creepy house." We were momentarily separated by some A/V kids wheeling an overhead projector down the hall. When we converged again, Phae seemed to be getting farther away, even though she was shoulder to shoulder with me.

"Were you taking some new kind of antibiotic?" she asked, frowning still and not looking at me. She was trying to puzzle me out, like a Rubik's cube. "I mean, that would explain the infection clearing up so suddenly, and maybe there were residual, hallucinogenic side effects that your body wasn't accustomed to . . ."

I could tell I'd already lost her, probably at the talking fox. Or, well, pretty much anything that happened last night could be shrugged off as a bad NyQuil trip. But I pressed on. "Phae, I told you, I just woke up like this! And I thought — hoped — it had been a wacky dream, too, except there was a fox on my bed who told me otherwise!"

I probably wasn't improving my case. We'd arrived at the AP English room, and before I could go on, Phae rested a heavy, fine-boned hand on my shoulder. "Roan, you are my best friend," she said, "and I'm not about to tell you what you experienced wasn't real, because it seems very real to you." I felt the tension in my face increasing; I had sensed the *but* coming from a mile away: "But, because I'm your best friend, and I want to support you in any way I can, I feel that if you see this 'fox' again —" her air quotes were painful "— you should really talk to a, uh, maybe a professional about it? That's not to say that I don't want you to come to me, because I really, really do. But this might be something physical, too. I mean, the nerves in your eye are all very intimately linked to neurological processes, and there may have been some serious damage there . . ."

My body sagged, the fake smile making as good a cameo as ever, however weak it was. "Hey, forget about it." I shrugged, trying to laugh it off a bit, backpedalling. "It's crazy. Too crazy to be true. It probably just . . . has to do with the eye. Yeah. Probably that."

At this point, lying seemed easier. It got a twitched upper lip out of Phae, but I had a feeling we were both being frauds, doing our best to console one another over my sudden psychotic breakdown, both failing miserably.

We took our seats. For the first time in years I was consciously brushing my wayward hair out of my face, unafraid of what people would see underneath it, almost excited to see what they'd say. It drew stares, mostly, along with whispers and people elbowing each other, nodding in my direction. This was more jarring than I'd expected — everyone had probably adjusted to the eye patches, or grown bored of the usual jibes, but I don't think they were prepared for the flash of amber that had been hidden beneath all this time. Maybe I should've sent out a press release? A Facebook status? (Not that I even had a Facebook account, but still.)

I realized all too quickly that, no matter what I did, I was still the same weirdo. So I just stared straight ahead, wishing I'd taken Sil up on her offer to stay at home today, and longing for my eye patch as I smoothed the hair protectively back in place.

Then the classroom door opened, with the teacher, Mrs. Mills, holding it ajar for the wheelchair-bound boy who followed her. I'd seen him in passing, climbing the school's steep concrete ramps with improbable strength in his lean arms. His hair was trimmed in a fade close to his dark skin, and his glasses always snuck down the sweaty bridge of his nose after long bouts of navigating the dense crowds clogging up the hallways. Just as I thought of it, he pushed his glasses against his face, parking himself next to the teacher as she introduced him. Barton Allen, moving up into AP English since, like a lot of us, he'd be doing the International Baccalaureate program, early prep for university next year. Nothing too exciting, though I still sat up to get a good look, like everyone else. I was happy for anything that took the attention off me.

Then he looked straight at me, and it happened again.

This time, the jolt to my body was more powerful than when I'd looked at Arnas this morning, so jarring that I felt like my bones were trying to fuse with my desk as I held on to it for dear life. The room swam and shadows leapt out at me, darting from my periphery and racing in the air. Then the shadows became shapes, grew legs: they were rabbits, enormous ones, fleeing something bloody and out of reach. Whatever it was struck out, cleaving the legs out from under one of the rabbits and sending its bloody body to rest on the hard-packed earth — on the tiled floor? — or both, maybe.

So much blood, but the rabbit was breathing, legless and alive, wild eyes racing, finding mine —

I shot out of my seat, grasping this new, however malfunctioning eye with both hands and nearly doubling over from the pain rocketing through my head. The shadows and the rabbits and the blood were gone (had they been there at all?), and I was left hunched over, trying to remember how to produce oxygen. I had to get out of there. The teacher stared, the students gaped, and I even caught Phae coming out of her seat and reaching for me, but I was out of the classroom and far away from them all before I could even register my flight response.

I finally stopped, trying to calm the shakes trilling up and down my spine. I crumpled into an alcove with high, bright windows facing the snow-buried football field, pressing my head against the glass. The sudden coolness quieted my pulse, allowing me to breathe again. *What's happening to me?* An antibiotic-induced hallucination, huh, Phae? List of possible side effects: nausea, dizziness, and visions of rabbit genocide as far as the freaky eye could see.

I looked out the window into the trumpeting sunlight, the clear day full of wondrous light — one of the only upsides to a Winnipeg winter. It struck the untouched snow and made the world look incapable of the violence I'd just seen. And then I saw her, enormous tail brushed over her feet as she huddled under the bleachers, watching me. Waiting. There was a look on her face that I knew all too well, that I'd seen for so many years peering up at me from the backyard . . .

I went down to my locker to gather my stuff. I'd worry about my school absence later, and maybe I'd be able to cover it up before they called Deidre. I beelined for the football field, and there I found Sil, sitting in the same spot. Still as a statue.

"You know, you look *awfully* familiar," I said to her, trying to frown as loudly as I could underneath my snowman layers. "And not just because you saved me from Death or anything." I knew that she had something to do with the destruction of the stone fox, and the creepy gem inside it. Or that she probably *was* the stone fox, since I had recently become an expert on the improbable. But she just tilted her head, pointing her chin at me with no trace of her earlier fox-grin.

"Fine," I puffed, looking around to make sure no one was watching. "Look, I have about a zillion questions, and if I don't get some answers soon, my head is going to explode. Literally. Not to mention that this new eye you gave me is totally faulty."

At that she scoffed, getting up and shaking snow crystals from her coat. "*I* didn't give you anything, pup. It's a spirit eye now, a gift and a burden from the Moth Queen, and something you'll have to get used to."

Her spiel didn't reassure, but I shrugged. "Well, that's the straightest answer I've got from you so far, so I'll call it progress." Just then, I saw a few kids coming around the fence beyond the football field. "Okay, we're going to have to continue this convo elsewhere. Come on."

But before I could protest, Sil jumped directly into my arms and was thrusting her nose aggressively at my parka zipper.

"What the hell!" I cried, scrambling and torn between keeping a good hold on her or flinging her into the snow. Either way, the spectacle was on the verge of drawing too much attention to us.

"It's *freezing* out here," Sil whined, finally snatching the zipper in her teeth, climbing inside, and burrowing against my chest. She clung in there defiantly, taking up a ton of space that I didn't know was under the jacket in the first place. "And besides, you rode here. It's faster if we travel together, and a fox running alongside you isn't exactly subtle. Now zip up!"

I teetered, but I had to admit she was a nice heat generator.

"For a wild animal from Manitoba, you're a bit of a wuss." I grudgingly zipped us up, making sure the passing kids were none the wiser, and with one arm protectively at my chest, I made my way to the bike rack. Just as I mounted, Sil repositioned herself and poked her head out of my jacket from under my chin. I grunted. She was panting, eyes wide and taking in the scene like a kid at Christmas.

"Real subtle," I sighed, feeling the snow tires grip the icy roads as I posted for home.

※

We slunk in through the back door, Sil on the lookout while I peeled off my tack. Deidre had texted that she would be out until the late evening due to some extended work meeting, and Arnas's car was mercifully missing from the driveway. Still, it didn't hurt to be careful.

"And you're sure he didn't see you this morning?" I hissed, following Sil's perked tail out of the kitchen and towards the main staircase. But the fox's mind was elsewhere, it seemed. She was peering up the stairs, considering what I assumed was the master bedroom on the third floor. My grandmother's room.

I jumped in her path as her paws touched the first stair. "No, no, *no*. We are not going up there. In fact, we aren't going anywhere. You promised me answers. No more distractions."

Sil looked as if she were ready to bolt past me in another demonstration of defiance or explode into the flaming creature I'd seen last night. She was as unassuming as a small dog, but I wondered seriously what it would take to cross the line with her. I stood my ground anyway.

Instead of exploding, she sighed with her whole body, looking wry but suddenly tired. "Answers. You always think it's as easy as an explanation, except you've forgotten to ask the right questions. The answers I have for you will never feel like the ones you want." She turned from the stairs and padded around the corner to the main floor hallway. She glanced back at me as I remained behind, perplexed. *Are you coming or not?* dared those penetrating eyes.

I sprang after her.

Sil was leading me down to the basement, which was more like a glorified storage cellar. As we descended, our path lit by a handful of struggling bulbs swaying over the grim affair, we found ourselves in a labyrinth of boxes and ghostly sheet-covered mounds. The basement had the same footprint as the house, and I had avoided coming down here for fear of causing an *Indiana Jones*–type cave-in or poking around in something I'd regret.

Sil navigated the box-corridors as though she'd set up the pathways herself. Spiders scattered overhead among wilting cobwebs and old piping, and just as the chill and musty smell was getting to me, we hit a wall.

"Man, I knew we'd get lost down here," I muttered,

folding my arms tight into my chest. "Can't you give me your extremely cosmic answers somewhere a bit more habitable? This house is full of *heated* rooms, you know." I touched the wall. It was cold, caked in mud and the grime of age. On this side, the foundation was stone, original and hundreds of years old. There was nothing there.

"But this is the only room I'm interested in." Sil tilted her head at the wall, pawing it.

"What room?" I started, but Sil had already performed a quarter turn, tail erect and pointed at the wall like a bushy finger. The tail ignited, flames catching the stone grooves of the wall. The fire extinguished just as quickly and the stone crumbled to dust, revealing a door that definitely hadn't been there a second ago. Pleased, Sil looked at me, dependent on my opposable thumbs to keep the plot moving.

"Okaaay . . ." I said, pausing before I grabbed the door handle to ask what I hoped was the *right* question: "Should I be prepared for booby traps, too?"

Sil actually rolled her eyes.

"Oh come on, it was a valid question!" I protested.

I clicked the rusted handle down and pushed inward until the door gave. An ancient sigh of air pushed past the threshold. What little light the basement afforded showed a set of rock-hewn stairs descending into emptiness. The last time I'd seen a pit that dark had been in the chest of the Moth Queen, and I wasn't about to lead the way.

Sil's tail lit up again, the fire moving through the bristles like bright water. Our only torch. "Handy," I quipped, and I followed her down the stairs, quick to close the door behind us, and somehow sure that the stone and dirt we'd burned away was gathering again on the other side.

The air around us was thick with shadow, and my hands stayed plastered to the wall as we made our way down. It was spongy and cool, pungent with the heady smell of peat. We were way beyond the house now, heading down a passageway that had obviously been dug out, but I couldn't tell more than that. I could see nothing beyond Sil's tail, and as I felt my way down each new step with my toes, I expected to pitch forward and crack my head open.

Naturally, I was getting nervous, and my worst response to anxiety was not being able to shut my mouth. You wouldn't, either, if you had visions of things fluttering out of every shadow, arms outstretched . . .

"Down into the inner sanctum, eh?" My voice was close in the narrow cavern of the stairwell, the words dying in my ears as the earthen walls absorbed the sound. "Like the Batcave! Or, um . . . a dungeon? Preferably not that, though. If I, uh, had a choice. Do I get a choice?"

The stairs curved. So far, what was the weirdest part about all of this? The whole nearly-being-dragged-off-into-Styx-by-a-giant-moth thing? The new eye that could see a bunch of wacky stuff I couldn't, and didn't want to, understand? Or the hidden staircase that descended into the bowels of the Earth beneath my estranged, comatose grandmother's house? These things all stacked up equally, and it was quickly becoming apparent they all had to do with the family I barely knew.

All in all, I really hoped Cecelia wasn't keeping a catacomb down here, with me as the newest addition.

"What do you know about your parents?" Sil asked suddenly. Could she read minds, too?

That stopped in my tracks — though not for long, since Sil was intent on keeping her pace. I swallowed that familiar stone of resentment, swelling with memories and things my parents and I would never get to do together.

"I . . . in what context? Like what they did for a living? What colour their hair was? Their favourite food?" *Veterinarian and horticulturalist. Crimson and blond. Thai food for both.* These things were written on the inside of my skull from trying to keep close the fading memory of these people who made me. And who were involuntarily fired from the job of parents, midstream.

Sil snorted. "So *not much*, then. Can't be helped. I'm sure they were just waiting for the right time. You were quite young, after all."

"Right time for —" I stumbled, trying to catch myself on the wall and scraping my hands instead. Thankfully, we had reached level ground, and my cranium was intact for another day.

When I composed myself, Sil was looking up at me, her body the only light in the room, giving off a soft halo where she stood. She tilted her head, appraising me as usual.

"There's almost *too much* to go over, and not much time to do it in," she huffed, shaking her head. Without warning, a shockwave rose from the base of her tail to the tip, finishing with a bright flash. I shielded my eyes, peeking over my forearm to see tiny globules of light floated around us. Sil flicked her tail, and they shot across the room like meteors until each found a home in the wick of a candle, or the heart of a lantern, and the room was fully illuminated.

The floor beneath us was polished black granite flecked with veins of silver. It shone in the candlelight and I could see myself in it clearly when I looked down. The patterns of the rock culminated in concentric circles, and as I gazed into them, I found the reflections of half-filled bookcases, closed drawers, glass shelves with plants and precious stones, and assorted bric-a-brac that I couldn't identify in the candle-light. Needless to say, though, compared to the house above us, this room was fairly empty, and everything was built into the walls to keep the ground clear. Whatever this was — chamber, glorified arena — I had zero ideas. Sil sat inside the centre circle, but by instinct I stayed rooted by the stairs, wondering what would happen if I tread farther.

The walls were made of earth, roots tangled like an intri-cate tapestry. Dug into the far wall was a hearth, but no flame burned inside it. I pointed at it, thinking I was being clever. "You forgot to light one."

"Did I?" Sil murmured. I think she was waiting for a reac-tion to this place, to her air of intense mystery. I puffed out my cheeks instead.

"Well, it's something, all right," I admitted, shrugging as my hands found my pockets. "I think I was expecting a lair filled with weapons and gadgets and whatnot, but maybe I watch too many movies." My attempted casual air was under-cut by my eyes darting around, waiting for an axe to fall.

The fox's eyes narrowed. Again I wondered how far I could push her. One minute she was a long-suffering side-kick, the next a prickling beast trying to choose between my jugular and my heart.

"You haven't asked why I mentioned your parents."

My spirit eye twitched. It hadn't acted up since school, and I was waiting for it to give me some clues, since Sil was making me work so hard for them. It was painful talking about Ravenna and Aaron at the best of times, especially down in the depths of God-knows-where I'd found myself.

Resentfully, I tried her avoidance tack.

"Give me a script so I'll know what to ask, then." I folded my arms. "You said the answers I wanted from you wouldn't be the right ones. So why bother asking anything?" Yes, I was dying to know what this chamber was for and why my grandmother had it under her house, but I didn't want to give the fox the satisfaction.

Maybe she grinned, maybe she snarled. But her lips crept back over her pointed yellow teeth. "The thing about foxes is that it's not in our nature to give straight answers. It's more important that we help humans find them on their own. You'll learn that soon enough."

"And *why* will I be learning anything from you?" I snapped. "Oh wait, no straight answers, right. So then, how about *I* write the story? How does it go . . . I'm the Chosen One for some bad-ass mission that's way over my head? There's a solid plot. Well, I mean, it's obviously *me*. I don't know how many other Winnipeg high-schoolers find themselves plucked out of reality by Death or crazy firefoxes, but maybe I'm just being narrow-minded. Yay, lucky me."

Sil scratched her ear with her hind leg, her uninterested pause successfully making me angrier, and she spoke to me almost as an afterthought. "'The Chosen One.' Mm. I never thought of using that term. But what a glamorous life a Chosen One has. Power, respect, infallibility . . ." She lay down in her silver circle, crossing her soot-coloured paws. "But let's see. What power you have is in an eye that you don't understand or know how to control. The duty I'm here to give you will turn everyone against you. And infallible? Ha!" This time it was a smirk, definitely. "No, you'll die; no doubt about that. There, how's that for a story?"

"So you brought me down to some shamanistic sub-basement just to make fun of me? Fine. Find someone else for your mystical power trip, then, or go back to the snow-bank from whence you came."

Her tail swept back and forth against the granite, the grin still there. "Ah, you see? You're already figuring things out on your own. Do you feel better?"

The burning sensation rose to my face. "I'm done."

I turned to stomp back up the stairs, but I was met with a wall of flame climbing from the floor to the ceiling, solidifying in the same black granite that the floor was made of. *Terrific.* I froze, my head turning slowly towards Sil, who hadn't moved.

"Taking on this fox form, getting you down here . . . pulling you out of Death's embrace. That was all hard work. Why would I find someone else when I've already put so much time into you?"

I seethed. "I. *Don't. Know.*" *Could I make that any clearer?*

"Good. Then keep your mouth shut and your teenage tantrums to a minimum, and maybe you will."

I stared into the hard blackness that blocked my escape, the wall that had pretty much entombed me. I didn't dare touch it. The remnants of my resolve lay in shambles at my feet.

"What the hell is this place and what do you want from me?" I asked the fox, and whoever else was listening.

She huffed through her twitching nose. "We foxes are good at avoiding the straightest path. I wonder what you say to other people when they ask you about your parents? Do you tell them that there is no way they pitched themselves into the Assiniboine like a procession of selfish gerbils? That you both hate them and wish you could understand why you couldn't go with them? Or do you just smile, and change the subject, and pretend their deaths happened to someone else?"

This time I was shaking, I registered that much. And when I was little, these were the things I'd creep out at night to tell the stone fox, the inanimate statue that I felt was my only friend and who might either make it all not true, or at least tell me why it was happening to me. I turned to her, not because it was my only option, but because I couldn't turn away again, not now, not when there was so much at stake.

"What does any of this have to do with them? With me?"

"Too much," Sil said, something like fire rising in her glowing eyes. "Come here."

My feet were following her voice before my brain could instruct them otherwise. I lowered myself to the floor, legs crossed. She was sitting up now, alert.

"Another thing you'll learn about foxes is that they don't run," she said. "They wait. Even when it's all falling apart around them, and the wave is coming, they wait."

The stone scene of my grandmother's menagerie made some sense now. "Why? Because they think they'll talk the wave out of it?"

Sil dipped her head down and the air around us suddenly became hot, far too hot to bear. And before I could do more than backpedal on my hands, her body had been ripped apart by swirling fire. It reformed again as a giant, flaming woman with the head of a fox and a wheel of nine tails behind her. The blaze was in my lungs, filling the room with its heat.

"It is because the wave usually doesn't know what it's dealing with." Sil's voice ricocheted inside my head, behind my eyes, and back out into the room.

"Stop, you'll burn the whole place down!" I cried, but the flames climbed higher around us and started closing in. "Can't you stop it? Can't you just go back to being the fox again?"

"Fire is hot. The sky is blue. The sooner you open your eyes and accept things as they are, the easier it will be."

"Is being incinerated *really* that easy?" I shouted back over the roar of the blaze, shielding my face with my hands and less than thrilled to die a second time in as many days.

I felt a hand on mine. It was cool and bright, and it pulled mine away from my face. Sil, or whatever it was she had transformed into, was pulling me back towards her looming shape in the middle of the room, guiding me with her human eyes. She was something older than me that knew what it was doing, so I put my trust in her. As soon as I did, the flames calmed and the heat fell away, but they still burned around us in a ring of fire.

I pulled myself back into a sitting position, shaking and watchful of the fire in case it got out of control again. But it seemed to have a mind of its own, leaping back and forth in playful coronas. The only difference was that it was now low and quiet, and I had the detached sense that it couldn't hurt me now.

"And it won't, if you trust it," Sil reassured me, even though I hadn't said a thing. "The fire is part of a Fox. It cannot be harmed by it."

"Well, lucky you," I said, looking back at her. But something strange was happening. She was still a fox, and still the fire spirit — an Ifrit, the Moth Queen had called her — ablaze and half-human and enormous. She was both at once, two shimmering images, watching me intently. I covered my left eye, the spirit eye, and she was the Fox. I covered the right, she was the Ifrit. Strangest of all, there was no pain in my head. Just warmth.

"Wait." I rewound the conversation. "You said fire can't harm a *Fox*."

Even the Ifrit grinned. "Did I?"

I glanced automatically down into the black unholy mirror of granite. I covered my right eye. Where I sat was another Fox, staring back at me. I blinked, and it was gone.

"That's . . . unexpected." I swallowed. "So, what, I'm . . . I'm a Fox? Like you?"

Her face didn't move. "The cold has always been a trial for you, here in the iciest of climes, but you are never broken by it. And you've never been burned, either, even when you touched every single candle on your fifth birthday cake."

I remembered that. My aunt's friends had shouted as though I'd done something wrong, as though it suddenly wasn't my birthday anymore. But I'd been used to it. My mother had been letting me touch fire since I first saw it, because I loved it and wanted to be closer to it. I'd forgotten all of that, and the memory made my chest quake.

"You know way more than I thought you would," I said, peering hard into the floor, even though my reflection didn't change again.

"Your grandmother was a Fox, and a powerful one. This room was her summoning chamber. Your mother was a Fox, too, but things moved too fast and you were marked too soon for any of it to be told to you properly." Her words grew heavier with the next breath. "And both were long gone before it could be made right."

Marked. The Moth Queen had said that first. "Marked? For what? To die? And my parents, is this why they died?

Because of . . . me?" In my darkest times of thinking about them, I blamed myself for their departures. It made my whole body hurt to think I was right.

The flames pulsed, and without knowing why, I felt like they were suddenly sorrowful. In this place, it didn't shock me that fire could feel. "Your parents died, Roan Harken, because they wanted to change something beyond them, to protect you and others like you. They did not know that it would result in your death anyway, that their sacrifice was in vain."

"But I lived!" I shouted, tears pricking my eyes. "I lived and I don't even know why it's important! Why *I'm* so important. Because I'm not! I'm just another body in a classroom, trying to pass my Provincials and be normal. *Normal*, for god's sake! This is pretty much the opposite of that." Phae's face suddenly flickered across my mind. My only ally, and even she felt further away from me the more this story developed. She and Deidre and Arnas were what kept me tethered to the world, to the normalcy I craved. And they kept me from looking sideways at the Assiniboine and wondering why it called to me, like it did to my parents.

"You said *their sacrifice*," I muttered, digging the heels of my hands into my eyes to stop the tears. "Like they had a plan."

After a long pause, and a silence that even kept the flames down, Sil said, "Yes. They had a plan. But they failed."

The form of her as a Fox and a flame goddess wavered like a mirage, but both sets of eyes were determinedly locked with mine.

"I want to understand," I said finally. "I need to."

"Then it's time." Her long arm, alternating crimson and

white and blue, like changing fire, extended out. I heard one of the room's shelves rattle, and suddenly a drawer opened, ejecting something towards us. I dove out of the way as a glinting dagger landed home on the edge of the silver circle that Sil occupied.

"A little warning!" I cried, feeling like a puffed-up cat spooked off a fence. I reached for the black hilt but reconsidered. The blade wasn't steel like I thought, but blood-purple glass. Garnet. "I bet this is for something unpleasant."

As usual, Sil ignored me. "I'm going to show you what you need, but to do that, I need to take you elsewhere. If you are going to spirit-walk at my side, you have to give something to the fire first."

I swallowed. "Um. Like a finger?"

The Ifrit cocked her head, the Fox's mannerisms breaking through the serenity of her blazing glory. "You'll need all those, I'm afraid, however powerful a gift it might be. And you've already given your eye to the Moth Queen. I was thinking your hair would do it."

"My . . . ?" I gathered it all up in my hand at cheek level. It reached my waist, and I didn't care for it or style it or pay too much attention to it. It was always tied back and stuffed under a bike helmet, so why bother? But it was one of those things that reminded me of my mother, or the idea of her, and it felt like another limb that I just couldn't part with.

But it was that or nothing. I picked up the garnet blade, which was at least a foot long, and so sharp it sang against my fingernail when I plucked it. I guess the importance of my hair paled to finding out the truth. "All of it?"

"As much as you can. Forget your vanity. It will grow back, and it is more powerful severed."

Severed. I steeled myself, slipped the blade under my hair at the base of my skull, and sawed. The hair whispered onto the floor. I gathered it up in a fist and held it up to Sil.

"Not to me," she said, holding up a glowing hand and flicking her head towards the fire surrounding us. It had risen like a hungry animal sniffing the air, tongues of flame pointing to me.

"But how — ?" I looked back at Sil, but her entire body was expanding, flickering into only fire with human eyes in the heart of it. Her body flames were leaving the inner circle and joining the flames that ringed the room. They seemed to be undulating faster than before, larger, hotter. I tried to calm myself as I had earlier and got to my shaking feet. I caught a glimpse of myself underneath me, head already lighter despite the poor hairstylist I'd turned out to be.

I looked scared. And I was. But I'd come this far, and I wasn't about to make another break for it. After all, Foxes don't run.

I turned my attention back to the flames, which were gathering strength and closing in on me. *Fire cannot hurt a Fox*, and since I apparently was one, I was safe. I hoped. I bunched the hair in both of my hands, and entered the silver circle. I hesitated, and then conjured up all the courage I had, wincing my eyes shut and holding the hair above me.

"Here," I shouted over the blaze, and the fire consumed me, taking my body and bones apart until there was nothing left.

⁖

But a body is just a shell, after all. And there was something left. Something that still allowed me to perceive, to know, and to imagine that I was moving. At first it felt like I was swimming through quicksand, like my limbs had been reprogrammed (if I still *had* limbs; at this point, I couldn't tell). All was darkness, but it was warm, and I hovered. Or maybe I walked. And beside me walked Sil. Beside me, or through me, or a part of me? Something else may have been carrying us, too, so I eased into the warmth I had become and let things change around me.

Everything went from darkness to brilliance, and Sil's voice was inside me.

"You're doing better than I thought," she said. "You're spirit-walking now."

Walking, I thought. *More like floating*.

"In a way," Sil said. It seemed all I could do was think instead of speak, mouthless as I was, but maybe that was enough. And maybe it was about time I shut up, anyway. "It is your spirit and not your body that exists here. They are two very different entities."

My spirit. Am I dead again? Where are we?

We were surrounded by the fire, though the form of it kept changing, trying to settle into recognizable shapes. As uncertain of the next step as I was, I felt as though it was waiting for me to tell it what to become.

"We are on a different plane. A place that will show you what I can't on my own." The fire flickered in approval, more and more alive the farther we moved with it.

So the fire's going to let me in on whatever you've been half prophesying all this time? Next time I'll just light a match.

"You're learning quickly," she said, a smile in the voice that rattled through my being. "But don't get ahead of yourself, because we need to go back before we can move forward."

Back? I asked. *How far back?*

"To the beginning," said Sil, her voice rocketing through the top of my soul and out into the fire, which assembled itself into what could have been a fire-painting of the world, rippling beneath us.

I could feel a creation myth coming.

"Myth and reality are two separate planes joined at the heart," Sil said. "They are the same thing for those of us who know them well, those of us who were born from them. Myths are dreams, and all things were born from a dream. Can you accept this?"

I guess I'll have to, I conceded. In the last two days, I'd seen so many embers of the world she was about to show me echoing into mine — the Moth Queen, the bloody rabbits, and Sil herself. I knew I would have to go beyond the limitations of my lizard brain and let it all in.

"Yes," she said in response to my silent musings, and as she continued, the flames danced and changed to illustrate her story. "The world was dreamed into being and kept by the collective consciousness of all those who passed before. We call this consciousness Ancient, for it is the spirit of the universe, and it is older than all of us.

"Ancient is the ember from which life sparks, and as each life ends, so it returns to Ancient. And the cycle continues. Ancient exists in all of us, from the smallest stone to the eldest mountain. And there are those of us whom Ancient has touched and allowed to see beyond the physical world and into the spiritual, into the realm of Ancient called the Veil. It is from the Veil that my power comes, and that yours will, too, in time."

That made my spirit body trill. *Really? I'll be able to light up like a powder keg and take on Death?*

Sil scoffed, "Not exactly. Animals and spirits and demons inhabited the world before man was even an inkling in Ancient's consciousness, and five creatures kept Ancient's peace: the Seal, the Deer, the Owl, the Rabbit, and the Fox. Each embodied an aspect of the world that kept it spinning on its axis: the Seal for water, the Deer for spirit, the Owl for air, the Rabbit for earth, and the Fox —"

For fire. The sun in the fire painting flashed like a medallion, a fox face emerged on its surface before it winked and vanished.

"Yes. The world grew and life exploded within it, and the Five maintained the balance. But there were darklings, too, the destructive aspects of Ancient that existed to keep the cycle turning, and they drew from Ancient one of its greatest dreams — a being that was a combination of the Five. Humans."

I saw indistinct figures climbing out of the earth, the enormous eyes of the five guardian animals watching them as they emerged. Knowing it was the will of the world that had brought them into being, the animals did what they could to allow Ancient's greatest dream to prosper.

"But as time went on, humanity grew out of our sphere of control. Goaded by the darklings that had encouraged them into life, they ceased to believe that anyone was their master except themselves, and they placed the Earth under their yoke. And as their eyes clouded over they buried us, seeing us only as animals — base creatures and a threat to their power. They hunted us and did as they pleased, despite our efforts to guide and protect them."

I saw Deer and Owls and Rabbits and Seals fleeing into the shadows of their world, but the Fox stayed where it was as an onslaught of men and women bore down on it. And then the Fox changed into one of them, and it went unharmed.

"We learned quickly that to protect this world, we would have to change with it. There are those of us who remained animal, who wanted to live simply and thus forsook the power that Ancient gave us. But those of us who still guard the Earth, who protect humanity despite its efforts to undo the fragile balance, we walk between these worlds. The Five Families live on, into today."

Where? Among humans?

"Yes. Everywhere. We have power, but that power dwindles as each season passes. Because the Earth and Ancient, the power at its heart, has grown silent. Trees are destroyed, cities built, and what was sacred is now a commodity. This is the New Balance, off course with everything we were made from. And the power we once turned to for guidance is harder and harder to reach. And so it was when Zabor came into power."

The Moth Queen mentioned that name, that thing . . . whatever it is. And that it was coming for me.

I saw an image of this creature flickering in the fire, which had turned black as oil. Red eyes cut through it like rubies, a heavy body pulsing in infinite coils.

"Zabor is a Celestial Darkling, a powerful demon that once tried to devour the earth. She is not like other darklings, many of which exist the world over with their own humble sort of machinations. Darklings themselves are not necessarily the opposite of my kind, as in the Veil there is no good or evil, only life and death. But they are the embodiment of the other side of creation, which is destruction. But the serpent called Zabor has her own vendetta against both man and the

Ancient creatures that once fought her, called Denizens. She is always hungry and has razed the land over and over using the scythe of her tail."

The tail shot out of the water, and the river rose in a tidal wave. I'd lived in Winnipeg long enough, endured enough winters, to know that the pervading fear of the whole city was the threat of the flood. And not just Winnipeg, but every town that grew out of the Red River Basin. It was pretty much what we were famous for, if widespread damage and destruction were worth bragging about. Lives were always claimed when a major flood happened, and beneath us, I saw Zabor swallowing every one of them.

"Members of the Five Families live all over the world, and here, in the Red River Valley, they live in fear. Long ago, Zabor made a pact with them that she would hold off the flood each year if the families were obedient and gave one of their offspring to her before the spring . . ."

What? Why would anyone agree to send their kids to the slaughter like that? Didn't they try to fight back?

"They tried, but there are few of us left with enough power to stop her. And with each descendent of the Five Families devoured, Zabor grew more powerful. It seemed like the toll was the only way to truce. Each year that a flood occurred, it was because the parents of those children marked for sacrifice rebelled and would not go through with it."

Marked . . . like me? I was marked for Zabor's springtime snack?

The landscape changed, and I saw myself at my parents' funeral. My father's coffin sat next to an urn, whose contents were symbolic; Ravenna's empty coffin had been cremated, a ritual of fire (and now I understood that). Their friends had all processed in with tokens and stories and pictures, lighting candles by a framed portrait of all three of us. We looked so happy suspended behind glass. A life just out of reach. My three-year-old self stayed behind a long while looking at them, wondering if the pictures would come to life and tell me it'd be all right, but the only thing that came to comfort me was a tiny yellow moth, the kind that loitered around our porch lights. It landed on my hands, shuddering dust before taking off again. I rubbed the tears out of my eyes, and I suddenly realized that's when it all started. When my eye went wrong and everyone said it was a grief tic, it was really the marking of the moth burrowing into my skull, waiting.

I still don't understand . . . why me? Is there a selection process? Did I do something wrong?

"The Moth Queen said it herself," Sil replied, and I dug around in my memory for the harsh words from Death's mouth: "It was the mother who interfered with the work, and there will be blood for blood . . ."

My mother? She interfered? But how?

There were so many images writhing around beneath us, but the flames were pulling back, dying out: Zabor, the black serpent; the flood she brought; the infinity of Earth; the Five Families that protected it . . . it was all melting away, and I felt as though I were falling through the abyss it left behind. My spirit clawed for purchase but I plummeted, Sil's voice gone as I cried out for help. In the dark I saw the shadow of a red Volvo falling along with me, and waiting underneath it, the open jaws of the snake.

⬥

I came to with my face plastered into the granite, torso inside the silver circle, legs splayed beyond it. I felt almost as bad as when I woke up that morning, but I figured there was room to improve my spirit-to-body landing. Since I was having a hard time moving, I closed my eyes, concentrating on breathing and bringing my scattered thoughts together.

So. 1997. The year of the second greatest flood this city had ever seen, and the autumn before that was marked by my parents' deaths. The flood waters came, wrathful as I could imagine, destroying lives and showing no mercy. And it was because of my parents.

"Are you all right?" Sil asked. Her muzzle brushed my nose, and I opened my spirit eye. She was a Fox again. That was something I could handle.

"Define *all right*." I managed to roll into an upright position, feeling my sinews realigning.

"You can talk, that's better than nothing." She shook herself, glossy coat ruffled. "You did well for your first time. It can be overwhelming, but you made it out alive."

I blanched. "There was a chance I *wouldn't*?"

Sil looked away. "Slim chance."

To be expected, I guess, out of so much *unexpected*. Words like *Ancient*, *Veil*, and *Zabor* raced through my head until it hurt. I touched my amber spirit eye. "Okay. So I was marked to be fed to Zabor to stop the flood from happening this year. But she didn't get me. You saw to that."

Sil was alert again. "Because your mother had found a way to stop Zabor, and stop the Families from paying the price with their flesh and blood. Even though Ravenna did not succeed, I think you can carry out her plan."

"Oh," I sighed. I felt like roadkill, but I realized this would be the least amount of pain I'd probably have to deal with.

"What?" Sil tipped her head, sporting that foxy grin. "You thought you could escape Death without having to work for it?"

"Something like that." I cracked my neck, feeling a bit better. "So, what's the big plan, then?"

"Simple." Sil picked up the garnet blade with her mouth and brought it to me. It was heavy, which seemed all-too symbolic. "You must unite the powers of the Five Families, defeat Zabor before her wrath consumes the entire city, and do it before the coming spring. And survive the endeavour."

My eyes rolled deep into my skull. "*Simple.*"

She ignored me and went on, voice sharp with prophecy: "Beneath the river ice, Zabor is waiting. And when she realizes her toll has not been paid, she will send her hunters for you. From now on, you will be prepared. You must expect death every day and be ready for it."

I snicked the blade to my fingertip, wincing as the blood oozed up. My mother's blood, and my grandmother's, too. The blood of the Fox. And it'd been there all along, beneath my skin.

My heart was thrumming with an exhilaration I couldn't understand. Certain death, zero help from anyone, and a mission I'd have to hide from every person I knew. And what was in it for me?

The truth, an unbidden voice murmured. And that was enough. I felt warmer already.

"Okay," I said. "I'm in."

Part II
SPARK

The COUNCIL *of the* OWLS

Barton sits in his wheelchair at the edge of his bed, rubbing his legs. Or what's left of them, since there are none from midthigh down. But he can feel all his legs, always could, even though he came into the world without them. He sometimes wakes in the middle of the night, flexing his phantom toes, stretching the invisible tendons in his ghostly knees. He swears that if he swung himself bodily from the bed, he could stand and walk himself to the bathroom, could rise from his chair and push his way through the plodding crowds in the high school's congested hallways. It always seems possible, especially in the middle of the night, fresh from dreams where he ran and ran for miles through endless woods, never tiring, blood pumping from his feet to his brain and back.

Every morning he is flush with disappointment. He'll never stride down to the breakfast table on the legs he coveted. He'll never see the exhaustion vanish from his parents' faces, replaced only with relief and delight that they no longer face the enormous handi-transit bills, could stop worrying that he gets picked on (though not that much anymore), or that his life will be fraught with challenges until it ends. Putting his parents out of their misery (and his) would've been the easy route. But Barton is no stranger to fighting, and he chooses to dream of his legs. In the dreams, he is free.

But the dreams have changed, lately. He runs and runs, and suddenly finds himself crouching on the ground. He passes a stream and catches his reflection — he's a giant rabbit, erect ears twitching in the abrupt silence of forest noise, then birds screaming overhead as they race into hiding. He watches a herd of rabbits cascading out of the woods, fleeing something that reeks of blood and rage. It is a blade, large and horrible and alive. Barton sprints at light speed, but the blade somehow always finds him, and when it has taken all the other rabbits down it swings for him, and he feels his legs separating from his flanks as he dives out of the way, feels the blood as it drains and drowns him, even after he wakes up, sweating and pale.

"Do you need anything, honey?" his mother asks softly from the doorway.

Barton's mother always does so much for him, and he knows he'll never be able to really thank her. But her pity makes his chest burn. He's devoted so much to honing his independence — he knows other paraplegics have done it — and he's even started saving for those beautiful carbon-fibre running blades, the kind that help Olympians achieve gold. He knows they will never match his dream legs, but he could stand tall in them, maybe run marathons, and that's all that matters. And dreaming of those things pushes him farther from the nightmare that his dreams have become.

"Barton?" she asks again. He swings back into focus, giving her an exhausted smile.

"I'm fine, Mom," he says, doing a quarter turn in the chair, snapping his brakes in place, and pulling himself into his turned-down bed. His greatest mistake was telling her about the dreams. Now her concern seems sharper, more insistent. Maybe dangerous.

Even though he didn't ask — and really doesn't want her to — she helps tuck him in, as though he were six again. He doesn't stop her. Her intentions are good, have always been. And he wants them to be close in this moment. Close enough that she will tell him what she's hiding.

"How was that new English class you got bumped up into? More challenging, you think?"

Barton's memory flicks back to the girl who had some kind of panic attack just before class started. He could've sworn she looked right at him, or directly inside him, before it happened. That maybe he was the trigger. He can't say why he feels guilty about it, but he didn't mind that the attention and whispers were directed at someone else for a change.

"It was pretty uneventful." He shrugs, putting his glasses on the night table and rubbing the bridge of his nose. "It'll be good for applying to those sports scholarships and stuff, so it's worth it for the extra homework." It's taken so much work to rise to captain of the school's basketball team, even in a wheelchair, and Barton will do everything to make it all count.

His mother smiles, the pity taking second place to pride for a moment. She touches Barton's face and goes to leave, but he stops her in the doorway.

"Mom — who came over today? I heard you and Dad talking about it." *Arguing, more like*, but he doesn't add that.

He can see his mother only in profile, but her face betrays her detachment for one second. The smile boomerangs back — much weaker this time, more plastered on. "No one important, love. Nothing to worry about."

She's out the door, her escape nearly complete, but his last words give her one more pause: "Was it Mr. Harken?"

Her hand is on the doorway, but her body is in the hall. She pulls the door closed behind her.

In the hallway, Rebecca Allen puts a hand over her mouth and closes her eyes. She has sacrificed too much to let it all slip now.

⋙⋘

From my bed, I traced the faint, uneven lines of the ceiling's paint job with my eyes. It was snowing again outside. It was weird to think I used to despise the snow and long for spring, but now it was a comfort, and it meant more precious time.

Sil was curled up on the floor beside my night table, face nestled into the bristles of her tail. I knew she was something from another world, but I kept forgetting she needed sleep and food, like a pet. She had put work into getting that body, she'd said, and she'd have to take care of it. Or, well, *I* would, anyway. It was up to me to take care of her and shield her from the world. Some first pet *she* turned out to be.

When we came up from the summoning chamber, I could hear Arnas pacing overhead, talking manically and hissing into his phone. We made it to my room undetected, and I went down to the kitchen to get Sil some smoked salmon and me a peanut butter sandwich. Since then I'd stayed holed up in my room, thinking about what I'd seen and the muddled things that Sil had told me. The more time passed, the more it seemed as though it had been a fever dream. Wishful thinking, though.

"You can't be unchosen," Sil had said to me as we ate, both of us trying to recover from the effects of pulling our spirits through the soup strainer that was the Veil.

I won't lie — that was the chief thought banging around my brain and giving me an emotional concussion. There had to be a loophole, a way to get out of this, even though I'd said yes. (What an idiot.) Whether I found said loophole before it was too late was another problem.

Now, on my bed, staring at the ceiling and remembering how it felt to be plastered against it by Death's personal army, I sat up, horribly aware that I was going to be a target until this all ended. *You must expect death every day, and be ready for it.* I pulled the purple garnet dagger out from under my pillow, laying it over my palms. Would this weird weapon be enough? Would I be able to draw it against whatever was coming for me and win? This wasn't an RPG, but I felt as though I needed to level up before ever leaving my bedroom again.

My concentration was broken by the *boop boop* of Deedee locking her car. Sil cracked a gleaming eye, ear flicking around like a satellite dish as I stuffed the dagger back in its (painfully obvious) hiding spot. Usually, I'd sweep my hair over one shoulder and twist it if I was worried about owning up to something, but there was nothing there from my throat down, and ironically, it was the lack of hair that had me worried. Just another thing I couldn't hide from her. Or anyone.

It wasn't Deedee's voice raised in greeting that made me slip out of my room, hiding around the corner from the stairs. I stopped at her sharp *what are you doing?* punctuated by the slamming of every drawer and cupboard in the kitchen.

"Arnas?" Deedee asked again, dropping her keys and purse on the kitchen island. My uncle rushed from the kitchen to the phone table at the bottom of the stairs, and I jerked back, heart in my throat. When I looked down, Sil was at my feet, her body rigid as the scene below unfolded.

Deedee stood agape behind her husband, putting a tentative hand on his back as he frantically dug through the table's contents. He shrugged her off explosively.

"What's the matter with you? Did something happen? Arnas, answer me!" Her normal steadiness had cracked, and that was scariest part.

"I'm . . . I'm looking for a p-picture," he stammered, ripping the drawer out and dropping it and its contents onto the floor. Deedee dove to help him pack everything back in, and even from the shadows of the stairs I could see him shaking. She stopped him and took his hands and, though he seemed to briefly take solace in her grasp, he pulled them back.

"Sweetheart, whatever's going on, you can tell me," she assured.

He got up, off balance, digging the heel of his hand into his forehead.

"What kind of picture are you looking for? I can help you if you just calm down."

"It's, um —" He paused before tearing open more cupboards. "A picture of Roan, I just need a picture of her. A recent one."

I felt icy fingertips skitter up my spine, and the mantle of fur at Sil's shoulders rippled.

"Why, Arnas? Just tell me why and I'll help you. Please —"

"I just *need it*," he bellowed. I had never heard him raise his voice before, but it was shrill and frightened and more commanding than I'd have guessed it could be. Deedee's eyes were wide.

Arnas softened in the wake of his outburst. I thought he would come to and give up the ghost, but no. "M-maybe it'd be in the boxes from the move, downstairs? I-I can check there . . ." He left the room, presumably to give the rest of the house that same post-burglary style.

Deedee put a hand to her mouth and sighed. Stiffening, she disappeared for a second, and I could hear her rifling through her purse in the kitchen. *No*, I hissed internally, *don't*.

"Arnas," she said, his name a stone in her mouth. The rummaging continued. "*Arnas!*" she barked again. This time, the noise stopped. Deedee was standing at the front door, waiting for him like a wary sentinel. He approached, and she held out her phone.

"Here's one of her from Christmas, okay? Is that what you wanted?"

Arnas seemed locked on the picture, and he took the phone from Deedee as if hypnotized by its digital glow.

"Yes," he mumbled. "Yes, that's . . ."

But Deedee stood firm, arms folded and blocking his escape. "Arnas, please. Just tell me what this is about. Why in god's name did you need to see this so badly? You ripped apart half the kitchen for a *picture?*" Even from where I stood, I could see her eyes glistening — they'd fought a lot over the last several months, but I'd never seen it this bad. "Arnas?"

"It's . . ." Again he let the thought fall, but that was because he was already onto the next move, running from the foyer, grabbing his jacket, and snatching Deedee's car keys in the pass. He held up the cell. "Can I borrow this?"

"What?" her eyes narrowed — so she hadn't meant to let him keep it. "No! I get work emails on that. Arnas, come on —"

He swung out of her way like a scarecrow midtango, ripping the door open and sending a sharp gust into the house and up the stairs. "I'll-I'll bring it right back, I swear!"

"Arnas! Wait!" Deedee stood on the front step as the sound of her car roaring to life and half grunting, half fishtailing, echoed through the house. Deedee stood in the cold too long, then finally came back inside and began cleaning up damage her suddenly possessed husband had left behind.

Way too engrossed in the drama below, I hadn't been keeping myself in check, and Deedee spotted me at the top of the stairs.

"Roan?"

I didn't try to escape. She was obviously shaken. I came into the light, self-consciously smoothing what was left of my hair. I watched every tightened muscle in her face fall.

She let out an empty laugh that faded into a sigh. "Nice. *Nice.*"

I wanted to explain myself, but I tried to take a casual approach. "I thought that maybe if university didn't pan out, I could go in as a hairstylist, whatcha think?" I fluffed out the jagged edges with an airy hand, pretending not to be shaken, too.

"Ohhh, *Roan*," she groaned, reaching out to touch it. "Don't tell me you did this yourself. I mean, it definitely *looks* like a hack job, but maybe that's trendy now."

I shrugged, my brain immediately rushing to the dagger under my pillow. Hack job indeed.

"You're lucky that I'm way too exhausted to care right now. And also that I'm partial to short hair," she tugged a bit on her bob, but there was still a *tsk* at the back of her throat.

"This is the part where the 'mother figure' tells you that she's getting *really* concerned about you."

"About me?" I said. "I think you've got bigger fish to fry. I mean, what was that all about?" I gestured towards the door, taking an exaggerated survey of the aftermath of Arnas's mini-rampage.

Deedee seemed to deflate as she moved around the kitchen, momentarily distracted from my hair loss as she tidied and shoved everything back in place. "Your guess is as good as mine, kid." She stopped, arms spread over the sink, and looked out the window. "Is there something going on between you and Arnas that I should know about?"

I tried to sidestep the implication. "Deedee, Arnas ignores me at the best of times. I don't know what he'd want a picture of me for. Honestly, it's like you said, your guess is as good as mine."

"*Honest*, huh?" she repeated as she turned to face me, tongue making a pass over her teeth as it often did when confronting my bullshit. "Well, if you're not going to bring it up, missy, then I guess it's up to me." She crossed her arms. We were caught in a deadlock, and for a second I really hoped she wasn't referring to the spirit-and-fire hopping I'd been doing with my vulpine sidekick in the secret basement. I waited for the axe to fall for the second time today.

"Your principal called me at work —" the relief I felt was a rush "— and said you had some kind of 'episode' in class.

And when your teacher tried to track you down, you'd left school property?"

I rubbed the back of my neck and broke eye contact. My gaze wandered up the stairs to Sil, still hidden by the corner wall. I was hoping for some support from her, but grimaced as she bounded away, a reproachful flash of her tail the last thing I saw. *So much for my spirit guide.*

"Listen," I started, not sure where I'd take this, "I know this might be a bit of a non sequitur, or a cop-out — or, well, as the psychs would say, *very telling indeed* — but . . . I've been thinking a lot about my parents lately." Deedee's lips were pursed, but she was nodding; she was always willing to hear my side of things, even though this topic was the hardest for us both. "And, um, about their deaths."

She stopped nodding and came away from the sink and took a seat at the island on one of the stools. She patted the one next to her, and I accepted the invitation.

"It's not a cop-out, hon," she said, reaching out to touch the jagged ends of my hedge-clippered 'do. "You know you can always talk to me about them. And that it's important that you do. You *do* know that, right?"

I got that familiar stinging in my eyes and nose when the tears were about to start, but I bit the inside of my mouth to stop them. "Yeah, yeah of course I do, Deedee. It's not about that."

She folded her hands and sat quietly. Even though she wasn't my mother — and she knew from the get-go it was a hole she couldn't hope to fill — I still considered Deedee way more than *just* my aunt. And I was grateful for her presence, especially now, in the midst of so much unspeakable chaos.

"I've just been thinking that, um, maybe their deaths weren't an accident. You know? I know that you'll say it's just a way for me to cope, but, maybe . . . it was because of something else? Some outside force?" With all the papers I'd been forced to write this year, I knew my thesis was pretty floppy without supporting evidence. And visions from fire-foxes weren't exactly scholarly sources.

But Deedee nodded. "Roan, I know it's a difficult thing to deal with, and that it always has been." She put her hand on my shoulder as Phae had earlier that day, same sympathetic *I-think-you've-lost-it* expression on her face, even though I hadn't said a damn thing about the tidal wave of spirit-crap I was now drowning in. "But thinking like that, dwelling on it, it'll just leave you frustrated. We can't know what was going through their minds, or what might have gone wrong when . . . *it* happened, and we probably never will. All we can do is try to heal and keep living."

"Yeah," I muttered, half agreeing, because that was the mantra I'd lived by and tried to keep close to my chest for so long. But now Sil had opened a devastating can of worms that would change everything. That my parents had a purpose for what they had done. *That they had maybe done it to save me.* I swallowed. Too many secrets about them were rising to the surface, with far too many plot holes. My parents had been pursued, like I was now, and their mission had become mine. I just hoped that my fate didn't lie at the bottom of the river beside them.

And the only person who could maybe give me some info was Arnas, my father's brother, and probably a Denizen himself . . . but I had a feeling that we were working in opposite directions.

I came back to the moment when Deedee's hand found my chin. "Hey, kid." She smiled at me. "You've got so much going for you. You're doing great in school, you're clever, and most of all you've got *moxie*. Remember that you can accomplish whatever you put your mind to. You just have to *go to class*, okay? And if you need anything, we're always here for you." As an afterthought she rolled her eyes and said, "Well, when Arnas is done having his out-of-body experience, he'll jump on board, too."

I smiled, because having Deedee behind me *did* matter. Hearing her say I was going to be okay (even though she really had no clue), it was worth it. "Don't worry, Deedee. I'll be fine. School is just stressful, and I guess I wanted a bit of a change . . . with the hair, I mean."

She waved me off. "Pah. It'll grow back. Besides, now we sort of look related." She got to her feet and flipped the kettle on for tea, snagging two mugs from the cupboard. "Let's veg in front of the tube for a while, I really need to wind down. Captain Crazypants can clean this all up later."

"All for it," I replied, giving the island a gavel-smack of approval then beelining for the couch.

"By the way," she added, stopping me before I could fuse bodily with the sofa cushions. "I made an appointment at St. Boniface with Dr. Yang about your eye. Hope you cleared your schedule for tomorrow."

I automatically looked up the stairs, but Sil hadn't come back. I figured I needed a day off from the shamanistic mysticism that would soon consume all my time. It was strange business that a jaunt to the doctor was now pretty much a vacation, but I'd take it.

Arnas pulls up to the legislative building. The parking area is deserted, save for the vehicle of the odd overnight security staffer. The building is an eerie megalith, especially after dark, the statues and intricate carvings of gods and historical figures frosted with ice. The shadows make them look sharp, scrutinizing. Unmerciful. Arnas feels their limestone gazes penetrating the SUV and boring straight into him. Spotlights pepper the front and rear façade, not only to present the city's architectural crowning glory at all hours, but to make sure nothing and no one gets past the eyes in the dome.

And the eyes are expecting him.

Arnas tries to get control of his shaking hands and pops the car door open. He shoves his left hand into his jacket pocket, clawing it tightly around Deidre's phone as he kicks the car door closed and hurries to the building. The other fist grips the bauble around his neck. He steels himself.

He knows better than to access the building through the back, the much less direct way. No, *they* would not like that. He's lucky he even managed to get them to assemble tonight at all, so he'll do things their way, despite how it makes his soul shrink inside his body.

As he paces, the figures set inside the looming pediment call to him: the Indolent Man beckoning to the land of promise, the goddess Europa leading the bull, the Lady Manitoba with the rays of sun behind her and the trident in her outstretched hand. And the entwined twins: one the Red River, one the Assiniboine. Both fair maidens, one monstrously feared and the other longed for. Arnas avoids them at all costs.

It's the north entrance he seeks, knows that's what they prefer. The direct approach, the kind that Arnas hates. He climbs the stone stairs with the forgotten speed of his youth, regretting it immediately. The door comes up faster than he's ready for, and his breath catches. He tries to compose himself as his knock stammers against the glass.

The young man on security looks up, narrows his eyes. They flit from the screen he was watching to the phone by his wrist. He answers it, meets Arnas's gaze again, and nods. The door buzzes, swinging inwards. He hesitates but remembers he called this council meeting, and he has worth to them — so he enters, upright, as much as he can manage. He hopes his forthright behaviour has at least curried *some* favour.

Arnas approaches the grand staircase, flanked by twin bronze bison guarding darkness. It's been years since he was last here under cover of night, but those who wait for him show no pretense of giving him a warm welcome. The bison bear down as if they would launch from their marble perches to gore his heart and weigh its value. Its *loyalty*.

He glances quickly over his shoulder to find the security guard is watching him closely. His head swivels, eyes bright and piercing. Arnas swallows and wastes no more time, ducking past the staircase and the bison that mind it and walking underneath dark arches until he reaches the white room, round and dimly lit.

There it lies. The Pool of the Black Star. Traipsed over by thousands of tourists who would never know the implication of the black star painted on the white marble like a compass rose. Arnas circles the star, hesitating. Though some people walk over it and feel a chilly reverence, they could never do what Arnas could inside of it, and for a moment that cheers him — even if what power he has left is borrowed, and dwindling at that. He clutches the trinket at his neck again and swallows.

Every moment he waits is a moment that pushes their patience. So he exhales, not realizing he'd been holding his breath, and steps inside the star. He knows it's not just paint; it's power. He glances up at the circle cut out of the ceiling. He is as ready as he's going to be. He closes his eyes, steadying his shaking hands as he crosses them, spreads them, and tents his fingers in the way he was taught but has not done in years. "I present this spirit in the hall of the Star, under the gaze of Ancient, as it turns to us all, and by the grace given to the Five that came before us."

His hands dance wildly as he invokes what influence he can from the ether. "I call to those loyal to this sphere, to rouse and place yourselves on my name, as is my right to ask."

Though he is not watching for it, he can feel it happening — the golden circles in the floor coming to light among the marble veins. They wake, orbiting the star, and Arnas inside of it.

"To the earth that is the element my house bears, yield to my name. Rise."

His hands stop. His voice carries the wake of an echo, and when it comes back to him, it sounds as though it belongs to one who knows what he's doing, who can command respect. But Arnas knows it's an illusion.

The tremor in the floor is faint, but Arnas has inherited the keen ability to sense the stone's ripples using his legs. The black star shifts under him, separating from the rest of the floor as a jagged platform. It ascends through the round alcove above and takes Arnas with it, towards his destination. To anyone else, the brilliant dome atop the Manitoba legislature is a *trompe l'oeil*, an illusion; there is no floor or chamber beyond the second floor and never was. Arnas's face, craned towards the ceiling, feels the slight burn as he breaks through the illusion that hides the boundary, his heart thuds loudly in his ears. Because there is and always has been an upper chamber in the dome. A roost. The governing seat of the Owls.

The star *chinks* into place in the transparent floor of the Mercury Chamber, the dark, candlelit temple where the current leaders of Manitoba Owl Family, the justice and authority of the Five, confer during times of crisis — and crisis there has been in these parts for some years. Arnas's hand defensively jerks into his pocket to find Deidre's phone when he realizes that each of the seven seats surrounding him are occupied, filled with faces sharper than the legislature's statues.

"You are lucky that you can still conjure the names and wills of spirits onto you, Arnas Harken," says a lilting voice from the fourth council seat. "You barely came through the seal unharmed."

Whether it was the dread and panic that had distracted him, Arnas only just notices the blood trickling down his face, the smoking singes in his jacket. He smears the blood away, embarrassed. The ghost of a laugh passes through the assembly.

His shaming finished for now, they resume business. A different voice, female and rigid, echoes from the second seat. "Arnas Harken, former neutralizer to house Rabbit and severer of gifts. You tapped the exiled leader of your House to initiate this council, and as a favour we have accepted. We will hear the case from your lips."

Sweat finds the wound in Arnas's forehead, stinging it with salt. He wants desperately to wipe it away, but he dares not make a sudden move in front of the shining eyes turned on him, the eyes of patient hunters.

"Council of H-house Owl," he chokes, "I come before you as near-kin to this season's toll to be paid to Zabor: my niece, Roan . . ."

"The Fox-kit," rumbles the large man from the sixth seat, leaning forward into the low light. "The last of a line of traitors who would have undone our carefully curated peace."

"Th-the same." Arnas tries furiously to master his stammer, wanting to power through his case. "She was marked to be taken last night, after fourteen long years that were g-granted in charity by this council. A-all the s-signs were there, I saw and noted them myself, have been w-waiting all this time, vigilant —"

"And?" says the voice from the seventh seat, the one raised on a dais at the head of the chamber. Arnas has never seen this council member before, but the whispers about this prodigy, the one Phyr Herself speaks to, were enough to make Arnas's mouth run dry.

He ducks his head, wetting his lips. "*And*, Ascendant, she was not taken."

The silence is heavier than the gazes they level him with.

"Not . . . taken?" repeats the second seat incredulously.

"This cannot be!" hisses the jowly man from the sixth, his chins rumbling. "She was marked *years ago* for this season. If she does not go to Zabor, the reckoning will be catastrophic!"

The third seat speaks for the first time, his Ojibwe accent clear. "How did she come away from the Moth Queen? What power does this traitor-child possess that she could do this?"

"She must have had help," muses the fifth. "Though who or what would intervene? And why?"

"I-I don't know," Arnas clamours, trying to reassert his presence and, above all, his innocence. "But . . . I think she has a spirit eye. I th-think someone is preparing her."

A current of shock rattles through every seat. At that, the seventh member rises, and the conjecture of everyone beneath him dies. Arnas steels himself for the sentence he is about to bear.

"Do you love your niece, Arnas Harken?" asks the young Ascendant, the outline of his lithe body shifting apart from the silhouette of the carved Owl, midflight, behind him in his seat.

Arnas clenches and unclenches his fists. "I don't —"

"A simple enough question," he muses. "Do you love her?"

Arnas deflects, knowing where this is going. "If the Ascendant thinks I'd risk all our lives to interfere with the plans of the Five —"

"Don't presume to know what I think, exile," he snaps. "You've defied the tenets of this council more than once to pursue your own motives. Don't think we've forgotten about the Allen child. That husk around your neck and the stolen power in it marks your betrayal."

Arnas is sweating profusely now, despite the coolness of the chamber. He can feel the sweat pooling at the small of his back.

There is an audible hiss, an undercurrent of voices, yet no mouth moves. Arnas lowers his head.

"Let me make this clear. Your niece puts us all in danger by virtue of remaining alive. She is more dangerous still, when we do not know who is guiding her or what their motives are

— a spirit eye means that the Moth Queen is involved. If she is being used as someone else's tool, then there is no other choice but to help this girl to her destined end. Though we, of course, cannot intervene ourselves, we must put things into motion. And we cannot do that if your loyalties lie with your traitor-brother's child instead of the greater good."

Arnas finds himself nodding and agreeing perhaps too quickly, willing to say anything, even besmirch his brother's name, to get this over with. "Y-yes, yes, that's exactly what I think, Ascendant. For the greater good. All I want is to be of s-service." Arnas produces the phone from his pocket, bringing the photo up for all to see. "I've b-brought it, just like you asked." He wants to throw himself at their feet and proclaim his obedience, and it takes every fibre in his body to restrain himself, to force dignity into his limbs.

In a flash of talons, beating wings, and a guttural screech, the phone is snatched from Arnas's outstretched hand. He recoils, the talons having nicked his skin, either as a warning for having let this happen, or as a show of power. The enormous Owl that bore down on Arnas returns to the seventh seat, form melting back into that of a young man. He scrutinizes the phone.

"Yes," he utters. "This will do."

The young Ascendant lays his palm over the LCD screen, and when he pulls it away, the image lifts out from the phone, suspended above his hand. Is this an Owl trick? Arnas dares not try to guess or even ask. The phone clatters uselessly to the marble floor, the sound making Arnas flinch.

The voices that ripple through his flesh fall away, satisfied. "You've done a great service to this council and this city, Arnas Harken. Once this issue is resolved, you can look forward to the restoration of not only your power, but your honour, as well."

Arnas straightens his back. His power? Dare he hope for an escape from the scrutiny of his Family, and the other Four? Fourteen years of cowering before his peers, cut off from his lineage, had sharpened his desperation — he would do anything to return to the way things were, before his brother's Fox-wife had meddled in affairs beyond her. Before her stubbornness had cost Aaron his life. What love could Arnas have for a child from a strange family, a child who was always destined to die?

"Th-thank you," he replies, making absolutely sure they don't question his loyalty again, that they see he is, once and for all, grateful. "I will do whatever it takes to have this matter resolved."

Lit by the rotating digital image floating over his out-stretched palm, the Ascendant of the seventh seat smiles. "Good."

Seeing his face for the first time, Arnas realizes just how young this "young Ascendant" is, and marvels at the power he must possess to hold the highest seat so soon. He has just arrived from his final training and selection abroad, they say, preparing to become the next Paramount of all the Owls. Though his gaze is that of a young man born to lead, he looks no older than Roan herself. And it is haunted, too, for what little experience his few years have afforded him.

Arnas tries not to think of Roan. This is for the best. *The greater good.*

The photo starts spinning, and a howling wind picks up in the temple, screeching around the dome. Arnas braces himself, the council members now standing, humming, chanting, hands outstretched and punctuating the air with gestures imitating ancient symbols. Golden circles incised in the transparent floor beneath them begin to revolve. They are calling them.

The Ascendant fixes his gaze on the photograph of Arnas's niece. "We cannot intervene directly — all we can do is aid Zabor and her hunters in taking her quarry. Your task, Arnas Harken, is to put your niece smoothly on the path of her destiny, for which there is only one intended outcome. Can you commit to this?"

Arnas lowers his arm from shielding his eyes, the wind piercing his ears and face. He knows his vision is not mistaken; the shadows in the chamber are peeling away, taking shape, and rippling around the room at the speed of the wind.

"Yes!" he shouts over the din, stammer forgotten in the wake of the storm rising around him. "I commit!"

At that moment, everything stops, suspended in time and the ether, the young Ascendant's body half transformed — dark wings spread behind him, eyes horrible and cutting, hands cruel talons. He sends Roan's image into the centre of the shadow-deluge, and Arnas realizes the demons they've called are all converging on him. Their scales and jaws and empty gazes, diving in slow motion to devour. And just as he cowers, time triumphantly spins back into motion, and they consume Roan's picture before they can reach Arnas.

Arnas watches, numb, as they shape a spinning, shifting column, the amorphous forms of the river hunters shrieking, *laughing*, as they split into hundreds, streaming out of the dome and over the city like a fume.

They are loyal only to their sleeping mother. They now know their prey. And so their hunt begins.

The SEVERED RABBIT

"Like I said, I really have no explanation for this," said my young Pakistani doctor as he pulled the light away from my spirit eye. I blinked, trying to dispel the spots twinkling in my vision. The doctor looked fresh out of med school, so I wondered what few "explanations" experience had given him. Probably not the one I had and was unwilling to tell.

He smiled all the same. "I think in cases like these, though, it's a moot point. The eye is healthy and there's been no residual damage, which is extremely fortunate. It's discoloured, yes, but changes in pigmentation can happen post-infection. It's not common, but obviously possible."

"But she's had this infection for years!" said Deedee. "I don't know how many rounds of drops or treatments or surgeries we considered. And it just *cleared up* overnight? Aren't you at all concerned about a recurrence?"

"It's not likely." He shrugged, adding the CT results to

my thick file. "But we'll *keep an eye* on it. Eyy!"

Deedee groaned but smiled. I wasn't as charitable, my eyes rolled so far back I could practically see my brain. This guy was way too young for dad jokes. "Anyway," he said, "Roan's got youth on her side. Youth equals a robust immune system capable of tackling anything the body throws at it. It's as simple as that."

"I'm just concerned," Deedee went on as I swung myself down from the examination table. I knew they wouldn't find anything, unless modern medicine had advanced to the point of detecting the astral plane. *The Veil*, Sil had called it. I wandered out of the exam room, crossing the waiting area into the hospital hallway to people-watch. Gurneys that were surgery-bound, patients meandering with their IV poles in tow, nurses pushing around equipment and supplies. Nothing out of the ordinary.

I took a breath, shutting my eyes and telling myself to focus. I pushed aside as much as I could in my mind, and when I looked back out into the hospital, it was with a sharper perspective.

There were more of them than I expected amongst the run-of-the-mill humans. Members of the Five, I mean — *Denizens*. I saw a doctor pass by, but laid over her face was that of an Owl, sharp gaze penetrating, head swivelling and bobbing as she walked purposefully towards another room, clipboard under one arm. I saw a Seal in a patient bed in the hallway. His skin was shining grey, and he was attended by a pup — a young, curvy girl who held his hand (flipper?) and probably assured him he'd be seen soon.

There were Rabbits, too, and lots of them. Coming in and out of rooms, watching clocks or televisions in the waiting area, eyes darting and bodies tensed for flight. I wondered how fast their hearts were beating, and if anxiety was common amongst the Rabbit Family. I thought of Arnas and winced.

I was grateful that the visions of blood-soaked, ruined rabbits had taken a back seat. I'm sure there was enough death in this hospital to fill years of visions, but I focused on the living and breathing, keenly observing them as they passed by. It was the first time I felt like a fox, watchful from my den of secrets as the others moved around me, a part of the scenery. *Foxes wait.* At the moment, I didn't know what I was waiting for, but when he looked up from signing something at the nurses' station, I felt my chest go still. It was just a man, a random stranger, and as he walked by he didn't even glance my way. But I felt his heat, and saw the air of a fox suspended over his body. For the briefest second, I caught my reflection in the bank of windows on the other side of the hall, and as he passed, we looked almost related. Two Foxes crossing paths. We didn't even sniff.

I watched him turn around the corner and disappear. I desperately wanted to follow him, to find out if maybe we *were* related (unlikely), but I realized, as my heart fell, that I longed for my own kind. That I'd always try to find family wherever I could, and would defend it to the death when I found it. And this is probably why the loyalty of the Five was so divided. All of us willing to protect our own at the cost of the others.

"Hey," said a voice behind me, breaking my concentration and setting everyone back into their normal human façades. I whirled to meet the eyes of the stranger but had to look down to find them.

"Oh. Hey," I replied to the wheelchair-bound boy in front of me. It was the new guy from my class. His name totally escaped me, but I guess I had a good excuse: mental breakdown mid-introduction can do that to a person.

He obviously remembered me, though. "I think we're in a class together," he said, semisheepish, as if too considerate to say any more. "I'm Barton."

I shook his proffered hand. "Roan. Yeah, you just moved up, right?" I swallowed, hoping that I wasn't about to be bombarded by more bloody visions. I didn't feel up to being carted off to the psych ward when it was so close by. I could feel it coming on though, something on the fuzzy periphery of my spirit eye's vision. I concentrated, and there it was, the double vision of Barton's face: I saw Rabbit in him, but this was different than when I'd identified the others. The essence of him as a Rabbit wavered like a mirage, like bad television static, flickering so faintly that as soon as I had seen it, it was gone. I could still see the others from earlier in the background, so it wasn't my spirit eye losing reception. I glanced quickly at his jeans, which were pinned back at the knee. I remembered the Rabbit suffering and bloody on the floor of my classroom, a giant blade having just sliced its legs away as though it had been harvest time.

I swung back into the conversation, hoping I hadn't been silent for too long. I could feel sweat beading on my forehead, and I smiled. "Well, it's a pretty easy class, to be honest. Let me know if you need any help, though, I've got kind of a tutor group going. Not like they pull their weight, or anything." I saw a flash of movement down the hall at the nurse's station. A woman looking up, nervous. Another Rabbit. And when she looked directly at me, her colour seemed to drain.

She changed tack and was suddenly coming towards us. I don't know what made me blurt what I did, but I couldn't help myself. "Barton this is going to be a weird question but . . . Have you been having weird dreams lately? About rabbits?"

He frowned at me for a second, then looked over at the nervous woman, now waylaid by a doctor a few feet away from us. She was nodding in their conversation, but she kept looking over at us, twisting and untwisting her purse strap.

Barton faced me again, lowering his voice. "How did you know?"

She was breaking away. I had to act quickly. I'd had only two major insight-visions into people with the help of my new eye, and I felt that meeting Barton was significant. I wondered if my new awareness of my foxiness had heightened my gut instincts. Barton had a prescription folded in his hand, and I snatched it from him.

"What's this for?" I said, darting to a sign-up sheet pinned to a nearby bulletin board, yanking the pen-on-a-string from its moorings.

"More pills. To help me sleep at night."

I scribbled my phone number on the back of it and passed it back. "I have a feeling we've been having the same dream. Sort of." He looked blankly at the number, then stuffed it into his pocket. "I think it's important that you keep having them, even though they're, uh, kind of awful. Maybe lay off the pills for a while?"

"Barton." The woman — I assumed Barton's mother — was suddenly there, had her hands on his wheelchair. "Who's this?"

"Oh, this is Roan, Mom. She's in my new English class."

I held out my hand, but she just looked at it and started turning his chair away. "That's nice," was all she said. "We have to go, honey. Transit is waiting downstairs."

"Mom, I can wheel myself," Barton argued, but she seemed determined to get away from me as quickly as possible. He turned around quickly. "See you in class, Roan."

I waved back weakly. I hope I wasn't wrong about him, or that I'd just made an idiot out of myself for talking about wacko things even my best friend didn't believe. I felt my phone go off in my back pocket — speak of the devil. Phae had been texting me all day, but I was ignoring her. Too much had happened for me to forgive her just yet. I wondered if I'd ever get the chance to prove I wasn't completely off my rocker.

I hadn't noticed Deedee behind me. "Was that Mrs. Allen you were talking to?" she asked.

"Huh?" I twitched, startled. I looked back at Barton and his mother as they slipped into an elevator.

"That's Rebecca Allen and her son. It's too bad. They've had a lot to deal with. Birth defect, that's what happened with his legs." I raised an eyebrow. I wasn't so sure it could be explained away that easily, as with most things I'd come across in the last couple of days. Deedee went on. "He's a pretty gifted athlete, though. He's got a lot going for him. Shall we?"

As we made our way to the elevators, I asked, "So how do you know so much about them?"

"Arnas grew up with Rebecca," she said, pressing the down button. "They were pretty close. Almost like family."

Like family, I thought, remembering my first vision and Arnas's bleak face when he saw my newly minted eye. An image of a Rabbit over his face.

Family, huh? Maybe Deedee wasn't far off.

※※

Arnas was nowhere to be found. Probably holed up in his office, doing god-only-knew-what. I was keen to avoid him for as long as I could, his episode with my photo fresh on my mind. With Deedee downstairs, Phae's texts going ignored, and rabbits haunting my brain, there was only one person I wanted to see right now.

"Sil?" I hissed as I entered my room. She wasn't in her usual spot. I had a package of smoked salmon bunched in my hand, hoping it'd help ply some hard-won information out of her.

I tried puzzling out where she might be and how I'd find her discreetly. She was either hiding out in the summoning chamber (though she knew I couldn't get in there without her), or . . .

When I reached Cecelia's room, I darted into a spare room across the hall to avoid a nurse wheeling out soiled bathing supplies. I'd gone from one hospital to another, it seemed. The nurse gathered everything up and started for the laundry, so I took my opportunity to tiptoe into the sickroom. I shut the door.

"Sil?" I whispered again. If she was in here, she would be somewhere the nurse couldn't catch her. Sure enough, her giant tail flicked from under the bed, and she emerged, shaking herself with a yawn.

"Napping?" I said, unwrapping the salmon and offering her some. I put it on the floor and she ate quickly.

I finally got a reply between mouthfuls. "Observing."

"Seems like we're on the same wavelength," I said, taking some salmon for myself.

"Oh? How was the doctor?"

"Educational," I sighed, wondering if Barton would keep my number out of his mother's reach. She didn't seem too eager for us to be in touch. "I decided to practise with my spirit eye. There are a lot of you animal-types wandering around. Rabbits especially."

"That Family has a habit of being overly prolific." Sil licked the salt from her muzzle and pawed her jowls for leftovers. "And those who are of the Five that retain their human bodies prefer to be called Denizens. And I'm *not* to be grouped in with them."

I faltered at her insulted tone. "Why's that?"

Sil twisted her head towards my grandmother lying quiet — but clean — in her sickbed. The heart rate monitor beeped. "Because I'm something else entirely."

She leapt onto the chair at the bedside, peering down at the old woman. She sniffed.

"And will I ever know what you are, exactly?" I knew she was powerful, that she commanded fire and could go past this plane easily into the next. And I knew that she was probably as ancient as the Ancient-thing she came from. But I wondered what had called her here, who had sent her. If she had any family, or a home, or if she was just some entity that had reached out from the nothing to help me for her own purposes.

"Just consider me a guide. That's all I'm here for. To help you grow into your power." Sil placed a paw on my grandmother's smooth hand lying palm down over the coverlet. "I knew Cecelia."

I took greater notice of my grandmother then. She looked barely there, barely breathing. Maybe the end was coming soon. "Knew her? Were you close?"

Sil barely moved but to sniff. "I was *her* guide, once. In a way. But she didn't think she needed me. Cecelia was very powerful. Stubborn, but stronger than any Fox that then lived. She was the Paramount of the Fox Family."

I frowned. "Of the Foxes here, in the city? Or . . . are there more?" I hadn't stopped to think that this is how it was in the rest of the world; continents near and far chock full of these Denizen people just wandering around with powers. It was an enormous machine coexisting with humans — and here I was, the faulty, uncertain cog.

"She was leader of them all," Sil replied.

The entire world. Why was Sil being so direct?

"The role of Paramount isn't one given based on age. It is awarded on merit: power, experience, the ability to perceive Ancient's will and act as its conduit in this world. She started out as the Ascendant, one of many training for the role, and then was chosen to lead. She had to visit each clan, mediate disputes, defeat darklings. Train younger Foxes to come into their powers."

"That's why she travelled . . ." I could feel my chest getting tight again. The resentment took hold faster than usual. "She went out of her way to help strangers but didn't bother with her own grandkid."

Sil finally pulled her paw away and looked up at me. "There was nothing she could do. Once Cecelia had taken on her role, she had more responsibility beyond her family, had to see to it for the greater good. And once you were marked with the sigil of the Moth Queen, she could do nothing to interfere. She only wanted you to live your life, oblivious to the world that cursed you."

"Curse is right." I wiped the grease from the salmon onto my pants. I tried not to show as much anger as I felt. But I laughed bitterly all the same.

"What a piss-poor excuse," I seethed. "She could've broken the rules, could've trained me to fight back. She could've helped me. I'm obviously going to need it." I paced to her letter-strewn vanity. "Do you know what it's like, being the kid with the dead parents who probably committed suicide? When everyone else is trying to live up to their parents, I was living mine down. I needed her. I needed *anyone*. Instead she has her errand-dog do the job she wasted years neglecting. I mean, I know she and my mom didn't see eye to eye, so it's not really a stretch that she wouldn't want anything to do with me, either.

"Face it, Sil. It wasn't just 'duty' or the 'greater good.' She stayed away from lack of interest. Figured a postcard every now and then was enough. Fine. She can die alone."

Like me. The thought rose up hard, but I pushed it away, slapping the twine-bound letters on the vanity table and letting them topple over. I turned to go; the air was getting too close in here.

"Your grandmother should've done more for you," Sil agreed sadly. "But you're not alone."

I stopped and looked back. Sil had come off the bed and to my feet in the span of a moment. I couldn't help smiling at her wry little face, her wide eyes that snared something in me since the first night I saw her. I tried to let the resentment go, but my muscles were still tight where the possibility of disappointment — and death — weighed them down.

"And what's going to stop you from leaving, too? I'm not really a sure investment for you."

She shot into the air in one of her trademark vertical jumps and landed in my arms — a perfect ten. That penetrating little snout was pressed into mine. "We are bound by fire," she said. "Spirit to spirit, nothing can break it."

I sighed. "I can think of a few things that can put even an inferno out. Like a river with a score to settle." I huffed. "But . . . well, I just hope the fire's big enough." I put her down, trying to feel better. "Anyway, I've got food, so you'll stick around, I think."

I was glad to know I'd have a sidekick (even though I felt more like hers), but we'd had enough drama for now. I had come in here to talk to her about the hospital, anyway.

"Listen, Sil. There's this one kid in my class — Barton Allen. He's definitely a Rabbit, but . . . there's something off about him. His legs are sort of, um, missing and —"

The floor in the hallway creaked, cutting me off. Sil froze, too, taking the cue from my nod to bolt around the bed and out of sight. I pulled the door open and found myself nearly bumping into Arnas's narrow chest. How long had he been there? What had he heard?

The first thing to catch my eye was the thing hanging around his neck on a leather string, something I hadn't seen before. (He wasn't the jewellery type.) It was a curious brass sphere that had a clasp, as though it could be opened — as though it had something inside it. I looked away, finding his blank eyes frowning down at me. He seemed determined, and that was also new.

I cleared my throat, pushing my hair behind an ear. "Um. Hi, Arnie." He hated when I called him that. *Good.* I slipped around him into the hallway.

"Who were you talking to?" he asked, blocking my path to the stairs and the safe haven of my room. I'd need to get around him again, but he was poised to stop me.

I tried to sidetrack him. "It's not uncommon for people to talk to the comatose, you know. Haven't you ever watched a soap opera?"

I darted to the left, but he slammed his hand into the wall, arm at my eye level. I took a step back. He had gone from years of being an aloof, stuttering pile of apathy to an aggressor, and I had no idea what had changed. I tried to turn my spirit eye on him for some insight, but when I did, I felt hot pain travel down my optic nerve and into my skull. I hissed and put a hand to it, unable to stop myself.

"How's that new eye of yours?" he asked. He was suddenly a sly private investigator, too. But I had his number. I now knew he was a Denizen. Which meant he probably knew I had been marked. But with the way he was acting, maybe living to tell the tale didn't sit well with him.

Great. Like I needed an enemy sleeping down the hall from me. But had he always been an enemy, or just an indifferent bystander? Had he, like my grandmother, just counted down the days until I was given over, sacrificial-lamb style? What had he to gain or lose?

"I'm fine, Arnas. But the twenty questions are killing me. I've got things to do." I decided I wasn't going to take a chance and let anything slip. I'd rather he thought I was still oblivious.

He almost looked about to lunge, but whatever he was thinking of doing, moving wasn't on the list.

All right, time to review: what power did Rabbits have? Speed? From the spirit walk Sil had taken me on, I remembered that their element was earth. What did that mean? Could he summon a mudslide from the suburbs to crush me? Cave the house in on my head? In this hallway, it didn't seem as though he had much of an advantage except his height (three inches on me) or his weight (barely thirty pounds more).

I took the visualization route, tried to imagine my blood becoming magma, my veins volcanic passageways. My heart rate rose and I was getting slightly warmer, but what heat I could conjure felt more like a menopausal hot flash than Sil's mythic firestorm. Even if I suddenly developed pyrokinesis, there wasn't much stopping me from accidentally burning down the house and everyone in it. And the garnet blade was a few floors away, hidden in my room . . .

This standoff had gone on way too long. I chose the aggravated teenager route and shoulder-checked my way past Arnas. I made it around him, but he grabbed my wrist. When his hand made contact with my skin, we both got a surprise. There was a hissing, a sudden reek of burning, and a shrill bawl that didn't come from me.

"What?!" I cried, whipping around, suddenly concerned for his well-being.

He took a step back, cradling his hand and glaring at me, disbelieving. He let it drop, trying to make it seem like he was unfazed, but I saw the flash of rising blisters and the red-hot flesh of his palm. Arnas had burned himself on me.

It wasn't pyrokinesis, but it was a start.

All I could say as I backed away was, "I — um, I'm sorry, Arnas. Find the nurse, maybe?" I couldn't believe I was blurting apologies to someone who was probably out to get me, but I still didn't have a handle on this hero-villain dynamic yet and figured I could at least be gracious for now.

I reached my room and slammed the door shut with my body. I looked down at my wrist and felt it myself — it was cool to the touch, to me. Maybe the visualization had worked after all.

I caught a flash of red as Sil appeared from behind my bed and began to pace. I didn't bother asking how she'd gotten around Arnas and me; I trusted her methods.

"Well, that was awkward," I sighed, smoothing my hands on my jeans, waiting for the shakes to stop.

"Things are moving faster than I thought," Sil grumbled, tail stiff and twitching. "Your uncle is obviously working against you, and he isn't alone. He was desperate for that photo last night. I wouldn't be surprised if he's aligned himself with the Owls . . ."

"The Owls?" I remembered the one I saw at the hospital; head swivelling, eyes piercing. "How can Arnas be working with them? I thought you said the Families were divided?"

"They are," Sil said, "but the Owl family controls most things, in their way — especially this city. The Families look to them to deal with Zabor, despite their archaic methods and shifty alliances. The Owls all have positions of power within the city itself, as well. They've been allowed to become the authority, and they are capable of doing terrible things to keep it that way."

I felt my phone go off in my back pocket. *Ugh, Phae, not now. There's intrigue afoot.*

I checked the screen anyway, and found a number I didn't recognize.

Hi Roan. Barton here. We met at the hospital today

Jackpot. I quickly texted him back and pocketed the phone, trying to refocus. "Okay, so let's rewind. The all-powerful Owl family and my uncle are working together. But why? What have they got against me?"

"Think!" Sil barked. "The Owls are the ones who deal with Zabor. They are set on appeasing her and keeping this city intact. What role do you have to play in that?"

Expect death every day. Okay, I got that part. But from everyone on all sides? "So the Owls just want to hand me over to the river demon. To save their own asses. Right?"

"Right. And as I'm sure you've already seen, Arnas is a Denizen of the Rabbits. But I don't think he has much favour with his Family. Whatever power he had was taken away from him. He seems the type to do whatever it takes to earn it back."

I groaned, sliding down my door all the way to the carpet. I suddenly felt so tired. My small uncle-burning victory vanished fairly quickly. "So I've got a crazy river demon waiting around with her mouth open, an uncle giving me up to the city's Owl Police, and a bunch of talons scrabbling for me." Good thing I was sleeping with that dagger under my pillow. "Am I even safe here?"

Sil came and sat beside me, whiskers and muzzle twitching in a half snarl. "Barely. I'll do what I can, but you will have to learn to protect yourself. And start gathering allies."

"Allies? From where? Should I start canvassing door to door, or start up a club at school?" I palmed my face, mouth twitching with laughter and fear. "It looks pretty much like every Family has me on a blacklist. How am I supposed to bring any of them together when throwing myself to the river is a better result to them?"

"You'll have to go to the fringes. If the Families are against you, it's because they're afraid. Because they would rather it be you than their children. You have to make them believe that you can end this." Sil's fatal tone made me cringe.

"I'm beginning to doubt I can," I argued. "All I seem capable of is burning people if I get riled up enough. I'm as useful as a baked potato."

"Just for now. That will all change." But Sil switched tacks. "Tell me about this boy, the one from today. He may be useful."

I felt my phone go off again. Sil cocked her head and pushed her nose into the screen as I read the message. *I need to know. How did u know about the dreams? The rabbits? When can we talk?*

I frowned. There was little I could go into just by hammering out a few characters on a keypad. *I think we've been seeing the same things.* I paused, thumbs hovering. *You aren't alone. We should talk at school on Monday.*

I rubbed my forehead. "Well, like I said before, he doesn't have legs — um, functional ones. Deedee says he was born without them. But I saw these rabbits, dying, running away, fleeing from a —"

"A scythe," Sil finished for me. "Hmm. Yes, he was born without legs. But mark my words — he is what we call 'severed.' Cut off from Ancient. He had his legs taken from him when he was still in the womb."

"Severed? Literally?" I winced. "But who would have done that to him? And why?"

"His parents, probably. To protect him."

I went so icy that if Arnas struck me now he'd probably get frostbite. "His own *parents*?"

"It's an old method. A terrible ritual steeped in blood that is dangerous to perform and irreversible. Zabor is only interested in the children of the Families, so if he was cut off from the power that connects us all —"

"Then Zabor wouldn't mark him. They did it to save his life." I looked down at my legs, grateful that my parents hadn't attempted something like that, but also sort of disappointed they hadn't taken drastic measures to keep me from my fate. *Maybe they had.* They were dead, after all.

I remembered Barton's worried mother's face as she hustled him away from me. She had done so much to keep him safe. No wonder she'd turned her back on me, the unwilling sacrifice. I would keep my kid miles away, too. "But why his legs? That I still don't get."

"The Rabbit family is rooted to the earth," Sil explained. "That is where their power lies. Take that away and you physically separate them from their element, simple as that. There are other methods of taking away their power, but they would still be considered a Denizen. Born without it, they have been forcefully made human, and thus not an agreeable . . . meal."

Great. I'd already tapped Barton, gotten my little issues into his head, and now he might be a lost cause. "Is it really irreversible? There's no way to restore his, um, power stuff? I got a spirit eye. Can't we get him spirit legs?"

Sil shook her head. "It isn't that simple. You would have to find the person who performed the ritual, a severer. Finding one who is willing to give themselves up, let alone the one we need . . . that's a task unto itself. Such rituals are forbidden, and those who perform them are dishonoured. Rebecca Allen used to be the representative of the Rabbits here, but she was denigrated for what she condoned. A small price to pay."

"For the preservation of her family, I guess. Do you know what happened to the guy who did the deed?"

"Dishonoured, stripped of his powers, probably fled. Whatever happened, the Owls kept it quiet. They did not get their authority by having it defied."

I stood up and stuck my hand under my pillow, retrieving the dagger. Hiding it in my room probably wouldn't be enough anymore. I'd have to carry it with me everywhere, what with Owls swooping in for the kill. But I'd need to keep this one-way ticket to expulsion out of sight on school grounds . . .

"There's something else," Sil said, leaping onto the bed so we were face to face. "The Owls won't come for you. Not yet. And your uncle won't harm you. All they will do is make sure you meet your end as it was intended, with as little fuss as possible."

"Yeah, but *I'll* make a fuss." I frowned, flicking the blade's sharp edge and producing a confident *twang*.

"What I mean" — Sil extended a long black paw towards me and lowered the dagger — "is that they won't intervene in Zabor's affairs directly. But they will do everything to help her. Your uncle will monitor your movements. And he's already given the Owls your likeness. I'm sure they've passed it on to Zabor's river hunters. They are dangerous, stupid creatures. They will go after any target that remotely resembles you — by process of elimination."

I caught my reflection in the jewel-blade of the dagger. Hacked-off hair, mismatched eyes, hardened skin from all the biking, hair almost red. I was starting to look like a Fox at the rate I was going. I wondered how recent the photo was that Arnas had handed over, and if my hectic hairstyling had bought me some time.

"Wait. These hunters . . . they're going to go around killing girls that look like I do, just to get to me?"

Sil just stared, the fading winter light casting odd shadows around her eyes. "This is why every day matters. This is why we cannot waste time. You have to be ready — *now*."

I put the cool blade to my forehead, hoping it'd ease the headache growing behind it. I hadn't had a migraine so foul since the night of the moths, but I could feel something growing there — a knot, a tight bunching of nerves, each strand something more powerful and dangerous and conspiring against me. Eventually the knot would become the size of my skull, busting through like a weed and consuming every good part of me. But I knew I had the will to resist and something germinating in my spirit that could untangle it. Or at least burn through it.

Just make it to Monday, Roan.

❧

Things did not improve when Monday finally came.

Sunday had been about avoiding Arnas at all costs while still trying to make it seem nothing was wrong. There had been no incidents with my grandmother and her nursing staff, so Deedee got a bit of reprieve there.

But the tension was heavy. She was holding things together with practised strategy, trying to downplay Arnas's strange behaviour and all my recent dealings. We ate together but I chewed more carefully, retreating to my room and marathoning TV shows. Trying to leave the house seemed even more dangerous than Arnas — what was out there, waiting for me?

While the three of us remained housebound, there was no chance of alone time with Sil in the summoning chamber. But Barton and I found time to connect, which made me feel productive. *I can't tell my parents about the dreams, but I feel like they know anyway. There are a lot of things they aren't telling me*, he texted. I kept reassuring him that I'd explain, that it wasn't safe to leave a trail of messages if he wanted to keep his parents out of it. I told him just to keep acting as though nothing was wrong, because it wasn't. Not yet, anyway. I knew that each day it would get worse, that the briar patch I'd found myself in would tighten.

On the way to school on Monday, the wild black thorns snagged me harder than I'd expected.

It's funny how, when it really happens, finding a dead body seems like anything else in the day. Like getting out of bed, or looking out a window, or crossing the train tracks on Wellington, like I had for years.

My bike jolted over the tracks. I wrenched the handlebars when I saw the girl in the road, and flew out of my seat as I lost the bike under me. I scrambled backward, yanking my face away from hers. At first, I didn't want to believe she was dead. I reached for her, squeezed her shoulder and shook it, but pulled away. She was stiff and staring listlessly into the iron sky with her one remaining eye.

It was just like Sil had said. A girl who looked like me, broken and tangled and dead, auburn hair and all.

One of her eyes had been savagely ripped out, but I forced myself to look into the untainted one. To look and to apologize from the depths of me, because this was my fault.

This was something that had happened because of me, even if it *wasn't* me. I silently promised the girl that I would stop all this, and that she wouldn't have died for nothing.

A flash went off nearby. I lurched away from the corpse and twisted around. A tall boy stood in the road, snapping pictures with an expensive Pentax. He didn't look like the press, didn't seem like he had any authority to be here. And I knew booking it now was my best bet. Shielding my face, I went for my bike and hustled, shoving past the vulture photographer, and snagging him with my handlebars. We caught a glimpse of each other in passing — icy eyes glinting in the harsh morning cold and, worse, a horrible smile on his face. Had he just been waiting around for a dead body to pop up for some sick art project? In my hurry to get away, I hadn't thought to turn my spirit eye on him. He was probably just a harmless, *human* sicko. I had gods and demons to worry about.

I got to school and found every bone and muscle and nerve fighting for control over my body. I had told myself to be ready for all the death heading my way, but I think actually seeing the body had fried my synapses. I could barely lock my bike up without falling apart. I couldn't believe I'd just run away, but what else could I have done?

I looked around, hoping Sil was hiding somewhere nearby to offer courage or comfort. No sign of her. School had once been a refuge from my problems, but it was now a prison, a waste of precious time that could be spent, *oh, I don't know*, stopping a city-wide cull of teenaged redheads and, ultimately, the flood that would drown us all.

At least school wasn't a danger zone (for now); I could be safe here in the crowds of kids who didn't know any better.

Find Barton. That's all I needed to focus on right now. I bit my glove off and fished my phone out of my pocket, checking for messages. Nothing from him, but still a few unread from Phae. She hadn't texted me in the last day; I think she'd caught the cue to give me some space. I wanted nothing more than to let her in on all of this, but I wondered if always-calm Phae could handle it. And was I willing to put her directly in danger just to have her tell me *it's all going to be okay*? It was probably best to keep her at arm's length; I wouldn't be able to live with myself if she suffered because of me, no matter how annoyed I was that she thought I was nuts.

I was in a haze, haunted by the chewed-up face of the river hunters' first victim: In my warped imagination, her good, dead eye looked right at me.

I careened back to reality when I found Barton in my path and nearly tripped over him. Luckily he had better reflexes than I did, and he manoeuvered to avoid me.

I tried (and failed) to collect myself. "Oh. Hey."

"Hey!" His face dropped when he got a better look at me. "Are you okay? You really don't look so good."

"Oh, uh . . ." I brushed my hand past my throat and jaw, pulse fluttering there like a caged animal. I needed to abort the oncoming panic attack. "I'm fine! Well, I mean . . . you know, things could be better. But we don't have to get into that right now."

I checked my phone for the time as we walked to class. I needed to be open with him, and it wasn't just because of this morning's dead girl; Sil's insistence that we couldn't waste any more time was weighing on me.

"Listen, Barton. I . . . I asked you about the dreams, and the rabbits, because something bad is happening. Not just to you or me. But it involves us. You know? I don't want to stress you out or anything, or make you think I'm some kind of wack job. I wouldn't blame you if you did . . ."

"You're really selling it," he snorted, "but look. I just . . . I need someone to talk to about this stuff, and I think I feel the same way that you do. That these dreams I've been having. They're . . . important, somehow. I thought you'd think *I* was crazy, but even if we both are, it's better than being alone in it, right?"

The warmth of gratitude spread through me, and for a moment I forgot the dead girl. Not alone in my crazy. I'd take it. "Right," I sighed, partially relieved but still shaken. "I've got class until two today. You?"

We'd arrived at the English classroom door. This was going to be a long, gruelling day, but I owed it to Deedee (and myself) to soldier on and see my school commitments through. After all, if I survived, I still needed to apply to university . . .

". . . classes till twelve, and a basketball practice till one thirty, so that works out," Barton was saying. "We can head back to my place. Take the bus, maybe?"

I couldn't help glancing down at his wheelchair, wondering how the logistics would work. He must've noticed — must *always* notice when someone stumbled over the fact that he didn't have legs from the knee down.

"I've used the bus for most of my life," he said tensely. "I just live in Wolseley, so it'll be a short ride."

I had my bike, but thankfully buses had bike racks on the front, or else we'd end up blocking the entire aisle.

"Sure," I said. "Sounds good." Going to Barton's house would prove challenging if we were going to get anything done; his mother would either hover or kick me out, but I hoped we could maybe keep our convo outdoors.

"Oh, hey, something's coming out of your bag." Barton pointed.

The heat flared from my throat to my cheeks when I discovered the garnet dagger was cutting through what I thought was my sturdiest bag. I shoved it back in and blocked the newly cut hole with my scarf.

I anxiously checked to see if anyone saw any more than the blade tip. Barton didn't ask, and as usual, no one noticed me or cared, so I think I was okay. Getting arrested would definitely throw a wrench into things right about now.

When I finally pulled myself together, Phae was suddenly at the classroom door, and I stiffened. Our gazes met, and I robotically waved. "Hi, Phae!" I tried to sound enthusiastic, like I hadn't ignored her all weekend. I must've made the incorrect facial expression, because she half smiled and hurried past us. My hand fell. I deserved that.

"Shall we?" I stepped out of Barton's path. He wheeled in, and I followed, focusing on holding my head high. Even with my eye all better, I knew I'd be grinding the permanent trench of my desk deeper, trying to keep myself under control.

Luckily my day was cut short. It took only one period for the news to flash through every grade and classroom about the girl found on Wellington Crescent. Police expecting foul play, teenager from the area, not sure if it was a targeted attack or a signal of more to come. And worst of all, she was a student from this school. *Mothers, lock up your daughters.* For once I agreed. At least until the spring passed . . .

Panic spread like an infection. Kids (mostly girls) were frantically calling their parents, asking to be picked up *like, right now*. Everyone was too distracted to focus in class. The principal called an assembly. I knew she was going to cancel classes today, knew she was going to tell everyone *it's okay to be feeling what you are feeling*, and *you have to be there for one another in this time of crisis*, and I didn't think I could deal with being surrounded by my stricken, tearful classmates, knowing that if I didn't do my job, it could be any one of them next on the menu.

As students streamed out of classrooms, talking hysterically, I turned against the flow, trying to swim through and find Barton. Once I did, I led him to the sidelines of the body-deluge.

"What about the assembly?" Barton snapped his brakes on as we were nearly crushed into the bank of lockers.

I tried to sound sure of myself, like the leader that I didn't think I'd ever be. "I just thought we could get a head start on getting back to your place, since we both know class is probably cancelled." I was already checking exits, feeling more like a bank robber than a fearless hero.

Barton checked his phone, frowning; sure enough, the coach had sent out a mass text about basketball being cancelled. "You're right. I guess we'll find out more on the news tonight, anyway. Let's bail."

We split up, prepared to meet again at the back entrance after we'd retrieved our bags. My chest hummed with anticipation: I expected shadows to spring out and take a chunk out of me at every corner. I kept scolding myself to keep my head, but I wondered if I'd have a choice about that after too long. This was definitely nothing like those Chosen One books, video games, or movies I'd consumed over my entire nerdy existence. I felt too human. And way too vulnerable.

On the bus, I kept a watchful eye out the window. As we crossed the Assiniboine on the Maryland Bridge, I involuntarily shuddered. I wondered which part of Zabor's body was lying there in dormant rage, suspended beneath four feet of ice. I wondered if she could smell me, if I had the same scent or taste that my mother did.

Get out of your head, Roan! I tried commanding myself using Sil's voice. I wondered where Sil was, if she was okay outside, if she was trailing me. Having her around when I spilled the beans about the not-so-normal circumstances surrounding me (and now girls that looked like me) would've been helpful. No one could argue with a talking fox. Believe me, I tried.

"You okay?" Barton asked again. I'd been too wrapped up in our whirlwind meeting to really get to know him at all yet, and I suddenly felt terrible. Here he was, concerned for me, a potential nutty stranger, and all I could say was, "Yep, I'm fine."

"I know what a 'brave face' looks like," he said, flexing his hand on the safety bar as we jerked to a stop. "It's okay. This thing with that girl. It's pretty messed up. Do you want to talk about it?"

Did I ever. The truth would come out soon enough, but I wove carefully around it. "Yeah, it's just . . ." I leaned in, lowered my voice. "I saw her. Before the cops did, anyway. I saw her on my way to school."

Barton's fuzzy eyebrows looked like they were going to rocket off his head. "What?" he hissed. "And you didn't tell anyone?"

There's a good point. Telling the authorities might have made me feel a bit better, in addition to being the right thing to do, but then again I didn't want to implicate myself, though I highly doubted city police would connect me to the crime via reasons of paranormal activity. Unless there were Owls on the force, which, now that I thought about it, was pretty likely.

"I don't know! I just . . . I panicked! Have you ever seen a dead body before? And there was this weird kid, taking pictures . . . he seemed like the type who had nothing better to do than alert the police." I looked away and physically tried to rub the guilt off my face.

Barton was proving way too quick for someone who'd had his Denizen senses cut off. "Roan . . ." he whispered. "You didn't have anything to do with that girl, did you? With what happened to her?"

I decided it was best to say nothing as the bus came to our stop. Barton had stuck with me this long, and somehow *that* revelation wasn't enough to push him away. I ducked out ahead of him as the ramp came down, reclaiming my bike from the front rack. We crossed to Wolseley Avenue and started walking west.

The sidewalks were clogged with snow, barely shovelled by the nearby winter-averse homeowners, so we stuck to the roads. "Thank god for snow tires!" I joked, trying to lighten the mood. I think I needed to just shut it. Could wheelchairs *have* snow tires?

"Yeah . . ." Barton was elsewhere, I think, trying to collect himself. "I really don't know where to start with all this. I get the impression that something big is happening. Something beyond just you and me, and maybe having to do with the dead girl. Yes? No?"

"Bingo," I sighed. We walked two abreast in the oncoming

lane, and I did my best to walk, talk, and keep my spirit eye activated, just in case. "Long story short, I asked you about the dreams, because . . . when I first saw you in English class, I saw them. Sort of. A bunch of Rabbits running away from something horrible. Because, um, I've got this sort of insight thing. It's hard to explain."

Barton paused for a beat. "Have anything to do with that new eye of yours?"

I chewed the inside of my cheek. So people *had* noticed. "Sort of. Yeah."

He yanked his collar up higher around his ears as a harsh wind snagged past us. "When I saw you in class for the first time, I didn't recognize you without the eye patch. Hard to miss, you know."

Was I secretly a high school celeb (for totally not-so-nice reasons)? It was the first time anyone had told me I was the centre of strangers' gossip. "I noticed you around, too," was all I could say stupidly in return, since it was true. I wondered how many other people talked about me.

"Let's just say that miraculously healing body parts are of interest to me." Barton smiled. I think he was trying to back-pedal, to make me feel less self-conscious. "In the dreams, I have legs. They feel so real. I sometimes wake up feeling like they're there, even though I've never had them. They feel just out of reach, but when the scythe comes . . ." He didn't finish, and I didn't blame him. "I know I was born without them. But I can *feel* them. They're real. And my parents won't tell me any more than *it's a birth defect*, so when I started asking even more questions, my mom just took me to the doctor, said I could use some medicated sleep for a while. That just made me more suspicious."

We passed a small lot-sized park whose treeline overlooked the river. "Anyway, this is . . . it's just nice. I felt like I was going insane. The dreams have been getting worse lately. I'm glad I can talk about it with you without being, you know, accused of being nutso."

Preach. It was nice to have an ally for once, someone who was dealing with the same strangeness.

I shrugged, smiling, letting my guard slightly down. "I'm no expert in anything that's happening, to be honest. I'm just as much of a newb at all this. A newb with *way* too much responsibility."

That's when Barton turned and snapped his brakes on right in my path. "Okay, this is the part where you finally reveal what your crazy ESP and this random dead girl have to do with the both of us. Are you in some kind of trouble? With a cult?"

I stopped short. "I, um . . ." Now I sort of understood Arnas's compulsive stammer. Sometimes words just failed. "Look there's . . . there's all this mythology and spiritual stuff. It's got a lot to do with death and a demon hiding in the river, waiting to drown us all. Man, I wish my fox-sidekick were here, she's way better at explaining it than I —"

A shadow flickered in my periphery. I tried to find where it vanished to, but it was quick. I tightened the grip on my bag and felt my blood leaving my extremities. I noticed too late how close we were to the river.

"What's the matter?" Barton twisted in his chair, clicking the brakes free.

"Shh!" I warned. I didn't take my eyes off the treeline beyond the park as I settled my bike against a tree then swung my backpack around to produce the garnet blade in one smooth motion. It glinted bruise-purple in the grey and white afternoon.

Barton tried to follow me, but I waved him off. "You're really freaking me out, Roan. I can't believe you brought a machete to school!"

My knees tensed as I took a defensive stance. "I have a bad feeling that risking expulsion was worth it."

I flinched in the direction of a low hiss and the rumbling snarl that followed. Concentrating, I turned my spirit eye into full wakefulness and stiffened when I saw a pair of sharp faces glinting black and oily between the trees. Their eyes were giant vertical slits on either side of their heads, mouths gashes full of uneven teeth, heads bobbing like grinning pythons.

"Barton," I said, trying to move my mouth as little as possible. "We have to get out of here *right now*."

"Why?" he asked at full volume. As soon as he spoke, the pack released a terrible chittering, like laughter, their grotesque, lithe bodies undulating as they rose upright to lick the air. "What do you see over there?"

Oh god, he can't see them. Maybe that was a consolation, but it wasn't going to help me any. Where the hell was Sil? Could I even kill these things?

"Just get the hell out of here!" I shouted, desperate to protect him by putting the monsters' focus on me. And that's when the two of them galloped up from the frozen riverbed at full speed, tearing through the snow and reaching out with jagged, splintered hands.

I dove out of the way, not knowing what else to do,

crumpling gracelessly in a heap on the sidewalk. I got a mouthful of dirty snow and whipped up my head just in time to see one of the creatures looming over me, winding up to strike. I stumbled to my feet and ran full tilt towards the river to lead them away from Barton.

"Hey! Over here!" The two that had been snarling after me looked suddenly displeased and drew up on legs I hadn't noticed they had. They were at least six feet tall, heads coming to a point and spines flashing along their backs. One of them broke the arm off its partner, and it liquefied, forming itself as a giant ice club. The mutilated hunter didn't seem to mind.

"Shit," I muttered, raising my feeble dagger in a two-handed white-knuckle grip, baseball-style. I was going to lose, but I needed to show them I wasn't willing to run. *Foxes don't run.*

They came for me in a flash and the first blow hit home, cracking my head back and slamming me into a tree. The second monster was hot on the first's tail, but I rolled out of the way as it crashed into the tree, ripping it clean out of the ground. It careened towards the ice, and I switched my focus to the club-wielding hunter diving for my legs. I flailed uselessly then remembered I had a weapon and came out swinging. Feeble though it was, my attack caught the hunter in the corner of its lips, ripping its wound of a mouth wider to what was probably its ear. Its keening wail stabbed my eardrums and made me scream.

"God, what *is that*?" I heard Barton shout, and I realized he was still here. He couldn't see the river hunters, but he could hear them? I got to my feet in time to escape the horrifically fast and out-for-blood monster that was gunning for me. I didn't have time to think as it twisted in an impossible way towards me and its club clanged against the dagger I'd raised above my head to meet the blow. The hunter pressed all its terrible strength into that club, and my legs buckled like an unsteady card table. I heard and saw the blade cracking under the weight — I was finished if it busted apart.

There was a rush of black. The hunter that had chucked itself over the bank had recovered, and like a bruised bolt of lightning, lunged out of the trees and straight for Barton.

"No!" I screamed, which broke my hunter's concentration. Its head cracked in the direction of its cohort, and I took that second to jerk out from under its club, pivot behind it, and stab down into its back. It roared and writhed, the awful pinging noise it made underscoring the fountains of black oil-blood spurting from the wound. It roiled against the blade, and with a pull, half of it broke off inside the monster. My dagger had been reduced to a shiv, and it'd have to do for the second one.

All this fuss did nothing to stop the other hunter from diving on Barton, knocking him clean out of his wheelchair and into the snow. His glasses flew into the street, and all I could hear was a human howl from under the black beast's girth as it clawed and snapped.

With a featherweight quarterback tackle, I launched everything I had on top of the thing, knocking it off and sending the both of us splay-limbed into the road. This one seemed a bit more sluggish than the one I'd just taken down, nice and slow on the recovery, and as I swung out wildly and awkwardly, I finally hit the mark and stabbed what was left of the dagger down into its stomach. The blade shard punctured the soft belly, and I got a faceful of black squirted back at me as I drew the shattered dagger out again. The hunter wailed, desperately holding its guts in as it scrambled away. It joined its wounded partner and they hobbled for the river from whence they'd come, leaving trails of blue-black muck-blood in their wake.

I finally caught my breath, wiping the offal out of my eyes as I twisted around to find Barton. As I got close to him, I tripped on the curb, landing heavily by his side. My mouth felt numb when I looked down at him. The dagger, slippery with blood and almost bladeless, fell out of my hand and into the snow. But I didn't care. I didn't need it now.

I didn't know *what* I needed. Barton's eyes were milky white, and his jacket was ripped open, a wide gash that already looked infected burning past the shredded cotton of his T-shirt. My hand hovered over it, trembling with fading adrenaline.

"Barton? Barton, can you hear me?" I shook him, but all he did was wheeze, then make a noise like the piercing wail of his attacker. For a second he seemed to see me, faded eyes catching mine as he grabbed my arm.

"What is it? What is it?" I wanted him to give me detailed instructions, wanted him to tell me exactly what to do. He only took a hard swallow of air in reply before collapsing back to the ground, sightless and unresponsive.

I let him go and looked around at the suburban street. So many houses, but the sidewalks and driveways were empty. We were alone. There was no help coming. Frantic, I dug through Barton's pockets until I found his phone, scrolling madly through the contacts until I found *Home*.

Mrs. Allen answered, and all I could say through my sobs was, "It's Barton, oh god, they did something to him, please, I can't do this. I can't. Help me."

A CROWN *of* HORNS

I'd been letting the shower run over me for the past fifteen minutes, my skin one overheated red welt. I sat in the corner of the tub, only just now satisfied that I had gotten all the black crap out of my hair and scrubbed from under my fingernails. The scene with the Allens as they collected Barton stabbed me afresh every time I pictured him, limp and reduced in his father's arms. They didn't bring an ambulance, didn't want to make a scene, but Rebecca Allen looked ready to assault me when I tried to apologize, tried to explain.

"You stay the hell away from my son!" she screamed as she got into the back seat with Barton's prostrate body. The car doors slammed and they peeled away, leaving only scarlet hatred in their wake. They earned that right. I had practically killed him. Or whatever was left of him.

I shut the water off. I wasn't ready to get out just yet, so I slicked back my dripping, spiky hair and drew my knees up to my chin, digging them into my eyes to calm myself. I wanted to let flow some loud, body-wracking sobs, but I heard a rustling from the other side of the shower curtain and drew it aside so I could check who it was before going all hopeless-weepy-shower-scene.

Sil was rifling through my ruined clothes, covered as they were in the scum from this afternoon. She recoiled in a savage sneezing fit, growling all the while.

"What is this?" she said through bared teeth in the direction of my laundry. "What happened to you?"

I let the shower curtain go, switching from despair to anger with the swish of the plastic. "Go away, Sil."

Her snout nosed through the curtain, and a paw followed.

"I said *go away*!" I snapped, pushing her head off as it tried to sneak through.

It was strange to hear her whimpering like a chastised dog. "Please, Roan. We need to talk about this."

"Sil, I'm naked and I'm upset and I *don't want to talk to you*." I pulled my legs in tighter. "If you had actually been there for me, you'd *know* what happened!"

Silence. I watched her shadow retreat out of view and was satisfied.

The next thing I saw was a ball of Sil crashing through the daisy-patterned shower curtain, which tore away from its moorings with her in it.

"Goddammit, Sil!"

Sil freed herself from her vinyl wrappings, shook herself, and came in for more investigative sniffing. "Are you hurt?" she asked, but I pushed her away again.

"Knock it off, okay? I'm fine." On the outside, maybe. Inside I felt ripped to shreds, and wondered what it was going to take to ever feel ready. "Where were you? I seriously needed your help and what were you doing, *napping?*" I stepped out of the tub and grabbed a towel from the rack to cover myself.

She sighed. "I can't follow you everywhere, Roan. I didn't think you'd be careless enough to throw yourself at the river when you knew those things would be there waiting for you."

"*I'm* careless? You knew I wasn't ready to face those things and you left me alone to get a crash course in demon dissection!" I cried. "If you had been there, you could've gone all Flareon on them and none of this would've happened!" I sank to the floor beside the tub, staring blankly at a clump of hair underneath the sink. I just wanted someone else to blame. "Barton got hurt. Bad. And I know it's my fault, okay? I know I couldn't protect him." *It was stupid of me to think I could.*

Sil rested her front paws on the bathtub lip and put her head against my arm. "Perhaps you set your sights on him as an ally too quickly. You should accept this and just let him go."

I levelled Sil with a disgusted glare. "So I put him in the line of fire and leave him to die?"

Sil shrugged her little fox shoulders. "What do you want me to say? What use would he have been to you, hobbled as he is? He was a target waiting to be struck. You need to focus and train, and most of all surround yourself with strong allies who can help you in this fight. What chance do you have of defeating Zabor with a powerless cripple, anyway?"

Sil yipped as I hauled her out of the tub, half-throwing, half-dumping her onto the floor, where she slid across the bathroom tile. She recovered gracefully, taking a defensive stance and turning her hot Fox glare on me.

Ifrit be damned. "You're a shitty excuse for a spirit guide, you know that?" I found myself shouting, now on my feet and ready to rumble. "I *know* Barton was meant to help me do this horrible godforsaken task you forced me into. Now he's suffering because of me, and your backhanded comfort is that I should just *move on*? You pathetic. Little. *Creep*!" I pitched my dirty laundry at her, then stormed out of the bathroom and tore through my drawers for fresh clothes. "I refuse to give up on him. I don't care what you say. I'm going to save him."

I tried to snarl at Sil with some authority and did a double take when I saw her sitting primly in the bathroom doorway, appearing calm and complacent from under my black-stained jacket. "Good. I thought I lost you for a second, there."

Sil's tirade had succeeded almost too well in getting me out of my black mire of misery and back on my feet. "Oh," was all I could say. Then I frowned. "Wait. Are you going to help me, then?"

She shook off my clothes as I pulled on fresh pants. "I'll obviously help you learn to better defend yourself. But you came out alive, and judging by your clothes you came out the victor."

"Not much of a victory," I muttered, pulling my socks on. I swallowed as my mind swept through the montage of this morning's dead girl plus Barton.

"Barton's not a casualty *yet*," Sil reminded me. "You may be able to help him. But we'll have to see him first."

I snorted. "Yeah, if I can us get past his mother." I dug through my bag and pulled out what remained of the broken glass dagger covered in solidified muck. I had forgotten all about destroying my only weapon. "Sorry, Sil. I really don't know what I'm doing."

"You will. Have some faith." Sil put her nose to the broken blade, and before I could do anything, it caught fire. I recoiled but didn't dare let it go; how would I explain a giant burn mark in the carpet to Deedee?

"What the hell?!" But the fire wasn't hot to me, and as I relaxed my hand around the hilt, the flames burned the black away. When they flickered out, I held a fresh garnet blade — longer this time, almost a sword. It glinted and I felt warm with possibility.

"Next time I'll be ready," I assured Sil. Assured myself. The day was young. I could fix this.

My phone went off somewhere in my discarded clothes. I lunged for it, hoping that it was Barton messaging me to say he was okay or that he hated my guts. Either would be okay, because it would mean he was alive and cogent.

It was Phae. Several messages asking where I'd disappeared to after the assembly. She said she was starting to worry, and that she just wanted to know I was okay. I definitely wasn't, but I knew I'd have to reply sooner or later.

I went straight home, I lied. *I've just been stressed. No need to worry. Going to a friend's house.*

She must've been waiting by her phone, because her reply came in a digital flash: *Which friend? Do you need a ride? I'm free if you want to talk.*

I didn't know when the time would be right to talk to her without double-dealing through my teeth, but it definitely wasn't now. *I'm fine, no worries.* The biggest lie I could conjure. And I left it at that.

For now, I had to concentrate on getting Sil and me undetected out of the house. "Can't you just go invisible or something?" I asked her. "How else have you been avoiding Arnas and Deidre?"

"Lots of empty rooms and unchecked beds," she replied as we left the bedroom.

We made it to the stairs, with me in the lead. I knew Deedee was a safe bet for being tangled up in her regular routine, but Arnas could be lurking anywhere, home-office layabout that he was. Sure enough, I heard the television on in the living room, volume set low. It was the local news, reporting on the girl I'd found this morning. She was my age and had so much ahead of her. Like all victims do.

I went to turn the corner towards the kitchen and, ultimately, the back door, when Arnas walked directly into my path. I was 0 for 2 for running into him. He was on the phone, and he jumped back from me as though I'd burned him all over again. "I'll call you back," he spat, and hung up.

I peeked around the stairs to see Sil within inches of me and tried to motion with my eyes for her to go back, but she didn't move.

"What are you doing here?" A fresh interrogation.

"Uh. I live here?"

He scowled. "Why aren't you in school?"

I thumbed casually at the TV. "You're the one watching the news. A student from my school was found dead this morning. They let classes out." *Try not to look guilty*, I commanded my face.

Arnas grimaced and walked into the living room to shut off the screen. Sil took the chance to dart around the corner and towards the door. I trailed behind, hoping to grab a spare jacket from the closet on the way, since mine was mucked up. All I could find was one of Deedee's fancy wool trench coats with a hood. Barely appropriate for subzero weather, but it'd have to do.

Arnas hurried around the corner. Man, he was a terrible set of eyes for whoever he was working for. "W-where are you going now?"

I opened the door just in time to let Sil out, undetected. Hearing his classic stutter made me feel immediately less threatened; this was going to be easier than I thought. So I got mouthy.

"Wouldn't you like to know." I grinned, saluting and hustling out the door and into the deep-freeze. I'd left my bike neglected in a snowbank after the morning's festivities and, pressed for time, I heaved it up onto my back and ran towards the street. Sil kept pace.

"I don't think I'll have enough room in my coat for you this time," I panted, dropping the bike at the road, letting it bounce on its huge tires while I steadied it. Sil skidded to a halt and leapt, deft claws scrabbling up my body until she settled over my shoulder like a living fur stole.

"Hurry!" she hissed as I mounted, and we both whipped our heads around as a jacketless Arnas rushed out to his car. He was coming after me. I instantly regretted mouthing off. He scrambled into the driver's seat, and for a split second he took the two of us in — delinquent should-be-dead niece and blatantly real fox in tow. I mounted my bike and pedalled hard, trying to ignore the slam of Arnas's car door or the tires struggling out into the street after us.

"Shit, shit, *shit*!" I gritted my teeth, pumping my battle-sore legs, determined to get max power. Sil and I shoulder checked as Arnas's SUV revved in our wake. The cold air burned my ears and skin as we cut through it. I wove into the oncoming lane, hoping that would deter him, but it didn't.

"There's no way I can outride him!" I shouted. "We're going to have to bail!"

We were coming up onto the train tracks and the river on our left. In spring there was a clear path up to the pedestrian train bridge towards Omand's Creek, but now it was buried in snow, and my tires could only cut through so much. I wrenched the handlebars and we plowed off the road, tumbling arse-over-teakettle down the short grade into the snow.

I heard Arnas's brakes slam, tires skidding on the black ice on the road; he wasn't desperate enough to pursue us at the risk of getting stuck in a snowdrift. I tripped to my feet, abandoning the bike, and Sil raced after me, clumps of snow falling from our respective coats as we bolted.

Arnas's diminished screams carried on the wind: "You leave Barton Allen out of this! You leave him alone! You hear me?"

"Keep going!" Sil snarled, and neither one of us looked back as we pushed our bodies up the hill and over the pedestrian bridge, over the river and around the corner, down to the creek and up again, onto Wolseley Avenue. I stopped us a few blocks from the park where we'd met our river hunters, and we ducked into a back lane.

Sil panted at my heels, clouds of hot breath steaming around us. "Why did you stop?"

We'd risked more than I'd wagered in the last ten minutes — Arnas attempting to turn us into a new hood ornament, broken bones cushioned by frostbite, and a river hunter run-in, since we were near their territory now. I was cold and sweating and my skin felt like it was going to peel off from frostbite. So naturally I burst out laughing, and it hurt my ribs and made me collapse against someone's badly painted backlot garage, but I laughed anyway.

"Pull yourself together," Sil snapped.

I sighed. "It's just . . . I have no idea where Barton actually *lives*." The laughter bubbled up again, turning into sobs. "Maybe we can go back and ask Arnas?"

Everything had happened so fast, and I didn't dare follow the Allens when they'd come for Barton. All I knew is that they lived in this general neighbourhood . . . but short of going door to door, I was screwed.

"Hmm" — Sil paced on the icy pavement — "did you touch him at all? When he was injured?"

The way things went down, I couldn't remember that fine a detail, but . . . images played in my memory like scenes from an old film: the gash on his chest as I peeled his jacket from it, the way he had grabbed me before succumbing to unconsciousness. "Yes. I mean, well, *he* touched *me*."

"Then there is a way to find him. His touch means that your body knows his spirit energy, consciously or not. You must try to pinpoint it inside you, and to see it outside."

I screwed my face up. "Oh wow, mystical fox lady, that sounds *so* easy to do, let me just tap into that." I tightened my face and strained. "Nope, nothing, sorry."

Sil's hackles lifted. I wondered if she could burst into flames just from being annoyed. "Do you want my help or not, you ungrateful pup?"

"Well, come on, you aren't helping anyone by being so *extremely* vague. How am I supposed to do any of what you're saying with zero context?"

"Focus, that's how!" she barked. "Focus, and concentrate. You've done it before with your eye when looking out into the world. Now, focus it inward, find the memory of Barton's spirit, because it has imprinted on you. You're a Fox, for pity's sake. You were born to hunt."

She was right. This was a hunt. I shut my eyes and held my breath.

I tried to visualize again, this time travelling inward and ordering myself to calm down. I felt a warmth spark and spread through me, banishing the numbness in my fingers and flesh, and kneading my muscles. If it was that easy to turn on my spirit-furnace, the harsh Winnipeg winters wouldn't stand a chance.

I frowned. *Okay, focus.* I pictured a series of nerve lines, of threads, and I followed the synapses as I searched for Barton, putting the memory of him reaching out and grabbing me on a loop, until it felt as though his hand were right there on my flesh. The warmth ignited into a flame, and I opened my eyes with a jolt. The feeling stayed there, as if he was beside me, and I saw — maybe with my spirit eye, or maybe it was a helpfully conjured hallucination — whatever it was, it was a silvery outline that guttered like frozen lamplight, and it was beside me and waiting. I got to my feet without taking my eyes off it, and it shot into the air, leaving a bright streak behind it.

"Do you see the path?" Sil asked. "Do you feel it?"

"Yeah. I see it!" Maybe I wasn't so dumb after all. I didn't know if I could help him yet, but this was better than nothing. "Let's go!"

It turned out that we weren't that far away, and we found the silver bulb of light on Telfer Street, hovering over the porch of a plain raised bungalow, the only house with a ramp. *Maybe you should've looked for that first, genius.*

As soon as I reached the stoop, the light fell to the ground, a fading star.

"What if we're too late?" I whispered. Was the light Barton's spirit? Was he giving up the fight?

I set a foot on the steps, but before I could even move, the outer door swung open, and Mrs. Allen's appearance paralyzed me.

For a second we were both lost for words, me swallowing the growing lump in my throat, her looking menacing with her pinched, reddening face, but she finally yelled, "Get off my property! Get out of here!"

I backed away, hands up, surrendering. "Please, Mrs. Allen. I know it's my fault, but I just want to see —"

"You think I'd let you anywhere near my son after what you've done? Get out of here before I call the police, you little . . ." Her tirade died out, and I followed her gaze down. She was staring at Sil — surprised, alarmed? Sil hadn't erupted into fiery doom, and she was trying to do as I was — keep things calm. But something passed between them, and Mrs. Allen had a look of frightened familiarity, especially when Sil spoke. "We are only here to help, Rebecca. If you care for your son, you will let us in."

She seemed to shrink back into herself, moving towards the door and clutching it for support. "But . . . you —"

"What's going on?" said a third voice, this time male. I recognized Mr. Allen as he appeared in the doorway, dark face pale, sleeves rolled up, glasses askew. He was the spitting image of Barton and looked like he'd been neck-deep in something haunting. I focused my spirit eye and, yes, he was a Rabbit. But where his wife was anxious and flighty, he seemed more grounded, more still and composed. And maybe he would listen to reason.

"David, keep them here, I'm calling the council!" Rebecca pivoted to get past him, but he caught her by the elbow.

"Becca, stop," he sighed. "We can't afford a scene right now."

"Don't talk to me about what we can afford! If she's here, she'll attract the hunters, and Barton will be finished. Think of your son!"

"I am!" he snapped, eyes darting from his wife to Sil and me at the bottom of his steps. He let the tension in his body drop as he gathered her to him, and she buried her face in his chest. But he was looking straight at me even as he comforted her.

"It's dangerous for you to be here — in more ways than you imagine." I thought of the Owls then, and wondered what they would do to not only me, but the Allens, if they found out I was here. "There's nothing you can do now. You should go." His warning was tender but firm.

"Please!" I found myself blurting, making up my case as I went along. "All I want to do is see him. I know I'm a total amateur and that giving me up for dead is the best solution to all of your problems, but . . ." I looked at Sil. "There might be a way to save him. And to stop all of this. But I need Barton's *help* for that."

Rebecca looked up from her husband's arms, eyes glistening. David Allen had the identical expression. His mouth twitched into what could've been a smile, but his face was too tired to hold onto it.

"Someone else came to our door, once, when Barton was

small. And she said something similar." He let Rebecca go but squeezed her shoulder. "Maybe we should have listened to her then."

I glanced around me, expecting the ghost of my mother to appear at my side or be reflected somehow in my shadow. In my mind, she stood taller, more solid than I ever could, with a backbone made of fire-tested iron and a resolve that was unbreakable. All I could muster was a slouched refusal to leave. Hopefully, that was enough to honour the woman I hardly knew.

After several moments' hesitation, David Allen tilted his head towards the open door. "Get in, then."

I scanned the street like a fugitive and went up the steps, Sil at my side. The Allens momentarily forgot me as they watched her, and she watched them back. They were wary of my bristling sidekick, and they ought to be.

Barton's room was at the back of the house, and we reached it so quickly that I hadn't had any time to steel myself. I stopped at the threshold and stared at the reduced Barton in his bed, my throat suddenly thick. His flesh was bruised with infection, skin turning purple with patches of black. His shirt had been removed, leaving only a blood-black compress to cover the wound in his chest. Rebecca hurried over to remove it and check the gash, but she inhaled with a hiss, and that was telling enough. With shaking hands she got a fresh compress and applied it, even though I could tell it was pointless. Barton looked ready to die, despite how his white eyes rolled around in his skull and his limbs writhed under his sheets.

What really made my heart tighten was how he was tied, stump and wrist, to the bed frame, probably to keep him from spasming onto the floor, and when I looked down, I saw that three concentric circles had been smeared into the carpet around him. Summoning circles. Looking at Mr. Allen, I recognized his exhaustion because I remembered feeling it myself. Had Mr. Allen begged the spirit world for his son's life only to come back empty-handed? If he couldn't do it, then how could I?

Rebecca was dabbing her son's rolling head, murmuring motherly comforts through her tears. I was sure he couldn't hear them.

"What . . . I don't . . ." I managed to squeak.

"He's becoming one of them," David said in a tone that had already divorced itself from the situation. "It won't be long now. He can hear the river calling him. If we let him go, he'd slither under the ice and go right to his new mother."

Barton seemed to blacken to charcoal the longer I stared at him. His skin, once deep brown, had gone greyish and was turning burnt in patches. Would his eyes migrate to the side of his head soon, his mouth splitting his face open in a slavering gash? I needed to get out of here, but Sil entered the room, and all I could do was tread behind her. She jumped onto the bed, onto Barton's chest, and flicked the compress off his wound with her snout.

"Don't!" Rebecca cried, but David held her back.

Sil favoured her with a glance. "If I was going to hurt him, it wouldn't do him any worse," Sil croaked, digging her face into the poisonous cut in the flesh. I wanted to look away, but I just slapped a hand to my mouth and kept my eyes and face forward. Sil seemed to be looking for something, like a dog nosing in the dirt for a bone, and when her head snapped back up, she had something black and oozing and alive in her teeth.

She crunched down and the thing screamed, then burst in her face. The black burned away as it touched her, though, and for a blessed minute, Barton was still.

"What the hell was that?" I cried, unable to control myself.

Sil continued nosing at the wound, the heat coming from her maw cauterizing the gash. But I could see it was only a temporary solution: The blisters still moved from beneath, ready to open afresh. "The infection is more of an infestation. It is alive inside of him. Let's just say I killed the infection's queen. The drones will be scattered, and the infection will slow. But soon they will rise again. I've bought him some time before his spirit putrefies."

Rebecca seemed all out of tears as she stroked Barton's clammy forehead. David was pretty much the only one present now. "So you bought him some time," he said. "What good is that?"

Sil just sat there on Barton's chest, considering him, until she said, "We will go to the Deer. They will know what to do."

I whipped my head towards her. The Deer? I had barely seen a Deer Denizen in the city, to the point where I'd forgotten all about them. David seemed just as dubious.

"The Deer have resigned themselves to pacifistic solitude for decades. They won't come out of that to help any of us. All the grace of the healers has been slowly fading as generation after generation rejects their human forms. There aren't any *left*."

When Sil looked up at him, the amber fire in her eyes and fur seemed faded, her hide slightly tighter than it had been only minutes ago. What was happening to her?

But Sil smiled anyway. "Roan will persuade them. She's very good at it."

Yeah, that's what got Barton here in the first place . . . I was also pretty unimpressed to be volunteered for yet another mission I had no idea how to accomplish. But when I saw the Allens' looks of feverish desperation, I swallowed and nodded. "I'll find a way to make them come." The words fell out of my mouth, almost meaningless in my ears. I hesitated, but I placed my hand on Barton's limp one. "I promise."

Sil jumped to the floor, tongue hanging free of her jaw in a silent pant. "I believe there's still a contingent of active Deer in the Assiniboine Forest, near Charleswood. We'll start there."

David helped steady Rebecca as she stared at her catatonic son. "And if they don't come?" he murmured.

"They will," I said, surprising myself. Even though I had no way of keeping my promise. I put a hand on David's forearm, tried to smile, and followed Sil out.

We tread in silence down Wolseley Avenue towards the dip at Omand's Creek Park. The creek bled out into the river, but it was as quiet as we were. I kept glancing at Sil to see if she was okay, or if she was going to reveal any reasons for her sudden fatigue. For now she kept pace with me, eyes and ears forward.

"Well?" I finally asked. "Will they come?"

Sil snorted, lips curling back over her teeth. "The Deer will do anything to stay out of this conflict. All we can dare hope is that *one* listens to us without spooking. Your friend has very little time."

I dug my hands into my pockets, shoulders hunched against the cold in my less-than-ideal winter jacket. The cold stung, but all I kept seeing was Barton, ruined body prostrate in his parents' arms, unreachable. Anger bubbled up inside me — equal parts anger at myself for failing everyone just because I was alive, and anger at the creatures intent on destroying innocent people to get to me. As the rage grew to fill my entire chest, I felt much warmer, and relaxed.

We reached the top of the hill and the path that descended into Omand's Creek, the brook beneath the Sharpie-vandalized bridge, and the river it led to, frozen and still. But Sil and I both stiffened at this crest, unable to press onward. Her ears pressed against her head.

"Do you feel that?" she snarled.

The air grew prickly, and I was all too aware of the tang of river mud, a smell that had been tattooed inside my nostrils only hours ago. I couldn't see them yet, but they were here.

The warmth inside me kept growing to the point where I could feel tiny beads of sweat pushing through the pores on my forehead. Everything was heightened, from the feeling of each hair on my neck rising, to the sharpened view my spirit eye now afforded me. Everything was clear. I felt a drumbeat far off, or maybe it was inside of me, trying to turn up the volume. A battle beat. The creekbed was alive with bodies drawing themselves out of ice crevices, seeping through the snow, slick as oil, jelly-boned and hungry. I whipped my bag forward, drew out the new-and-improved garnet sword, and threw the bag aside. I felt so calm and single-minded in what I had to do, even as I watched the river hunters multiply to dozens, chattering their mocking throat-laughter and eyeing us, claws and teeth prepared. My skin felt drum-tight over my bones as I gripped the black hilt of the blade and the heat inside me rose.

"Roan? Are you ready for this?" I heard Sil ask, but her voice seemed far away. I didn't wait for her as I moved through the gap in the bike path's gate. The onslaught of hunters watched and grinned, their muscles rippling under their tarry flesh. I raised the blade. They swelled as one, and I hurtled down the hill.

How did I suddenly know how to swing the heavy blade, cutting bodies in half like they were made of wet clay? When had I learned the steps of a murderous dance that made me pivot and duck and slice as though it was an art form? All I knew was that they had to die. All of them. And as I hacked away, I was safe in my warm bubble, enrobed by a comforting, powerful heat that drowned out everything else, even Sil barking at me as she fought by my side. Even my humanity.

The snow at my feet evaporated as I wove and cut down my enemies, these soulless monsters, and I swore I could hear them begging, in their keening way, for mercy. For help from their mother lying dormant beneath the ice just nearby. But no one was going to help them, and if they did, I would tear them apart, too. This was all I knew. I gave them no quarter because they deserved none. They had ripped apart an innocent girl, had torn into the very soul of my friend, and they would not stop. So neither would I. Their flesh and blood covered me with every stroke, but when it touched me, it burned away. I can't remember when I dropped the blade and started ripping them apart with my hands, with my teeth, but it didn't matter. They would all die.

And finally, in a rush of sound and fury, my warm bubble burst, and all I could hear echoing in my bones was *"ROAN!"*

I jerked forward and stumbled, hands and body shaking as I clenched a tree for support. The air was rancid with death, but it was silent again. There was something large and wet in my mouth, like a piece of meat. I spat out the gore and when I realized what it was, I threw up. I tried to catch my breath as the wintry air invaded my ears, perforating my skin. The warmth inside me was gone, leaving only a very human feeling of empty cold. I shivered, trying and failing to stand up straight as I looked around.

The creek was blackened, and the tarry remains seeped back into the ice from whence they had come. What had happened here? No, I knew. But it had felt like the agency of some other character in this terrifying story, someone acting on my behalf, or some terrible version of myself that only existed in a bizarro world. I had felt such rage, and I let it take over. I rubbed my mouth on my sleeve until it was raw.

Sil stood before me, ignoring the massacre around us, her fur thick with tar, burning away. "You have seen the power you are capable of," she murmured, "but you accessed it with anger, and the power took over. You may have conquered here, but at the cost of yourself."

I inhaled, finally feeling like I had control of my lungs again. I closed my eyes. "Well it worked, didn't it? What does it matter how I access it?" I had let fear get a hold of me when the river hunters had attacked the first time, and I lost. If I could slaughter them all in a matter of seconds just from being righteously pissed, then their mother didn't stand a chance.

"A towering inferno is powerful, but it consumes everything it touches. Don't think you can be protected from yourself if you let your fire get out of control."

My fire. I clutched my chest. I had felt it there, felt it coming out of my skin and burning everything around me. I felt like I'd become part of a greater flame. Most of all, I hadn't felt vulnerable. I felt alive.

I wanted to get into more firefox Yoda talk, but my phone went off in my pocket. I was surprised it was still in one piece given what had just happened. I answered automatically.

"Roan?"

My voice came out in a croak. "Phae?"

"Look, I know you're angry with me, I get it. You wanted my support for whatever is going on with you and I backed away. But when you just start running off during school without saying anything after a girl dies, and the last conversation we had was you telling me about a bunch of weird things that sound like they're straight out of a sci-fi movie, and then you avoid me for days when all I want to know is if you're all right —"

"Phae, look, just stop for a sec, okay? I'll explain everything. We can talk. Does your offer for a ride still stand?"

❧

I sank into the front seat of Phae's dad's Honda, totally conscious of my best friend's stare as I did the seat belt up and Sil readjusted herself in my lap. I held her to keep her balanced, but she shivered under my touch, the lustre of her coat turning almost brown. I knew I needed to ask her what was wrong, but I didn't know if I should risk chatting it up with her in front of Phae . . . who still hadn't put the car into gear.

"That's a fox," she pointed out.

"Yes," I said.

"Why do you have a fox?"

Sil and I looked at each other. "I'm pretty sure I mentioned her before."

Phae tried to keep cool. "Yes, but I didn't think —"

Sil sniffed in Phae's direction. "You're sure she can be trusted?"

I sprang forward, pulling Sil back into my lap. Phae had no visible signs of recognition on her face, so I don't think she could hear Sil, just like Barton couldn't see the hunters.

Then Phae became pragmatic. "Roan, you can't just go around adopting wild animals, especially if you're doing so to make me believe what you said last week. What if it attacks us while I'm driving? What if it has rabies?"

I sighed, because they were all valid questions, but we didn't have the time. "Phae, it's fine. Sil won't do anything . . ." *Don't say "unless provoked."* "Just don't worry about her, okay? We need to go to Assiniboine Forest, like ten minutes ago."

"What?" Phae quirked an eyebrow, knuckles tight on the steering wheel. "Why?"

I tried to gather my patience. "Look, I know I've been acting super weird lately. But someone is in trouble, and I have to help him. And the only way to do that is for Sil and me to get to Assiniboine Forest. And I asked you to take us because I want you to come with me. I want to actually *show you* that I'm not clinically insane."

I don't think my little speech inspired much trust. Yes, I sounded extremely delusional, but the first step to cracking the veneer of Phae's logical world was that there was a fox in my lap, and I hadn't bothered to hide my ridiculous garnet sword in the back seat, either.

She turned her eyes forward, putting us into drive and (I hoped) taking us on the right course. We had met her out on Wellington Crescent, now thankfully devoid of Arnas's SUV (and with my bike hidden in the trees to reclaim later). With the river on our right as we cruised towards Charleswood, I bit my lip. The river had claimed my parents and sent its minions after me. Even dormant, it was dangerous.

"Who's in trouble?" Phae asked after a while. We were turning onto Corydon.

I gnawed the inside of my cheek; my mouth still tasted like tar and blood but I tried not to gag. "Um. You remember that guy outside of English this morning? The one in the wheelchair?" God, had it really been this morning? It seemed weeks ago.

"You mean the new transfer student?" she asked.

I nodded.

"Yeah, why?"

Sil had her nose pressed to the glass, panting and watching the world go by through the fog of her breath. I let my hand rest heavily on her back, suddenly afraid she was going to disappear. "He's dying," I managed. Though what he was going through was much worse.

Phae shook her head, still not taking her eyes off the road. "He seemed fine this morning, though. Was he attacked, like that girl?"

Why sugar-coat it? "Yeah."

"Is he at the hospital? What did the doctors say?"

I dropped my head back against the seat. "Phae, it's a bit more complicated than that."

She scoffed. "Well, you can't seriously be taking responsibility for this guy. If he's in a doctor's care then there's nothing else you can do but trust they will treat him as best as they can."

"He doesn't *need* a doctor, Phae. He needs a healer."

"Roan, this isn't *World of Warcraft* . . ."

I felt very ready to tear my hair out.

Sil gave me some serious side-eye. "It's useless. She'll see for herself soon enough, or else her ignorance will prevent her from doing so. She's the same as any other human. Save your breath."

"She's not *ignorant*, she just hasn't had to deal with any of this yet," I blurted.

"Are you talking to me?" Phae glanced worriedly at Sil and me as she came to the stoplights at Shaftesbury and Grant.

"No, I . . ." *No, my talking fox and I were just shooting the breeze, s'all good.* "Anyway. I know it all sounds insane, and trust me when I say that, yeah, everything I'm telling you is pretty out there, but it's real. All of it. From the giant river serpent that's got it out for this city to the five animal-spirit-family-things that want to hand me over to it. I've had a crash course in ancient mythological superbeings over the last few days, and I thought I was losing my mind, but that'd be way too easy." I inhaled sharply, trying to keep myself from exploding. "And it's somehow all tied up with my parents, and how I've got to finish what they started before they died. I don't think their deaths were accidental, Phae, or suicide like some people say. So it all sounds wacko, but it's important to me, and it's been hell, so if I had your support, I'd appreciate it."

Phae sighed again as we barrelled down Grant Avenue, the Assiniboine Forest thick and dormant on either side of the four-lane road. "Okay," she said, reluctant patience in her voice. "Okay."

We pulled into the small parking lot attached to the forest's entrance. The Charleswood Rotary Club had closed the gate, but that wouldn't stop anyone from going in and out.

"Hopefully there aren't too many cross-country skiers or dog walkers," I muttered, noticing that we shared the lot with a couple of cars.

I hesitated before opening the car door, and Phae noticed. "Well? What are we doing here? Are we meeting someone?"

I brightened at the mention of "we"; maybe Phae was going to jump into the fray after all. I peered into the cluster of trees and the path that cut through them. It was a painfully bright winter's day, and the mix of snow and leafless trees seemed to stretch into blinding infinity. "Maybe. Sort of. Not really. We have to go in and find them."

"Do you have their cell number? Calling or texting would probably be easiest . . ."

Oh, Phae. So practical. Do I ever wish I could conjure some spirits with a phone call. Why couldn't the Five Families and all involved leap into the twenty-first century, anyway?

"Aside from that, how are we —"

I popped the passenger door open before Phae could hold us up with any more questions, letting Sil out into the snow. I poked my head into the car again and grabbed the garnet sword. "Are you coming or not?"

Sil padded several feet ahead, nose down. I kept my spirit eye open like a wide aperture, sword ready if anything came at us. And even though I felt calmer now that we were far away from the river, anything could be hiding in these trees.

"Maybe you should put that thing away. People might think you're —"

"Nuts? I'd rather people thought I was crazy than be caught off guard. I have to be ready." I blew a piece of hair out of my eyes, grumbling, "I always have to be ready."

Phae pulled her scarf in tighter and yanked up her hood. "So you're the hero of this story, then? The predestined arbiter of justice?" When I looked her way, her face held a kind of frank curiosity, even if it was because she thought I believed in my fantasy enough to act it out with integrity.

"Hey." I pulled her to a stop. "I'm not a hero, okay? That's not what any of this is about. I don't want glory or to be some awesome, venerated Chosen One that everyone bows down to." I tried to avoid her eyes, though they were drawn sharply on me. "People are getting — *will* get — hurt. All I want is to stop it from happening."

Her expression softened. Was it pity? Phae reached over and pulled my hood up for me, fastening the buttons at my throat. "And here I was thinking you'd want to be famous for your efforts."

I couldn't help but crack a smile. "Come on, you know how antisocial I am."

We continued on the path for a few steps until Phae said, "Wait, where'd your fox go?"

I stopped and looked around. How could we have lost her? The path opened into a wide field, a blank white snow canvas with nothing to obstruct the view. Maybe she had thought we were following close behind. *Dammit.* I jogged towards the trees and staggered when Sil materialized out of the thicket.

"I thought we'd lost you," I sniffed, collecting myself.

"Then keep up," she hissed back. "I've picked up a trail. This way." She turned back into the web of trees. I waited for Phae to catch up, then signalled for silence with a finger to my lips, and we crunched our way off the path.

The snow was up to midcalf. Trudging quietly, lifting

our knees high and avoiding clawing birch branches, was mind-numbing. My legs burned and my exposed skin was raw. Sil was too far ahead for me to ask how much farther we'd have to go. Then I felt a hand yank me back by the arm. "What —"

Phae slapped a gloved hand over my mouth and pointed to a place in the trees beside us. I squinted, but there she was: a big doe, staring at us with that blithe *what kind of deer are you?* expression, white tail flicking. How had we not seen her, not heard her? I exhaled, and she jerked backwards as if I'd fired a gun, vanishing into the woods.

"It's so hard to imagine they survive out here during the winter," Phae murmured as we trekked along. I agreed, and wondered what had made the Deer Family think it was a good idea to reject being human for this place, for the uncertainty of their lives out here. Did their withdrawal from the human world stop Zabor from devouring them?

Finally, we came out of the trees and into an opening hemmed in on all sides by the forest. It was remarkable how we were still inside the city, but I could barely hear any kind of car or urban noise. Sil was half buried in the snow, soaked up to her chest and sniffing the air. She really did look sick. I wanted to call out to her, but I wouldn't dare break the silence. She kept circling and circling.

"Is there something wrong with her?" Phae whispered, catching on right away. I clenched my jaw, not wanting to admit out loud that the creature I'd once thought invincible could get sick, or even die.

"I don't know, but —"

I raised my blade and pushed past Phae to shield her. Hundreds of shapes had appeared in the thick group of aspens surrounding us and had done so without making a sound. Wet black eyes — but not the eyes of the hunters whose taste haunted my throat. Deer. Bucks pushed cautiously to the front, antlers sharp and new and yearning to be bloodied.

"You said they were pacifists, right?" I hissed at Sil, whose hackles were cautiously up, though she made no sound. "Right?"

The crowd multiplied, and the deer crept closer, closing in on us and what had suddenly become a narrow, open field.

"Roan, what's going on?" Phae and I stood with our backs pressed together like praying hands. "What's happening?"

The bucks were bigger than the does by at least a hundred pounds, and they moved with their heads low, ready to charge. I stood, primed to fight, but the last thing I wanted was to let the fire rise in me again, putting Phae, Sil, or even my own life at risk. And above all, I didn't want more blood on my hands — or in my mouth.

"Lower your sword!" Sil suddenly barked.

"What?"

She threw a devastating glare at me. "Throw it away!"

"It's all I've got if we end up like gored matadors!" The Deer had all stopped moving, but I could see their shoulders kneading. *Great, a THIRD ambush in a day.*

Sil backed up into my legs, looking slightly rabid. "Do as I say, girl, or you'll get your wish!"

I squeezed the slate hilt, taking one last look at the assembled antler-firing-squad before throwing the sword to the side. It didn't make more than a muffled *perf* as it landed in the snow, now too far away to reclaim if things reached battle levels.

Phae jumped. "What are you doing? And who are you talking to? Roan, what's going on?"

I exhaled, dropping my protective stance and grabbing Phae's hand. Startled, she tried to pull away, but I held on tight.

"It's going to be okay." I smiled, though it faltered. "And if it isn't, I'm sorry I dragged you out here."

She looked on the verge of tears, unable to consolidate the scene we'd found ourselves in with reality. But she squeezed my hand back. There was nothing else we could do now but stand strong, and face it together.

I tried to speak loudly and clearly and keep the stammer out of my voice.

"We mean you no harm," I shouted, and I meant it. "Please. My name is Roan, and I'm a member of the Fox Family. There's a Rabbit that has been attacked by the river hunters. I've come here looking for a healer. Can you help us?"

Silence prevailed, my words lost in the white of the sky and the ground and the noiseless pocket we were sealed inside. The bucks raised their heads and stopped pawing the snow. The does looked carved from stone, the fawns they shielded with their legs sniffing the air and twitching with repressed energy. My memory flashed to the deer in my grandmother's stone menagerie, and how I would ride them through imaginary forests, holding tight to their antlers like reins. My mother told me that if I ever needed them, I need only ask. Was that a tenet that the Deer had to abide by, giving aid when needed?

"Please," I repeated, "I know that you've rejected your human forms for the sake of peace, but Zabor's carnage will continue even if you back away. I've come to unite all of the Families to stop her, and the dying boy is . . . key to that."

"We have heard this all before," said an oaken voice. A buck with huge antlers stepped ahead of the throng, his coat flecked with grey. My spirit eye gave nothing away; he was a deer, and that was all. "This claim was not yours to begin with. We knew your mother, and we grieved her loss. And we are saddened that you have been marked. But we will not return to fight a losing battle."

My throat thickened, but I tried to dampen my rising frustration. "You've already made it a losing battle by refusing to help! If all Five can't come together on this, then it's a self-fulfilling prophecy!"

"And the Owls?" questioned a honeyed voice, a doe raising her head. "How will you come together with they who work with Zabor, they who keep her pact from breaking?"

Admittedly, I hadn't thought that far ahead. "I didn't say I knew what I was doing," I said. "But at least I'm doing something, rather than hiding out here in the woods, waiting for the day I forget my human worries and die ignorant."

Another buck reared, shaking his head. "You Foxes! Always with your sharp words and empty promises. Our children die every day, Zabor or otherwise. What use is our Ancient Grace to humans or Denizens when they tear this world apart? Zabor is the product of human darkness, and the Denizens temporarily save themselves by throwing their kin to the beast. We will all die. The Deer are simply choosing to do so on our own terms."

I felt my face redden against the cold. "Then you're as guilty as the river demon!" I cried. "If you won't join me in this, fine. But you're not going to stop me, and I didn't come here to argue with you. Please. My friend is suffering because of me," it hurt to say it out loud, "and if you have any humanity left, you'll help me save him."

They had been so full of criticism before, so eloquent in decrying my cause, but now they were noiseless, empty-eyed prey animals again, looking ready to turn white-tail and vanish into the trees. My only reply was the sudden snowfall of heavy flakes drifting in the thicket.

The crowd parted then, and an old doe came forward. Her ribs pushed delicately against her flesh as she ambled towards us, head lowered, eyes milky and crusted in yellow. At first, I thought it was a trick of the swirling, gently falling snow, but the image of a woman walked with her, as aged and hunched as the Deer before me. Younger does trailed in her wake, like attendants. When she reached us, she dipped her head down to Sil, who looked about ready to collapse in the snow at my feet. They sniffed each other, and the old Deer sighed.

"It's been many years, my friend. We look quite the pair, don't we?"

Sil nodded. "Yes, Geneve. It's been a long life."

I held out my hand, and the Deer, Geneve, touched her wet nose to it. "I came to the woods to join my grandchildren after they came here with their parents. It was getting lonely, holding onto my ideals. I truly believed we could make a go of it, Denizens and humans. Some think it's still a gesture in futility."

Phae stood stock-still, still unable to process, asking me questions I couldn't fully answer. "Roan, *what's happening?*"

Geneve lifted her head and extended her long neck to Phae. She gave her a lengthy, meaningful sniff, then rested her old head against her chest. Phae just stood frozen, arms raised, looking uncertain and frightened.

"A human heart free of judgment or dilemma, and alive with loyalty. She came here for you, child." Geneve's blind eyes shimmered. "The heart of a healer."

As the old Deer pulled away, Phae and I exchanged glances. I tried to convey my feelings of *I have no idea what is going on, either* through that look.

"Don't do this," urged one of the does that had followed.

Geneve didn't turn her head, but her human outline grinned. "If we are asked for aid, we must give it. It is the oath that binds us to this world, and we cannot break that."

"Don't give up your life for this Fox we don't even know! Let her meet her fate!" another doe-attendant begged. I assumed these were her daughters or granddaughters, though I wouldn't doubt that the entire gathering was dedicated to this Deer.

"Wait, wait," I held up my hands. "I didn't ask anyone to give up their lives!"

Geneve nosed her way into my chest now. "You ask for life, you must expect life to be lost. In this case, my life is over, but my Grace remains. I would rather pass it on so that it could be used, rather than letting it seep into nothingness like the rest of us."

I still didn't understand. "Pass it on?"

Sil piped up, seemingly using the last of her waning strength. "She wants to pass on her power. To your friend. To make her a healer. A Deer."

"In a matter of speaking," Geneve muttered, nipping Sil gently to keep her from losing her balance. "We can't go back with you now. But your friend can."

I knelt and lifted my Fox-familiar into my arms, holding her close to me. "Sil? What's happening to you?"

"She needs rest," Geneve shook her old head slowly, as though it weighed the equivalent of her years. I saw her human outline reach out to touch Sil's head, and for a moment she seemed revitalized, eyes wider, fur brightening, though she still rested heavily in my arms — a temporary revival. "Those we protect are a heavy burden to bear, child. Can you bear the weight of us all when we are dragged down by the flood?"

I nodded automatically, even if I didn't know the answer yet. "If I don't, who will?"

Both the doe and her human ghost smiled. "Your friends, perhaps. This one seems ready to follow you to the edge of the darkness. Will she?"

I turned to Phae, who seemed to realize that every creature at this gathering was focusing on her now. "What? What's wrong? Tell me we're going to get out of this alive."

I lowered Sil gently and took Phae into my arms. "Phae. I know you always wanted to be a doctor, and that you love people enough to devote your life to healing them. And this is sort of a roundabout way to that, but . . . this Deer here wants to give you her healing powers. More or less." Was I selling it? Not really.

Phae tilted her head. "Listen, Roan, this is all very weird and troubling, what with the fox and the deer-based tribunal, but —"

I cut her off. She had to commit to this. "This is real, Phae. This is real. I don't know how else to say it. It's real and I need your help. I should've asked for it before and, yes, it's all hard to accept. I need you with me on this. Let's be real — I've *always* needed you." *Don't cry, don't cry.* "Please? Will you do this? Barton's running out of time."

Geneve watched us with her blind gaze that seemed to penetrate our flesh and hearts, and Phae reached out to touch her bristled face with both hands.

"How does it work?" she whispered, snowflakes stealing past us as a wind finally breached the thicket, whipping up the white.

"We kneel," Geneve said and, as though she could understand her, Phae dropped to her knees just as the old Deer did. Geneve's head was still in Phae's hands, and she pressed their foreheads together. "And we pray."

I watched, amazed, as every Deer gathered lowered their heads in reverence and knelt on their haunches, pressing their bodies into the snow as the wind grew fiercer. I kneeled beside Phae, putting my hands on her narrow, delicate shoulders, and we all shut our eyes against the world.

"I call to the Spirit of Ancient, the Spirit we invoke to give life and remove it," Geneve said. I heard it repeated amongst the throng, lower and undulating, like a wave. "I present this spirit in the corridor of time, the winter that suspends us all, under the gaze of Ancient and by the grace of the Five that came before."

The words and the wind blended now, and I felt it cutting a path in a circle — or maybe several? — that intertwined, passing through us and around us. Geneve was turning this thicket into a sort of summoning chamber, and I felt the snow shift with urgency.

"I call now to my Family, that they might commend me to my rest in the heart of Ancient, from which we spring and to which we return. Rouse and separate me from this flesh, leaving only my Grace, to place on the name of this child."

The chanting from the Deer sounded more like a funeral dirge with Geneve's words. She was asking them to help her die. I held tight to Phae; her breathing had been shaky and uneven until this point. I felt her small body press into and pull away from mine as I held on because I wanted her to feel I was here with her on this, as she was for me. But now she didn't move and, afraid that something terrible had happened, I opened my eyes. Every Deer rippled with an icy light that pulsed through their bodies until it reached Geneve and Phae. Their eyes were open, but empty and clear and shining with that bright incandescence, and Geneve's words started falling from Phae's lips. "To the Spirit that is our conduit, the element that this house bears, yield to my name and pass this power forward. Spirit, heart, hand. Heal."

The frenzied wind and the snow it bore on its back froze everything. The flakes suspended mid-air twinkled like daytime starlight, and Phae's long, ebony tresses climbed up her back, possessed and hypnotizing. They rose and knit on her head a heavy black crown of horns, all at once dark and shimmering, until they crackled blue, pulsing with veins of light. The light cascaded from the antlers and lit up beneath Phae's dark-brown flesh. As it passed down her head and neck, her eyes came back to her, and she breathed.

The crown fell away slowly like shifting feathers, and the snow followed suit. Phae's hands released the head of the Deer that had passed on her power, and her life, and Geneve's body fell limp in the snow before us all.

"Phae?" I whispered, alarmed that she was staring catatonically into the distance. I followed her gaze and watched as the does got to their feet, each ducking their heads in a sort of reverent sadness towards us as they turned to leave, returning to their self-imposed exile.

The old buck with the large antlers hung back. "You now have the Grace of our Family on your side, young Fox. Use it wisely and well in your quest to dispatch the river demon." And he looked to Phae then, who seemed to be fully awake and aware now. "And to you, New Daughter. Guide your friend well, and return to us for guidance should you need it. You bear an Ascendant's power now."

"Yes," was all she said, tears running down her cheeks.

He blinked his great black eyes and faded into the trees with the rest.

When I thought I would have to now reach out to Phae to offer a hand of support, instead her hand found mine. "I'm sorry," she said. "I'm sorry I didn't believe you or understand."

Perhaps it helped that the element of the Deer Family was spirit, because something had reached down into Phae's core and rocked her. She seemed different. I smiled. "Ah well. No one's gonna believe *you* now. We're even."

Though something great had been moved in her, I was grateful that pragmatic, brass-tacks Phae remained. "Take me to Barton. We have to hurry."

◦◦◦

I would have been lying if I didn't admit to feeling a bit envious that Phae knew what she was doing more than I did, and she'd only been at this for less than an hour. She got us to Barton's place with singular purpose, and she led us into his house without restraint. I wondered if the power she had been given came with the years of experience of its former user. If only I'd been so lucky. Sil still seemed diminished, but at least she was alert, and I stood back with Rebecca and David as Phae laid her hands on my friend.

She seemed to be searching for something, hands floating uncertain over his chest, calculating. After a moment, she said, "There's so much darkness inside him. It's hard to see his spirit anymore." She spoke with certainty, and for a second it worried me. "It will have to be drawn out."

Barton had been writhing, drooling, and snapping his teeth since we arrived, and even with Phae at his side, this didn't stop. It seemed Sil's solution had been more temporary than she'd hoped, and what was left of him seemed alien and beyond saving. But Phae looked at him like a practised surgeon, ready to cut the affliction out with her bare hands.

Her eyes drew back into her head, the whites fading to the same blue I had just seen in the forest, and her hands pressed hard onto Barton's chest. He howled, and the wound in his chest seemed to pucker like a mouth and, worst of all, laughter chittered out of it. Rebecca's knees buckled, but I was there to catch her. David bolted and took her from me as a tremor ran under our feet, and Barton's sports trophies and alarm clock and anything not nailed down rattled. Phae seemed unfazed, but I ran to her side and did my part to hold Barton down.

"*You cannot have him*," the wound-mouth croaked in too many voices. "*We are hungry and we have eaten him and Mother wants him.*"

Were these the voices of the thousand black worms Sil had said were inside him, crowding around for a taste of Barton's soul? Phae concentrated harder, and the mouth twisted. When I looked down, I saw that her hands were *inside* Barton's chest, past muscle and bone and up to the wrist in oozing black tar. I wanted to scream, but I wouldn't show fear to these monsters, not when I had cut so many of them to pieces in my righteous vengeance.

Phae spoke to it in a calm, professorial tone. "He is not yours to have, and his spirit remains. Your mother has too many children, anyway." The tarry offal that Phae was buried in tried to resist her, until it turned as blue as her eyes and started to dissolve.

"*No, no!*" the wound screamed, its cries for mercy blending into Barton's. But the light dug into his flesh, and she wrenched her hands out of him, pulling fistfuls of black mass with them. The light ate it up greedily, and it dissipated into spectral dust. At last, Phae put her hands on Barton's head and chest, and the wound closed, his skin returned to its healthy shade. His spasms weakened until his breathing was the only movement he made.

He opened his eyes and took us in. Phae came back to herself and looked worn out and slightly troubled, but she smiled down at Barton almost beatifically. No one moved, afraid to break the spell of the miracle.

"M-mom . . . ?" Barton croaked, throat probably shredded from shrieking like a banshee all day. "Why am I tied to a bed and surrounded by girls? And also half-naked?"

Phae and I jerked back as the Allens untied their son and wrapped him in their arms. "Gah, guys, you're choking me," he said weakly. They pulled away, shaking and relieved and crying. Barton still looked mildly disoriented.

"These girls saved your life, son," David said, running a hand over Barton's fuzzy hair. The small family turned to us, and I knew that this was what I had been searching for in the last few days of struggle and death. The look that comes with life restored, with a happy ending that no one dared think was a possibility. A family would not be torn apart today.

Sil and I met gazes across the dishevelled bedroom, and she dipped her head at me with newfound respect and something that had always been there — belief that I could make things happen. Make them right.

Barton smiled at us, despite looking like he needed to sleep for the next ten years. "Makes sense. I had a feeling about you." He nodded at me.

"I had one about you, too," I shrugged, unable to keep from grinning back. Not knowing what else to do, I half-hugged Phae and pushed her forward. "But she's the real hero. Phaedrapramit Das, your healer."

Phae raised a hand in a shy half-wave, still not sure what to do with herself, flung as she was into something she probably didn't fully understand. "Hi," she said quickly, averting her eyes, since Barton was still mostly naked. If he'd had the energy, I'm sure he may have blushed.

"Thank you," Rebecca muttered through her tears. "And I'm sorry."

I felt suddenly taken aback, my smile faltering. "Why are you sorry? I got Barton into this mess. The least I could do was get him out —"

"It's not that," she sighed, reaching for Barton and speaking more to him now. "If we hadn't have done what we did . . . none of this would've happened."

Barton looked confused, and I realized how little he knew about any of this, or the sacrifice his parents had made on his behalf to protect him. I suddenly felt as though we were trespassing on an intensely private moment.

"What do you mean?" Barton asked.

"Rebecca," David warned, putting a hand on hers. He looked at us with sad eyes. "We have a lot we need to talk about. But Barton needs rest."

Thankful to take that as our cue, Phae, Sil, and I turned to leave. "Wait!" Barton yelled, sounding desperate. "Wait."

We stopped, hesitant to go any farther, but unwilling to leave it like this.

"You came to me because of the dreams. Because there's something about them that's real . . . because there's something coming for us, isn't there? And it's not just whatever attacked us today. It's something worse."

That was about the size of it. "Yes."

"I could . . . I could see it. I could hear it. Hear *her*." He shuddered, grasping his sweat-stained sheets. "She was whispering in my ear, calling me to her and to the dark place. I tried to get away from it, but the voice followed me. Until I realized that the voice was inside me. And it was so cold." I could follow this vision clearly, because whenever I passed over the river I faced the same dread. I clenched and unclenched my fists.

"I know," Phae said before I could. "I saw it when I reached inside of you. And I heard her voice, too. She tried to come inside my head and talk me out of helping you."

David ran a hand over his face. "Zabor is more than a voice or a bad dream," he said. "Right now she's half asleep and still able to control an army. Things will only get worse. And now she's starting to realize that she might be opposed for once." He looked directly at me. "She won't lie down if you face her."

Barton stared at his parents with a mix of awe, exhaustion, and frustration. "So you guys . . . you know what Roan's talking about? You knew about all of this?" His jaw tightened. "You knew my dreams were real, and you tried to convince me I was sick."

Rebecca's face twisted as if holding back a sob. "We just wanted to protect you. That's all we wanted." I knew her intentions had been good, but I had to summon everything I had to stop from scoffing. If only she'd been honest with him. *If only my parents had been honest with me.*

Barton was a better person than I was, though; he searched his mother's face, and instead of allowing himself to become instantly angry, he looked back at me. "I know I'm not much, and that I'd probably just be a hindrance . . . but I want to help you in whatever you have to do. I sort of . . . have a feeling that it's my destiny. Maybe I've always known that." He took his mother's hand, though she tried to hide her tears behind it.

Sil finally spoke up, sounding confident despite how ragged and tired she looked. "A Rabbit, a new Deer, and a Fox cub." I let the "cub" jab go. "All five Families must unite to stop Zabor. At least now we have a start."

And that was when Rebecca's vision seemed to clear, waking up to Sil's words and the brevity she once possessed as a leader within her Family. "The Owls are against you. They know everything you're doing, every move you make. I know, because I've been passing information on to them." Her eyes fell. "They will do everything they can to keep you from uniting the Families. You must avoid them, and stay away from Arnas at all costs." I had forgotten all about that. Deedee said that Arnas and Rebecca were close. No wonder he'd screamed at me to stay away from Barton after trying to run us down.

"Arnas is my uncle," I said, more for Barton's benefit, "and living with him makes it pretty hard to stay away from him. He's . . . well, he's *mostly* harmless." I hoped that streak would continue, since he was resorting to brute force with SUVs to getting his point across.

"Don't be fooled," Rebecca warned. "He might seem harmless, but he has some power now. He's the one who . . ." She looked at Barton, trailing off. Colour rose in her cheeks.

And then I knew what she was going to say, as though all this spirit-ness had given me prophetic autocomplete. *He was the one who severed my son.* Arnas was the one who performed the ritual on Barton. I flashed back to him on the phone all those times.

I stopped her there, because I knew this was something the Allens would have to cover in private. "It doesn't matter now. All we can do is move forward."

David nodded, though his slight shrug made him seem skeptical. "It's a good attitude, but the past is tangled up in this, too. Arnas has more than just a desire to save himself. It has a lot more to do with your parents than you think."

This day, really. Barton nearly turned into a demon, Phae at my side full of wisdom and power, and everything coming at us with the smothering force of an avalanche. All I could do was stuff my hands in my pockets and try to seem calm.

"I think we could all use some rest." I smiled, trying to call up some essence of leadership I knew I'd have to work hard at. "We just have to stay strong. And do it together." It wasn't much of a rousing speech, but it seemed to do.

When we left the house, I kept Sil's observation of us, this patchwork "team," close to my heart; a restored Rabbit, a brand new Deer, and a Fox with barely a clue. There was still a long way to go, and two other Families to convince, but now it wasn't so much a mythological pipe dream. We could bring this demon down.

And maybe we'd even survive.

Part III
FLAME

The OWL'S OFFER

Eli has always preferred the old-fashioned method of film development. There is something about the tactility of images, the achievement of chemical composition making a moment in time physical. He built the darkroom himself — *because my whole life* is *a dark room*, he heard in a movie, once — and he spends much of his time here. His Family is all about big spaces in the air, suspended within and beyond the sky and the universe, but sometimes it suits him to burrow deep into the earth in an effort to appreciate it when he takes wing and leaves it behind.

He rubs his chest absently. It is also here that he's as alone as he can be.

Photo development by hand takes patience and care, and he prides himself on having these traits. They are what have raised him, along with the Ancient power he's been given, to the great annals of his forebears. Towards the Seat of the

Paramount. And perhaps these traits will take him beyond that, but Eli has never been one to speculate that far into the future. Everything hinges on each step, and each has as much significance as a single note in a powerful score. You cannot jump to another measure when you haven't completed the first. He smiles as he drags the photopaper through the development fluid, sweeping his hand like a conductor.

Shapes begin to coalesce into an image. He has seen her face before, in digital form (what a lazy means of photography), and then once face to face. They'd had a moment. She had no interesting features, nothing to set her apart (aside from that very Bowie-esque set of mismatched eyes), and Eli doesn't find her to be particularly pretty. But as her face blooms in the photo, he finds himself mesmerized. Something fearsome lurks beneath that pallid, naïve visage. It fascinates him, the haunted eyes and the lips parted in confusion, how she looks more a sheep than a Fox. But perhaps she is deceiving him with intent. She is an obstacle to be removed. For now, he can look at this picture of a troublesome idiot and puzzle over why she bothers him, and why he cares enough to look.

The voices rise and shuffle inside him uneasily. Eli winces, flexing his chest tighter and asserting control. *Not here. Not now. Leave me to myself.* The voices seem to chide him, but whether by his will or no, they dissipate. For now.

Recovering, he clips the photo next to the others in the series he has snapped in days since; pictures of the dead girl at the train tracks and the empty-gazed Roan, who was just as culpable of the crime as the river hunters who exacted it. Eli is proud of his work, and the work that will come of it. He casts a glance at his large computer monitor, which is currently streaming the live news broadcast of another body discovered at the Red River bank off Lyndale Drive. Same trauma as the first victim — eye ripped out, heart gored, red hair — except this new victim seems to have had her hair sawed off with a blunt instrument, maybe even chewed off. Some initially thought it was an animal attack, but now officials suspect foul play, possibly gang related, and very indicative of serial killings. *Who could be responsible for such violence? Why are they doing this? We must stop them before it's too late.*

Eli looks back at the picture of Roan Harken, and smiles.

❧

"Ouch. You look rough."

"Um, thanks," I said, trying not to rub my cheek. I'd covered the massive bruise there with some of Deedee's thick and creamy foundation and didn't want to think about how that only made me seem *more* obvious.

But Barton didn't pull any punches, despite being in rough shape himself. He wheeled up, grimacing. "What happened to *you?*"

I leaned into the bank of lockers, wondering if I could get away with taking a nap inside of one. "Sil and I spent a lot of time in the summoning chamber last night, fifth night in a row. She's, um . . . she's showing me how to conjure spirits and fight them. For practice." I didn't bother lowering my voice. If anyone was listening in, they probably thought I was talking about a long night of LARPing.

"So it isn't going very well, hm?" Phae interjected as she appeared beside me. I self-consciously touched my face and, in doing so, rubbed off some of the makeup.

"Damn!" I hissed, wiping it on my pants. Before I could make it any worse, Phae took my chin in her hand, and I felt warmth rush into my face. The ache in my cheekbone vanished, as though my cells and nerves had undergone a sudden case of amnesia.

"The fewer questions about what you're doing in your spare time, the better," she said, fingertips sparking effervescent blue until she hid them in a fist.

I sighed. "Looks like we all have a lot of work to do." Phae had been experimenting with her newfound powers and insights for the last few weeks and found them trickier to tap into than when the Deer elder had first transferred her powers over. It suited her to practise on me, since getting injured had become the norm lately.

"Yeah, you guys have it *real* tough," Barton muttered. "Roan gets to learn how to hone her firepower, and you get to heal her minor scrapes. And then there's me. You still sure you can't regenerate these?" He motioned to his legs. "I'd appreciate getting in on the action instead of being constantly benched."

Phae hugged her books tighter to her chest. "It just doesn't work that way, Barton. I can't heal what was never there."

He scoffed, kneading his hand into his forehead. "But I can still feel them!" Then he looked at me, and I bit the inside of my mouth. "What about your uncle? He's the one that did it. Can't you get anywhere with him?"

"I've already *told you*," I groaned, "he's never around, at least not when I'm there. And the last time I confronted him, he did something that made my spirit eye go all crazy, some kind of protection. And what would my aunt say if we started beating on each other? The cops would get involved and then we'd *all* be screwed." I took a breath, feeling suddenly guilty as I noticed how much redder Barton's face had become in the wake of my excuses. "I'm sorry," I mumbled.

"Well, what about me?" He switched tacks. "What if I talked to him?"

Phae and I exchanged glances, which I'm sure didn't do much to take Barton off the offensive. She stepped forward before I could open my mouth. "We need to focus on getting the Families together on this whole thing. We can't risk more conflict right now." I could see that Phae's pragmatism wasn't holding up against Barton's dissatisfaction, even though she was right.

The bell went off and Barton snapped his brakes up, eyes cutting us both. "Yeah, well, it's easy for you two. I'm supposed to be a part of this, too, you know, and I'm still on the sidelines. Maybe it's time you thought about finding someone else."

Phae reached for him uselessly, trying to offer comfort. "Hey, we know that your dreams mean that something interrupted in the ritual, that it wasn't fully complete. There's still a chance it can be reversed. We just need a better plan than ambushing someone who could do a lot of damage to us."

"Yeah, yeah." He waved her off.

He turned to wheel away, but Phae held her hand up. "Wait a second." She turned to me suddenly. "Did you find the book?"

"Oh, yeah." I jerked my bag off my back and dug out a small heavy journal. "Cecelia apparently got it from a Rabbit a while back, as a gift. She said it's a primer on rituals and all kinds of stuff from the perspective of the Five Families. Hope there's something useful in here."

"Well, if there is, Barton will find it." She passed the tome to him. He looked slightly perplexed as he flipped through the pages of cramped writing and faded diagrams.

"What am I supposed to do with this?" He quirked an eyebrow, but he seemed brighter than he had been a moment earlier.

"From now on, you're the intel," Phae said. "We need all the information we can gather on the Families, anything we can find that will help us get rid of that river snake."

He was already caught up in reading. Pushing his glasses back on his nose, he looked up at Phae with the same gratitude I'd seen on his face the day she brought him back from the dead. "The intel, huh?"

She nodded. "The more we know, the better prepared we'll be."

"Okay, okay." Barton flapped his hand again, but this time it wasn't dismissive; there was a bit of a smile on his face. "I'm on it." He tucked the book into his bag, nodded, and wheeled off.

We let out a breath simultaneously. Phae and I had felt equally frustrated in our inability to help Barton, but at least this would allow him to contribute.

"Nice going, homie." I patted Phae on the back. "That'll keep him busy. And knowledge is power." She'd done Barton a solid, of course, but she still looked defeated.

"I really hope there's another way to reverse the severing that doesn't involve your uncle." We turned together and made for the chem lab. "And even still, if we can reconnect Barton with Ancient, it isn't going to give him back his legs."

I patted her on the back again, feeling just as useless as

ever. "I know. We'll figure it out. It's just been a tense couple of weeks."

Well, that was an understatement by half. Things had gone downhill since Phae and Barton had been dragged into the hazards of being Denizens (and associating with the one that everyone wanted dead). Once Barton's parents finally let him in on the secret world they'd kept him from, he didn't come to school for days. He didn't answer texts, either, and Phae and I worried that he'd never come out of it. I didn't blame him for being so mad; they'd laid a bombshell right on him just after he recovered from demon possession — a situation that rivalled his nightmares.

And here's the kicker: I had tapped him to join us, to take part in this weird epic we were all tangled in, but until we could figure out a way to bring him back into the Ancient fold, he would always be on the outside looking in, and we'd still be one step away from bringing the Families together. Even the local Rabbit elders, who had been visiting the Allens since they tried reconnecting with the Family, had nothing to offer except looks of pity. The one thing Barton hated most, and the last thing he needed. He finally came around, though, determined to make a difference in any way possible.

In the past week, we hadn't made much of a difference at all, and we all silently shied away from that fact. All we could do now was try to work with what we had in front of us, though Barton's power-revival side quest was dividing our personal time. We needed to learn how to control these powers, and soon. It was almost February. The impending spring was haunting our steps.

Meanwhile, Arnas kept a cold eye on me from time to time, but he had basically checked out of reality. I started sleeping with my dresser pushed against my door, just in case. He'd gone off his hinges now that he was aligned with the Owls, and I'm sure trying to run me over was just the beginning.

Poor Deedee had been rocked by what was going on, too, completely in the dark as she was about all the Ancient shenanigans going on around her. But she was still trying to hold things together. I tried talking to her about Arnas, tried reassuring her, but she had built an impenetrable suit of emotional body armour to keep her heart in one piece.

So she just smiled and pulled a Roan — "I'm fine. Don't worry," she'd mutter, and off she'd scurry, burying herself in her work. And this worked in our favour, because we could effectively stay out of each other's way, and that was key to what Sil and I had been up to.

Sil still hadn't let me in on what had caused her sudden illness, a basic power-outage in her being, and Phae had been unable to heal her. But as the days passed and she recuperated at home, her familiar vitality and bullying persona had returned in full force, and she had plunged me back into the summoning chamber and all it entailed. *Pull it from the Veil, concentrate, focus, what are you doing? Use the fire, become the fire, earn your power. Rinse. Repeat. Wax on, wax off.* I was still sustaining injuries, unable to keep myself as grounded as she wanted me to be, the power I'd let consume me at Omand's Creek now out of my reach. Sil had said I didn't want that kind of power. But I did. It's all I thought about. And I wondered how long I could go on ignoring it as I took beating after beating, unable to defend myself against ghosts.

We reached the chem lab and started setting up our station. Phae had gone off to collect materials for the experiment that was written on the whiteboard, and I was in charge of paper-work. It was surreal to be going to school when you had an enormous threat looming just after the three p.m. bell, one that hung over your life, the life of your friends, and the fate of over 700,000 people. What use was the periodic table when the thing you needed to destroy didn't follow logic, reason, or reality? If ever there was a need for Demon Sealing 101, now was the time to petition the school board.

As I got our lab packages sorted, my ears twitched, turned to a conversation in the back of the room that was very much out of human earshot, but not mine. My senses had become almost painfully keen as I became more involved in the world of Ancient, and sometimes I had to rein them in. But not now. A bunch of kids were talking about the most recently mur-dered girl who had been discovered on the bank of the Red a few days ago.

"I hear the police are coming to each school, advising redheads to dye their hair and stay inside at night . . ." one whispered, fear threaded through her tone as she clutched her safely blond locks.

"Ugh, my curfew is balls right now," another girl groaned.

"They're calling the victims the Red River Girls, I heard," one boy cut in. "It's a horror movie waiting to happen."

Another boy joined his line of thinking, one from the group I was supposed to be tutoring in English, and he sneered. "I bet it's a serial killer with some sick, twisted past. Totally *Silence of the Lambs*. Maybe they *will* make a movie out of it and this one-horse town will get some respect."

Sigh. *Kids my age, seriously*.

One thing from their convo stuck with me, though — the police were coming to every school. At first, that seemed innocuous; it was probably to talk to us about protecting ourselves and staying safe, seeing as we could so closely relate to these dead teenagers. But this wasn't fourth grade, where you get a special presentation from a policeman showing off his regulation sidearm and telling you not to cross the street without a grown-up. Maybe they were coming to gather information about the victims, to link them to possible suspects. Not like they'd ever find the culprits, since testifying that the murdered girls had all been torn apart by spectral river beings was grounds for insanity. Or expulsion. But —

"Roan Harken?" came Mr. Godinez's voice from the front of the classroom. Phae had just come back with our beakers and tools, but we both froze as though we'd been caught midcrime. I gaped.

"Can you come with me, please?"

All eyes laced into me, and I felt their judging weight on my back as I obediently stood and shuffled out of class. I gave Phae a backwards glance, knew she wanted desperately to follow, hoping that it had nothing to do with our secret affairs. *Don't do anything stupid*, her face urged. As I turned back to Mr. Godinez's penetrating stare waiting for me in the hall, I knew I couldn't promise anything.

"Did I do something?" I asked. His typically placid face seemed more ashen than usual, and he shifted his lip, making his thick black moustache dance.

"I don't really know what this is about. There's a police officer in the main office asking to speak with you. He wouldn't give any other details."

I went cold. I tried to summon the fire that Sil was coaching me to control, but I just imagined my heart had turned into spent white embers at the bottom of a pit. Why were the police looking for me? What could they possibly have on me that wasn't related to Ancient and my questionable adventures throughout the wintry city?

The reason dawned on me before we even crossed the office threshold, and I confirmed my suspicions almost instantly. The police officer stood in confidence with the school principal at the back of a conference room. Principal Fraser, a thin, progressive woman with a blond shock of well-manicured hair, saw me in the doorway and hushed their conversation. When the officer turned, his head swivelling and grey eyes latching onto mine like precise talons, I knew what no one else did. An Owl. He was one of *them*.

"Thank you, Hector." The principal nodded dismissively to Mr. Godinez, who at first seemed uncertain if he should leave me or not. He shuffled his feet and headed back towards his classroom, his transient moment of loyalty fading with his footsteps.

Principal Fraser smiled at me, but her eyes stayed serious. "Come in, Roan." She said my name familiarly, though I'd only met her a handful of times. She paced towards me with leonine agility, pulling the conference room door shut. She gestured to the other end of the table, where the officer, eyes still on me, had taken a seat. I took the opposite chair, the principal at the head. She folded her manicured hands on the linoleum tabletop, pinning me to my seat with her plastic smile. "Now, I know this must seem quite alarming, summoning you here like this. But Officer Seneca has a few questions for you."

My eyes narrowed as I turned my attention to him. He certainly wasn't going to smile anytime soon, and that relieved a bit of the tension in my jaw. This was business.

The outline of his Owl-self was as unmoving as his human face, and his eyes seemed carved from glass. He knew who I was, he had to. As I levelled him icily, I hoped he realized I knew him, too. Equalling the playing field. I looked back to the principal.

"Can I ask what this is about, first?" I wanted to sound as cool as possible, though my hands were hot, twisting in my lap.

She kissed her teeth as though my question had been an inconvenient fluff on her blazer. "As I'm sure you're aware, there is an ongoing investigation into the *tragedies*" — she sidestepped *murders* with the grace of a politician — "and they unfortunately started with this school. The police are just asking any students who knew the victims if they can offer any information to stop these heinous crimes."

I frowned. "But I didn't know the victim at all. This school has, like, over two thousand people in it. So why bother asking me specifically?"

For once, the principal's even facial expression broke, and her eyes darted to the officer. "I don't understand."

"I didn't *know her*," I repeated, trying to keep the shakes out of my voice. What was going on here?

Officer Seneca made his first move, hand entering his jacket and producing an envelope. He didn't say a word, merely started unlooping the string around the cardboard dial that kept it sealed. The principal finally spoke up. "Officer, you said this girl —"

"Is this you?" His light tone tinkled in my ears as he fanned out the photos on the boardroom table. There I was, in perfect focus, standing stricken over the body of victim number one, each photo a frame in a dance that saw me turning, horror-struck, to face the photographer.

My mind peeled backwards to that day in the cutting cold morning, the flash of silver eyes and the mean smirk beneath them. A character in this tableau I had completely erased until now. Maybe that's what he'd wanted, so I could be implicated in this, instead of him. And I could see it now, etched over the memory — a smirk that curved into a beak, and the same slicing glare that I was being served by Officer Seneca.

I just stared at the pictures, and the principal sat agape. "What is this?" she asked the room. "What's going on here? Is this even legal? Due process —"

The officer finally flicked his gaze from me and looked at the principal, his expression reaching out and stroking her face. A catatonic glaze relaxed the tense muscles in her forehead as his voice carried her elsewhere.

"Thank you, Mrs. Fraser," he oozed. "You have been most helpful. You will forget this encounter as soon as we leave the room."

She nodded and stared straight ahead. I knew that she would be silent for the rest of this conversation, a virtually empty seat that had left me alone with a hungry predator.

"I'd read that Owls were given the power of suggestion, to use all their limitless wisdom to tap into people's minds," I spoke evenly, quoting Sil as though I were doing a classroom presentation. "But I thought Ancient decreed the Owls were only allowed to use that power in cases of 'dire urgency.'" I poked the oblivious principal. "Or, you know, something like that."

Seneca eyed me, jaw tightening. His features were severe — like all the other Owls I'd seen so far — and if it wasn't for his absolute, hungry confidence that I immediately hated, he would've been good-looking.

"When you're this far from the Authority, you tend to make your own rules. Isn't that so?" The sound of his voice prickled in my eardrums. Would he try to control my mind, too? Would I let him, without knowing it? The frustration of my vulnerability lit the flame inside me, and it climbed protectively.

He tapped a finger against the photos, as though bored with them now. "Don't worry. I'm not here to harm you or wrangle you. Just to warn you."

"What, that you could arrest me at any time? I've seen enough crime procedural TV to know that I should have a lawyer present to be even talking to you. If this *was* in any way legal." Though, what would it matter, if the Owls controlled the police? But I needed him to know I wasn't afraid of him or his Family. Even though I was.

Seneca raised an eyebrow at me, almost pityingly. "This isn't about human law. This is about *our* law. I know you aren't familiar with it yet, but you will be, before the end. You can't run from your fate forever."

I cringed, biting back a snarl. "Go ahead. Arrest me and hand me over, then. It's what you all want. What's stopping you?" I was taking a chance, but I knew if that's what he wanted, he wouldn't be standing on ceremony by summoning me here.

Seneca eased back into the plastic chair, taking in the creaks of the wheels as though they were prey-bones popping beneath his weight. "Nothing really. Nothing's stopping me, or anyone, from snatching you and tossing you to the river. But we do have some rules we must abide by. We can't intervene directly, unless at the moment of *dire urgency*." He threw my words back at me. "Which we fully intend to do, if you don't co-operate."

"*You're* the ones who sent the river hunters after *me*! You're the reason they're out killing people who have nothing to do with this!" My hands shook, and I felt the air around me getting hotter. He sensed it, too, and instead of turning fearful like I so desperately wanted, he grinned.

"And until you give yourself up willingly to the Council of Owls, for the good of this city, they'll keep killing those girls: Their blood will be on your hands." The smile dropped from his mouth. "It's as simple as that."

Simple. I said nothing. I felt numb, trapped. I couldn't burn my way out of this. Sil was right, I needed to control the fire before I unleashed it; I was going to need the Owls on my side, after all. This wasn't something I could do alone, or without their help.

"I can do it," I said, stilling my sweating palms in my lap. "I can bring down Zabor. I know I'm green, but I can try. You just have to give me a chance."

Seneca blinked, not expecting that. He shook his head. "I'm afraid we can't allow that. You'd be upsetting a balance that goes beyond this little speck in the universe, and we won't be a part of our undoing." He started gathering up the photos, shuffling them carefully. "If you don't give yourself up, you will be tried by human law for the murders of the Red River girls. And by our law, we'll see to it that you're executed in a manner befitting a murderer. Which, through your continued inaction, is what you are."

He was right. They were dying because of me. But I held onto my resolve.

"Every year that you help this monster more people will die," I murmured. "Even members your own Family. And when there are no Denizens left here, Zabor will swallow you, too. You're just as culpable as I am, preventing me from stopping this."

For a moment he stopped shuffling. Had the inanity of what they were trying to uphold ever really struck them? That eventually, all that would be left of the Denizens of Ancient would be crumbling bones and forgotten lore locked away in basements until the stewards of their world dissolved into obscurity?

Or was it simply about power?

Seneca got to his feet and the moment passed. "Your mother. She suffered when she attempted to change what we were charged to do." I clenched my fists and jaw and levelled him with a glare. "See how her quest ended. See how you have to pay for her sins. Don't make any others pay for yours. Especially your friends."

I went numb at that, their faces flashing in my mind. The envelope of photos was just within my reach, but he snapped them up and tucked them under his wing — under his jacket — and began to leave.

"Think about what I've said. Reconsider. Do what's right." For a second, Officer Seneca sounded as beaten as the stones of his words, but he believed he was doing what was best for me, for us all. And I couldn't turn him away from the certainty of his conviction.

"You think about what I've said, too," I shot back. He paused in the doorway, composed himself, and kept walking.

The principal jerked forward, looking around the room as though she'd just been scared awake. She put an unsure hand to her face and jolted again when her eyes fell onto me.

"Oh! I'm sorry. Did we, um . . . did we have a meeting?"

I stood and put a heavy hand on her shoulder. "It's all good," I lied. "Don't worry about it."

The EMBER DANCE

.

D eer. Rabbit. Fox. Seal. Owl.
I traced my fingers over the totems of the five Families, laid out in hundreds-of-years-old ink in another book I'd found in the summoning chamber. United, the Families could defeat Zabor. What that meant, I still didn't know. Too many questions, and this book lacked an answer key.

In any case, we were still shy of a Seal (and I'd barely seen any in weeks, or ever had a Barton-esque vision about them) and an Owl. But after the interrogation at school, it seemed more and more hopeless that the birdbrains would fight on my side. And if they did, how long would it take them to betray me?

I closed the book. I'd been reading it carefully, but it was more a primer on the Families, their characteristics, histories, and global distribution. When it mentioned unity, it was only about *protecting the realm*, *maintaining the Great Narrative*, and the Denizen connection to humans. Darklings were a big part of the history, too, but the Families were meant to co-exist with these manifestations of nature's destructive tendencies. Because they were as much a part of the world as the rest of us. Only if they got out of hand were they to be dealt with — but that was for Ancient to decide. And Ancient had been dormant, Sil told me, for nearly a thousand years.

I'd read the book over and over until I felt like the pen marks were scratched into my eyes. This book wouldn't help me get Barton his legs back, let alone restore his connection to the one power we all drew ours from. It wouldn't make Phae an instant-expert, even though she worked hard at it. It wouldn't help me find a Seal, wherever they were, or to become the Great and Powerful Leader that everyone expected me to be. I wasn't going to get answers here.

But . . . from behind the book, I pulled the letters. Letters penned over decades and never sent, envelopes sealed and left to pile up with their secrets. I shut my eyes and went back to the night I'd found them.

It was the night after Phae and Barton and I had made our pact, and Sil had disappeared somewhere in the house. She was still sick, and acting strange.

"Sil? *Sil!*" I kept my voice down as I crept into my grandmother's dark bedroom, nostrils assaulted by the room's antiseptic sterility. I shut the door behind me and turned on the overhead light.

I stood at the foot of Cecelia's bed, feeling like she'd shrunk since I last saw her. Deedee had warned me that she probably didn't have much time left in this world. The day of the dead girl, and the attack on Barton, her contingent of remaining nurses had been on vigilant watch, as her heart rate dipped lower and lower and seemed to hover over death with reluctance. What was she waiting for? What was she holding on to? I leaned in and waved a hand in front of her face. *Just get it over with, already.* She was such a stranger, and I wished it could just be finished. You can't mourn someone's passing — or the passing of your entire family — if they're still there. Not really.

I heard a very low whine come from under the bed, and I immediately knelt. "Sil?"

She lay with her head tucked between her paws, brow furrowed. She had been alert enough on the ride home, but as soon as we arrived, I had carried her to my bed to let her rest. When I returned to check on her, she had vanished, but now . . .

"What are you doing in here? Can you hear me?" I put a hand on her head, and it was warm, which must have been a good sign. The light creeping under the bed showed that her fur had brightened back to its proper copper hues; she looked better, but she only opened one eye. It passed over me like a shade, then closed again.

"If I can help you, you have to let me," I said. "Can't you let me in on what's going on? You can't have forgotten how to talk. You'd miss badgering me too much."

I couldn't tell if that had elicited a fox-smile, but if it had, it was already gone.

Unwilling to be defeated, I pulled myself fully under the bed and nestled beside her, one arm tucked under my head. My free hand stroked her fur. She didn't move and didn't seem to mind; her breathing was regular. It was strange, though, being with her in this way. She was supposed to be my teacher, the only thing keeping me tethered to the world she was offering. But seeing her like this made her seem fallible, which is not what I needed. I was fallible enough for the both of us.

"What are you?" I whispered, letting the bristles of her winter coat prickle my palm as I swept my hand down her back.

"Just a shadow," she replied, her voice low, but her words coming with less effort than they had that afternoon.

"Was it something to do with the river hunters? Did they poison you?" It couldn't have been because of the attack, though; she'd already started looking spent as soon as we'd reached Barton's place. But I saw no other explanation.

I didn't expect her to answer. When I thought she'd gone back to sleep, she mumbled, "Yes . . . and also no. It's not an easy thing, being me."

I frowned. "Is that all I'm gonna get?" The fox-grin came back, and it stayed there a little longer. I sighed. "Ah, well. Guess that means you're on the mend." It seemed that being in this room was improving her spirits. "Are you getting better because of your connection with Cecelia?"

Both of her eyes opened and seemed to swallow me. Beautiful, bright eyes, old and full of memories both primordial and immediate. She was about to reveal something really meaningful. "Yes . . . and also no," she said again and closed her eyes.

I rolled onto my back, arms out, studying the underside of Cecelia's mattress. Deedee had pulled me aside earlier, telling me to prepare myself for the end. Maybe my grandmother's life *was* tied to Sil. And maybe I should stop letting my resentment of being ignored by her all these years control how I felt. If she lingered on and kept Sil alive by doing so, then I'd pray with every fibre of my being that she held on. Until the end.

"Can you tell me about her?" I asked, picking at the bed frame with a fingernail. "What she was like, what she enjoyed . . . or do you bother with character sketches when you're training would-be warrior queens?"

For the first time since I'd come in, Sil raised her head stiffly, stretching until all of her foreclaws poked out, a long-tongued yawn showing all her sharp, yellow teeth. She stared forward. "She was pigheaded and stubborn and always thought she was right," Sil snuffed. "Seems genetic."

I ignored the jab. "You knew my mom, too?"

Sil shivered, fur prickling, even though it was warm under the bed. "Yes. I spent time with her as well. But she did not have Cecelia's penchant for power. She was more connected to the earth than to the flame; to the fire of life, you could say."

"Explains the vet thing," I mused. Everyone told me Ravenna could calm any animal that went through her clinic, rabid or hysterical. "So there's a spectrum of Family powers, then?"

Sil ducked her head in a lazy nod, but didn't answer me directly. "And dancing. Cecelia liked to dance. She liked to be the centre of attention, in general. Did you know she used to be on the stage?"

"What?" I squawked, maybe a little too loudly. "No, but what I don't know about either of them could fill an arena . . ." On the stage? I thought I'd come from a long line of brooders and introverts. I really had no grounds to blame my retraction from a social life on genetics, then.

Sil finally turned her head in my direction. She wasn't looking at me, but through me, to somewhere else in the room. "Have you ever looked through her things?"

I cocked an eyebrow and turned over, looking in the same direction, at the vanity table. "Why would I do that?"

"Because her history, your history, is in this house of hers. And it's yours for the taking. You were her only grandchild, after all. It's all yours."

Sil put her head back down and settled in. She was through reminiscing.

"Wait, no! Don't go back to sleep! Aren't you going to tell me where to look?"

"I need to rest," she exhaled in reply, as much of a bark as anything. "Consider this part of your training."

The house was filled with relics and antiques, and the basement was piled to the ceiling beams with what could be meaningful memories or just garbage. Needle in the haystack times infinity.

"You know where to start," she assured me, before her breathing became low and calm, and I knew she was asleep.

I groaned and crawled out from under the bed. I got to my feet and crossed my arms, almost unwilling to start the hunt out of spite. But really, what else was I doing? Staying out of Arnas's way was one thing, but it was boring. And I was hungry for answers. Sil was right — there were parts of this I'd have to do on my own. At least I didn't have to kill anything. For now.

I caught my reflection in Cecelia's beautiful vanity mirror. It was ivory with gold trim and seemed to glow. The vanity was strewn with jewellery, old photos, and dazzling things from an era of glamour and beauty. I pulled out the prim, plush stool and thumped inelegantly onto it. It was the perfect height for me, and I had a good view of myself from the ribs up. It really did feel like something a stage actress would go for, and that's what she'd been.

What did Cecelia think about, sitting at this mirror, primping and pulling the gilt silver brush through her hair for a hundred strokes? Officially, everyone told me she was an anthropologist or archaeologist, someone who was always on her knees in the dirt, digging up history, or presenting it to classrooms of intellectuals. Not exactly a glamorous career choice. But that's not what she turned out to be; it'd just been a cover for her Denizen tendencies. I could see her as a *Relic Hunter* or *Buffy* type — fighting baddies with her wicked fire-power, solving ancient mysteries, sending evil back where it came from. There was so much I'd never know about her, and fiction only bred more fiction.

I looked back at the real Cecelia on the bed. Her hair lay wilted on her pillow; I couldn't picture it red, like mine and my mom's. There were a few pictures of her, though. I put the brush down and looked at the photos tucked in the corner of the mirror. I plucked one out that was flaked at the corners: Within its white Polaroid borders was a woman with long waved hair, black in the sepia picture. She was tall, with slender legs, embarrassingly big boobs, and a smile that promised what you desired but didn't guarantee delivery. She was a stunner. A real star. She shone with it, shone with the knowledge that she had a conflagration at her fingertips and wasn't afraid to use it.

I looked at myself guiltily in the mirror, like I'd failed to live up to her — my chop-shop hair, flat chest, some-what thick, soft body. No. Looks were definitely not genetic. Maybe I'd gotten my father's body, instead.

I tucked the picture back. She had it all. Beauty, charm,

outgoing personality. I'm sure she was horribly intelligent, too, what with being the great leader of her tribe, everyone coming to her for advice and help . . . and the power. The power that maybe I had inherited, but couldn't pull out of my back pocket without struggle. I felt more robbed than usual. From what pictures I'd seen, my mother had been shorter than Cecelia, and wasn't as "out there," but she was beguiling, lovely, plump like a Botticelli painting, with the reticent eyes of a witch. And she could touch any creature and hear its heart sing. Was I destined to come from so much fire, only for it to fizzle out?

When I looked in the mirror, I tried to subtract the things that I knew were mine, tried to compare my features to my mother's, my grandmother's, to grainy photos. The women in them were strangers.

I looked away. I needed to put a hold on the pity-partying. I'd indulged in it too much lately and now wasn't the time. I started shuffling through the papers on the vanity. There was a pile of letters there, one I had knocked over a couple of days ago in frustration, so I figured I'd start there.

The letters were yellowed by time and looked sealed, never opened or sent. I picked one up and read the address.

Roan Harken
39287 Lipton St.
Winnipeg, MB
R3G 2H1

When I was little, Ravenna used to make me repeat that address over and over, like a song, so if I ever got lost, I could tell it to a grown-up who could safely deliver me home.

Home. It was the address of our house in Wolseley, with the vines and the greenhouse and the fading memories. The return address was in Beijing.

I tore into the envelope, rabid, like it had been a hard winter and all the elk were dead, but here in my hands was sweet, restoring manna. I ended up ripping part of the letter, but I smoothed it out with shaking hands and started reading.

December 9, 1994

Dear Roan,

Whatever your name ends up being, I will fill it in later. Hopefully I hear word soon, as I won't be in contact with anyone from Canada for several months after I leave Beijing. I am writing this from a hothouse in the city centre — a greenhouse, where plants and flowers are grown to sell — and will be consigning myself to the country for a long time in a few days. I am sorry that I am not there to see you in your newness. Hopefully you'll forgive me later down the line.

You're just a baby now. Maybe your mother will read you this letter someday. Maybe you'll come upon it on your own. Or maybe she will burn it before it gets to you. Either way, I think I'm writing this more for myself than for you.

I frowned at the letter, not sure if I'd maybe read it out of order. But it was the first letter on the pile, which had been neatly stacked and tied with twine. Cecelia had taken great pains to get them in order and keep them that way. And the date was the day I was born.

My frown fell away as I cast a glance at the prostrate letter-writer herself. Icy fingers penetrated my guts. She was talking to me now, from the depths of her coma, and she was three feet away. It was too surreal to think about, so I dove back into reading.

> *I'm not even sure if your mother* ~~talks about me~~ *will talk about me. I know you probably haven't even opened your eyes yet, but I should let you know that your mother and I are not on the best terms. You could say that it's just a difference of opinion, or you could say she has made the wrong choice for herself, and you, by bringing you into the world at all.*

Wow, ouch.

> *But that would be petty. You're just* ~~a baby a kit a leveret~~ *a baby. You are innocent. It isn't you. It isn't Ravenna, either.* ~~Maybe it's me. It probably is.~~ *I don't like to think that it could be me. I've been told that too many times by too many people. It also pains me to admit that they're right. I don't know why I'm telling you these things. I thought it would make me feel better to write, because what I do is lonely work. Ravenna* ~~hates~~ *resents me for it now, but what she doesn't know is that I would rather be there with her than here on the other side of the world. I don't think I'm ready to admit that, just yet. What she can't understand is that we are appointed certain duties, and I learned a long time ago to face mine head-on, rather than turn from them. Even though it cuts me off from everyone.*

I could see her sitting at a small table in a Chinese green-house, barely dewed with sweat, great black mane kept up from her neck as she sipped green tea and grimaced at her clumsy attempt at saying *hey, you were born today, welcome to the world*. It filled me with a bit of familial pride, knowing that I edited myself in the same way, always wanting to do and say everything just so (and usually failing). The paper was even slightly crumpled, as though she'd consigned it to the trash before reclaiming it and smoothing it out.

> *You are my granddaughter. Nothing else matters. I am glad that you're here. I will see you soon. And that will get me through the months of wandering through the country-side like a cursed nomad, wishing this "duty" on someone else. And it will keep me burning strong.*
>
> *Still, I wonder if you're a Fox or a Rabbit or simply a human. Maybe I will never know, and maybe it doesn't matter.*

Love, Cecelia

What?

I read the last line over and over again. *I wonder* . . . My eyes flicked back to the mirror, and with a hitch in my breath, I flashed my spirit eye on. A Fox stared back at me, sharing the subtleties of my human face. *A Fox or a Rabbit? What did she —*

I exhaled — sort of a laugh, sort of a hitched sob. Since the Moth Queen had come for me, I'd been caught up in my mother's legacy, my grandmother's lineage. The fire that burned and the Fox that I was born to be. I had barely given my father a second thought.

Hands shaking, I put the letter down. I turned my left palm up in supplication and traced the lines of my skin. Arnas was a Rabbit. He was my father's twin brother. Which meant that there was Rabbit in me, too — or could there be? This only brought up more questions, like why was I manifesting as a Fox in my reflection, with fire in my blood and heat in my heart? Had my genetics abandoned the Rabbit side for the stronger power? Or was there no Rabbit in me at all, because . . .

I wanted to drag Sil out from under the bed and shake the answers from her. But Sil needed rest, and I couldn't move holding further proof that I would never truly know myself. When the tears splattered the letter in front of me, I realized that I was finally mourning the loss of something I never had, and I was hot with the futility of losing it.

I sniffed hard, dragging the back of my hand over my eyes and refusing to let confused sorrow get in the way of my current task. I was doing all I could, sleuthing through the remnants of Cecelia's life to put together the pieces of my own. I couldn't ask any more of myself, and the tears were actually a reassurance that I was on the right track.

I read the last part of the letter over again. *Wandering through the countryside like a cursed nomad*? Was she just about to embark on a demon-banishing mission, or was this some kind of self-imposed penance for whatever stood between her and my mother? The answer was obviously right in front of me, though; Cecelia had hinted that it was something about *me* that had thrown off their relationship, and I would bet what little money I had that it was more to do with Ravenna and Aaron's marriage than with me. The daughter of the Fox

Paramount running off to marry a Rabbit probably didn't sit well with the strict, primeval traditions that Cecelia seemed so enamoured of. It was a wonder she wrote to me at all.

What I do is lonely work. My heart thrummed with the pang of her words. I had been so angry at her for neglecting me, but I hadn't really realized the full scope of responsibility to the Family at large, eclipsing, as it did, her family by blood. I understood lonely work, all too well. I had Barton and Phae, true. But those were tentative ties, and none of us knew where to start, what we were doing. The three of us were now hunted. And we could tell no one about it, seek no guidance from those we loved. Alone together.

I picked up the second envelope and was pulling the letter out before I registered that I'd ripped it open.

March 8, 1995

Dear Little Fox,

Today I am writing from Inverness, Scotland. The air here is cool and damp, and there are hills and mountains and lochs (lakes) that I think you would like. Someday I will bring you along with me, when things are simpler. For now, your mother should be showing you the fire, which you were borne of (thankfully) and will keep you warm while I can't be there.

You must be learning to walk, by now. Or dancing before even that. Did you know that I used to dance? Oh yes. I loved it dearly. I loved a lot of things, but they had to be given up. You'll find that out someday, too, but for now you can revel. You can do what you like without much pressure

*or pretense. I envy you. Maybe that is why I love you so,
aside from the blood ties. Aside from the fact that a part of
you is me. It is because I want nothing more than to be you,
to go back to that place where I could be myself without the
weight of everyone pressing down.*

*I tried to run away from what I was, once. Because I
heard drums in my blood, and the dancing made me powerful. In Scotland, there are drums. They are called bodhrans,
and they sound when you have to go to war. I always feel
like I am going to war — in a way, I am — and maybe it
will help you if you ever have to. Because the soft lightness
of childhood ends too quickly, and you might have to fight
battles of your own. Dancing brought out the rawness in me,
and allowed me to do things I don't think I was supposed to
do. But I liked it. And I couldn't stop dancing. Maybe that
is what got me here in the first place.*

Will you dance, too?

Love, Cecelia

My heart beat a little faster. There were endearments
in this letter. Words that I'd longed to hear. Even though
Deedee had spent countless years asserting that I'd been
loved, I refused to believe it unless it came from the lips
of the dead and disappeared who should've been there to
say it. But Cecelia had used "love," and addressed me as
"little Fox." What if I'd turned out to be a Rabbit? Not that
it mattered; she'd left me out of her life despite the fire I'd
inherited . . .

But here it was, plain before me, and I was paralyzed by
the enormity of it. I was loved.

Her words ricocheted through me again. *Things I was not supposed to do.* There had been drums of my own calling me when I had been consumed by vengeance for Barton, when I'd attacked Zabor's monsters with the brutal efficiency of the monster I, myself, had become. I hadn't heard the drums since then, but I wanted to.

I liked it, she'd said. I clutched the letters close.

⤳≪

"Roan!"

I snapped to, reeling aside as what could only be called a *shard of fire* glanced past my face at eye level. It exploded on the far granite wall of the summoning chamber, leaving no trace.

"What the hell was that for?" I rounded on Sil, getting back to my feet in time to slide around another shard, this time with a bit more grace.

Sil herself landed with molten poise, as she'd been firing the things through her tail like clay pigeons. Yep, she was definitely back to her old self, and these training sessions hadn't abated since her strength came back.

She sprang up again, turning end-over-end until she was a fiery, airborne saw blade. The shards came out of her in multiples, sending me careening and jerking out of their paths. It was a little more than obvious that she was pissed.

"For god's sake, Sil! Gimme a break!" I whirled around, and the fire-disc Fox in the air had grown bigger, bristling with flaming shards. I glanced at the summoning chamber doorway, which was sealed as usual.

"You are here to work," her voice roiled with the blaze, "not to daydream."

I cringed, and what I'd been thinking of flashed through my mind unabated, which just annoyed me more — Cecelia's letters, the Owl cop Seneca, the first dead girl by the river. And the boy. The boy at the crime scene snapping my picture, setting me up with each flash, teeth gleaming. Those teeth. They seemed to get sharper every time I thought of them. I wanted to reach into the memory and smash them out of his —

"Focus!" Sil bellowed, then the sulphur meteor that was now Sil rocketed over my head.

I turned my face to the heat, pivoted with my arms out, and turned the blaze aside on my own. At first, the fire met my flesh but seemed to wrap around my arms like ribbon. I closed both hands around the flames, testing for a sure grip.

And I heard the drums, like Cecelia predicted I would. The steady beat in my pulse set the tempo. It was leading me, reassuring but firm, and this time I wouldn't let it turn me into something *wrong*.

The fire bobbed around me like something liquid, or something with light ballast. It listened to my movements, obeyed me, and when I felt it was growing too heavy to support any longer, I slammed it down into the unforgiving black marble of the chamber floor, where the fireball shattered like a glass balloon. Shards of brimstone skittered around my feet, then disappeared into the dark.

Sil stood in front of me, eyes filled with golden appraisal. "Well," was all she said, swishing her tail like a pendulum.

It was only when she spoke that I remembered to breathe, and that I registered the megashakes quaking through me. I was standing in a half-crouch, arms spread out, like I had just executed a triple Salchow, waiting for the judge's score. My knees gave out, and I fell to them, panting.

"This is why I push you," she said, coming closer. "You have to stay focused and present. And you improve when you do."

"I know," I grumbled, pressing my hand into my thigh as I got to my feet. "I get it, okay?"

Sil snuffled. "You're letting your frustration dictate your skills again, and that will get you nowhere."

"That's not true!" I argued, but it was feeble. I'd been thinking about ripping that photographer apart when things seemed to click and the fire yielded to me. I crossed my arms, pacing. "I just . . . I can't get to it any other way right now."

"The power of the Five can only be accessed with a tranquil heart, and you carry a dangerous element in your blood. As destructive as water."

I couldn't stop my derisive laugh. I whirled on her. "Oh c'mon, Sil, you think this giant demoness is gonna just roll over with a *tranquil heart* when I come at her? I have to *fight*, and yeah I'm mad! So why not use it if it gets the best result?"

At this she sat without breaking eye contact. "What did you do, just now? To master the meteor?"

I stopped pacing. "I just . . . I grabbed it and smashed it? I don't know."

"You *danced*," she said.

"I . . ." I had heard the drums. But they weren't the harsh, rapid pealing of staccato beats that led my fury weeks ago. They were steady as a heart. There was *some* tranquility to it, I had to admit. "I guess I did." I scratched my cheek. "That's good though, isn't it?"

"It's better." Sil inclined her head. "But not yet good enough." She thrust her chin up, and I smiled, seeing the flash of pride in her eyes. I was getting there. And if it meant dancing my way to victory, then I'd learn as many moves as I could.

Her head tilted, the ruff of her shoulders rippling. "Where did you learn that?"

"Cecelia." I shrugged, cheeks warm and feeling pride of my own. Then I pulled the garnet-bladed sword free of my belt before I could get sappy. "Shall we continue?"

Sil nodded. "We shall." And the fire rose again; this time, I was ready to meet it.

The BROKEN TENET

"The spring is nearly upon us." Anton Bel shakes his large, ponderous head. "This has already gone on far too long."

Eli, unmoved by this token and extremely useless observation, goes on feeding live mice to his enormous snake. The snake pushes out its muscular coils, sliding backwards to strike. Eli closes the tank lid and stands aside so that all assembled have a view of the snake pulling back, tight as a bow string, before it snaps out and devours its quarry.

The assembly of elders, advisors, and dissenting Owls keep silent. Eli exchanges a glance with his father at the other end of the room but doesn't linger. Eli can handle this himself.

"Thank you, Mr. Bel," Eli intones dryly. "But I've access to several calendars. We all know what time of year it is."

A hand slams palm down on the round oak table in the centre of the gathering hall. Eli flicks his eyes in the direction of the obvious dissaproval, and the culprit, Bel himself, slowly retires his hand to his lap, consigning his eyes to the floor.

Eli turns to fully face them now, aware of each muscle and bone beneath the flesh of his face. He knows his manner has so far worked to unnerve this small-town council, but also puts them at ease; after all, he is their highest authority at the moment, and at least they can rely on him to remain impassive in the eye of ruin. Even though he's only twenty-five, a youth filled with promise, and they are mostly quivering old men haunted by their imminent graves.

"Gentlemen. Ladies. Yes, spring is near. No, the blood has not been paid. We are behind schedule." Arms folded, he moves to the hall's eight-foot wall of windows overlooking the grounds of the manor house in which he's been a guest since arriving from Seoul weeks previous. It was his father, Solomon Rathgar, who had been tapped to offer guidance for this year's cull, but Eli, newly minted Paramount though he was, had more authority now than even his pious father could offer. This surprised everyone, since Solomon had always been a fixture, and now he had been replaced by the son no one knew he'd had. Eli glares out the window at the snowdrifts the size of a man.

A hatchet-faced councilwoman gestures to the window — Eli catches the movement in the reflection of the glass. "But winter's grip is still firm. There is time enough, no?"

"Time enough to sit idly by and wait for our destruction," mutters Bel from under his enormous bushel of a beard.

Eli narrows his eyes, favouring Bel with a glance, but the response is taken up by an incredulous squeak out of Gregor Fellin's teeth. "Do you dare suggest we break the tenets of Ancient for the sake of your *patience?*" he cries. *Classic fundamentalist.*

"Those tenets were laid down when the spirit of this Earth commanded itself!" Bel barks back. "*Back then* it could be relied on to keep the balance, but now —"

"Enough." Eli's cool tenor has ripples skittering across it, the bickering fools wearing on him quickly. Their eyes go round on him, and he can't help but smile; they look so much like their Family's sigil — collars puffed, dander up, faces flushed. And yet, none of them are willing to draw blood where required. But Eli is.

"The tenets of which you speak," Eli begins softly, pacing the table, calculated, "are guidelines given to those charged with protection of this realm. The Five must keep destruction neutralized and maintain the balance. We are slaves to these rules, yes. And since the Families have shrunk, the full burden of this task falls often to the Owls. It is a heavy burden to bear. It always has been. Many sacrifices have been made, all for the greater good. And we are not dealing with a lesser darkling here — this is Zabor, a Celestial, from the beginning times. She would destroy us all if she were to wake, unsated.

"Yet how can we protect our world when we are commanded to sit back and wait for 'fate' to intervene? I'm not a stranger to this frustration. We have all felt it in the past, and Ancient has a purpose for these tests of our patience — and in the end, it always prevails."

Eli stops, trying to master the tremor pulsing in his chest like a starburst. They must hear the voices, too; the Owls in attendance exchange almost-terrified glances, either because of his speech or the hissing oaths seeming to rise from the room's dark corners. Eli feels his spirit flex. "But it has come time to realize that the old tenets are useless to us, especially when Ancient itself sleeps idly. We must act independently, yet still for the greater good."

Fellin purples instantly. "Are you actually agreeing with this — this — *dissenter?*" he blusters, flapping his hand at Bel, who looks equally perplexed at this turn.

The other assembled members rasp to each other in shocked whispers, a shudder of doubt, rage, and absolute fear rankling through them. Eli expected all of this, but even without the influence of his hidden advisors, he knows it is the only tack.

Eli pivots towards Bel. "You've suggested that time is running out. And you're right. Six-foot-high snowdrifts are no barometer for our doom. A melt could come at any time, and when the ice breaks up, the flood waters will rise. Someone intervened in the Moth Queen's delivery of our sacrifice. Rather than fumbling around wondering *why* or relying on the hapless misfires of Zabor's children, it has been suggested we take matters into our own hands." The outcry rises, and Eli finds, to his annoyance, that he has to speak over it. "We have done all we can to assist the river hunters, but the Fox-girl has evaded them. Their tactics can no longer be relied upon."

Eli's father rises to his feet, and the Owls elbow each other to hush. Eli has seen this protest coming. Solomon Rathgar is Eli's personal dissident, always ready with pro-test. Ever since Eli had been chosen as Paramount, their already tenuous relationship has eroded nearly to nothing. "You are being unfortunately reckless, Elias," his father intones like a war gong. "You are suggesting we take the girl to Zabor ourselves, that we break the tenets that govern the Denizens of Ancient and the Five Families to hasten the task. To make it seem like we are loyal to a darkling, and not Ancient."

Eli catches Fellin nodding his head like the sycophantic dipping-bird he is. "The law *clearly states*," Fellin argued, "that any appeasement given in blood can be given only by Death, taken by the darkling independently, or given willingly by the sacrifice themselves! These are laws made to protect us all and maintain the balance —"

The balance . . . the word echoes in a place deeper than Eli's soul, repeated over and over in the hollows of his head. Mona Fawkes, her face carved from crystal, has cut in: "— laws that, if broken, could end up waking the demoness no matter what we do, and put us in the path of Ancient's fury for disobedience. We are guardians, not executioners. Let the river hunters deal with her. To get involved directly could cost us everything!"

Eli smiles. Then, letting his control slip, he laughs — and the sound is so alien it jars everyone. "You seek authority and comfort in the Old Laws," speaks a hundred tones that aren't his, and yet must be, "and yet it is my Law here that will be absolute." His hand creeps up to his chest, to the solid, cold thing that lives there. A shard of his mind curries for control, stopping the hand from unbuttoning his shirt and exposing it to the room.

Fellin removes his spectacles in disbelief. "It . . . it cannot *be*."

The rest of the gathering remains still, as though they might perish for moving. Anton Bel is agog. "The Moonstone? But . . . it was lost —"

"It is here. It is supreme. It is the wisdom of the forebears that impel me to act. Let none of this Family speak against it."

More murmuring, a mixture of awe and fear. He lets them turn it over in their minds — that these orders come from their very ancestors, and how can they be wrong? Eli is momentarily furious that his authority isn't enough, but he doesn't dwell in anger long. A soft suggestion reaches tentatively out of the group, a shadow of a thought, but Eli swoops down on it, clutching it to him as he whips his head towards the inner voice.

"Whose thought is that?" Eli and the voices thunder, choking the rabble further. Their eyes go to him, then around the room. Only one head is dipped, but Eli forces it up by the power of his will: Jordan Seneca, the police officer sent to question the girl, Roan Harken, to see if she would meet her fate head-on. An offer she obviously refused. Seneca meets Eli's eyes guiltily, but does not pretend to hide the intent in them.

"Stand up and repeat your thought for all to hear, cousin," Eli invites, his voice now his own, the effort of controlling it and his cruel smile enormous. But though the edge of Eli's words strike Seneca hard, the accused stands firm, clearing his throat.

"We could leave her be in her mission," he speaks clearly, despite knowing his words betoken treason, "and be rid of Zabor once and for all. Have our ancestors spoken of this alternative?"

The gathering had yet to reach utter silence, and now it does. There is nothing to say. Eli has the room again, looking to each assembled Owl and carefully recording their complete shock. It steadies him.

"Oh?" he can't help but smile again, placating. "And you imagine that this *girl*, along with the band of misfits she's gathering to her, will be able to subdue a darkling older than time, and without the use of the targe that sent Zabor here in the first place?"

Seneca tries to defend himself. "Someone is training her. There is a great power in the girl that will soon emerge. I could sense it when I met her. She may be able to —"

Solomon dismisses Seneca with a sharp glance; for once, father and son are on the same page, though perhaps Solomon only seeks to spare his nephew. "It takes tremendous power and will to seal a darkling. This girl is a child. And so are the allies she gathers and pretends are worthy of the task."

"Yes, I had heard she was spotted with the Allen child, and a human-turned-Deer," Fawkes muses with a tone that hints at gross fascination.

Fellin scoffs. "A *severed* Rabbit child! An abomination, at that. No connection to Ancient whatsoever. And this Deer girl? The Deer haven't fought a battle for centuries. They wouldn't know what to do with themselves. *Prey*, the lot of them." He glances reverently at Eli, as if trying to curry favour. "We cannot go against what our very ancestors have willed. The girl must be stopped."

"And what of the Seals, the ocean-born?" says someone in the crowd; Eli does not see whom. Eli sharpens his mind, searching everyone else's and finds the source.

"Enough," he seethes, turning to Seneca and pinning him down with a glare. "We are here for one purpose: Roan Harken's expedient demise. She stands in the way of our total destruction. I will not waste time entertaining hero fantasies. There is too much at stake."

Most nod, grunting or murmuring assent. They will not dare disagree now. Eli goes on: "I want a call put out to all of the Five that none are to fraternize with the Fox-girl Roan Harken. Anyone found helping her will answer to their respective Paramount or Ascendant on charges of treason. Zabor must be kept sleeping." But he can feel that their loyalties are shaken; they must obey the will of the Owls that have come before, though murder doesn't sit well with them. He scoffs. They are weak. "We will allow the river hunters a wide berth to do their duty. If intervention is required, it will be done."

"And is there to be a reward for *killing* Roan Harken, cousin?" Seneca retorts, though he speaks with the tone of sweet allegiance.

Eli narrows his eyes, hands clutched in a vise grip behind his back. The question is a trap. "We cannot put a price on peace." He indulges a lucid fantasy of tearing into his cousin's mocking face with the black talons he is capable of conjuring. But he only smiles back, inclining his head deferentially, for he knows they all think this new, strange Paramount seems almost too bloodthirsty.

"Do not fear," he reassures them, "Ancient may be silent, but our ancestors are with us. They are our compass towards the path of the greater good, and their wills are to be trusted." Eli pivots away. "You are dismissed."

They are placated, for now. As council members and the heads of important Owl families murmur their goodbyes and depart, Eli can see it clearly: fear.

It steadies him. The voices under his flesh hum their approval. He is pleasing them. For once.

Seneca lingers, casting a glance behind him as he joins the exiting throng. Yes, an eye would have to be kept on him.

They nod to each other, carefully hiding their thoughts, as Owls do. Eli met Seneca only recently and knows he has a bit of authority here. But Seneca has a different code of honour and ethics, one that could pose a threat. Eli needs him to stay as loyal as he knows him capable of being. As much as Eli balks at being challenged, Seneca is blood. Eli doesn't want to punish him, not really. But he might have to.

The heavy doors swing shut, and the gathering hall emptied but for Solomon and Eli. The light outside the high windows is fading. The setting sun heightens the power of the Owls; it clears their minds. But the tension coming off Eli's father stings. His mind is far from clear.

"I thought I dismissed this meeting, Solomon," Eli says coolly as he joins him at the window. He will never call him "Father," because this man has only just legitimized him, and he doesn't feel anything close to gratitude for it. Eli stares straight ahead, even when Solomon turns to him, his weathered, aristocratic face dropping some of its edge. The expression is sad. *Good.*

"I blame myself for this," he whispers.

Eli snorts. "If you want to blame yourself for something, then blame your failure to reach your potential. Then the stone would be yours, and you would see reason."

"Reason?" Solomon spits back, his mouth pressed in a grim line.

Eli eyes his birth father with a mix of dislike and curiosity. "Careful," he warns. "You are being weighed with every word."

"Let them hear!" he explodes, and Eli is taken aback. "Let that cursed stone know what a world we've made. You think it brings any of us joy to have to do this year after year? To sit idly as we deplete Denizen-kind because we can do nothing else? I can tell you now, Moonstone or not, killing children for no other reason than our impotence ages you, Eli." He reaches out, but doesn't touch his son; such gestures are reserved for *real* families. The hand drops.

Solomon stiffens again. "If you would only put the stone away. I may not know you well, but I knew your mother. I knew that she had a mind for justice and serenity. That you shared her pure heart. The stone . . . it changes you. Destroys what makes you good. The girl is *just a girl*. You cannot let this happen. You have the power to make this end."

Eli's eyebrows shoot up. Something of his true, old self emerges, and it is frightened with fury. "*You* sent me on the task to find the stone! Said that with it I could overcome a terrible evil." Eli finally masters himself, shrinking back from the man before him. "Zabor cannot be defeated. The evil here is the weakened devotion of Ancient's Denizens."

Solomon's eyes fall. "You weren't there when the pact with Zabor was made. Members of our family were. Your own ancestors died there, and she has killed many more since then. I thought with you, there might be hope . . ."

Eli suddenly snags Solomon by the shirt and slams him into the window. His strange eyes are not his own. "You are a fool," hiss the hundred voices.

Regaining control, Eli drops Solomon and backs away. He can feel Solomon's thoughts — disappointment, fear, and a loss he dares not examine.

"You are *weak*," Eli scowls, speaking from the place that keeps him rooted, that assures him he is in the right. "The stone chose me, not you. Because I am willing to do what is *necessary*. I seek to defend our world and all Denizens."

"What frustrates you more?" Solomon asks, genuinely curious. "That the girl is alive, or that you can't kill her yourself?"

Eli takes a step back, slightly jarred. He makes doubly sure that his mind-wall is up and well guarded before he indulges the thought: If the opportunity arose, yes, he would kill her himself. He should have when he took those damn pictures, but he had been foolishly fascinated by her — an average, unremarkable specimen touched by destiny. For a moment, he had been able to keep the ancient, mysterious stone out of his thoughts, and he wondered if it had been because of the way she looked so deeply inside of him . . .

"And how easy killing her would be." Eli lets the smile creep over his mouth like a shade.

This time, Solomon has no retort. The Denizens cling to their dwindling power and the hope that one day Ancient will return and answer their prayers, will cast back the darklings that humans and Denizens have allowed sway over this precious world. But they all rely on a primordial concept that has not spoken back for nearly a thousand years. And likely never will.

The sun now fully set, Eli feels his skin bristling with the ache to transform. "This Fox scion has her part to play in the Narrative. And if I must do what is in the best interest of all, I will do it, for I was chosen for it. The girl will die, by the authority you yourself gave me. And that is a tenet you cannot break without admitting treason."

Solomon just shakes his head, turning back to the window in resigned silence.

Eli approaches the round table, which has an intercom console in the centre. He presses the call button. "Send him in."

The doors swing wide moments after, and Arnas Harken is escorted through them, looking as anxious and flighty as always.

Eli erases any emotion from his face as he nails Arnas in his place with a glance. "Now, then. Your part is next to be played."

The SLEEPING JAWS

I always find myself standing at the riverbank, half aware and exhausted, like I had to cut my way through a thousand-strong army to get there. I can't understand why the river isn't moving. It isn't frozen, the water is just still — an artery blocked, a heart stopped. But I can still tread on the surface — like I'm walking on Jell-O, sinking a bit with each step. Less a river and more a carrion field, like the ones you read about in History class, like the crusades. Bodies, bodies everywhere, the crows turning above in the slate-dark sky as though they're stuck on an axle. And the bodies are many, and for a second I think, They're like the fruity chunks in the Jell-O mould, then I am ashamed. Their eyes follow me as I progress, faces contorted in death, arms reaching out, so much blind hope that maybe it's just a dream. It occurs to me that I am not in my dream. I'm in theirs.

I stop walking, sinking, sinking. I look down. I realize the bodies are stuck in a spiral, a silent maelstrom, all being pulled *into the place where I am sinking. An open mouth, inhaling them in. I look up at the crows stuck on their axle. And all at once the world explodes, sucking me into the undertow of a hungry breath —*

Phae grabbed a handful of my jacket and yanked me back onto the sidewalk. I hadn't processed that the traffic light was still red at Osborne and River and was about to get fatally intimate with the #16 bus.

"Yeah, that would've been cool. The Chosen One splattered at a crosswalk." Barton was joking, of course, but Phae's lips were pursed sourly.

"Sorry, sorry," I mumbled. I looked around, a soft pinging noise in my head softening into the regular sounds of Osborne Village — honking horns, loud teenagers, the splash of tires intersecting with melting snowbanks. *Yes. Yes this makes sense now. We're going to Phae's.* I yawned, desperately trying to keep my eyes ahead and not meet Sil's.

To say I was sleep-deprived was an understatement, and the rules of the waking world didn't seem to apply to me anymore. Over the last few weeks, nightmares swirled around me constantly, the kind where I found myself questioning whether or not I was actually awake. At least there were buses and decent friends to remind you of the difference.

If I was going to be assaulted in my sleep, then I wouldn't be caught dead dozing. This led me to spend more and more time in the summoning chamber with Sil, immersing myself in fire until my eyes were bloodshot and I reeked of smoke. Even my furry Yoda thought I was overdoing it.

"Well, at least you're committed." Sil rode in the basket underneath Barton's wheelchair, out of sight but well within earshot. "But rest is as vital to your training as the training itself." Easy for her to say, considering she spent about eighty percent of the day napping . . .

Phae, who was adjusting nicely to the concept of a talking fox, nodded solemnly as she linked her arm in mine. "If Sil is telling you to take it easy, then you should know better." The white crossing-man flashed. I let Phae keep a hold of me as we moved on. I wasn't about to shrug off support when I desperately needed it, even if I wasn't asking.

We were headed to Phae's parents' house nestled in the narrow streets of residential Osborne Village, beyond the numerous boutiques and cafés that made the area a big people magnet, even in February. Thankfully the snow had been melting (definitely not a Winnipeg normality), making the sidewalks and streets passable for Barton and everyone's mood lighter. Everyone's except ours. I tried to keep positive, but as the snowdrifts shrank and the asphalt shone slick and black, it made my chest tighten. Time was running out.

"You've got the same look you used to get when your eye bugged you," Phae said, snapping me out of my gloom.

"Phae, could you maybe not use *eye* and *bugged* in the same sentence?"

She rolled her black-coffee-cool, untroubled eyes, and we all kept walking. "So, Barton, are you going to tell Roan about what you found?"

I gaped at both them. "Am I out of the loop?"

Barton and Phae exchanged a meaningful glance, which annoyed me. "Well, you *have* been busy . . ." she said. I wanted to retort that I thought *Barton* was in charge of the intel, but I held my tongue. After all, I was the muscle of the (current) team, so I had more physical work to do. But I also thought I was sort of the de facto leader, and if the two of them had been hanging out *alone* together, that meant . . .

"Yeah, yeah." I rubbed a hand hard over my face. I'd think about the implications of that later. "So what's the dealio?"

"Oh man." Barton shook his head; he was looking tired, too, but flushed in the determined manner of Indiana Jones knee-deep in a lost tomb. I envied him. "Where do I start?" He looked up at me. "Did that moth lady tell you anything about this Zabor thing? Its origin story?"

I huffed hair out of my eyes and tried in vain to tuck it behind an ear. (It was still too short to co-operate.) "I only remember bits and pieces, but nothing specific. Specifics don't seem to be a Denizen strong suit." I shot Sil a sharp look, but she had hopped out of Barton's basket to pursue a mouthy grey squirrel.

The flurry of fox fur brought us up short. "Shouldn't you . . . ?" Phae started, pointing.

I waved her off. "Nah. Let her be a wild animal for once. Maybe killing something will mellow her out." I acted casual, but I hoped she'd be back soon. She seemed to be doing okay as long as she didn't use her powers. I hoped mine were useful enough now that she wouldn't have to. I'd brought her along for this specific reason, though — so she could enjoy herself. And do something other than badger me.

The pause had allowed Barton to shuffle through his backpack and produce the book he'd been studying dog-gedly. The book, he told us, had belonged to my granddad, Aaron and Arnas's father, who, according to Rebecca Allen, had been an influential neutralizer — a Rabbit that could per-form the Rituals of Ancient, talk with the spirits, and open portals.

"Portals to where?" I asked.

"I'm getting to that," Barton muttered.

This was the province of the Rabbits; only they could tune into the earth and open gateways or channel Ancient in ways that other Families couldn't — they weren't just nervous game, after all. This explained Arnas's former abilities; he struck me as a guy who couldn't summon a sock from a dryer, but what did I know?

"Well, that narrows it down to who can reverse the severing ritual." I folded my arms. "So what does this have to do with Zabor?"

Without a word, Phae took up Barton's wheelchair when we reached a particularly icy stretch, and we continued onward. It was a familiar, affectionate gesture. And for some reason my stomach did a backflip and my face went red. *Yep, they definitely have a thing.* Now I felt *really* left out.

Just as the queasiness set in, Sil appeared at my side and filled the sudden void. I even forgave the faint bloodstains smearing her jaws, the ghost of the squirrel's corpse still lingering in her smile. Circle of life, I guess. Just like teenage relationships. It wasn't like these two were a bad match, but I'd never heard Phae *once* express any interest in boys. She was too focused on prep studies to care, and she was a notorious scoffer at high school romance in general. I guess semi-apocalypses brought people together. I didn't think it'd be important, but my chest buzzed.

". . . at the beginning of time. Hey, Earth to Roan?"

"Hmm?" *Oh. How long had he been talking?* "Can you repeat that last part?"

Barton exhaled loudly and started again. "Okay. So let me break down the mythology. Ancient equals the consciousness of the world — where things come from when they're born-slash-created and where they return when they die. A big recycling plant. It's treated like a living thing but is also the cradle of creation as well as the underworld. *Comprende?*"

I rolled my eyes. "*I* could have told you that, dude."

"Anyway, Ancient used to speak and be independent, but about a thousand years ago, it just stopped. Radio silence. And over time, the Denizens' abilities and powers started to lessen. Like, a thousand years ago, Zabor wouldn't be a problem. But she only popped up recently."

"How recent?"

"Around about the time when Lord Selkirk, the Scottish guy who settled the Red River Valley, showed up. The First Nations peoples tried to warn the settlers about the malevolent spirit that had been causing terrible floods and eating anyone who went near the river. Of course, the regular folk thought it was either superstition, sacrilege, or raving, so they went on their merry way. That's when the Denizens realized it was Zabor."

Barton turned a page in the book in his lap. "And she's notorious. She isn't some random bogeysnake bent on causing havoc for the sake of havoc. She was around at what the Denizens call the Narrative, or the beginning times, back when they were all animals, and humans were barely a sparkle in Ancient's brain-eye. They call her a Celestial Darkling. The story goes that she was born out of a giant emptiness caused by three dying stars, which also made her brothers, Balaghast and Kirkald."

We rounded a corner and were within spitting distance of Phae's. The air was comfortable, but a chill zigzagged through my marrow regardless. "There are *more* like her?"

"Yep, and the three of them embody this bigger, ultimate

darkling. So basically the Three Muskefears fell to Earth and tried to eat Ancient, gain its power, and bend creation to their will. They're pretty much pure darkness. Separate they're terrible, yeah, but together they're the end of the world."

I shook my head, tightening my arms to my chest. "Man. And one would just *have* to turn up in Winnipeg, wouldn't it?"

Barton was thoroughly enjoying himself. "See, that's the kicker. Ancient forged three seals — or 'targes,' that's what the text calls them — that could imprison all of them in this place called . . . wait for it . . . *the Bloodlands*."

Phae's mouth twisted. "No, that doesn't sound morbid at all."

"Sounds like a hot vacation spot," I said. In my reckoning, that made three planes of existence in the Denizen world: our reality, the Veil, and now this Bloodlands place. "So Ancient put them away for good, saved the world, et cetera?"

"No, no, Ancient *made* the targes. It was the Denizens that managed to put them all away. It takes the power of the Five Families to activate the targe. That's why —"

"We need a Denizen from each of the Families to close the door on her." Relief washed over me.

"And," Phae put in helpfully, "a Rabbit can open the Bloodgate, which is the doorway we need to open to send Zabor back to her cage — once we use the targe on her, anyway."

"Okay!" I felt brightness lift me out of my sleepless stupor. "So then, all we need is to get us one of these targe thingies, find a Rabbit who can do the thing, and try to recruit a Seal and an Owl. Then we're done!" Saying it made me feel like we were bearing down on the finish line, even though reality

226

told me to *grip myself*. At least a big part of the enormous puzzle had been filled in.

And then a big piece fell under the sofa, and we were back to nearly square one. "Well. Sort of," Barton sighed, massaging the bridge of his nose. We were at Phae's now, but we were heading round the back. A pathway had been carefully dug in the snow, and plywood laid down, which made getting Barton to the backyard so much easier. I'd never seen this set-up here before, which just confirmed that Phae and Barton had been spending far more time together than I'd originally thought.

"The targe." Phae picked up where Barton had left off. "It's what kept Zabor imprisoned. But she somehow managed to break free of it and come through an open gateway between our world and the Bloodlands. When the Denizens found out she was here, they tried to send her back, but they weren't able to. Not without the targe."

I could see where this was going. "We don't know where the targe is, do we?"

"You think if the Denizens did, they would've dealt with this themselves by now, instead of leaving it to a handful of teenagers, hm?" Sil picked a fine time to add some much-needed — and long overdue — commentary. She shook herself out.

I gritted my teeth, holding myself back from punting her clear across the yard. "And you didn't tell me this stuff sooner, *why?*"

Sil snuffed. "You didn't ask."

Fury trembled through my bones until I buried my face in my hands and muffled a scream. Heat surged out through my boots and the snow around my feet evaporated. Phae yelped.

"Hey, chill!" Barton held his hands up, signing peace. "Like literally."

I huffed, the breath cloud in front of me as good as seething dragon smoke. "Whatever. We still don't know where this targe thing is. Unless you're sitting on that info, too?" I glared at her, but she didn't seem to notice. "So I guess the next step is finding it and shoving it right back down Zabor's gullet." I ground my fist into my palm, trying to affect ruthless courage, but as soon as I said "gullet," the dream-jaws and their whirlpool of death flooded my spirit eye. I had only seen shadows of Zabor in my nightmares, but I doubt the image of me shoving *anything* at her was a plausible one.

"Easier said than done," Sil confirmed, loping ahead of us as we came into the yard.

Phae's house was the only sanctuary we had. It was private, quiet, and safe from the scrutiny of our parents, other Denizens, and the river hunters. We were headed for the shed in the back — Phae's mom's old studio. She did all kinds of art, spending hours on huge installations, but since they'd done an addition on the house last spring, she was able to move her artistic operations back into the house. She'd given Phae the space to use for whatever she needed: studying, working . . . facilitating meetings of the Secret Demon Hunting Squad that her best friend coerced her into . . .

There were four Deer lying around the shed now, each at one of the four corners. The fifth was a thick-coated young one nosing around nearby. The four does raised their heads as one as we appeared.

Normally I would have been content to stop and watch them, afraid I'd spook them altogether, breaking the spell. But Phae kept up the approach, pushing Barton and navigating the bumps of the plywood path as if they weren't there at all. Sil went for the baby, which made me give a strangled cry.

"*Tch!*" I sucked on my teeth. "Sil!"

Her ears pricked straight up, and she swivelled her head in my direction. Her pupils were small, and she looked entirely like the carnivore she was. The look passed. She trotted over, panting.

"I don't need you going for the full woodland buffet, all right? A squirrel's enough!" She had the grace to look abashed.

"I wasn't going to *eat it*, you silly pup!" she barked back, as Phae dug in her pocket for the key to the shed.

"What's with the entourage?" I whispered loudly, which made them all tilt their heads at me inquisitively, some having been nosing around in the exposed, semifrozen grass and munching away like we were no more than curious talking shrubs.

"Protection, I think," Phae replied. "This is Geneve's family. I think they still feel a connection to her through me. Or they're just loyal."

I glanced over at the grey-brown bodies, hooves tucked neatly under them, faces impassive. There was no tension for them here; I'd never seen a Deer so at ease around humans before. I couldn't tell the difference between the lot of them, either, or even pick out familiar features from that day in the Assiniboine Forest when everything changed for Phae. At least they still had her back, despite the fact their grandmother had given her life to pass her power on to Phae.

"Do your parents mind?" I looked over at the big kitchen window facing the backyard. The curtains were drawn. I hadn't seen Phae's parents at all recently, come to think of it.

A shadow passed over Phae's face as her long black hair fell in front of it. She finally had the key, the lock undone and hanging from the latch. But she didn't go in.

"I think her parents are scared," said Barton. "There usually aren't Deer at all in this neighbourhood. But they've been showing up more and more every day. They just stare at the house for hours. I think it freaks them out a bit."

"Yeah, but, I mean . . . they're harmless unless you're really attached to your garden . . ."

Barton frowned. "You know Mr. and Mrs. Das are deeply spiritual people, Roan. And Deer can mean a lot of things. Deception. A curse. Death."

Well, thanks for making me look like the worst friend ever, I wanted to say, but I just looked down. I had never taken the Dases to be so devout that they'd do anything rash, or maybe see more into Phae's new life than other parents, but I felt abashed and sorted the snow with the toe of my boot.

"Pitā tried to get rid of them one morning," Phae said, her voice low and guarded at the mention of her father. "I had to stop him. Then more Deer came. They think I'm in danger."

I could see the scene clearly, a standoff in the pre-dawn snow between a frightened teenager and her confused father, a small herd of Phae's new kin watching silently. I imagined Phae's hair climbing into sparkling blue antlers in front of her father. Had she just demonstrated Geneve's gift, or had she done something she regretted? I wasn't about to ask. I let the closed curtains speak for themselves.

The shed door swung inward, Barton wheeled past us. The Deer all looked up at Phae — eyes wet and questioning. I couldn't blame the Deer for being here to protect Phae; in light of what I'd just heard, I was glad she had them. We were all in danger. It wouldn't be long now.

Phae forced a smile. She was getting as good at it as I used to be. "My parents are just like anyone else's right now. Everyone is afraid for their daughters now that so many of them are showing up dead on the riverbanks. I'm no redhead, but I just . . . I had to show them that they shouldn't worry." She looked down at her smooth hands as if they were someone else's. "Now they don't know what to think of me. My mom's gone off to the West Coast for an art showing. Pitā stayed behind, but I rarely see him — he's always taking extra call shifts. Maybe it's better that way, for now."

I hadn't realized I'd been holding my breath until we went inside and shut the door. I pulled Phae to me. How could anyone be afraid of such a strong person? "They're afraid because they *love you*." I said the words with such force that Phae looked up at me, startled, cedar eyes clear. "You have to know that. You have to always remember that. Okay?" I had her by both shoulders now, my reassurance turning more into begging. It was all I could offer. She had joined me in this crazy mission with no thought of what it would do to her life. Barton had done the same. No. I wouldn't let anything touch either of them.

Phae smiled, hands on mine, and I let her go.

I tried to diffuse the sombre mood. "Whew, cozy digs, Phae! Did you redecorate?" There were throws and cushions on the floor, a few space heaters humming their ancient electric spell to keep the cold out, and a single window letting in the afternoon light. I unzipped my jacket, and Barton shed his, his shirt momentarily sticking to it and riding up. The scar that the river hunters had left shone pink and white against his brown skin.

He caught me looking and grinned. "It's okay. Makes me look tough now. Next time they won't be so lucky."

I smiled back. "Yeah."

Phae was settling in on the floor, and Barton passed her his books from the basket on his wheelchair. I frowned. "The river hunters. They've been pretty quiet lately. No more dead girls or random attacks. It's wishful thinking they've given up, but . . ."

"It's just a clenched fist winding back for the KO." Barton shook his head. "They might be planning something. Or their semicomatose mother is. When the Denizens tried to subdue her the first time, they were pretty much facing total decimation. She could've just ended it there and then. But just when Zabor was about to wipe the last of them out, a Fox came forward and made the deal with her."

"The deal?" I looked around, suddenly remembering Sil — she was snuffling about in the shadows, just on the outskirts of our conversation. I wondered suddenly what would happen to her when Cecelia finally slipped away. Would she disappear?

I swallowed a knot in my throat. I watched the fire-coloured creature — fierce and powerful with a body of fragile bones easily crushed. I didn't know what I'd do without Sil, though I knew exactly where I'd be. Double-dead. She was busy kneading a particularly lumpy scatter pillow, a look of amusement dancing in her golden eyes as they met mine.

"It's always a Fox," she said, "trying to talk the world out of ending."

I twisted towards Barton. "Think I can *talk* Zabor out of killing everything inside the Perimeter Highway?"

He rolled his eyes. I turned back to Sil. "Didn't think so. So what were the details of this deal. Any loopholes?"

"It was made so Zabor would stop her rampage, and in fact *protect* the people of the Red River Valley from the flood waters. But in exchange for sparing them, each year she wanted the blood of the Denizens' children. One a year. Sometimes more. She's powerful and fickle and has the upper hand. She made this the stipulation so that the Denizens would always be reminded of their shame. Reminded that they couldn't stop her." Barton grew quiet then and looked down at his jeans pinned back at the knee. His own reminder that some Denizens weren't prepared to give their children up. But there were dozens more who felt they had no choice.

I hadn't heard Phae move across the tiny shed to Barton, but there she was, sleek as a shadow and suddenly kneeling in front of him, face frank and stern as ever. But the edges of it softened, and her hair began to move of its own accord, climbing her head and twining in a pronged, delicate dance. Blue static weaved in and out of the strands, but she did not touch Barton. Her body was stiff with the powerless desire to heal what couldn't be healed. So she laid her head upon his legs, knowing that touching him would do no more good than she'd already tried.

"We'll find a way." She spoke with clear determination.

I looked away. My chest got tight again, and my exhausted eyes darted to Sil. There was pity in her stare as her ears flicked.

"There's always a way," she said.

". . . So, that led me to wonder, since Geneve passed her power on to me, maybe another Rabbit could give their power to Barton."

It was just after sunset as we made our way back from Phae's, the powdery fingers of dusk streaking everything with colour. The street lights had come on well before sunset, and the wind kicked snow up in their halos. The three of us had clung together as long as we could throughout the day, but I couldn't stay away from Cecelia's place forever. As much as I wanted to. Deedee's worry-texts were blowing up my phone, and not in a pop-song way.

"I dunno, that Deer had to sort of, um, *die* for that to go through. Right?" I looked to Sil for reassurance. She was trotting openly beside us as we made our way up the Osborne Bridge and to my bus stop. I'd had to retire my bike after my ill-fated encounter with Arnas. I dared any of the curious passersby to make a comment as I walked stiffly beside her, but we were met with stares and the occasional tripping side-step as people tried to avoid her. *God, what is it going to take to show everyone in this city there is something weird going on right in front of them?*

No one volunteered to answer my question about the open possibility of sacrificing some hapless flufftail, taking his powers, and letting Barton devour them, tribal-heart-eating-ritual style. We may have been moonlighting as a fringe secret society, but we weren't at the sacrificing part just yet.

Sil stopped just as we passed the Roslyn building and the bridge started over the river. Her nose was in the air, seeking.

"What's wrong?" I hissed. We were leading the pack with Phae and Barton a bit behind us; I'd wanted to give them some space. I hadn't wanted to so blatantly walk over the river that wanted to eat me, but there was no way around that in this city.

"I can't tell," Sil murmured, still sniffing as we came to the middle of the bridge, the Assiniboine as still as death underneath us.

The Manitoba Legislature loomed nearby, and I'd fixed my gaze on it just as Sil barked "Wait!" and I lurched to a stop, looking around. Phae and Barton came up short behind us as I wheeled my bag around, grabbing the hilt of the garnet blade. I didn't draw it yet — not with a crowd on all sides.

"What is it?" Barton asked in a tight tone, as though the wrong words would set off a bomb.

The street lights flickered above us. I was the first to see it, even though I didn't know I had. A black shape parted from the sky above the dome of the legislative building, heading straight for us with grim intent. It banked towards the river, momentarily vanishing in the darkened treeline. "What —" I muttered, but Sil snarled, "Owl!" just as a torrent of screeching wings barrelled into me, sending me flying from the sidewalk and smashing into the concrete partition just separating the bridge's north- and southbound lanes.

Breath knocked out of me and head ringing, I summoned enough sense to get out of the road and scramble onto the partition just as a sedan swerved to avoid me. The slick roads didn't work in the driver's favour, sending him careening into a van that braked hard and swung straight for Phae and Barton.

"*NO!*" I screamed, reaching. All I saw was a bank of flame, and all I felt was the white pain that came after a claw as big as my face snagged my outstretched arm and threw me backwards into traffic. This time I bounced off a windshield, and was stopped only by the railing on the opposite side of the bridge.

Everything hurt, no big shocker. I was surprised my body hadn't just burst open like a garbage bag of vegetable soup. But I was coming back to with a strange awareness as I tried to remember that *getting up and getting away* was the goal. No. Before that. *Phae. Barton. Sil.*

Panicked drivers had stopped the flow of traffic in light of the teenager being thrown around the bridge like a badminton birdie, and I felt someone's hands on me, saw a troubled man's face as he searched my bloody one for signs of life. He was saying something, maybe asking me if I knew my name, but it was behind a curtain of nonsound, of a pinging alarm. *You look so worried about me*, I thought. *But I'm the least of your problems.*

My blood surged like lava, and the nonhuman part of me wrenched my body back into motion. I grabbed my pedestrian saviour around the middle and tackled him backwards as the flurry of murderous feathers descended once more. I got the guy to his feet.

"Get out of here!" I shouted, shoving him back towards the Shell station. Cars honked, people screamed, LED cellphone screens flashed as the unhelpful uploaded the scene to Everywhere On The Internet. Could they see the thing coming after me, or was I the spectacle? I ducked, my pursuer now hidden in the darkened sky somewhere, waiting to strike again. I stumbled into the street, weaving through the stopped cars. "Phae! Sil!" I screamed over the din. The wall of fire I'd seen was now just a bundle of flames coming from the hood of the crashed van, front end crumpled into a light post, my friends not readily visible.

But there was another light, fingers of crackling blue coming from behind the van. I slipped as I rounded the crash, praying for a bloodless outcome on the other side.

Barton's wheelchair was overturned but not crumpled. Phae looked at me, appropriately a deer in the headlights. She was crouched over an unfamiliar body under the bent but wrenched-open passenger door. Probably the driver. She took her hands off him, and the obvious head and neck injury he'd suffered seemed to be knitting itself right again under her shaking hands. I fell to my knees at her side as Barton plucked away his busted glasses and rubbed his eyes.

"Couldn't have taken the flash off, huh, Phae?" he coughed.

Sil was sniffing the body. "He'll live. Leave him. We must get out of here. The Owl won't be satisfied until he takes out his mark." I didn't need to meet her eyes to know it was me. This was getting old already.

I ignored Sil and stared at the side of the van that faced us. "Phae . . . what did you do?" The van's exterior was bent around us in an embrace. It was like it'd crashed sidelong into a steel sphere. Or a crackling blue one . . .

"I just —" She was still shaking, rubbing her hands on her thighs as though they'd fallen asleep. "I couldn't help it. I just wanted to stop the van."

"With a *force field*?" I cried. "Since when can you make force fields?" Phae just shrugged. *What answer did I expect?* "You guys have to get out of here." I righted Barton's wheelchair, and we helped him into it. "Get off the river. Go back to Phae's place. Lie low."

Phae grabbed my arm in a vise grip. "You're coming with us."

I put my hand over hers. "I'll follow you," I lied. "Just get to the other side of the bridge, okay? I'll be right behind you."

She touched my face, and I felt the blood leaking from my head recede back into its rightful place, the gashes on my arm closing up and starting to scar. Sure, she could heal me, but as long as I was near her she was a target, and so was Barton. The only one here with literal firepower to fight back was me.

I broke our staring contest to look over at Barton, who nodded at me. I glanced down at Sil. "Besides, I'm not alone. I've got a bona fide firefox. It'll be easy." Sil looked dubious but said nothing about the last time she had used her powers. I turned back to Phae and Barton. "Go on, before the crowd thins out. I'll see you soon."

Phae hesitated.

"Go!" I barked and, as she retreated, I looked back onto the bridge from behind the van, stepping over the extremely-lucky-to-be-passed-out driver. Sil and I searched the skies — evening was settling fast, creating thousands of places the monster could be hiding.

"So what're we dealing with here, chief?"

Sil's fur rippled. "A Therion. A powerful Denizen that can take on the Ancient form of the Families."

"Sounds pleasant," I sighed. Though my adrenaline was still pumping, I had the presence of mind to look down at my arm, the slash marks huge under my ruined coat sleeve. Definitely not your average city owl.

"Yes. And if it dares to attack you out in the open, then it's gone rogue. Direct conflict is against their code of non-interference. It may be working for Zabor."

"Oh good. Well, whatever it is, it sucks as usual. So what's the plan?"

A growl rumbled through Sil's small body like a thunderstorm, and before I could ask, I felt the tiny hairs on my arms rippling to gooseflesh. I caught it, too: a familiar scent, faint but menacing, cutting through the breeze like ozone. We both knew it was coming.

"We flush it out into the open," she snarled. "We kill it."

Sirens were fast approaching as the first responders pulled up from River Avenue. I crouched down, trying to keep out of sight. We needed to act fast before more people got injured. "Look, I'm all for killing river hunters and their pissy mom, but that's a *person* we're talking about, aren't we? We are *not* killing other Denizens!"

"It means to kill *you*, Roan! Now it's time to put your training into action. There are greater things at stake than the life of one villain."

I froze, heart pounding. "But . . . but there are so many people around —"

"Who will die if you do nothing. Hide here, and the Therion will just start killing anyone in its path." *Aren't you responsible for enough deaths already?*

I knew she'd never say that, but the accusation still sprang to mind. I turned my head, watching the movement of bystanders and evacuating pedestrians as though I was floating above it all.

"Now it's your turn," I said.

"What?" Sil half barked.

I smiled, but I was less than thrilled, trying to keep my head. "Go and find Phae and Barton. Make sure they're safe. And get as far away from here as you can."

She was silent. She didn't beg me to let her stay, to fight by my side. She knew that this was my fight, and that I'd need to get used to it before this ended. She whined nonetheless, paws hesitating on the pavement. I didn't look at her. Then, in one fluid movement, she turned tail and ran off.

I sighed. I half wished she hadn't gone, but what was done was done. I took stock: My bag was lost somewhere in the chaos of the bridge, and with it the garnet blade I'd come to rely on. Not like this thing would stay still long enough for some hack-and-slash. I just needed . . .

I looked up at the street lights. They were flickering again, and I followed the trail of lights all the way down the south side of Osborne Street. Light standards with traffic signals blinked out first. Then the building floodlights, then street lights, pops and showers of glass preceding the darkness. I stumbled up and checked out the north side. The lights were going out, too, extinguishing towards me. Time slowed. It knew where I was. The final light standard was just above my head, warm and persistent. *Warm.* I closed my eyes, reaching for it without the intention of touching it at all, just holding that warmth within me. Kindling it into something greater.

I felt the glass *snick* past my hand, through my blunted hair, bouncing off my shoulders. But I didn't need the glass. Just the spark that followed, the one that touched my hand and set me on fire.

And in the light of the flames, the darkness split aside to reveal the Owl hurtling talons-first at me. I sprang up on the bridge rail and met it. My quarry howled in a voice of startled rage and pain as the flames climbed up the outstretched leg I clamped on to. *The fire is in the dance,* Cecelia whispered to me from her letters, and I twisted around, all elegance while vaulting onto the wreckage of the van and hurling the Owl headfirst into the concrete partition where I'd been only minutes ago. Another thought: *Imitation is the sincerest form of revenge.*

The flames had welled up my arm and stayed there, the heart of them cool and calming against my skin as the van toppled, and I leapt onto the hood of a nearby Honda Civic like I was playing hopscotch. One foot stayed firmly planted on the roof and ready to spring. The street went quiet, and I wondered how long it'd take before the video went viral on YouTube.

Enough of that, though. The Owl's dark body shimmered like a mirage. Sil was gone. She'd keep my friends safe. She trusted me, and I her.

I raised my flaming arm-lance. Time to show the haters what they were up against.

The Owl gathered itself up, trying to find its feet. I hadn't yet seen its eyes, but its head, which had gone almost all the way around with the impact, swivelled back and pierced me with an unforgiving glare. It stretched out its burned leg, which steamed in the cold as it shed feathers more like scales. The looming, six-foot Owl stretched out its enormous wings, pulling arms out of them with the sound of bones breaking and viscera slopping to the ground at its feet. I didn't think the bird suit was more than just a bad Owl mind-trick, until human hands tore the wide Owl face away with a sucking exhale, tossing it aside with the rest of the ripped-up bird body newly disposed of on the asphalt.

I swallowed my gorge, but disgust was quickly replaced with fury. I was staring down my paparazzi, the one who'd caught me over the body of the first dead girl — silver eyes and all.

"*You.*"

He only smiled, and moved to raise his hands . . .

"*STOP!*" came a booming cry over a loudspeaker. Cops. I glanced sideways, resisting the urge to stand down obediently. I saw raised guns and frightened people. *Sigh. Talk about a pile-on.*

"Put down your weapons immediately and put your hands in the air! We will come to you."

I lifted an eyebrow. *Weapon?* Maybe they thought my arm was a flame-thrower. But come on, they couldn't think *I* was the guilty one here. Hadn't they just seen birdbrain strip down in the middle of the street? I didn't want anyone else getting hurt, but I wasn't about to back down. I hoped that if I ignored the cops, they'd go away.

My adversary, meanwhile, seemed pretty amused with this turn of events. "Don't you just hate it when the rabble gets uppity?" He had an educated, arrogant voice that I immediately hated. Scottish, maybe, but I wasn't in the mindset to trace accents. And he was talking to me as though we were buds. Those piercing eyes sparkled for a moment above his well-formed cheekbones. I clucked. *Gimme a break.*

"Yeah, well, best-laid plans and all that," I shouted back, trying to match his casual air. "Why don't we take this party elsewhere? Or better yet, you go back to roost under the bridge you came from. Wouldn't want to ruffle any more feathers." I brandished my arm, the shrugging motion causing the flames to leap from shoulder to shoulder, hand to hand, as though I was shuffling a deck of cards Gambit-style.

His hands dropped to waist level: Was he conceding

defeat? Doubtful. "Your concern is touching, truly," he admitted dryly, hand to his heart. "But I must apologize. Tight schedule."

The feathers and gore at his feet shed only moments ago lifted from the ground, changing to the consistency of ash as they swirled around him. Another Owl illusion? I kept my face blank as I checked my senses: Sil had taught me to close myself off from the psyche-infiltration the bird-baddies were known for, but you could always feel the prodding. I had felt it with that cop, Seneca, but now . . .

Speaking of cops. "Drop your weapons, or we *will* open fire!" Damn, the rabble *were* agitated. Something bad was about to happen, and bullets were no mean thing to avoid, either. I wasn't made of Kevlar.

I couldn't help but bark out a laugh, though. "Ha! Oh man. It's a *firearm*," I waved it around, the irony almost too good.

The Owl's face had dropped to implacability. He was done with the banter. So was I. I took a defensive stance, ready for whatever he was about to throw at me in the middle of his char-cyclone as it sped up. I could hear the fuzz shouting again, locked and loaded as they were, and was prepping to jump back behind the Honda, but my sharp-eyed compadre swept his hand towards the police, sending a massive gust of ash right for them. I was nearly caught in it, too, bracing myself in a crouch on the car roof. Through a gravelly sheet of black, I saw the assembled crowd — police, pedestrians, et al — suspended mid-air, contorted and unable to land, tangled in the ashy threads of the Owl's former body. The lines cut into their throats, choking them to silence and paralyzing them.

I let out a guttural howl, which should've been a dignified *Stop it, you giant assface!* but the fire had exploded inside, and I rushed him like a comet. I slammed into him — or what I thought was him. I was suddenly careening around his body, trapped in the vortex of wind that he still controlled. Whipping me aside into an abandoned Lincoln, he came at me full force, face contorted in vicious delight.

I rolled just as his hand, now a bladed talon, cut through the hood. "This is just what I needed!" he cried gleefully, whirling and striking blows that seemed almost too easy to deflect. "We should've done this *ages* ago."

White-hot rage couldn't begin to describe the fire as it blazed higher in me. I felt like I was slipping out of control again as I grabbed his temples and slammed my head into his. That sent him reeling, enough for me to conjure the blaze back into my hands, hurling what felt like molten lava after him. The vortex whipped back up, pulling him out of the way as the railing behind him melted, the hot remains dumped into the river.

The adrenaline pumped through me with the beat of the drum — one, two — and then I crumpled, strings cut. The fire had gone out and blood whooshed behind my eyes. I threw up. I'd reached too far. I wiped my mouth with a shaking hand and saw my dumbfounded contender staring at me with renewed interest — maybe even respect. He cracked a genuinely pleased smile.

"Well, well." The smile gave in to pain. The head-butt had left a massive burn scar over his entire forehead, part of his eye. His talon hand reached to it dumbly, then recoiled, the disbelief palpable. "You bloody, fiery *bitch*."

"Yeah, yeah, big words," I panted, the frozen air cutting

into me now that I'd lost the heat that kept me moving. I tried to get to my feet but that wasn't happening.

"Here, let me help." I heard him above me before the claw clamped around my throat, lifting me from the ground and squeezing at the tender windpipe beneath. He brought me close to his face, and all I could smell was burning flesh and hair.

I must've smiled, because his fury grew. "Yes, it *is* funny, isn't it? No juice left and you've lost the whip-hand. For a second I thought you had a chance. Now I see you're just a stupid child with power you can't even control."

Maybe it was the tunnel vision coming on, but I could've sworn I heard more voices than just his in my head. I coughed, weakly scrabbling at his claw. He liked that. He carried me farther into the street, where I could get a better view of the bystanders still trapped mid-air. Without the street lights I couldn't see much, but my waning spirit eye told me that these victims were awake and aware — I could even pick out their disappointment in me. Heroes fall fast around here.

"You will be an example, Roan Harken," said the thousand voices, "of the courage it takes to dig your grave and lie still in it."

I may have been weak and hanging a foot off the ground in his horrible Owl hand, but I had enough left to reel back and kick him in the leg I'd already burned. He stumbled, concentration broken, and I heard shrieking as bodies thumped to the ground. The threads were cut, the people free. At least I could do that.

The talon's grip tightened, and I found myself smashed into multiple cars with the precision and rage of a whack-a-mole mallet. Maybe your senses level-up before death, but

I could've sworn I felt blood escaping from the bones in my skull.

The Owl brought me up to his face again, eyes slanting at sharp angles, feathers growing out of his skin like blades. I felt the sweeping air, the beat of wings. We both lifted away from the ground, and he floated down to the broken bridge railing. He turned me around, shifting the talons to the back of my neck as he hung me over the now open river.

"The debt will be paid," he — they — whispered, "for the good of all, at the hand of Eli Rathgar and his ancestors. Tell it to your forebears in the land of the dead."

As I dropped, limp and broken, I thought of my parents. I wondered if I'd see them immediately, if they were waiting on the other side. All I saw now was the black of the sky, and I forgot to take my last breath. The water was hungry as it sucked me down.

Part IV
Inferno

The HUNTER-CHILD'S SECRET

Deidre clicks the bathroom mirror back into place as soon as she's retrieved the nail clippers. Her forehead crinkles as she cuts away a self-inflicted hangnail. She hasn't chewed her nails since grade school, priding herself on the self-control required. But everything has fallen out of control in recent months.

Her stomach twists as she clips the hangnail, and the flesh gives way to blood. She drives the finger into her mouth, sucking for relief. But it's only fleeting; her next thought runs to her husband, as her troubled thoughts often do. And shortly after, they go to her niece, and her stomach drops again.

She sees Roan's distant face, eyes clouded and looking to a place that she won't share with Deidre. When she catches her aunt looking, she hides behind an empty smile, an *I'm okay*, and a rush off to school, to see her friends. A practised gesture. They've shared nothing since she sheared her hair and her eye changed.

Her husband has been worse — nervous and preoccupied and waiting for the hammer to fall, the worst he's been in the last year. Of course, he too shares nothing with Deidre, but the shock of it is much colder. He shies away from her reassuring touch, flying from fear to rage in a breath. He looks at her like she is a stranger and treats her like one, too. He's moved permanently to the guest room, has abandoned his freelance work, and seems to spend his days behind that door, eating little and growing more emaciated and drawn. *Haunted.*

Her work and focus at her job has faltered. Her superiors, showing concern, have suggested an intervention — to perhaps get the police involved, maybe even psychiatrists. But that would be admitting that Deidre's control is slipping . . . She examines her finger — the bleeding has stopped, but her nail is ugly. They all are. She balls them up into a fist. *What are they hiding from me?* The tears well up and she sobs freely, alone in this enormous house of strangers.

When she came home tonight, the stillness was deafening. And she knew, with the exception of their unconscious host upstairs, she was on her own. Roan had at least texted her: *"I'm going over to Phae's for a bit. I'll be back by six."* But six had come and gone. And when she'd gone to check on Arnas, his room was abandoned, the door wide open. No note, no message. Just silence.

Arnas must be in trouble, she thinks as she washes her hands. *He acts like he's being watched, or chased, like his life is in danger. . . Or else he's done something terrible*, and Deidre doesn't dare entertain that thought further. *Arnas isn't capable of that. No.*

But there are probably a hundred things she doesn't know. She splashes water onto her face, trying to wash away the desperation. Her resolve is already cracking. How long until she herself does something rash? For all their sakes? Her suitcase is still flung open and half packed on the bed she once shared with Arnas. But if she leaves, where does that leave Roan? She's already been having issues in her graduate year. Would it only make things worse? Could Deidre survive with a plastered-on smile until the end of the semester? She gives a sidelong glance to the suitcase. If only Roan would answer her recent texts . . .

As she replaces the towel on the rack by the sink, she hears the front door open. Certain and relieved that it's Roan, Deidre starts for the living room.

"Roan?" she calls. Her phone goes off in her pocket, and she pauses in the hallway to check the screen. Texts from a co-worker. *Are you watching the news right now?! I think Roan is on it!! Something really crazy is going on at the Osborne Bridge . . .*

Phae Das lives in Osborne Village. Deidre's heart catches.

"Deidre? Are you there?" The voice that carries clear as a bell from the front door stops her at the foyer. It is not Roan.

Arnas stands silhouetted in the open doorway. It's snowing out, and the wind that sneaks around him chills her synapses. He smiles, pivoting with unfamiliar grace as he closes the door behind him. His eyes never leave her.

"Arnas . . . where were you? Are you all right?"

Concern overwhelms her desire to yell or throw things at him for all his absences in recent months — absence from their home, their marriage, their confidence. But he looks so utterly changed — spine erect, stance relaxed but confident.

Skin waxy and glowing as the smile disappears from his mouth. He looks like an impression of himself.

"I've never felt better. You mustn't worry — everything is going to be fine now." He holds out his arms to her. She steps back and away. He is visibly displeased by this.

She is shaking now, and it is not from the cold. "Arnas . . . you haven't been honest with me in months. And I've had enough." Her ruined nails bite into the flesh of her hand. "You'll tell me what's going on right now, or I'm leaving. And I'm taking Roan with me." Seeing him like this steels her resolve.

His eyes change, and she covers her mouth. The irises and the pupils seem to rotate, focused and cutting. "Roan," he says. "*Roan.*" The word is a curse in the air. His head tilts and bobs, and he steps closer to her. All at once she is sure that this is not her husband.

"Stay away from me!" she screams, backing into the table by the stairs.

"It's not me you should be afraid of," says this thing with her husband's voice. He clasps her by the arms. "It's Roan, don't you see? It's all her doing. If she had only died like she was supposed to, none of this would've happened. No one would be dead. And we would not have to suffer."

He raises an arm and flicks his wrist at the television screen in the entertainment room beyond the foyer. It turns to the news, showing repeated footage of a standoff between a man and a woman on the Osborne Bridge. No, a girl. The camera zooms, pictures flash, and a photo she recognizes from last Christmas, a photo she took with her phone, aligns with the panning view of multiple car collisions and fleeing people. And in a loop, the girl falling off the bridge and into the open ice below.

Roan. Her name is plastered alongside *Terrorist Attack* and *Possible Link to the Dead Red River Girls?*

Deidre has nothing. Her words are gone. She turns back to Arnas, but he is inches from her, and his bony hand is already around her neck. Not tight, just a gentle threat.

"She's dangerous," the anti-Arnas assures. Deidre's tears return. For a moment, she is sure she can see the real Arnas behind this horrible stranger's eyes. He's trying to get out. But he's losing.

"Dangerous," he hisses, the fingers closing. "She has to be stopped. And we tried to, today. But she's persistent. She is selfish. And she could still be out there. We must be vigilant."

"Arnas," Deidre whispers, vocal cords straining against his hand. "If you're in there. Please. Don't let them hurt her."

The head bobs and tilts again. "And what of your life?"

"Don't let anything happen to her," she repeats. "She's all you have left of your brother."

For a moment, the grip falters. The eyes seem to be trying very hard to stay focused. She is certain she's reached into him, that there's hope.

"She will die," he says. And in a squeeze, Deidre's world goes dark.

❧

The stars are beautiful in the land of the dead. They wink at you mockingly, pinpricks in the great black. You *are* dead, after all. The Great Joke.

Ugh. Why am I bothering being petty now? Just enjoy the scenery, you bodiless, stupid consciousness. You belong in a primordial mire with the stars laughing at you because you're a dumbass and you got beaten and this is what you get for thinking you could do otherwise.

Something bumped against me in the sluggish swamp of the dead. A bolt of sharp lightning pinballed through my neurons and, against rationality, I realized I definitely had a body. I wanted to scream the stars out of the sky, but all I could get out was an *ughhh*.

The stars were obscured by the cloud of my breath — my hot, stinking, living breath. I tasted blood. I was in a lot of pain but I couldn't move at all. I felt numb. I was alive, but had I broken my spine? Was I still in jeopardy? Had the Owl — Eli or whatever — continued his righteous rampage against my friends? Were they all dead and now it was too late?

I started to panic, as the recently dead are wont to do.

"Whoa, whoa!" someone said, bumping into the prostrate pain-sack that was my body. I groaned and coughed, the pain thick.

"You gotta calm down, eh?" the someone grunted. It was hard enough concentrating on anything but the pain, let alone trying to make out my captor in the dark. I'd decided he and anyone else making an appearance near me must be a baddie, because I was vulnerable and cranky, all things considered.

"G-get away!" I rasped with zero menace. My throat was raw. And there was another taste in it, one I only faintly recognized. It was black and bitter, bile mixed with putrid river water and . . .

My captor had pulled a flashlight out of the pack he'd been rifling in. He held it in his mouth, and when I looked down, I saw that I was wrapped tightly in some ratty blankets lashed with old jumper cables and belts. He started undoing these, but as each came free, the pleasure of free movement never seemed to come.

"You 'otta s'op 'at," he said around the flashlight in his teeth. "You shoul'n't moo' righ' now, ish not gooh."

My futile struggling and sudden resurrection had straight-up exhausted me. I tried taking note of this guy's appearance in the dim circle of light: overweight, ponderous in a parka, cheeks burnt flush. Couldn't make out much else, and I wasn't in the mood. All I knew was *Pain bad, thinking hard. Need to go home.*

Then the blankets were fully loose, and I saw why I couldn't move. I was encased from the neck down in a solid block of ice, woolly-mammoth style.

"The hell?!" I gargled, stupidly trying to get free. What I first thought was futile led me to think that maybe I was on to something; steam issued from the block as I struggled, a warmth spreading into my limbs as the ice melted . . . which only made the pain worse.

"Don't!" my captor cried, like I was a dog that was caught peeing on the carpet midstream. The flashlight fell out of his mouth with the exclamation, and he groaned over me. "You gotta stop that, okay? You broke a lot of stuff. No good moving around and makin' it worse."

In the dark I could tell he'd taken off his gloves, blowing into his palms before resting the weight of his hands against my frozen confinement. Whatever I'd melted in my struggles solidified back into place, and I actually felt the pain slide back, wayward, swollen limbs amply supported. I felt insulated rather than cold and marvelled at my surprising comfort. I relaxed; it was all I *could* do.

My captor's hood slid off, and a tangle of ripe-smelling hair tumbled out as he bent over me to retrieve the flashlight. The shine guttered, and he flipped it at his face, smacking it with an open hand. I realized my captor wasn't a he, but a *she* — around my age, maybe younger. And my spirit eye woke up to tell me she was also a Seal, wet coal eyes shining enormous in her round face.

"Who are *you*?" I rasped bluntly as she clumsily shoved her hair back into her hood, human face swimming into a grimace.

"Natti Fontaine," she grunted, hitching her pants up, and retying all the jump cords and belts. "We gotta long way to go still, Fox-girl, so get comfy." There was a scarf wrapped around my head, too, which she retightened. She followed that with a slap to my bundled body, and when I didn't issue a moan, she seemed satisfied and went around behind me.

"Hey, wait, what are you . . ." Then we started moving again, snow *shush*ing and ice scraping under me. "Wait, am . . . am I frozen to a *sled*?"

"Yup," she said, pulling me along as my personal sled dog. "Good thing you're skinny." And so we plowed along like this, and I didn't have the energy to protest.

"Are you taking me to the Owls?" I sighed, resigned to my fate and getting frustrated that the longer I survived the more this whole thing would drag on and on. *Either let me die or leave me alone, already.*

Natti just laughed. "Man, I woulda just left you back there if I wanted you dead. Less work. I'm takin' you to my aunty. She wants to talk to you."

She was probably lying. But at this point, I didn't care.

My eyes adjusted to the darkness, and my spirit eye filled in what night obscured: We were on a wide-open plain, banks of snow bookending us. It was a familiar place. I swallowed the pain as the sled bumped over an uneven surface and gagged when I realized we were actually still on the river. Far from Osborne Village, though, and the horror show I'd left in my wake; the traffic sounds around us were dim, with few lights in the distance save the odd street lamp seen through the bracken of winter-stripped trees. We were somewhere near the Exchange District, or the Alexander Docks, but I didn't think too seriously about way-finding. Flashes of being torpedoed down under inescapable ice shuddered through my mind lockstep with my heartbeat. *God*, my head hurt.

"You remember anything?" Natti asked as she pulled me along seemingly without effort.

I was silent for a bit, weighing my options. Could I trust her? Then again, what else was I doing? At this point, I didn't much care for restraint.

"I was dead," I said. Then I scoffed. "*Again.*"

"Close but no cigar." She snorted, Clydesdale-esque. "You wouldn'ta made much of a snake snack. Nearly did, though. That Owl guy got you good."

My body remembered each car it had smashed against, glancing off bumpers and hoods like roadkill. *Good way to immobilize someone before sending them to a watery grave, I guess. But what if I get thawed, and I am as good as dead anyway?*

I looked down. "Do you know . . . how bad . . . ?"

"Nothin' your Deer friend can't fix up." I could hear the grin in her voice. "So I thought puttin' ya on ice was better than leavin' you as is. Better to avoid the hospitals. I'm sure the whole bridge thing is all over the news now, along with your face."

I blinked in the darkness. "Why are you helping me?" I blurted. Her lack of murderous intent was unsettling.

She snorted again. "Heard you needed a Seal on your side. And nothin' makes me happier than to piss off the Owls. They told everyone not to go near you. So I went lookin' for you, naturally." She pulled me deftly over a small snowbank, the rush of the air past my face a temporary relief to my headache. "They'll think you're dead for now. It'll buy us some time."

Time. Something I didn't have enough of. Instead, I had an abundance of people that I owed my life to. The Moth Queen kept reaching out to me, and so many people kept pulling me back. Made a girl feel wanted, at least.

"I remember . . . water," I coughed, the images a jumble. I turned my spirit eye inward and bade it to find all I'd forgotten. "The water was moving so fast. And . . . the ice . . ." Suddenly, I was there again, overcome by the suffocating feeling of my body being pulled up, dragged along the underside of the ice. There was nothing I could grab hold of, no strength to stop myself, and no fire left. It was endless black under there, but I could perceive glinting things rushing along beside me. Hunters. Hundreds of them. Their red, terrible eyes raked the water like bloody boat lights. I remember wondering when my lungs would explode as they filled with the Assiniboine, but I finally stopped moving, body grasped in the claws of the hunters, teeth gnashing. They dragged me down, down, down against the current.

To *her*. To a body coiled tight as a threat. To the face enormous, upturned, jaws yet unopened. Slit nostrils flaring, scenting me, the meal she'd been denied. The giant eyes opened, white and unawake. No recognition in them, just raw hunger. I felt my world blackening as the maw split, the heart of the maelstrom from my nightmares now real.

Then a different torrent snagged me — a fist of water, powerful and determined. The penetrating, submerged screams that came after still echoed in my memory. I thought my ears would burst from the pressure of the sound and the fury. The water-fist ripped me away, pulled me back, smashed me up and through the ice.

I cried out, a new wave of fresh pain crashing in my skull with the impact of a baseball bat. The last image that flickered was a looming shape — a person standing over me, hands taking my broken body up and draining the water from my lungs. I gasped, both in the memory and outside of it, as familiar hands bound me up in an icy cushion. I knew this person was Natti without seeing her face in the memory. I must've finally succumbed to the dark after that, locked in dreams that assured me I was dead.

But I wasn't. Natti had saved my life with her power — an element whose strength could rival the destruction of mine.

And she wasn't done yet.

My gratitude was lost in a sudden flurry — the sled cracked against a horn of ice, and something rattled on the skis under me.

Natti righted me but stopped. The rattling turned desperate. "What's that?" I asked, my range of motion compromised so I could barely tilt my head. The rattling became banging, and Natti dove around me as a box sprang free from the sled.

"Shit." She grabbed for the box just as the lid strained against the jumper cord holding it closed.

Then the cord broke, and the river hunter inside burst forward, howling its agonizing horror cry at us with its vertical mouth. Part of it was still in the box, and it raged to get free.

"Why the hell do you have one of those things in a *beer cooler*?!" I screeched. I was definitely going to be zero help in this situation.

"You musta thawed it when you got all microwave back there!" Natti barked, hands twitching. The hunter gave up trying to get the cooler off its back end, reduced to a clumsy Coors hermit crab now, and under other circumstances I would've laughed.

It was small, but probably just as dangerous as its brothers, and it focused on us and snarled. Just as it lunged murderously, propelled by its scrabbling claws, Natti reeled back like a major-league pitcher. Her hands spun water from the moisture in the air and locked the hunter in a sphere of ice. It crashed heavily into the snow a foot away from us.

I shuddered out the breath I'd been holding. Natti went to the ice ball and pressed her hands into it; the sphere compressed neatly to the body of the hunter, and she manipulated the shape until it fit back into the box. *Evil genie, begone!*

"What are you carrying it around for?" I asked. She seemed to know what she was doing. "Why don't you just kill it?"

She gave me a hard look as she carried the box back over and secured it to the sled again. "You in the habit of killin' stuff for no reason?"

I felt slighted. "No! I —"

"You don't destroy what you can use. That's what my family says." She tested the tension of the cables, then stood up. "He's gonna tell us about his mom. So no one else dies. Okay?"

She was still glaring at me. I averted my eyes like a chastised kid. "Yeah. Okay."

"Okay," she said a second time. She went back to pulling me towards her mysterious aunty, with a river hunter tied to the sled that bore my frozen, broken body. We went on for the rest of the way in silence.

Above me, the stars had stopped laughing.

☙

The bridge is still in chaos. News crews are on the scene, reporters interviewing pedestrians who don't seem to remember much of what happened. A series of car accidents and a fight between two people. Many were injured but can't recall how. *A girl*, some say. *There was a girl. She was on fire. She went over the bridge.* But when the newscasters try to get them to repeat the story, they've suddenly forgotten that, too.

But there are people who have been documenting it on their phones. Taking pictures. Uploading video to YouTube, to Facebook. The onlookers prove useless in their testimony, stunned they'd filmed something they don't recall happening. Some pictures even vanish from feeds. But CTV gets hold of one video and broadcasts it before it can be stopped. A girl falling over the side of the destroyed bridge. A vague, blurred image of her face. Who is she?

The news scrambles to identify her, but with the faulty memories of the witnesses, reporters can only speculate. *Terrorism*, *troubled youth*, *conspiracy*, and *cult tactics* — words broadcast in place of truth, until they *become* truth. An anonymous tipster submits a picture of the girl, Roan Harken. A redhead. Maybe she is just another victim of the Red River murders. Or maybe she is the perpetrator.

Perfect.

Yes, a wave of amnesia seems to have hit all witnesses. But Eli has made certain of that. Their minds have been easily probed, their memories changed or erased. All anyone has to hold on to is that a girl has fallen over the bridge. Rescue crews are down on the ice trying to piece together what happened. Detectives are baffled by how the rail seems *melted* from its moorings. And if a girl *has* fallen under the ice in the Assiniboine, her death is almost certain.

Almost.

Eli moves unseen in the crowd of reporters and bewildered police, a strong psychic shield cloaking him from onlookers. He pulls his wool coat closer to himself in the night chill. The thrill of the fight has long ebbed away, replaced by a feeling of cautious victory, as well as pain in his face and burnt leg. He curses under his breath while passing the police line unnoticed and leans over the bridge rail, staring at the ice and the workers below. They will try to break through and retrieve the body. Eli knows they won't find one.

But a trill of worry still hisses in his chest, and he scowls against it, absently rubbing his head. Is she well and truly dead? Is it over? How can he be sure unless he finds out himself?

"It's neat work, cousin," says a voice behind him. Eli resists the urge to whirl around, angry at himself for letting Seneca sneak up on him. But his face betrays nothing, for he really has nothing to hide, and he turns casually, his mental wall intractable. He probes into Seneca's mind, but it is just as resistant.

Eli smiles and shrugs. "It seems she finally succumbed to guilt. Hopefully this will be the end of it for the spring."

Seneca joins him at the railing, staring down into the ice. "Seems so."

Eli is carefully erasing himself from the memories of the onlookers of the entire affair. Soon, all the news would have is the girl's name; soon, recollections would surface that *she* had caused all this damage — that is, *if* she survived. She would be watched for, noticed, unable to hide from him. It was an insurance policy if Eli himself couldn't catch her. Let the humans do the work — his mind is busy enough.

Harken's friends had also been in the crowd but disappeared before he could get to them. They are his next target. He can't risk them trying to tap another Fox, or even a Seal, and picking up the crusade where Harken had left off.

But now he has Seneca to worry about, even though the voices assure him that nothing can threaten this new Narrative. Has Eli been sloppy in his ancestors' plan? He has the skill to manipulate multiple minds while changing forms but had he lost control in the moment the Fox-girl bettered him? He resists touching his throbbing leg or drawing attention to the burn across his face.

"Are you sad to see her go?" Eli asks, a harmless enough question, but filled with accusation because of what had transpired at the council meeting. He fears Seneca's loyalties have changed. Best to redirect the tension for the moment.

But his cousin doesn't move, the wind pressing his sandy hair against his skull. He is deep inside his mind, either troubled or indifferent, his face conveying nothing. "What's done is done. It's over." He turns to Eli, eyes full of knowing. "There is no going back now."

Eli's eyes narrow. What was over? Their peril, or the ill-advised loyalties to Ancient, and all its mighty, weak tenets? "Indeed," is all Eli replies.

Seneca nods, pulling his hood up against the cold. "Be well, cousin. And be careful."

Seneca leaves Eli's side, melting into the dazed crowd. Eli tips his head to the stars. *Your cousin's hope makes him weak — none can defeat the river snake.* Eli nods at the words dancing behind his eyes, right and eternal. *It will make him a traitor.*

Eli's wings beat hard as he lights from the bridge, body and misgivings swallowed by the night.

〜〜

I must have fallen asleep; the sound of the snow beneath the sled, coupled with the sheer exhaustion of the past few weeks, had taken me down into darkness. No nightmares this time, no visions. Just quiet, heavenly *nothing*. No images, either, just sounds, impressions.

Roan, a voice whispered. *Little Fox*, rasped another, in many dry tongues. I felt Sil's presence, but not that of her Fox form — it was Sil as flaming animal-woman, a wheel of nine tails spinning behind her. She bled through the black, leaning her huge body into a flaming garnet sword stuck in the ground. Her battle mantle was a corona, her fox head still on fire. Behind her, looming large and still, was the Moth Queen. Her wings shuddered. They both stared at me, into me, but allowed me my rest. It wasn't a warning. Just a reminder.

The Serpent stirs, the Moth Queen said, her children

fluttering around her in a ring. *It is almost time*, the Sil-god nodded. The Moth Queen rested the thousand needles of her hands on Sil's golden mantle. Sil held out the garnet blade.

Are you ready? they both asked me.

I opened my eyes. The mocking stars had been replaced by street lights. I took a look around. We were no longer on the Red, but a sidewalk, surrounded by houses instead of riverbanks.

"Where are we?" I yawned, groggy but feeling much better.

"Point Douglas," Natti sniffed. "Nearly there."

I flashed to full alertness. "What? The North End? You pulled me *that far*?"

Though I couldn't see her, I was sure Natti shrugged. "How else were we gonna get there?" She didn't seem phased by the distance, or really anything so far. And I must've slept for hours. Geez, I wondered how high and mighty her aunt was that she couldn't just pick us up or something.

Then we turned up a driveway. The yard was lost in snowdrifts, but you could see old car bodies insinuating themselves out of the snow like zombies who'd given up halfway out of the grave. Point Douglas was a far cry from Wellington Crescent. Any thoughts of high and mighty were well and dead as we got closer to the rundown North End house.

The sled stopped suddenly. "Oh. You're here," Natti said.

"Who? Who is it, Natti?" I tried craning my neck as hard as I could, but it revealed nothing in the dim outline of the porch light.

Tiny footsteps pattered down the concrete steps. "Me," Sil said as she came towards me, golden eyes round and huge in the winter moonlight. She got up on her hind legs, sniffing my face before pressing her forehead to it. I could've wept for relief.

"You're a sight for sore everything," I sighed.

"You too," she said and licked a tear away from my cheek.

"What about Phae? And Barton? Did you get them off the bridge?"

Before I could get an answer, I felt a jerk as Natti started hauling me, sled and all, up the front steps. She obviously didn't have time or patience for heartfelt reunions. The front door opened behind us.

"You finally back, eh?" said whoever held the door. As Natti struggled to get us up the last step and inside, I saw that the voice belonged to an old woman. She was huge; as tall as she was wide, wearing a ratty terry cloth robe and holding a cigarette. Her iron-coloured hair was clubbed back in a thick braid, big glasses hanging on a black string around her fleshy, brown neck. Her eyes glowed when the light shifted, and I saw her for the big Seal she was, a selkie wavering in the doorway. Sil followed us in, the old woman nodding at her, and the door closed.

"Look at the set-up you've got here!" the old woman laughed as we settled into the cramped living room. There was clutter everywhere — the sofa looked fifty-years-used, the box-sized television crackled, and there were pop cans and overflowing ashtrays strewn beside dusty table lamps. "You did good, little *nattiq*. What else did you bring Aunty?"

Natti had already started undoing the cooler from the sled as I took in the environment. It smelled stale and slightly mouldy, but at least it was warm. Sil sniffed around, investigating, but she came back and settled beside me without comment. Having her near was a reassurance we were in a safe place.

A hulking guy came in then, another Seal, as big as Natti and her aunt. "This the Fox-girl everyone's hatin' on?" he said, leaning in to my face. I lifted an eyebrow at him and his awkward proximity, but I guess he was just as curious as I was. He was older than Natti, taller too, but when she pushed him away he backed off.

"Yeah it is, Aivik, so step off." He scratched his head but didn't challenge her. "Ignore my brother," she grunted to me. "He needs a hobby."

"Yo, I got hobbies!" he cried defensively, adjusting his skater hat and drooping jeans.

"Yeah, if *Warhammer* counts . . ." Natti mumbled as she undid my blankets and revealed my icy sarcophagus.

Aivik whistled. "Nice." I looked over at Natti's aunt and saw her resting her large hands on the beer cooler.

"You brought an *atshen* here, Natti?" She meant the river hunter. She didn't seem angry or even pleased.

Natti looked over at me. "It basically means demon." Then she shrugged, brown cheeks colouring a bit. "It came after me after I pulled her outta the river. Thought it'd be useful."

"Mmm." Aunty nodded, chin merging into three deeper ones.

There was a hesitant knock at the door, and Aivik went to it. A small voice wafted on the wind as it passed through the entryway. "Hi, we're . . . I'm . . . looking for —"

"Phae?" I shouted — if I'd whipped my head any harder, I'm sure it would've cracked the ice holding it in place. Aivik turned aside as she rushed towards me.

"Roan!" Her arms were poised to fling around me, but she stopped short when she saw my ice-cubed status. "What . . . are you — ?"

Aivik had disappeared out the door, only now returning as he shoved Barton and his wheelchair unceremoniously into the house. "You forgot this outside," he grunted. Phae looked slightly sheepish.

"It's all good, thanks," Barton said, wheeling as far into the room as he could. "Glad to see you on your f— well, alive, anyway." He cringed, rubbing the back of his neck.

"The same goes for you crazy kids." My heart lightened past the pain. But I frowned.

My phone suddenly clattered onto my ice-covered chest. "Pulled it out of your jacket earlier," said Natti. "It isn't in such good shape after your swim, but the case kept it good enough that I could text your friends."

"Lock it up, kids. We've got business," said Aunty, and Aivik shut the door, then moved around the living room, closing the drapes. "Time to thaw her out. And you, girlie" — Aunty pointed at Phae — "get your Deer stuff ready, eh? She's in bad shape."

I winced as Natti laid her hands on me and the ice began to liquefy. It didn't melt all over the carpet, but rather left me encased in a fluid bubble. Natti split the water in two halves, then rejoined it over my head, compressing it into a dense ball about the size of a watermelon. She refroze it, then grumbled, "I'll go put this in the sink."

My broken bones seemed to jut up against one another as my body settled into the sled, and all at once I felt like I was going to puke or pass out — or, regrettably, both. I tried not to make a sound, but the pain was too much. It hurt to breathe. I sucked on my teeth.

"It's okay, it's okay," Phae tried to soothe, and next it was *her* hands on me. Bones and bruised flesh knitted together, but even that came with unique pain. I cried out, looking at my friend for support. Her eyes were the glowing white of the healer, the antlers in her hair solid, but blue sparks flickered along their lengths, and her brow furrowed.

"The damage is extensive," Phae muttered, surprised. "Your vertebrae are out of alignment. And your neck was close to broken."

I swallowed, unable to hold back the tears, but the pain was finally dissipating. "Well, when you wanna kill someone, you don't half-ass it," I groaned. "That guy wanted me good and dead. It was . . . almost personal to him. A real . . . *honour* . . . to do me in."

Sil snarled, her ears pinned to her skull. "I'll rip that Owl's throat out for this."

Aunty fixed her glasses to her nose and considered Sil through them. "Sure and you could've, Fox. Why didn't you?"

I wanted to interject on Sil's behalf, tell the old woman that I'd sent her away. But my breath came out in hitching gasps as I felt my back return to normality. Next was my shoulder — dislocated — and a shattered wrist. Nearly done. But I had enough presence of mind to glance from Sil to Natti's aunt.

Sil's eyes narrowed at her. "You know I can't intervene."

Aunty's mouth tightened, but she nodded. "Mmm. The Preparation."

"The what?" Natti asked when she returned, but Aunty waved her off.

"Never you mind. How you feel, girlie?"

I think that one was directed at me. Phae stood back but had to sit down on the arm of the sofa behind her. Scrapes were easy. Bones were tiring work. I flexed my hands, tilted my neck. Full range of motion. Natti bent over and offered support as I got shakily to my feet, finally free of the sled. I was whole again. Though for how long, I couldn't guess. "I feel like a cat that's running out of lives."

"Hope you saved one, at least," Aunty said, undoing the cable on the beer cooler and wresting the lid free. "You're gonna need it."

Natti pulled the sled away and went to shove it into an overflowing closet. We watched as Aunty waved her cigarette-free hand over the cooler, pulling the block of ice loose with an invisible tether. It floated in the centre of the room and, as I'd seen Natti do earlier, she unfolded and reshaped the ice until it was a sphere. In a flash, it turned to water, but it stayed airborne. Aunty took off her glasses, and we all watched as the hunter confined inside began to wake.

Its eyes opened as the sphere revolved, looking into each of us with the understandable hatred of a caged animal. It lashed out against its watery prison, but it couldn't get free.

"*Atshen*, killing spirit, you are trapped in your own mother's water. Ease yourself." Aunty's lilting Inuit accent had changed. The tone was like a rushing wave, or a glacier shearing into the sea. It echoed in our heads, and I sensed that the river hunter understood. It turned towards her, eyes wide in shock.

"Where is she?" it said, a voice both a child's fearful whisper and a monster's hissing knell. "Where is Mother?"

Barton wheeled over to Phae. "What's it saying?"

I'd forgotten that Barton was out of the loop when it came to Ancient happenings. I answered him without looking away. "It wants its mom."

"Kinda sad," Natti admitted, but none of us was moved to agree. The hunter took another look around the room, its hatred turning into desperation.

"Did you hurt her? Will kill if hurt her!" The fear became rage, the teeth needling out of its terrible mouth.

"It's only a baby." Aunty clicked her tongue, shifting momentarily back to her normal voice. "A hatchling."

It was thrashing inside the water again. "How are they even *born*?" I grimaced, uncomfortable with the idea that these things could reproduce.

"They are made from the victims the river claims," Natti said. "It was human once. Now it doesn't remember."

I imagined a child unfortunate enough to not only fall into the unforgiving waters, but to be made into a monster for its innocent folly.

"Man, this is *dark*," Aivik complained. "I'm gonna get my DS . . ." He slumped out of the room. If only the rest of us were so lucky.

I turned to Phae. "Can you . . . change it back?"

She pressed her lips together and shook her head. "It's not like when Barton was infected. There's nothing human left."

Figures. These were efficient parasites. Natti stepped up to the water prison. "Can you tell us about your mother?" she said, her voice a probing ripple in an Arctic stream — inviting, patient. The hunter whirled towards her, pressing its face against its confines.

"Mother is all things. Mother loves us. Mother hates the Spirit Walkers and the dirty folk. Mother will make them all suffer." The spiteful whisper cut away the warmth in the room, and the red, empty eyes found mine. Its vertical teeth made a poor imitation of a smile. "Mother wants Fox most of all."

I crossed my arms, feigned disinterest. "Thanks, Captain Obvious."

It lashed out again, but Aunty rushed both of her hands into the sphere. The hunter howled, covering its head as terrible currents rushed through its cage. All at once they died away, and Aunty shoved her guilty hands into the pockets of her robe. "The hatchling must learn respect in the house of its captors."

The hunter was balled up now as though in a womb, visibly in pain. It wept bitterly. "No respect for Mother when she was held in the Dark Place! Mother suffered and screamed and no help! We will help Mother with revenge!"

"The Dark Place?" Natti repeated.

"The Bloodlands," Phae, Barton, and I all replied in unison. This time I stepped forward, taking Natti's place. "Your mother was there . . . a long time, wasn't she?"

The chastised hunter-child turned over to face me. "A hundred forevers. Mother will not forgive. Mercy is a mistake Mother will correct."

It seemed open to spinning its sob story, so I dove in: "Your mother was kept down in the Dark Place because of a . . . a *lock* that was put on her before the hundred forevers. It kept her trapped. Did your mother say where it is now?"

This elicited another smile. At first, I thought that's all I'd get, but the wretch spoke again. "Mother cunning and has many lovers. The Hero heard her call and freed her of her cage, but mother knew the lock would be useful. She gave it to the Gardener for keeping-safe."

I glanced at Sil questioningly. "The Gardener is Urka, a guardian at the prison of the Three Darklings," she spat. "It has lived in the ash-woods since Ancient created it."

"So the targe is still down there somewhere with this Urka? In the Bloodlands?"

Aunty suddenly looked very tired. She flopped onto the sofa and patted her pockets for a light and a fresh cig. "A lot of good that'll do you, girlie. Woulda been easier to get down there maybe fourteen years ago, when the gateway at the Forks still worked."

The hunter had had enough of us after that. It screamed and thrashed and cried out for its mother. "Shut that thing up, Nattiq." Aunty waved her hand, exhaling smoke through her teeth like she was at the limit of her patience. All Natti had to do was press her index finger into the water, and I knew it would freeze instantly, but I shoved her aside and, against my better judgment, thrust my hand inside the sphere. I touched the river hunter's ghastly slick flesh, and my spirit eye flashed me out of Natti's living room, into the future.

Maybe it was less a prophecy and more an insinuation of future events: The sky was bruised and in swirling tumult, the sun red and ruined. The flood waters rose and swept away the fleeing people. Heaven opened a thunder-wave cataract and dumped it on the screaming people below. The city burned then drowned. Any cries were cut to silence. And in the centre, holding out her massive, powerful arms as though she was conducting a symphony — Zabor. The head and torso of a woman, and the skyscraper-long tail of a snake.

River Serpent. Mother of Doom. She smiled in her benevolent destruction. The flood waters returned to her like a loyal dog as she moved downriver to the next city, and the next, until she had swallowed all life to her bare, scaled breasts.

The glassy globe hit the ground with a careless *thunk*, the hunter prostrate inside. I was vaguely aware of a ratty carpet rubbing against my cheek, the smell of what had to be a mix of cat pee and cola sticking in my nose. I was back in the North End. Natti hauled me to my feet.

"Roan!" Phae came to my other side. "Your eye —"

I knew which one she meant immediately, and my hand rushed up to the spirit eye Death had given me. It was bleeding, but I brushed her aside. "It's fine. I'm fine." I broke out of Natti's grasp, too. No more signs of weakness. Not after what I'd seen, what was coming. I wiped the blood away.

Aunty laughed as if we were all being too melodramatic. "She's had a vision. Nothing serious. Not with that little Fox at her side."

We all looked at Sil, the fire in her eyes kindled. "You've seen it, too, haven't you?" I asked her. She only nodded.

"Saw what?" said Barton.

But Sil cut in. "How it will be, if you fail."

I scuffed my shoe near the ice sphere with the river hunter inside. It seemed less like a vision and more like the propaganda that all Zabor's children had been fed.

"What'll you do with it?" I asked, meaning the globe of ice and the creature inside.

Natti's placid face seemed to twitch with pity. She shrugged, shrinking the captured hunter and the ice that encased it down again. "Put it in the freezer for now, I guess. No use sending it back to its mom to rat us out, and I don't feel like cleaning tar-blood off the rug." She hefted it up into her arms. "And what are *you* gonna do?"

Aunty cut in for me. "There's no going back now that Zabor's had her prize meal taken right out of her mouth." She frowned. "She's wakin' up, all right. And nothing's gonna satisfy that appetite 'cept *everything*."

I came to her side at the sofa, but she avoided my eyes, brown cheek resting dolefully on a fat fist.

"What did you mean about the gateway at the Forks?" I asked. "What happened to it fourteen years ago?" I wasn't sure if I wanted to know, but I didn't take it back.

When she finally looked up at me, it was with the sadness I knew she'd been trying to hide. "It's called a Bloodgate. Only Rabbits can open them. Your father opened that one. Your mother went through. You know the rest."

My chest felt like it had been slammed into an SUV all over again. What *I* knew, or at least thought I did, was that Ravenna and Aaron had gone into the river in her car either accidentally or on a suicide mission. A lie, then? *Or a story fabricated by the only people I knew who could control minds and memories?* My world tilted.

Sil joined us, ears tight against her neck. "*Ravenna* went through?" she asked. "Into the Bloodlands?"

Aunty fell into a coughing fit, waving her hand wildly at Natti until she came back from the kitchen with a glass of water. She drank, gratefully, but her forehead was creased in irritation. "That girl, I swear she had a rock for a skull. Couldn't get it through her head that it couldn't be done, that she'd *fail*. No. She was determined. And lord love Aaron, he'd do anything for her. For *you*." She thrust a bent finger at me, and I backed up a step.

I looked at the blood smeared in my palm from my eye. My mother's blood. "They knew I was marked." And so they went to do what I needed to now — find the targe. To stop it all. And they'd failed.

"Of course they knew. And as foolish in love as the two of 'em were, I was the biggest fool of all." Aunty leaned forwards with her hands between her knees, staring into the past. "They begged for help from everyone. No one would listen. I was dumb enough to believe in them."

"What . . ." I started.

"*I helped 'em do it*," Aunty spat, a mix of shame and anger flaring in her old face. "The Bloodgate was at the fork of the two rivers, and while Aaron performed the opening, I split the river aside so Ravenna could pass through it."

The scene played out with sick detail in my mind's eye, as if I'd been there. My parents' faces were, of course, obscured. But what they were willing to sacrifice to save me, and to stop Zabor . . .

"But she didn't come back," I said, breaking the spell of Aunty's words, not wanting to watch as my father let the Bloodgate snap shut, my mother lost inside forever.

Natti took her aunt by the hand.

Aunty stared into the couch cushion as though she'd find some solace there. "When you pass through the gate, the opener tethers you to the Earth. A physical lifeline, you could say. But it doesn't last forever. If the opener is compromised, or the traveller is, the tether snaps. The gateway shuts. And some gates can only be opened once."

My knees started going to water, and I sat down hard on a nearby footstool that was partways crushed from use. "What went wrong?" was all I could get out of my tightening throat.

"Oh, *guess*," Aunty sneered. "The Owls came. Can't stand it when their little plans go all to hell. Not like they would've known, either; it was broad daylight — they don't like that — and Ravenna played it close to the chest, didn't tell a soul. But they got their spies everywhere."

"They were betrayed," Barton murmured from the other side of the room.

Aunty turned and surveyed him, openly ogling his missing legs until her sharp glare met his passive one. "By the same person who did *that* to you, kiddo."

The fire had returned. It was spreading through me as if my bones were dry kindling. The air around me shimmered. "Arnas." Aaron's own brother.

"Did it to *protect* Aaron, he said. Didn't want him getting hurt. But since the Allen incident, Arnas would do anything to get his powers back. The Owls had stripped them from him, and they did the same thing to Aaron. Gave Arnas an amulet with his brother's Grace sealed inside, said *this is all the power you're getting from us.*

"Then they threw Aaron to the river hunters. Chum for the sharks." She slammed her cigarette into the ashtray as her bitter tale ended, her head whipping up as I rose suddenly to my feet. I ignored the surprise in her eyes, in the faces of my friends. I saw nothing but what lay ahead.

"Roan?" said Phae. I felt as hot as a new star. The Owls. Arnas. They had ripped my family apart for the "greater good." I was ready to let the fire take over and incinerate everything around me, but I held it back, turned the fuel down. Saved it.

I steeled myself, finally managing to unclench my jaw and my fists. "I think we can kill two birds with one stone. Barton, Phae, we're going back to my place." I turned to the Seal that had saved my life. "Natti. You said you wanted to help me. Now's the time." She nodded and zipped up her parka.

I looked down at Aunty. I think she'd waited a long time to tell me all this, had thought I'd be dead before she ever could. "Thank you," I said quietly. "For telling me. And for helping my parents when they needed you."

Aunty set her mouth in a thin line. "Your father let me get away once the gate shut. Didn't tell a soul I'd been there, and the Owls never found out. It takes a lot to keep a secret from a mind reader. So I owe him my life. Sure we're all gonna owe you ours, too, when you pummel that snake back to the pit she came from."

I nodded and moved to leave, but Aunty snatched my wrist, holding me back.

"There's another Bloodgate, kiddo. In the house of the Owls — the Pool of the Black Star. If you want that targe, it's the only place left you can go through to get it."

She let go of me, leaving behind a cool pulsing handprint on my flesh. But to open that gate, we'd need a powerful Rabbit. "Two birds, one stone. Get you back your power" — I nodded at Barton — "and beat Arnas dead with it."

The FIRST RABBIT

*D*on't *be rash*, Phae had warned.

You can't just walk in there and go all flame-thrower on your uncle, Barton had chimed in. I didn't want to hear them. I wanted this to be simple.

But when we got to the front door, ripped off and dangling from its hinges, none of my three companions, or my Fox-Yoda, said a damn thing. They were all waiting — to see if I'd explode or if I'd be the leader they needed and keep my cool.

My fists shook at my sides, the cold air evaporating as I cut through it towards the house. *Cool* was the furthest thing from me at that moment. The snow shrank away from me; I pretended it was out of fear.

On the way here, all I could think was *He will pay. He will pay*. Arnas was the reason my mother was trapped in the Bloodlands — either torn apart by monsters (the most likely) or still alive. He was the reason the man I called my father was dead — his *brother*. His cowardice. His complicity. And he'd been sleeping down the hall from me all these years. He would've let me die, too. He'd even tried to do the deed himself.

And I'd left him alone with Deedee. The only person in my family who *didn't* want me dead. Who genuinely loved me. I had tried to call the house. The phone rang and rang. Deedee's phone went directly to voice mail. Seeing the ruined front door made me fear the worst.

Sil darted into my path as I reached the stoop, her ears flattened. "It could be a trap."

I sidestepped her. "Of course it could be. But Deedee could be hurt. And I'm willing to take the chance."

Phae reached out for my hands — gloveless, newly healed. I didn't feel anything other than the fire. And when she touched me, she stifled a cry, which was enough to stop me.

Phae cradled her hand, flinching as the blue light from inside her spread over her burned palm and healed it before a blister could form. She looked up at me, hurt ringing in her troubled eyes.

I was startled back to myself. "I'm sorry, I —"

"— can't control it. I know that." Her words were acid. "But you're going to have to."

Barton piped up in a harsh whisper. "You can't just go in there and blow him away, Roan. Not with the Owls waiting to see if you're dead. And not with your comatose grandma upstairs, either."

I froze, having completely forgotten Cecelia. I glanced down at Sil, who seemed to be faring just fine. But Cecelia was just as vulnerable as my aunt — worse so. What if —

"I can't show him mercy," I seethed, trying to calm down. "I just can't. Not after . . . and he could still do a lot of damage to us." I turned towards the ruined door, wondering what else had been destroyed inside. It was as dark as the secret stairway underneath the house. What if he'd found the summoning chamber, too?

Sil pawed my shin. "Your power has grown quickly," she murmured. "And you will need that power to fight Zabor. But Foxes are not defined by their strength. It's their cunning that gets the desired result."

I thought of the stone menagerie. It seemed like eons since I'd found the statue of the fox crumbled in the backyard, with a real one waiting to save my life. While the others seemed to be running, the Fox kept still in the path of ruin. The Fox waited.

"Yeah, cunning," Natti muttered. "Wasn't it a Fox that made the deal with Zabor in the first place?"

I straightened my spine at her words. "Well. I guess it'll take a Fox to rectify that." I turned around to face them all. "He's my uncle. And it's my beef. You guys don't have to come with me. I can do this alone."

"Ha! Yeah, right!" Barton laughed. I started in his direction, but couldn't help the twitch at the corner of my mouth. He was still on the bench, but he was willing to be on the front lines and have my back. "Besides," he shrugged, seemingly reading my mind, "maybe after this I'll finally have something to do around here."

Phae stood firm beside Barton, hand gripping his wrist. Her hair sparked up into antlers as smooth as lightning. She nodded.

Natti just grunted affably. "A promise is a promise, Fox-girl. If I can help you, I will. And if you *could* do this alone, we wouldn't be here, anyway."

I huffed, the fire that had blazed earlier now cradled in me like the heart of a blowtorch — controlled, calculated. Ready. Four was better than one, anyway. And though I knew Arnas would probably be an easy takedown, the hairs on my neck rose like needles. I stepped through the door.

Furniture overturned. Windows shattered. TV smashed. *Deedee will kill me*, was the first thought. *If she isn't dead already*, came the next. I swallowed.

The lights were out. I reached for the switch and flicked it on and off. Nothing. Power cut. Phae and Natti flanked me, forming a protective V in front of Barton.

Sil's tail lit up like a roman candle. "There's a strange presence. Like a Therion, only . . ."

I nudged her with the toe of my boot, pressing a finger to my mouth. Silence fell, save for the sinister, sentient creaking that coalesced through the bones of the house.

Or the earth around it.

A seismic quake seized the house then and I pitched forward, landing hard on my palms. Phae cried out behind me, and I twisted to see the foyer light fixture falling towards my head. My eyes bugged as I raised my hands, ready to fire-blast it into oblivion, but it slammed into the white shield Phae had cast around us and bounced off like a toy.

I scrambled to my knees, grabbing Natti in an attempt to support the both of us — her haughty, hard veneer had broken and, despite our protection, she covered her head.

Then the earthquake stopped. Phae had herself wrapped around Barton, keeping his wheelchair from toppling, her antlers rippling blue in the dark of the foyer. She let out a hard breath, forehead glistening and face ashen as the shield flickered away.

"What the hell was *that*?" Barton hissed.

Sil's tail sparked in cadence with her growling. "Whatever it is, it's hiding beneath the house. And it's taunting us."

I jolted. "Could it be in the summoning chamber? Do you think it's Arnas?"

Sil looked away. "I think it *used* to be Arnas."

A chill vibrated up my spine, an internal earthquake. "Then we better go down there before the house crumbles on top of us."

I got to my feet, shucking my coat and tossing it on the askew sofa. "Phae, stay with Barton. Natti, you're with us."

"But what if —" Phae jerked forward, hand on her head. Barton reached out and caught her, his arms steady.

"You're drained," he whispered, smiling ruefully. "You're no good to anyone dead. I'll only be a burden for a little while longer, I swear."

A pang of sadness and sheer anxiety lanced my heart. What if this crazy power-stealing mission didn't even work?

Phae's eyes went round with dismay. "You're not a burden! Don't you dare . . ." Her plea was lost as another wave of dizziness overcame her. Barton gathered her as close to him as the wheelchair would allow.

I didn't want to break their embrace, so all I could do was rest my hand on her reassuringly. "It's going to be fine. Just rest here and keep watch. If I get broken again, I'll let you know."

Sil urged us on with a whine. "We must hurry." I caught her looking worriedly upstairs instead of towards the basement door. Cecelia. She was torn.

I frowned; I'd need Sil to help me take care of Arnas and couldn't risk sending her off again. I'd made that mistake already today. Natti was taking off her winter tack, too; underneath she wore wrinkled cargo pants and a black sports top. She was primed to fight. But first . . .

"Natti." I turned towards her. "Upstairs, third floor. First bedroom on the right. I need you to check on . . . on my grandma." The word felt foreign in my mouth. "Just make sure she's okay. If anything's disconnected — IVs, tubes, whatever — call 911." I tossed her my miraculously working phone. "The power's out, so her machines probably will be, too. And if it's all fine, lock the door and get to the basement. Your Sub Zero trick will probably come in handy."

Natti grunted, cracking her knuckles and making for the stairs. Sil turned those gold eyes on me, ears flicking. I nodded, and she took off ahead of me. I looked to Phae and Barton one last time. "Put up the shield. Stay behind it. I'll be right back."

"Famous last words," Barton sighed, but he saluted. "See you soon, chief."

A globe of white light flashed around the two of them. I didn't know how much longer Phae could keep it up, and I felt a clock start up behind my sternum. Time was already running out and I hadn't even started. The dark corridor leading to the basement loomed like an infinite tunnel.

I turned away from them and followed Sil into the shadows, feeling my way down the stairs with as much stealth as I could manage. I touched the solid concrete floor and felt a shudder rise to meet me. I froze, waiting for the quake to come. Ten seconds. Twenty. Nothing. I breathed, then hissed. "Sil?"

She lit up right at my feet. It took everything I could to clamp down and silence a shout.

I swallowed instead, taking comfort in her heat while it made mine flare. I touched her blazing tail, and my arm lit up like the torch I needed. *God, I wish I could make my own fire, already.* Unfortunately, basic training had been put on hold. I raised my arm, stiffening as the disarray before us came into view.

I had grown accustomed to finding our way through the winding piles of junk and storage, but this time boxes, furniture, shelving units were overturned and scattered. The labyrinth had shifted. Now there were new columns, new pathways, blocking old ones.

All the better for whatever hid down here, biding its time.

"It's trying to get in," Sil murmured, her voice a susurrus of embers as her fur flickered.

I didn't bother asking if that were even possible, if anyone besides her could open the door to the summoning chamber. Anything could happen now. "What would he want down there?" I led us forward, waving my torch arm in search of a passable way to the hidden doorway. "I thought each Denizen had a chamber. For personal practice."

So silent was the basement that I could hear Sil sniff as she scaled an Easter Island head with ease, scouting ahead. She grunted, finding no way through, and returned to my side. "Cecelia was in the business of hiding secrets. Things of great value. A bird loves a shiny object." Her whiskers twitched.

I frowned in the black. *Cecelia was in the business of keeping secrets. Great. More secrets. More lies. More riddles.*

We made our way far enough to reach the west wall of the house. Boxes and debris had toppled to create an enclosed tunnel the width of my shoulders, and it might just reach to the back wall. I flashed my arm towards it, careful not to kindle the surrounding cardboard, and Sil bounced in. She signalled, and I followed.

"You think the Owls are looking for the targe, too?" Maybe they thought Cecelia had it, that Ravenna had maybe succeeded and given it to my grandmother, before . . . I tried not to think about it, my mother trapped in the underworld all these years.

But why would the Owls put so much effort into stopping Ravenna, stopping me? Was the balance really so important?

Sil read my thoughts . . . or maybe she was talking to herself. "Those fools will stop at nothing to maintain their precious Narrative. They'll break their own rules, work with the monsters they claim they're protecting Denizens from, feed helpless children to a snake. Cowards. All of them. Power mad. They'll be the end of us all."

I tried to swallow my rising pulse. Sil seemed far chattier than usual, and I hoped it wasn't a sign she was as anxious as I was. There was always so much she wasn't telling me, locked inside that thousand-year-old head. She knew something and she wouldn't give it away. Something that riled her and made her seem to blaze up with each breath. And was she getting bigger? I kept quiet all the same. I needed her to stay controlled, and her nervous energy was catching.

The tunnel was running out; I could see the clear exit in front of us. "Yeah, well, too bad we need an Owl to finish the j—"

The ground shook. We'd arrived at the back wall, and we crouched close to each other as the quake passed. I clamped my mouth shut, the echo of my voice ringing stupidly in my ears. The wall was a crumbled ruin, concrete churned into playground pebbles, but still somehow holding. The secret doorway that led to the summoning chamber was a rimey outline in the debris but was yet unbreached.

Above it, buried in the man-made stone, was a horrible hulking shape that writhed its body, drilling itself deeper into the wall. With each of its movements, the ground shook.

"So close now," said a greedy, reedy voice from inside the wall, hungry and angry and wanting.

I got to my feet; the aftershock hummed under us. I glanced at Sil; her fire seemed to be whistling in a hundred different directions, a flame for each hair on her body. She *was* growing — her back was as high as my hip now. "Nothing worse than a burrowing Owl," I said loudly, trying to assert myself and maybe calm Sil down.

The shaking ceased so suddenly that I stumbled and caught myself. The shape rolled over, a keystone in a knot of soon-to-collapse rubble. Its eyes were huge and semihuman, leaping off its face, arms and legs tucked tightly to its body. My jaw tightened, but kept my arm alight. When I flashed the flame, I could clearly see its pupils contract.

They were my uncle's eyes. The shimmer of a Rabbit danced across my spirit vision; a Rabbit trapped, a Rabbit afraid. A Rabbit begging for mercy.

"He's being controlled," I murmured. "Or possessed." It all flashed clearly in my head; he was controlled, all right, by the Owls who had been using him all along, promising him a return to power, the protection of his wife — promises already broken. Now they were fed up with his lack of results, and they'd decided to make him useful. To see what else he could get from the home of the former Fox

Paramount and to make sure her granddaughter didn't come back from the dead.

"Leave this place, you filthy wretch!" Sil barked, her voice as big as her, her body growing larger still. I suddenly worried the whole basement would go up in flames around us. "There is nothing for you here!"

His smile was ragged like a stamp's edge. "There is. You are hiding it. A great power. A deep power. Here all along. And it could be mine. So shiny. I hear it calling me."

My spirit eye twitched, a whisper, an insistence — a shadow and a gem and a broken statue. I shook my head. Is that what Arnas — or not-Arnas — was after? A rock?

Whatever they were doing to not-Arnas, it seemed as though their influence had made him into something as ugly and twisted as all his fears and desires. Our combined firelight made something flash at his throat — the dark bauble I'd seen on him before. Could this be what was left of my father's power? And was it being warped now?

"Any power you have is stolen!" I cried. "Give it back, and maybe I'll consider keeping your face intact!"

The Rabbit shadow flashed again, pleading. But the Owlish monster inside the wall only deepened its smirk, swallowing the real Arnas back behind its horrible crunching teeth. His wide, twisted arms released, and I saw another shape, separate from its drilling body, come into the light.

A pale face. A dark halo of hair. *Deedee.*

"Come and get it," the Arnas-thing mewled. And the house began to heave.

❦

Natti braces herself against the wall before she can be flung across the hallway. She's just made it to the third floor and to the doorway of Roan's grandmother's room, but there is nothing but bedlam. The walls shudder like they will shake loose; the ceiling cracks, threatening to cave. Luckily, the pipes from a bathroom down the hall have already burst and are drowning the carpet. With a flick of her wrist, Natti shoots the water from the floor and onto the ceiling, freezing the cracks and buying some time.

Another sudden rumble pitches Natti through the doorway. Even before she can collect herself from the ground, her face registers a sudden heat, and she rolls, looking for the fire. Maybe one of the hospital machines exploded? It's blazing in here, and —

Well, it's not the curtains or the bedspread or the machines. Even as the house caves in around her ears, the grandmother lays peaceful and still as a wax figure. Except the grandmother *herself* is up in flames, serene and unharmed in the heart of the blaze. The heat carries to the hall, and Natti wonders how long her ice-patch job will hold.

Shit. She scowls as the house lurches again.

～✹～

I feinted and leapt backwards, trying to avoid the storage landslide and the tumbling concrete and rebar. Arnas had wrestled his way out of his hole, each struggle of his mutated body shaking my resolve. The juddering threw me off long enough that he managed to nest Deedee in the rubble before he rocketed out and landed in front of us.

He stomped his foot, heaving the stone floor apart. I thudded against the wall, rolling out of the way of a falling bookshelf as the seismic tremors heaved and worked the house from its foundation. I got to my feet in time to see Sil flash into her Fox-woman form, launching at Arnas with her mouth open.

"Wait!" I screamed over the din, barely able to hear myself through the reverberations. The two of them locked together and rolled, the Arnas-thing shrieking as Sil lifted and slammed him face-first into the ground.

"Traitor!" Sil howled, and she picked him up again. She didn't seem at all like herself, all wisdom and serenity dissolved. "You killed her! *My daughter*! I'll rip you into nothing!" Her face was animal and monstrous. I stopped breathing.

She crushed his face in her massive hand and hurled him aside. Despite it all, the Arnas-thing seemed to be laughing, and he got to his broken legs easily, scampering into the dark like a shattered beetle. Sil-the-warrior fell to all fours and rumbled after him.

I didn't have time to register shock. *Daughter?*

"Sil!" I shouted. "Stop!" But there was something wrong. Something had taken hold of her, too; something I had felt in myself at Omand's Creek. There was little that could penetrate righteous rage when it was personal. I tried to follow them.

Sil *was* the fire, now. And it had caught all the boxes and furniture around us. Hot and fast, it swallowed everything, and I lost them in the blaze.

I pulled up short of a crackling wall of fire, shielding my eyes even though I knew it wouldn't hurt me. Old reflexes I guess, but this was the angriest heat I'd ever felt. I dove in, regardless, and it hissed away from me as I peeled through, trying to find them.

"Sil!" I screamed over and over until my throat was raw. I chanced a glance up, and wondered how long it'd take until the inconveniently wooden ceiling caught, too.

I found them at the heart of the inferno. Sil stood over Arnas in all her brutal, mighty glory, so hot she was white, flickering *blue*, and she looked prepared to tear him in half. The creature laughed and laughed. The Rabbit-silhouette over him still flickered, though it was nearly gone.

But he was still Aaron's brother. He still needed help, even if he didn't deserve it.

Sil's hand came down for the final blow and, without thinking, I leapt in front of it.

※

Phae holds tight to Barton's wheelchair. The room is spinning, and she knows it isn't really, knows it's just reverberating, and she tries to dismiss the black spots in front of her eyes.

"Phae?" Barton shouts. He holds tight to her, the best he can offer. His complete uselessness pounds hard into him. But he will give his life to protect her, just as she's doing now for him.

"You can't do this forever," he says into her ear. Her eyes are closed in full concentration, her hair-antlers brushing against his head. "You need to get out of here!"

"I'm not leaving you," she replies almost too quietly to be heard. Her beautiful brown skin is turning grey. She has nothing left.

"You're killing yourself!" Barton protests, hoping the hyperbole will make her snap out of it. Hoping that he isn't right.

Nothing would be worse than losing Phae. She protected him without question. She supported him without words. And if she did so at the cost of her life, his would be worth nothing in the end.

It's getting extremely hot, and Barton knows the destruction will only worsen. The heat probably means fire; fire means Roan. Hopefully she's winning, but he can't count on her now.

Barton grips Phae tight, pushing her gently away from him. This causes her eyes to flash open as the house rocks apart. They look at each other for a prolonged moment; even though Phae's eyes are a clear, glassy white, Barton knows she sees him. Just as she did when she saved his life for the first time.

Now it's his turn.

With all the strength that basketball games have given him, he picks her up and hurls her into the upturned sofa nearby. The shield is broken, and even in the chaos he can see her features relax past the surprise. She breathes again, colour coming back to her.

Then the floor crackles beneath him. And he hears Natti scream, *"Fire!"* from upstairs before he plummets through the burning living room floor.

❧

Sil's ancient power shuddered through my forearm like an axe hitting a stump. But I stood my ground, feet planted over the bloody pulp of mutant-Arnas.

Her fire cowl erupted. "Get out of my way! He's *mine*!"

I gritted my teeth so hard they should've turned to paste. I put up my other arm against her, bracing my body on hers. "We . . . need . . . him . . ." My fire started climbing, and I felt myself *becoming* the blaze around us. I was so dialled in that I could hear the flames goading us on. Begging us to stop. Telling stories of the dead.

"He killed her! It was his doing! She's gone because of him!" Her eyes were hatred, her gaze was death. Gold and iron and horror. And she had it all turned on me. Her nine enormous tails whipped the blaze up higher, faster.

"I know!" I screamed back, my hair becoming fire, my body growing. "But this isn't the way! Killing him won't bring her back, Cecelia!"

I didn't know if I'd said it intentionally, or if it'd been an accident, or if I'd known all along. But I'd said it. And her eyes turned to glass, massive teeth and jaws going slack with sorrow. The burning house closed in.

"My *daughter*," she moaned, her flames still high, arm locked in my grasp. "I couldn't save her. *I didn't know*."

"I know," I said again. "I know."

Then a scream ripped through her that made my head split, and her fire went out. She crumpled to the ground, and the light in her gorgeous, fearsome Fox face was gone. I stumbled backwards with the next tremor and heard a crack like thunder above our heads. The ceiling split open, eaten by the blaze. Not-Arnas was still laughing, choking on the smoke, and probably not long for this world. I scooped him up into my flaming arms and he howled, either from the heat or from his broken limbs, and I dove out of the way as the living room came down on top of us.

That was the last of the tremors. The earthquake stopped. And by some ridiculous stroke of luck, we'd avoided the majority of the cave-in, but the fire still raged. Sil's body was still somewhere in the debris, but I'd have to stop the fire first. It was only a matter of time until it swallowed the whole house, and my friends were still up there. I stowed Arnas aside, and rounded on the fire, hands out.

"Stop!" I cried. If I could light it up, I figured I could bring it down. It was a gamble. But I shut myself off to the heat, and coaxed it calmly. "It's done, now. It's done. Come back to me. Rest."

The fire seemed to pause, the smoke receding into it like a black gasp. It swirled backwards, then climbed down. It came to me as an obedient pet, wanting to please. When it reached my skin, I felt it fuse with my blood and marrow. It was part of me, now, even though I knew it had once been Sil's. Cecelia's. My grandmother's. It came to me because my blood was familiar to it. I would've cried if I'd had the energy left.

The silence of the house was deafening, especially after what had seemed like hours of uncontrollable mayhem. I felt myself shrinking down to the Roan that sort of resembled a normal girl, and I let my lungs relax. I looked at the Arnas-thing, still in one piece but moaning and writhing. I stumbled over and ripped the bauble from around his neck. He arched and screamed. I staggered back, and his body writhed as it reasserted itself into my uncle, looking slightly charred and terrified.

"Roan!" I heard Phae shout. I scrambled over to the massive hole in the ceiling, and before I could ask her if she was okay, I found myself tripping over Barton and his wheelchair. He groaned and I fell to his side.

"He's okay!" I yelled back up at her. She was already at the top of the stairs, themselves badly damaged, and trying to climb down. Natti wasn't far behind.

"Yeah, speak for yourself." Barton scowled. He had a big splintered piece of wood jutting out from his shoulder. I recoiled.

"Shit." I ran to Phae. "You'd better —"

Natti was already ten steps ahead of me: She'd cobbled together a set of ice stairs from a leaking pipe, and Phae was skittering down them.

"You idiot, you *stupid idiot*," she was half grumbling, half crying. Her antlers shot up and she ripped the wood out, the wound searing together as soon as it was discarded.

"Gah!" he winced. "Heal, don't hurt!"

"I'll do more than *that*, you moron," she muttered. "I had everything under control."

"I don't think any of us did." I smiled. "Just hope there's insurance on this place . . ."

Then I sprang back up. "Sil!" She was buried in this, somewhere.

"What happened?" Phae croaked, leaving Barton for the moment and finding Arnas in the corner.

"Sil, she just . . . she got out of control. Then she collapsed." I didn't want to give away anything else yet, especially that my mentor and trusted semifamiliar had been my grandmother all along, invested in this personal mission as much as I was.

"Yeah, your granny got pretty out of control there, too," Natti sniffed. "She was pretty much *on fire*. I didn't want to risk the ceiling to caving in on her or the machines burning, so I sort of, um, put her out."

"That'd do it," I muttered. I pulled aside plank after plank, but I couldn't find her. "Sil!" *Please don't let her be dead. Not now.* I couldn't keep the sob out of my throat. "*Sil!*"

"Here," she said. She was still the Fox-woman, though now she looked ashen and cold. Her nine tails drooped and dragged behind her, her shoulders were bent, and her cowl looked soaked. She held a body in her arms. Deedee.

I swallowed. "Is she okay?" Sil had her cradled close to her chest, feeding what warmth she had left into my aunt.

"She'll live," she sighed, like a candle going out. She put her down gently beside Arnas. Phae had her hands on him, but she hadn't gone to the trouble of healing him yet. She just stared up at the beautiful, beaten Fox goddess that was my grandmother.

"What will we do with him?" I asked Sil, who regarded Arnas through hooded eyes that had seen far too much. She sneered at first, but Arnas didn't look at her. He just reached a broken, bloody hand out to his wife's face and sobbed uncontrollably.

"He'll live," she grunted, and she nodded at Phae. Phae rested both hands on Arnas, and his myriad wounds were righted. He didn't stop sobbing through the ordeal; the more his bones refastened, the closer he edged to Deedee until he could pull her totally into his arms. Once she was there, he was quiet.

After a long pause, he reached up to his neck, patting it absently. He sucked in a breath.

"Looking for this?" I dangled the brass-encased bauble between my fingers.

"D-don't!" He reached out then recoiled. "They've d-done something to it. They made me . . ."

"No one made you betray your own *brother*," I spat. "This is him, isn't it? Or what's left of him. He's dead, and you're here, and this is your prize, right?"

Arnas cast his eyes down, clutching his unconscious wife tighter. "I never had a right to it. I'd never use it for ill. I just . . . I didn't want them to hurt Deidre. I just wanted to live. But I'd . . . have to live with the shame. *That* was my prize."

Sil reached up and grasped the bauble between two large fingers, which were sharp and deviously clawed. She cracked it between her nails like a walnut, and something black and foul sludged out. It hit the floor with a hiss, then slimed across the concrete.

"An old spell," Sil murmured absently as she crushed it beneath her boot. She discarded the shell and passed what was inside to me. It was dry and small. A bone, maybe. Delicate and frail and tiny. But it was warm.

"Bring the boy. It's time you made good on your shame." Sil's knees buckled, and she steadied her huge body with a fist to the ground. She was wavering.

I tensed my arms, which were growing sore as the adrenaline of the last hour wore off. "And what about . . . Cecelia?" I had to crunch my teeth down on saying *you* before it slipped out. But with the power off, and her great flame snuffed out, seeing Sil in this state made me wonder how much longer she had left.

We all froze as the sound of sirens and shouting grew nearer. I glanced at Sil when she spoke: "The machines Cecelia is hooked up to have a phone line attached. If the power goes out, it puts out a 911 call directly. She'll be all right, if they're quick about it."

We didn't have much time, then. I saw what happened to Sil when she was too far away from Cecelia . . . from *her* body. The ambulance would take her straight to a hospital, especially with the house in the state it was in.

Sil read me easily. "The summoning chamber," was all she said before I started mobilizing the troops for the trek underground.

Arnas moved to pick up Deedee, but Sil stopped him. "Leave her."

"But —" he said, and I stepped in front of the still-menacing Sil.

"The paramedics are coming," I said, and I could hear them pulling up on the front lawn, coming in through the door. "It's better that they find her and care for her now. Right?"

Arnas hesitated, but as soon as he looked down at his wife, he nodded grimly and rested her comfortably in the debris at the bottom of Natti's ice steps, which were nearly melted away.

After that, Phae, Natti, and I managed to assist Barton and Arnas down the earth-hewn steps to the secret chamber below the house. I felt strange about bringing so many strangers there, since the chamber had always felt like Sil's and mine, like a fortress against doubt and the disappointment of those counting on us. I had no idea what would happen next, but I hoped Sil did. I was helping her gingerly down the last of the steps, as though she really was the old woman in the bed I'd stood over so many times. I tried to summon up the fire she'd lost in her tirade and warm her with it. She sucked in a breath, but was unable to act grateful yet. Too many regrets hung between us, and we weren't about to explore them now. This crisis wasn't over.

We reached the chamber's entrance. I'd forgotten about the candle-lighting. Sil was able to push herself off from my support but, without even thinking of it, I sent flames eddying from my pores into the air, and the baubles of light found their candles. I shuddered. *I'd made my own fire.* But no one else seemed in a celebratory mood as they put down their injured charges on the obsidian floor amidst the silver circles. No one knew I'd changed drastically in the last hour except for me and maybe Sil. I caught her eye, and she nodded at me.

Arnas joined Sil in the great circle, and he and Sil sat cross-legged on either side of Barton. The rest of us stood aside, steeling ourselves for the show. This was the circle through which I'd passed into the Veil. I wondered if that's where we were going now.

After a long silence, Sil spoke. "Bring the relic forward."

Natti and Phae looked at me. I had the bone of my father clasped protectively in my palm. It was still warm. I placed it in Barton's hand and tried to smile, knowing I was giving him the only piece left of the father I didn't really know. Barton didn't smile. He just nodded, gravely.

"We find ourselves in a difficult situation," Sil spoke again, voice low. "A severed Rabbit in need of restoration. The neutralizer who performed the severing has no power left to reverse it. But we have the boon of the bone. We are going to need the assistance of the Veil and the Old Powers . . ."

"You mean the original Ancients, don't you?" Natti scratched her cheek. "Do you think they'd help us? The Matriarchs?"

Sil shivered, her muscular, goddess frame seeming more human and fragile as each moment passed. "We'll need to appeal to the First Rabbit to restore the connection to Ancient for Barton. If she doesn't help us, no one will."

"Better plan than nothing," I exhaled. "But it sounds pretty lofty. More like something a Paramount could accomplish than a ragtag gang of Denizens." I looked straight at Sil, arms folded tight into my chest to keep my nervous heart from bursting out of it. Knowing who Sil was now, that she was Paramount of all Foxes, their champion and conduit for the other realms, the onus should be on her to fix this mess. I had no right to be angry or bitter with her, but I couldn't help it. She deserved some reparations for lying to me this whole time.

Sil regarded me from heavy eyes, the colour of them faded and barely lit. She glowered. "My powers are now severely limited, thanks to a well-intentioned oversight." Natti raised an eyebrow, but Sil didn't elaborate. "And I don't know how long my body will last off medical support. I'll need your help, Roan."

I swallowed. Since she'd thrown her fiery self into my life, Sil had never asked for my help, not directly. She'd never said *anything* to me directly, come to think of it. She'd spoken in glances and riddles and withheld secrets. I realized suddenly that this wasn't Sil the Spirit Guide beseeching me now, but Cecelia, my grandmother.

"I don't . . . what do you want me to do?" There was no use in hesitating, I thought. If I wasn't ready now, I'd never be.

Sil turned away from me and shut her eyes. "I need you to open the gateway. We will not be going through. Instead, the Veil will come to us. I will summon the First Rabbit. Her name is Heen. What happens to Barton will be up to her."

She opened her eyes and let them bore into Arnas. For once, he didn't look away. "You will speak for the boy, and use your actions against him as a bargaining chip for mercy. Do you understand?"

Arnas only nodded again, numb. What else could he do? He was culpable for Barton, and he'd done other terrible things for which he'd never fully atone. Sil glared at him, weighing his reliability. While there'd be a satisfaction in *really* bringing Arnas to justice for what he'd done to Ravenna and Aaron, I had finally come to terms with the knowledge that killing him would only make the loss inside me, and inside Sil maybe, too, linger larger and more infinite.

But that still didn't help me. "Sil, I . . ." I choked, uncertain. "How am I going to know what to do?"

She closed her eyes again. "Use your spirit eye. Look into yourself. You're more capable than you give yourself credit for. The words will come, and you will be able to bring the two planes together. I trust you."

Stunned, I could only swallow. I put a hand on Phae and Natti, directing them to stand aside. I came forward and stood on the edge of the centre circle, closing first the eye that saw the Rabbit visions to begin with and directing it deep down into the place I'd probed before. I felt a vibration from the cold obsidian under me shimmer up my boots and through my legs, a murmur into senses newly opened and flexing. I forced myself to breathe as I held my hands out over Sil and Arnas, forming a triangle around Barton, and opened my mouth. "I call now to the flames that started this world, that they might hear my petition and rise."

Was it Sil's fire, now in my blood, that called the silver rings so easily? They flashed awake, and a wheel of fire crawled up from their crescents. I heard Phae yelp and Natti try to silence her, but I didn't stop as the blood rushed in my ears. Sil's words, or maybe the words of all the Foxes before me, tumbled out of my mouth.

"Spirits of the core, of the heat of creation." I raised my hands, palms up and fingers twitching. "I implore you to consign our spirits to the hands of the Veil and those that walk there. Open the door, and let your world into ours. I place the fire on my name." The flames were high around us now. In the heart of them I perceived Sil's utter calm, Barton's wavering nerve, and Arnas's sheer panic, but I let the blaze tower in my control. "*Yield now.*"

A bright flash quivered inside me, the reverberation of a gut punch threatening to bowl me over, but I kept my ground. The summoning chamber was gone; instead, we were inside a wavering mirage of light and colour and nothingness. I looked down at my hands, or what I perceived as my hands: they moved and shifted each time I lost the requirement of them, and I remembered that any form I had here was of my own making. My body solidified once I recognized how much I still needed it.

I turned to look at Phae, but she and Natti had vanished. Only the four of us in the circle remained. I looked down at Barton and Arnas; they looked the same to me as they would without the Veil filter, but maybe because I was projecting my memory of them onto their spirits. Out of the two, Barton seemed the most solid, still clutching the frail bone close to him, with Sil a beautiful inferno of body parts, a fire still and quiet.

Her flames jumped with her words. "Well done." She smiled at me from the heart of the heat.

I swelled with pride, but I shrugged. "It runs in the family."

But there was no time left for commendation. She reached out her blazing hands and placed one gently on Barton's arm. He gawked at her.

"Where are we?" he whispered, the words ricocheting around our shifting, uncertain landscape.

"We are in Limina, the Place in Between," the flames of Sil said. "This is where you will be one again."

She folded his palms together over the Rabbit bone, encircling his hands with her own. "I call now to the authority of Rabbits, to the First Matriarch. Heen. I commend to you a lost leveret."

A great trembling engulfed us then. I felt it in my marrow, but I was not shaken by it. The Veil and the world we came from intertwined and flexed, both reasserting themselves in a unified matrix. When the pieces clattered into place, I saw a deep forest, trees as old as time and scratching the surface of a heaven we couldn't see. At the heart of a tree with roots that reached into the chest of the universe, there emerged hundreds of small, inquisitive forms. Rabbits, or the fleeting memory of their spirits, flitting around us like camera flashes.

"You took us to the *Warren*," Arnas seethed. I'd almost forgotten he was there. "I can't . . . believe . . . ." He looked around, seeming like he was about to rise and look for someone he was expecting.

"Break this unity we travelled here in, and I will break *you*," Sil snarled. "You won't find your family here. They can't see you anymore. And they wouldn't look on you if they could."

Arnas thumped back down, expression hollow. This must be a sort of afterworld for the Rabbits, I guessed. My stomach dropped when I realized that Arnas would never see any of his family again, because of what he did. Harsh punishment, and even I was doubting that it fit the crime when I said, "Does that mean that my father . . ."

Sil shook her head before I could finish the thought. "He was fed to the river. He is one of *hers* now."

I tried to focus on Barton again instead of my kindling anger.

He was spellbound, taking it all in with a childlike awe I'd never seen on his affable face. I remembered then that he'd never been able to see any of this, had never been a part of it. He'd only ever trusted us, that we were really and truly surrounded by a world of talking foxes and river mud demons. And now he could see it.

But he still did not have legs. I don't think he'd even noticed yet. Sil gripped her hands tighter over his, matted muzzle peeling back over her gleaming, crackling teeth. A smile.

"This is the legacy of the Rabbits. Your Family." Barton finally looked at her, clamping his slack jaw shut. "And the mother of that Family is here. The first Rabbit."

I hadn't noticed until Sil ducked her head in that direction, but the roots of the great tree before us were moving aside, revealing a massive hole in the spirit earth. The smaller Rabbits shifted and sniffed the wavering air, but they did not flee in alarm as a massive brown creature emerged from the heart of the tree. No, not emerged — came into existence from the dark earth itself, the tree roots her ears, topsoil her fur, loam her paws. Her eyes were white glittering quartz, and they were not turned on us, but the Rabbit spirits flocking to her. She nuzzled them, sniffed them, as she pulled herself fully into the open. Hers was a benevolent energy, and I felt my spirit sigh as she came closer, behind Arnas.

She ignored him completely, even though his lamenting whimper could be heard across the Veil. I couldn't understand why he'd be frightened of her, until I saw that he was crying. I couldn't help but pity him.

"Dear daughter of the fire, creation-sister." Heen spoke in a voice that was a whisper through the grass. "You are my sister's walker in the world? And you have brought me a child of earth?" Her great head entered the circle, nose snuffling Barton carefully. She surveyed him this way for a long while, taking special care to note his severed legs, until she drew her head back, curious. "The scent is faint. There is more blood here than earth. How are you sure he can be mine?"

Sil turned her burning eyes on Arnas. Stung back into usefulness, he reached around Barton and placed his hands over his and the bone cradled there.

Heen didn't move, but her ears flattened down hard with a whip-crack of willow bark. "*You* were once mine." She thrust her head at Arnas and bared her long file teeth. "But my gift was taken from you. You will tell your mother why."

"I deserved my shame," Arnas said plainly, eyes on the ground. For once he didn't stammer, despite the tears. "I severed this boy from your gift before he was born. So he might never be sacrificed to the Darkling Zabor. Then I betrayed my brother. The punishment was just."

Heen's eyes widened. She sniffed Barton again to verify Arnas's truth. She pulled herself up on her massive hind legs, lifted one up, and beat it rapidly against the ground. The sound was thunder ripping through my senses. The Rabbit souls popped and flashed until the warren was full of them, large and small, old and young, their empty eyes shining on us.

"So that your ancestors may bear witness," Heen explained, coming back down on all fours. "You come now to ask that this boy be returned to the fold you denied him."

"With the shame of my crime weighing on my spirit, I ask this, Mother." Arnas looked up at her now. Ready for her judgment, whatever it would be.

Heen weighed us all, Barton in particular. Then her voice echoed through the cavern of my heart. "A severing to save a life from a darkness long remembered. And your power stripped for it. How do you intend to restore the boy?"

The three peeled their hands back, then, six protective flowers over the bone.

"Another of my children parted from me." Heen's heavy words trickled down.

"My brother." Arnas swallowed. "He died for my cowardice. I concede his power to the boy."

Heen surveyed him over lidded, incalculable eyes. "You would give this to *him*, when the power could be yours again?"

"Yes."

The Warren grew still as if holding its breath. Heen dipped her head down, touched her mouth to the bone. It shimmered until it melted away into the light of Barton's hands and went inside of him.

Two blaring-white Rabbit spirits bounded forwards and made for Heen's bowed head. Their teeth went to work felling the ancient roots that were her ears until a shower of tangled green and brown cascaded around Barton. Sil and Arnas stood up, and the spirits flashed away.

I suddenly felt as though the entire world was crushing

me: I was the link keeping these two worlds open, and now my strength to keep it up was unravelling. I held my arms out and steadied my spirit. My hands quaked.

The Warren shook as the circle threatened to break. Barton still sat before Heen, gazing into her eyes until he cried out in agony. The roots she had offered writhed and wound around him, then all at once they lanced into his chest. His screams rocked us all, and the Warren began to dissolve.

"May the grace of the Rabbits shine in your spirit, little leveret. Put my gift to the use it was intended, for the Rabbit that bestows his power to you was a noble child of mine." Her words were only whispers, so faint as to be only in our heads. The Veil faded, and all went black.

※

I was the first to wake up. Natti rushed to me, but I waved her off, pointing at the others. Sil had reverted to her tiny Fox form, and I crawled to her first, scooping her up in my aching arms. She was still warm.

"Barton? *Barton?*" Phae was taking tentative steps towards him, but there was still a bright light that kept the two apart.

"Phae, *wait!*" I choked, but she reached out and was thrown aside by the buffer. There was a loud ringing, and we all shielded our ears until the wall of light came down and all that was left was Barton.

Arnas came to then, hand to his skull. "What —"

Phae fell to her knees at Barton's side, hands hovering just over him. He wasn't injured, and he wasn't dead. There was nothing she could do for him. But I knew she wanted to touch him.

He blinked awake, eyes bleary like he'd only overslept. "Hey, Phae. You all right?" He sat up suddenly, hands to her cheeks that seemed pale in the dark of the chamber. "Phae? What is it?"

We all stared. Barton's legs hadn't changed. But his arms and hands had.

Shimmering roots intertwined around his muscular forearms and throbbed there like new veins.

Phae looked numb. "It didn't work."

"I think it did," Arnas murmured, legs crumpled under him. "Not even a Matriarch can . . ." He tightened his jaw. "But she gave you back the link."

Barton looked up again to Phae, who broke out of being stunned and threw her arms around his neck. "You blessed idiot."

Levering himself onto his hands, he pulled himself to Arnas, who jerked in surprise. The room went quiet.

Finally, Barton put a pulsing, rooty hand on his shoulder. "Thanks, Mr. Harken. Really."

Arnas still had that old look on his face, the spot-on impression of a scared Rabbit about to bolt. But the look faded. "I don't think you can celebrate yet."

Sil was still resting quietly in my arms, but her breathing had become regular. I got to my feet, careful not to jostle her. "Arnas is right." I bit my tongue down on the *for once* that should've followed. "Barton's got his power back, but he'll need to learn how to use it. Plus, we need the power of the Five to use the targe, and we're short an Owl, much as I'd like to keep it that way. So all that," I sighed, "plus, we don't have the targe to begin with."

"But it's only February," Natti argued. "You know how

long winter here lasts. There's still time."

Phae shook her head, palms cupping her elbows as she calculated. "It'll be March next week. And you've seen what it's like outside. *Unseasonably warm.* And they're calling for an early melt, even before the first day of spring."

"*Someone's* in a hurry for breakfast." Barton clicked his tongue. "So that gives us three weeks, more or less, until the official first day of spring . . . if the weather forecast is right. Not like we've ever been able to rely on it."

Arnas brow furrowed. "This happened before. In 1997. The melt was sudden, and then it rained for days. You can't think of Zabor as just some brute monster. She's a force of nature. She has influence over the river and the weather. And no one was prepared for the river to breach the Red Line. I have a feeling it's going to be worse, this time."

The Great Flood of '97 raged through not only Winnipeg, but the towns around it. Houses were decimated. People drowned. The destruction was felt across the country for years. I always walked under the Osborne Bridge and stared down those lines, trying to picture the river being as high as the highest mark, the Red Line. The Say-Your-Prayers-And-Hold-On line.

I stepped forward. Fearless leader time. "Three weeks. We've come this far in four. I'm not turning around now." I came up to Arnas, then, my impulse to smash his face ebbing away, but ready to come back should the need call for it. "You tell me right now: Whose side are you on?"

He looked petrified of me but swallowed. "The side I should've been on."

I refused to smile or feel relief. I nodded, then I turned to face my friends. "So what's the next step?"

"The targe . . ." Sil whispered from beneath my arms. Sil's golden eyes were still dark, but they took me in completely. "You will need to go . . . through the Bloodgate."

I forgot for a second that she was my all-knowing grandmother, Paramount of all Foxes, because in that moment she was once again a riddle-spewing forest dog I had no patience for. "Uh, okay. And who do *you* know who can open one?"

"Me," Arnas volunteered, hand raised halfway until it dropped back to his side. "I mean. I know *how* to do it. But now . . ." He looked down at his open hands. Without my father's bone and the power sealed inside of it, he had nothing.

"But you can teach *me*!" Barton smacked the ground. "Just tell me how and where, and I'll do it."

Arnas looked skeptical. "It'll take more than some beefy arms and a good attitude. It's one of the most treacherous things a Rabbit can ever learn, let alone survive long enough to keep the door open."

"Hey," Barton protested, pointing at me, "if Roan can bring the entire *Veil thingy* through to this plane in her grandma's basement, I think I can manage opening the gateway to hell."

My mouth twitched, but I didn't mention that I had more experience than him, or the toll it took every time I did something witchy.

"And that's another thing . . ." Arnas turned to me. "You're supposed to be dead. So any ease you felt running around the city without consequences are gone. They'll want to make sure you went where you were supposed to. The reason Rathgar turned me was for insurance. If you somehow survived, I was supposed to . . ."

After all the excitement, I'd totally forgotten that the house we'd all called home was now partly incinerated and totally unlivable. And that my aunt had' nearly died in the middle of it all. There'd be paramedics inside now, taking care of Cecelia and Deedee and getting them to safety as soon as possible. But after that, there'd be insurance claim adjusters. Press. Rubberneckers. And worse, *police* swarming the place as word spread of the domestic earthquake on Wellington Crescent.

And police meant Owls. Owls meant everyone had to lie low.

Arnas suddenly looked more ill than I'd seen him before, though, as he looked down at my aunt. *"Deidre."*

It was then her part in this horror show dawned on me. "You were going to use Deedee as a bargaining chip against me. So I'd turn myself in to the Owls in exchange for her life."

Arnas didn't nod, just stared at his hands.

I did the only thing I felt I could. I got over myself. For the moment.

"It'll be all right," I lied.

The BLOODGATE

It was early morning, and I still hadn't slept — I was too wired from the events of the last twenty-four hours. If I could be on the edge of death, entrenched in visions, stop a fire god, and bring two planes together, I figured I could survive a few hours more.

I sent Phae, Barton, and Natti home so they could get some rest. I told them I had some *family business* to take care of. It was the first time in my life I felt I had a family I was responsible for.

I stood in the doorway of Deedee's hospital room, but I didn't go any farther. Arnas sat beside her, not touching her. In these few moments before she woke, he was still innocent, didn't have to ask forgiveness just yet. The heart rate monitor beeped its senseless staccato. Her injuries were only moderate, and she was stable.

I couldn't go in.

I ducked away from Deedee's room and paced down the hall, hiding my face in my hood. I zipped my jacket up higher.

For once I wished I was an Owl, wished I could hide myself from prying eyes by just *imagining* myself invisible. Sil was tucked against me, inside my jacket, growing warmer as I walked. I knew it meant Cecelia was close.

I was relying on Sil, tucked in my jacket, to locate her body; I didn't dare ask a nurse or even look anyone in the eye. It'd been all over the news, apparently, that I'd caused a scene and then leapt to my death. And now my name was being mixed up with the murders of all those girls found on the riverbanks. Probably the doing of that super-psychopath Eli who'd thrown me overboard *for the greater good*. The story was picking up now with the juicy twist of my grandma's ruined home, probably in connection with my crimes. My high school career was over for the foreseeable future. And I was so close, too . . .

"There," Sil said. I backtracked to the room we'd just passed. And, sure enough, there she was.

By some stroke of insane luck (or excellent health insurance), Cecelia had the room to herself. I made sure no one was passing by, and closed the door.

Unzipping my coat, I was careful to keep a hand under Sil's body so she didn't tumble out. I held her under her front legs and lowered her on the end of the bed. She could only keep standing for a few seconds before her paws crumpled underneath her. Cecelia's body didn't move or even register the disturbance — but then again, it wouldn't.

Cecelia's body was Sil's. Sil wasn't her guardian after all. They were one and the same.

Sil closed her eyes, but she seemed to be relaxed rather than in pain. "I'm sorry," she said.

Finally, my legs buckled and I thunked into a plastic chair by the bed. "It's . . . Well. No, it's *not* okay. At all. But there's not much I can do about it, is there?"

Sil — Cecelia? — sighed. "I couldn't tell you. Not until you bested me. Those are the tenets I'm bound by. But I knew you'd come through eventually. You're my granddaughter, after all."

"Oh don't start that," I snapped. "I'm your granddaughter *now*, when you need me. But all this time I've just been an *ungrateful pup*." I was exhausted and cranky, but my hackles were raised, and I was fully awake now. "You spent my entire life keeping me at more than arm's length. Then you turn up again to make me watch you die? Are you going to explain any of that?"

She still hadn't opened her eyes, but her lips were peeling back from her teeth. "I had hoped I could. In time. I didn't plan —"

"Well who did?!" I got to my feet and came around to the back of the chair. I needed something between us. I tried to swallow my words, tried for reason. "Look. I know you saved my life. I know there's a lot more to being a Denizen of Ancient, or whatever, than just getting fed a line, that I've got to earn it and do it myself. I get that. I'm grateful. I am full of grate. But you're my *family*." I choked on the word and cursed myself for tearing up. "You're all I *had*. And you couldn't be bothered to spend time with me because of *duty*, because of some dumbass *rules?* You pretend that you loved Ravenna so much, but you —"

"Ravenna was everything to me!" Sil barked, loud enough to make me nearly topple the visitor chair. At least being closer to her human body was reviving her, but maybe not to my benefit.

She came down from her anger quick, but there was still a bitter snarl on her lips. "I loved my daughter. I loved her enough to stay away." Her eyes were open, but I could see it was a struggle to go on. "She wasn't born with power like mine, but she could do wondrous things. And I liked having control over everything in my life, including her. She wanted a different path than the one I imagined. So she married a Rabbit, went against me to do it. And I hated her for it. I'd been cursed to be Paramount for years, and there was always some enemy I needed to fight, some plot I needed to uncover — never a chance to stop and live. So I threw myself into what needed to be done. And she could be free to live her life, even though I didn't agree with her."

I remembered the letters, then. So many unopened missives to me that ended abruptly when my parents died. Cecelia had admitted on those lines that she'd regretted not being there when I was born, that she couldn't abide Ravenna's marriage to my father. But most of all, I remember, she was relieved to find out —

"Wait. My father was a Rabbit. And my mother was a Fox. What does that mean for *me?*"

Sil looked at me sideways, seemingly irritated that I was making her spell it out. "Aaron raised you. But he was not your father. He couldn't have been. If two separate Families come together and have children, they make humans. Not Denizens." Her voice was sad. "And you are a Fox, through and through."

I definitely didn't need this right now. I shook my head hard. "It's too much." I stifled a half sob, gripping the plastic chair so hard I was afraid I'd melt it. "It's too much for one person. I just can't." Not my real father. Another part of me I thought I was on the way to reclaiming fell away. I felt even further from knowing who I was or could be than ever before.

"I know it is." Sil tried to crawl towards me, a gesture of comfort, but she hadn't the strength to leave the bed. "I *know*. I tried to see you when I could, even though Ravenna and I always ended up arguing . . . and suddenly she was gone. And there was only you." Her ears flattened back, teeth glistening again in a scowl. "And they *marked you* when you were three years old. It sent Ravenna over the edge, and I knew the tenets I'd come to rely on needed undoing. I had to stop it from happening."

I jerked my head up. "What do you mean? I hadn't seen you in fourteen years. You just —"

"Fell off the face of the Earth? Yes, that's exactly where I ended up. I left this world so I could get this body. Because the Paramount is never allowed to intervene with the Moth Queen. But the Paramount's right here" — she pointed her chin at her comatose, shrivelled body on the bed — "and a fox is free to go where she likes. Especially if she knows the way."

I sat down again, too tired to keep up the rage and disappointment. My own body was having a hard time keeping my blood pumping to my brain as I absorbed her words. "It took you *fourteen years* to trade up bodies?"

Sil didn't look at me, just kept her eyes on her human form. "I had to go deep to a place few have been able to in the history of the Families. I did not know that much time had passed. All I knew was that I had to keep going. I couldn't let you slip away from me, like Ravenna. I told her her quest was foolish, selfish. That it wasn't our problem. That she was risking the lives of thousands for one. But I was the foolish one. I should have been at her side."

Her eyes met mine, and the look inside them made my stomach twist hard. "But what I saw down there in the depths of the universe bodes ill for us all. Denizens. Humans. Everyone. Everything. That's why we need to succeed. That's why you must stay alive. Because you need to be the next Fox Paramount. And maybe the last."

As yet another bombshell steamrolled me into silence, Sil's head fell heavy between her paws, and she said no more.

﹏

Sil rested after that. But I felt, for once, like I'd heard enough. I drew my knees up to my mouth and just cried for a while. When I said it was too much, I'd meant it. I'd gone years without really knowing my parents, thinking about them mostly in wild hypotheticals beside what few memories I retained. Deedee filled the role of mentor and mother well enough. Arnas was distant, and now I knew why, but at least he'd been there. My grandmother was an enigma, and while I entertained fantasies of her taking me away on her grand adventures, those wild notions didn't last into my teens.

I could've been okay. I could've moved on with my life despite it all. I mean, aside from the *marked for death* thing.

I'd like to think that now I could've gotten myself out of it, beaten Death back and not asked any questions. Gotten on with things.

But now my story had split off into a high-fantasy redux with lots of horror and enough drama to topple me. There were things I didn't have time to reconcile, or really the brain space to do so. More responsibility. More expectations. More big revelations I couldn't do a damn thing about. More people relying on me *not to fuck it up*, because their deaths would be on my hands.

And now the promise of an end in sight was gone. Because having to kill a baddie in my hometown wasn't bad enough; but the entire world could be at stake, and now I had to take that on, too?

I can't. I CAN'T. I wanted to disappear. I wanted to be the invisible nobody again. *I just wanted to pass my English provincial exam.* I'd always longed for normal, but I'd had it all along. *Roan, you gigantic idiot. You gave it all up for THIS.*

I was all cried out, lobbing these useless, dark thoughts back and forth until I was finally numb. I wanted to get as far away as I could, but I stayed rooted in my misery.

Then something rustled against my cheek — a dust mote, or a curious finger. I opened an eye, and saw a moth flutter by. *Real hygienic*, I thought miserably. Then I opened my spirit eye.

The Moth Queen herself stood silent over Cecelia and her Fox avatar. And me. She was still and all alone, a hundred hands all folded against her furred chest in expectation.

Bleary-eyed and absolutely done with everything, I lifted a hand. "Hey."

She nodded, curious leaf-antennae swivelling like tiny

satellites. "Fox-girl," she said, in her burning cornfield voice.

Her wings flexed but did not open. I looked from the abyss of her sloe eyes to the bodies of my sleeping grandmother. "Who are you here for this time?"

The Moth Queen didn't move — didn't have facial features to arrange in any emotion, really, but I could've swore she smiled. "That is up to you."

There was a thrill in suddenly having agency, a chance to make a choice, but I was too exhausted to run with it. "What do you mean?"

Whatever I'd thought was a smile had become so razor sharp I could cut myself on it. "Death does not explain itself. It only gives. And takes. When it arrives is up to those that need bearing." She reached out a hand to me. It was beautiful, and it was prickly, but I wasn't afraid of it anymore. Death was not the enemy, and this wasn't the Moth Queen of my nightmares. She touched my cheek. She sounded sad. "I wondered if you had had enough, Fox-girl. If you needed me now."

The hand was still close. Though it had been only a vague memory in the passing weeks, the comfort of the Moth Queen's darkness came back to me. The reliability of it. The peace. She was offering me a way out from the responsibility, from the consequences of failing. She was here to grant my wish.

I wanted it. My whole body screamed, *Yes. Please. Make it stop.*

I took her hand in both of mine and held it there. "No. But thanks for thinking of me."

Her wings unfurled like blossoming shadows. She took back her hand and bowed her head, dissolving into so many tiny bodies, each in search of souls that *did* need her. The only thing left of the Moth Queen was a face when she said, "We will see each other again, very soon."

It was just Sil, Cecelia, and me now. I'd given up my get-out-of-jail-free card. But it seemed that Death herself respected the authority of my failing courage, had as much said *now isn't the time to run.*

It wasn't much. But if Death believed in me, I'd better start doing the same.

The hospital room door creaked open, and I threw my legs out of the chair.

"Whoa! Sorry 'bout that, just checkin' on everything in here." The nurse, a tall dirty-blond guy with stubble, strode in around the bed to check Cecelia's various monitors and fluids. I was too startled to pull my hood up and hide my face. Too late now. He'd looked directly at me, glancing away from the IV drip to smile across at me.

"Geez, you look wiped. Your granny here'll be just fine. Just leave 'er with us and get some rest. You can always come back later."

My eyebrows twitched. I looked down at Sil, motionless and breathing slackly at the foot of the bed. "Um," was all I could get out, but the nurse didn't stop looking at me and never even gave the fox a second glance.

And his hand was still on Cecelia's IV line, slowly crushing it.

"Go home. Get some rest," the nurse said again, and I wavered slightly. *Yeah. Rest. Man, I'm so tired. I need . . . I need to sleep —*

My eyes grew heavy, but the one I needed, the one I could rely on, saw through the haze, and I snapped awake, clutching the chair and melting it in my grip as I twisted and hurled it across the bed at the Owl on the other side. A gale whipped up from nothing, and blew me, and the chair with it, back against the hospital room door.

I slammed hard into the door, wind knocked out of me and my back screaming from the impact. I crumpled to the floor, wheezing, trying to keep my spirit eye open and alert against the pain.

The nurse's face, formerly buddy-buddy hippie, rippled like a disturbed parking lot oil slick. "Sorry about that," the face burbled as it rearranged itself. "But I had to make sure it was you."

As I tried to split my focus 50/50 on recovering quickly and not letting my guard down, I realized that somewhere in that murk of sound, was a familiar voice. I forced myself to my feet despite the pain in my back. Whoever he was could still harm Sil. Cecelia. Both.

"I know we've met before, but I'm terrible with faces. Especially when they don't keep still," I choked.

Then the face smiled, and it was whole. Maybe it'd been there all along, but it was taking my brain a bit to catch up with the Owl's illusion. It was that police officer from school. The one with the grey, sad eyes.

"Jordan Seneca," he said, bowing his head slightly. He gestured to the half-melted chair he'd just lobbed back at me. "Do you need to sit?"

"Thanks, I'd rather stand," I shot back, shifting my weight, on the defensive. I felt the air heating up around me; he felt it, too. "What did you mean you had to make sure it was really me?" The hairs on the back of my head crackled like embers.

He held up his hands. "There's no need for that," he sighed. There was another chair on his end, and he pulled it up. He slumped into it, and my pulse calmed. "I don't want to fight you."

"Answer the damn question. Because I'll fight you just for the sake of putting my fist through something, I'm *that* done." I kept my squeezed fists at my side, waiting.

He puffed his cheeks. He looked defeated. "I had to make sure it was you and not another Owl. In case I was walking into a trap."

That got my attention. My mouth scrunched. "What? Trap set by who?"

He smiled. "My cousin. Vindictive little shit. You met him." He clasped his hands between his lean legs. "Eli. He suspects I'm going to try to help you, if you're found alive. Unfortunately for me, he's right."

"What? Wait . . . what?" I felt like I was dreaming of myself onstage, in front of a full house, and I'd forgotten my lines. Where was this coming from? "Don't you and all your winged besties *want me dead*?"

Seneca scoffed. "I don't think anyone knows what they want anymore. Least of all the Owls. All the other Families think we've got it together, that we're this pious pillar of wisdom and guidance and that we *know what's best in the name of Ancient*. But we're questioning things now. We're tired. We want it to end. And we didn't believe it before, but . . . you might actually accomplish what we've resisted for hundreds of years. And it's got them scared."

I came closer to the bedside, antsy about having this guy close enough to Sil to smother her if I wasn't quick enough. I put a hand on her head and she leaned into it, but she didn't wake. I kept Seneca's eyes locked on mine as I stood over my grandmother's two bodies. He blinked. *Owlishly*.

"So the Owls are on my side now? Why?"

He raised a hand. "Slow down there. Mostly just this one." He thumbed at himself. "The majority still think the best bet is to let Zabor have you. But some think otherwise, having now seen what you're capable of. You left a nasty mark on our precious *Paramount*, and the lot of them won't soon forget he's actually fallible." He sneered slightly at that. With all the excitement of *nearly being dead*, I'd forgotten that I had fought back, that I had the upper hand for a second, but blew it. My current running guess had been that this Eli was the de facto leader of Winnipeg's Owls . . . but now I knew he was the Paramount of them all. And I could see why. That kind of role was decided by power, and I wasn't shocked.

"None of them believe you're dead though, least of all Eli, who hates to see a project unfinished," Seneca went on. "So he has us pounding the pavement. Hunting you. Interrogating Denizens. Reaching into human minds that may have seen you. I volunteered to lead the main task force. To be honest, finding you wasn't too hard after what happened at your grandmother's house." He glanced from her to me so fast I barely registered he'd moved his eyes; a true prey bird. "They won't stop. They'll come for your friends. For your aunt and uncle. They'll draw you out. You've seen Eli at work already, not only on yourself but on Arnas. He won't stop until he's fulfilled the task he's being made to carry out. He's sure you'll fail in defeating Zabor, so your only option left is to die."

I let out the breath I'd been holding and closed my eyes, looking inward. It was quiet inside, and I followed my veins as they shunted life through tiny corridors, keeping me upright, holding me together. A body pummelled and hunted and hated, and it still trundled on. Momentum demands that you keep going. The world keeps spinning even when a part of it burns.

Because the world was a body. It had its own order. The Owls believed they were the reason that order was protected, that they were what kept it going. Little did they know that without them, it'd still be what it was: a cycle of death, of a demon's petty revenge. The sleeping god they feared had nothing to do with it.

"It won't stop with me." I opened my mismatched eyes. "And I won't stop, either. Until it does."

We'd exchanged these words already. Seneca, like Death, had come to test my resolve and see if I had any left.

"Good," he said. "Because I'm going to keep them off you, off your family, your little A-Team, for as long as I can. So you can do what you need to."

"Oh yeah?" I challenged. "You'd put your life at risk for me?" But I was grateful for his offer and suddenly felt the relief I'd been craving.

"Not just my life. Everyone's. For their own sakes." And that was it. After all the doubting and the anxiety, we had our Owl. We were Five. All that left now was the targe.

He smiled a little, probably reading my thoughts. "Now, I know you need to get into the legislature, to get to the Bloodgate. They'll have it heavily protected, but there are ways to get in undetected. And I can show you how."

※※

Seneca has promised them a week of lying low and safety. Seven days. This is all they get before they have to dive into hell and somehow come back out.

Barton is in the summoning chamber that his parents had

sealed up years ago, beneath the house he'd grown up in. He could never go to the basement before, anyways, so he'd never been curious enough to check it out for *magical secret rooms*. It smells like Roan's chamber: warm earth, walls made of peat and stones.

"They'll help you," Arnas Harken is saying, nodding towards these miraculous arms. "They'll keep you grounded, which is what you need." The broken man smiles for a second, remembering his training, maybe, but the smile doesn't last. "For this you need to be still. Everything. Your heart. Your brain. Your soul. You're trying to open up the earth, and it answers only to itself. You've got a week to learn how to tame it, so quiet your mind."

Barton's mother and father stand aside from the silver circles glowing dim under the loamy soil. They nod. Barton has learned not to resent them for what they did, especially after seeing the look of desperate understanding in the eyes of the First Rabbit. She had understood their sacrifice. And so does he.

Barton squares his shoulders, the tension there built up from years of compensation. His mind races. The possibilities are endless. He can become the hero he's dreamed of. And most of all, he can stand tall (if only metaphorically) beside Phae. He can be her equal.

Yes. He grounds his palms into the earth, clenching the wet. He thinks of Phae. His mind is still.

"Okay," he breathes, feeling the world in his hands, his heart.

Arnas nods. "Let's begin."

Four days.

Natti stands on the porch of her aunty's house in Point Douglas, staring out into the neighbourhood, into nothing. She thinks about Roan Harken and her friends and the mess they'll be in. She thinks of how different their lives are. She tried not to think about it when they found themselves on Wellington Crescent before the throwdown with Roan's uncle. Now *that* was an eye-opener. White girl from the wealthy suburbs forced to save the world. Not like Natti hasn't heard that story before. But Roan knows less than Natti first assumed. She leans heavily on her friends, asks for help. She needs them. Doesn't presume she can do it without them. At least when it comes down to it, they are all just a scared bunch of kids. But they are willing to do this together. At least she can rely on that.

Natti shakes her head. Her aunt has already warned her that a lot will be resting on her when the *big* throwdown comes — there are very few Seals this far inland in Canada, and she is one of the strongest Winnipeg has. It'll be up to her to listen for the water. And it's already angry. It's already coming for them. Nothing they didn't already know. But Natti can hear it from miles away. The chattering of the river's children with the side-slash mouths. The ice is breaking, and Natti can't freeze it all.

She looks at her hands. She's going to have to try, though. Or at least keep the water at bay, keep Zabor's hunters out of their hair when the big momma herself wakes up. Natti glances back out into the neighbourhood, which reeks of road salt and thawing sewer pipes and smoke, babies crying and women screaming and men yelling. This is *her* place, despite how decrepit it is, despite how someone like Roan

Harken would never come down here for a social visit. This is Natti's stock, and she's always had to prove herself against it. But she wonders now if maybe, despite the world telling her she can't do much . . . that this place is a part of her, and it is worth protecting.

She finds herself slumping down the basement stairs, assaulted with a deep chill and the smell of mildew. Spiders scatter as she removes the cinderblocks on top of the freezer. There's no sound from inside. She unlocks it slowly, steps back a few steps, waits.

The freezer hinges crack like a thunderclap as the baby river hunter bursts out, landing wetly on the cracked concrete of the basement floor. It keens wildly, gaping mouth wide.

Natti doesn't move or try to stop it; she waits.

"Hello, little one," she says in the water-tongue that this creature would know. The language Natti's mother taught her, sang her to sleep with . . . before she became another statistic and disappeared.

The hunter whips its head towards her, a tentative claw in the air, grotesque face hemmed with concern. "Mother?" it mewls, sniffing the air around Natti cautiously. It can smell the Arctic Ocean in her veins — a cleaner, richer scent than the dank death-water it once knew.

So, Aunty was right (was she ever wrong?): kept in seclusion long enough, these things forget where they come from. Forget their loyalty. Most die of loneliness, but this one is strong.

But Natti will not start this creature's second chance at life with a lie. "No, little one," she says. "I am not. But I could be your sister instead, and you could be my brother. Your own creature. If you needed me."

Before she could think, the hunter is in the air, nearly on her, but she puts out a hand and stops it. Her face is stone. She must be the waters of life. She needed to get close to the hunter, to see if it was possible that they could come back. That any hunter could be human again.

She holds firm, as still as a lake. She could be a tsunami, but not yet.

The red eyes of the creature have changed. Now they are a murky green. It looks at Natti's hand, wrapped around its bony wrist in a loose grip. It pulls back its arm and tentatively touches her chubby digits, comparing the hands. Thinking.

"Hm," it grunts, transfixed, still considering. "Sister?"

"Yeah," Natti says, slipping back into English, nodding. "Sister."

❧

Two days.

I flexed my hands, staring at them underneath the table. Only a couple more sleeps, and that'd be it: we either did it, or we didn't.

"You sure you don't want anything, hon?" Deedee asked me, concern filling up the visible part of her forehead underneath the cranial bandage. "You can't just have iced tea. They have red velvet cake, you know!"

I half smiled. *Yeah, we're in Sals . . . I know about their trademark delectables.* "I ate a little while ago, Deedee. No worries." I was lying, as usual, but it came naturally now. I couldn't remember when I last ate. And there were lots of worries more important than red velvet cake. Heapings.

Arnas was elsewhere. Things had been going well with

Barton, but there wasn't much time left to hedge our bets. That was step one; opening the door. If he could do it, I'd still have to go through. I'd volunteered, after all, because I had more experience in other realms than anyone else, and I'd know how to handle myself down there.

But the hypotheticals piled up: If I made it through and couldn't make it back out, then Zabor would still go hungry, demand blood, and it'd be for nothing. My mother had been strong, but even her lifeline snapped.

Couldn't think like that. I needed to relax. Everyone said so. Even Sil, when I went to visit her in the hospital. She'd taken up residence in the bottom of the supply closet in her hospital room, and Seneca made sure everyone thought she was just a pile of old linens that no one could ever move. She still needed rest; she'd had a lot taken out of her. But even in her exhaustion, she just nodded, knowing I could do the thing. And on the rare times I'd seen her in the past week, I hadn't even asked what would be down there waiting for me. I didn't have the energy to think about it.

I pushed the iced tea away. We'd been eating all our meals out and sleeping at the Viscount Gort Hotel. Seneca had fiddled a bit with Deedee's brain while she was out, making her believe she'd come home early and the destruction of the house was due to a water main break and ensuing electrical fire. She'd be fine if her manufactured memories held, and if she never remembered that Arnas had nearly killed her in a possessed fugue state.

I glanced out the window, watching a car slam through an enormous road-puddle. "I can't *believe* this weather!" Deedee crooned, her voice a mix of ecstasy and concern. "I've never seen a spring this early in all my years here. And I can't believe the animals — birds disappearing, deer fleeing upland. It's lucky your grandmother's house is on the safe side of Wellington. Though either way, we might find ourselves house-hunting soon, or kicking out the tenants from your parents' old place, if what they're predicting about the flood is true . . ."

Finding a new home would be the least of our problems, if the river had its way.

※※

Four forty-eight a.m. on the day of the Bloodgate.

Soon.

Seneca is exhausted. His head throbs. He made this commitment to Roan and her friends because he feels in his bones that Denizens must write the Narrative now for themselves if their power, their gift, is to survive in this world. Ancient is too far away to reach, and they have one another for now, at least. That in itself is worth protecting.

But the cost of his promise has been great, even for seven days. It's meant no rest, no sleep, even. It's meant constant vigilance, knowing exactly where the four of them, plus Roan's aunt and uncle, are at all times, and protecting himself from prying questions of his colleagues, his Family. He doubts that any single Owl has attempted to cloak *that* many people at once for more than three days. Since the sheer skull-bleached feeling of insomnia had taken away his ability to care, he wonders if this means he's nearly as powerful as Eli, the main creature he's fought to keep out of his mind.

And the one who batters against his psyche openly now, without restraint.

Just another hour. Seneca thinks, restless and weak. His heart knocks inside him like the victim beneath the floor-boards. *Please, Horned One of my House. Grant me your grace.* Seneca was never one to pray, but he reaches out desper-ately to his First Matriarch now, here in his dark apartment, sprawled on the floor, trying to send his mind out in seven directions. Stretching himself this way is starting to make him hallucinate, make it more difficult to focus on reality. It warps at the edges, threatening to choke him. He resists. He has to stay strong if their plan is to go forward.

Roan Harken. Barton Allen. Phaedrapramit Das. Nattiq Fontaine. Arnas Harken. Deidre Beaumont.

Jordan Seneca.

Protect us.

He was not expecting The First Owl to reply. He barely registers the window crunching from the impact of massive talons. Seneca turns his head, his mind growing fuzzy as he perceives the enormous Owl swooping towards him. *Horned One? Phyr? Queen of the Moon?* Seneca asks it inside his imag-ination, stretching out a hand. The talon wraps around it, squeezing, he at first thinks, in reassurance.

But the feathers melt away like a burnt offering, and the talon becomes a hand, crushing the fine bones of his fingers. Seneca screams, his concentration broken now as Eli pulls him up off the ground. His huge black wings beat a torrent as Seneca's full weight hangs from his broken hand.

Eli is inside his mind in an instant. But it is not just Eli, Seneca realizes dully. He howls in pain from both his hand and his head, filled with the voices of all the Owl Paramounts who came before. They sting his thoughts with poisoned barbs.

Eli sneers. "The Bloodgate under the Black Star? You were going to let them *desecrate our roost?*" He squeezes the hand harder, and Seneca has nothing left in him to fight. "You would go against the Narrative and everything we protect for a worthless *Fox-girl?* Answer me!" Seneca's head dips, limp, but Eli shakes him awake. His silver eyes meet Seneca's exhausted ones. They are defiant. Eli's hand crunches down with such force Seneca can feel his wrist and the bones in his forearm intersecting.

"Traitor," the barbarous voices whisper as Seneca's face whitens. "You will be alert when you're judged for your crimes."

Now Eli is rising higher from the ground, beating backwards through the window and dragging Seneca behind him. His feet catch on the broken glass in the pane, but he clears the window frame, hanging three storeys over the ice and concrete below.

"Please, Eli," Seneca chokes, reaching up weakly with his unbroken hand.

Eli's mouth smiles. "Traitors will not be spared —"

"Not me," Seneca blurts. "The girl. Eli. Please. *Help her.*"

The smile turns into a glistening sneer. Eli lets go of Seneca.

※

I fumbled in my pocket for my phone. It was still early, still dark, but that worked in our favour. The four of us gathered in the shadow of the greenhouse just behind the legislature. This was where Seneca has promised to meet us.

"Where the *hell is he?*" I hissed, spine hunched.

Arnas ducked back amongst us after doing a survey of the area. It was fairly calm down Broadway at this time of morning on a weekend, and we knew where the perimeter cameras were. They were pointed away from us, just like Seneca had said they would be, but without him here, we didn't know how long that would last.

Was he dead? Was he trapped? Had he been caught out helping us? Or maybe it had been a trick all along. Despite my worry, all I could think of was that horrible psycho Eli, grinning over the body of the dead girl all that time ago. My spirit eye revealed nothing, and part of me didn't want to know.

I wished that Sil were here — underhanded, lying, devious grandma or not. She'd always been by my side to tell me off or to save my hide. But this time it was up to me, and she couldn't do much but sleep and gather her strength.

And if I failed . . . I didn't want her to see.

Phae put a reassuring hand on my hunched back. Some of the tension eased off; not sure if that was the Deer in her, or just her homegrown calm. "We all know the plan. We know what we're doing. If he's been compromised, we wouldn't still be here, untouched."

"Phae's right, as per the norm." Barton shifted in his wheelchair, eager to launch. "We'd be swarmed by now, either by Owls or those creepy river-things . . . Uh —" He stopped short and glanced in Natti's direction. She had a river hunter fledgling standing beside her, sniffing the air experimentally, but neither seemed to take offence.

"It's fine," Natti muttered. "Brother will scramble the other hunters if they come. He knows what to do." She didn't touch the creature she called *Brother*, but they shared a significant look. It was hard to believe we'd managed to bring one of them to our side, and while I initially kept my hackles up when Natti had brought him along, we were good so far.

Arnas checked his watch for what felt like the hundredth time, his waves of nervous energy enough to shake me. He was the only "responsible adult" amongst us, but he seemed dubious. "Seneca should've been here half an hour ago. It's the drop time in two minutes. We need to move."

All this time waiting for the big moment, limbs ready to leap in and mind ready to get it over with. Now they froze in the pre-dawn darkness. Point of no return, here we come.

"Right." I exhaled. "Getting in is the easy part. Arnas, Barton, time to set up at the Black Star. Phae, feeling juiced up and ready to cover them, and me if it comes down to it?"

Barton and Phae nodded solemnly.

"Natti, you still good on offense?"

I caught her nod and the jerk of her head towards the river. Brother perked up at her signal, but seemed to hesitate, staring off towards his former frozen dwelling with what might have been fear in those freshwater eyes. He finally took off in a flash of black, slithering up onto the statue of Louis Riel pointing his scroll towards justice and curled himself around the arm, stiff and waiting.

"That leaves me . . ." I shook out my arms, loosening up. "You've all got places to be. But this level's boss is mine."

Barton smiled. "Plus ten bad-ass over here." He squeezed my arm. "We know you can do this, Roan. We've got your back."

I looked round to the lot of them. My friends. My new family, mixed and ragtag as it was. But still mine. They all nodded.

It was time.

Natti did one more visual sweep of the area around the greenhouse. She turned to us and signalled with a raised hand. *Time to fall out.*

Arnas tapped Barton's wheelchair, ducked, and dashed off. Barton peeled after him. They were headed for the back entrance, a service door with a ramp. When they passed through, according to Seneca, they'd look like the next shift's janitors — hopefully this illusion still stuck, seeing as Seneca was nowhere in sight. Natti and I took off to the east side of the building, rounding it as close to the Tyndall stone wall as possible. Phae fell in behind us, but kept back, in case an attack came and we needed shielding. The three of us were headed for the front entrance. Our disguise was admin staff, familiar faces that wouldn't set off any bells. And if we went in the front and were compromised, we'd be the first they'd see — hopefully we could hold any Owl offense off long enough for Arnas and Barton to set up shop on the level below.

I scanned the eaves and crevices of the sculptures surrounding us. Nothing roosted amongst them that I could see, but the stone gazes were relentless, and we felt watched anyway.

I pulled out the keycard that Seneca had given me. "Here we go."

Before I could swipe it, the auto lock clicked and the door swung open.

"Shit," Natti said for us.

I heard Phae's voice catch. "Trap. For sure."

I sighed. I'd seen this coming, but there was no going back. "We're going in."

No one argued or called me crazy. They knew our options were limited.

"Barton . . ." Phae whispered. If the Owls knew about us, then they may have gotten to them first.

"Natti, with me. Phae, head to the Pool. As fast as you can. We're going up."

In my peripheral vision, I caught her nod and, without further comment, we walked in.

The security desk was empty. All the lights were up, as if they were prepping for a gala. The silence was full and alive and treacherous. My heart slammed in my throat.

I signalled to Phae and she slunk off to the left, under the arch. I prayed the others were all right, but the sensible part of me knew better than to hope. Natti took my right, legs spread almost in a boxing stance.

We waited. Silence. I was finally fed up.

"I'm done playing!" I shouted, my words echoing until, by the time they got back to me, the conviction was dead. "Proper hosts would show themselves when a guest arrives!"

Natti inhaled sharply, and I reflexively danced aside from the Owl that had appeared beside me. He stumbled in his strike, and I had my chance to spin, light up an arm, and slam him to the ground with it.

And then the real onslaught started.

A horrible bird-scream clanged like an angry bell in our heads, a sonic wave of rage. Owls peeled from balcony shadows into the light. Figures we'd thought were just other statues melted into men and women. We were surrounded, naturally. Home team advantage.

I grinned. My heart had moved back into its rightful place, and this time it hummed with animal lust for a fight.

I was warming up. Good. "Well, we're all here," I said to the assemblage of assassins, all young, all spoiling. "Might as well do the thing."

A horrible torrent of wind came rushing down on us. I blocked my face and tried to stop myself from getting flattened against the marble tile. I looked up; a clutch of Owls was casting a hurricane, it seemed, more coming in and adding to the surge.

But we could use it to our advantage.

"Natti!" I screamed over the gale.

Despite how loud it was, I could still hear her cynical grunt as she planked hard against the wind. "I can't do anything — not enough . . . moisture."

I raised my head enough to check out the high ceiling. Buried in the beautiful gilded stonework, sprinklers.

"One sec," I shouted, getting into a crouch to face an oncoming Owl skipping in and out of focus from the tornado she was beating with her long, graceful arms. My arms lit up like powder kegs, flames flickering in the gusts but strong enough to overcome them. I eased forward, and found the eye of the storm.

The fire awoke inside; I felt it behind my eyes. I focused it upwards in a pillar, and it caught the turn of the wind. My personal firenado rocketed into the ceiling, and the sprinkler system went off.

The Owls fell back against the blast and the blaze, and I pulled the heat back into me just as Natti launched a tidal fist that knocked them aside.

I shook myself loose. Had to keep moving. With the first wave of Owls broken back, I made for the stairs. The second wave came after us like human bullets, hurling themselves from the balconies around us. I scrambled out of the way, grabbing an offending fist and flame-launching its owner into a bronze bison.

Natti fared better; the sprinklers were still going full force, and she commanded the downpour as though she had made it with her bare hands. Right now she was gathering straggling Owls in a dripping hydrosphere, keeping their heads above water as they struggled. At least she was being gentle.

She caught me half grinning as she pulled a wiry, protesting twenty-something into her baddie bubble. "Don't look at me, get up there!" she grunted. Keeping them contained was obviously putting a strain on her, and who knew how long a window we'd get before the Owls' backup arrived. I snapped to and jogged up the stairs, two at a time.

Inside the rotunda, I stumbled towards the banister and the opening that hovered above the Star we desperately needed.

"Phae!" I threw my head over, searching. There was no one down there that I could see.

But there they were, pushed suddenly into view. Back to back, standing over the Star, and looking up at me. They, too, were surrounded. Barton's wheelchair was overturned, and Arnas was holding his head. Phae was unharmed, but her hands were pinned. They looked done.

Another sonic screech threw me aside; it had come from the entrance. I heard an enormous splash and startled cries. Down went Natti. The stairs and the balconies filled with soaked, beaten Owls, glares fixed on me as they assembled, blocking all exits. Just me, now.

I caught movement above and looked up. Not alone, after all.

Eli Rathgar's charred-black bulk plummeted down from the vaulted dome above, body whistling through something shimmering — a force field, maybe? — and landing heavily on the marble opposite me. He drew up from a crouch to his full height — he wasn't in full Owl-regalia, but some in-between that made him look like a fallen angel after the spin cycle. And I saw his face. Rage didn't begin to describe it.

It was quiet again as we surveyed each other. He drew his wings into his broad shoulders, and I straightened my spine, squaring my feet. His sneer was too deep to even favour any of his redeemable features.

What better time to prod the bastard?

"Sorry I'm late." I turned my palms up. "Thought I'd pop by, seeing as we had such a good time when we saw each other in Osborne. I see you kept my parting gift, though." I gestured at the scar slashed across his forehead under his messy dark fringe, and I saw his fingers twitch, as if he was going to raise his hand and cover it up. His cool façade was slipping.

He moved around the circle slowly, and I followed. A measured, tense dance.

"You know, the last time we met, there wasn't much time for intros, but since then I've heard a lot about you, *Eli*." I figured I could buy us some time. "I'm Roan. Harken. You know my uncle." I motioned down the hole with my head. "You guys hung out recently, I hear. Wasn't a social call though, from my understanding." My chest burned. "I dunno what kind of coward it takes to hurt innocent people to get to *one girl*, even after you'd already killed me. But being smarter than everyone else must bore the hell out of you, so I get that possessing my uncle and trying to kill my aunt was probably just *recreational*."

Eli scoffed. "Spare me the rhetoric." He slid his hand along the balustrade, glancing down into it like a cat over a koi pond. "Rebels have loved ones. They're useful, and they yield results. But your friends are more powerful than we first thought." His fist tensed and then relaxed, nails turning black and flashing into talons. "Tell me who it was who uncursed your snivelling Rabbit uncle. Call me curious."

I knew he meant Sil, but I wouldn't give her more than a flash of a thought. I wiped my mind clean and laughed. "You think I'm that easy? C'mon. Thought you were tired of the rhetoric. If you're here to kill me, get it over with."

Eli wanted my blood there and then, but he rearranged his face, forcing a sadistic smile as he looked down into the Pool of the Black Star. "Why expend the energy? You're going to do that for me."

I stopped and followed his glare. My cool was wavering, breaking. I feigned indifference. "Oh, what, you're going to kill my friends, then, if I don't do what you want? Man, that's getting as old as your vendetta. Either do the job right or don't do it at all."

He chuckled and shook his head as though I'd told a good-natured joke over cocktails. "Me? You want to heap the blame on *me*? You bring harm to anyone who rallies around you. You lie to them, promising you'll save them. Speaking of, after all he did for you, you haven't even *asked* about Seneca. I can see how much loyalty really means to you."

I clenched my fists so hard my nails bit into the flesh. My spirit eye rumbled, and pasted over Eli's smug, lean coolness, was the image of Seneca howling and broken, flying through space and smashing into pieces. His light was faded, but not gone. Nearly, though. But from the periphery of his pain, I caught no regret.

"Yeah. He helped me. Because he's sick of this, just like all the other Denizens you lord over. Seneca wanted to end it, and he did a damn good job until you *jumped him*. Which is pretty messed, since I heard you were family."

I caught the uncertainty of Eli's gathered thugs, especially those down below — exchanged glances, shifting feet. Eli whipped his head in their direction, and there was stillness again.

This time, I spoke more to them than him. "Did you or any of your cronies ever stop to wonder *why* they're on your side? That maybe you're the batshit lunatic in all this, seeing as your solution to keeping the death toll down is *more killing*? I'm sure no one's doing your bidding out of *loyalty*. But lies get the job done, too, I guess."

No one spoke to defend themselves, and I hadn't expected them to. I just wanted to hear the rusted cogs in their brainwashed, fear-addled heads turn.

I felt air on my cheek and saw that Eli's wings were flexing. I cringed against it, which made him smile.

"They're not loyal to me, no." He put a hand absently over his chest. His eyes changed; the one that Death had given me twitched. What was I trying to see . . . ?

Then his voice changed, too. "They're loyal to Ancient. To tradition. To the Narrative. This is the way things are. And they must be carried out for the good of nature's unfolding story. That's what the Owls protect; the Ancient knowledge. Deviating will bring our ruin."

My spirit eye wavered but lost the transmission it'd been searching for. "Oh, blah blah with your bullshit!" I shouted, my skin a warming stove element. "The greater good argument is for fascists and people too stupid to open their eyes. Your fight is with me. Let my friends go, and we duke it out. If you win this time, I'll do it. I'll fulfill your little horror story. Everyone will know that I stood here and called you out because I want that water witch gone, and we aren't going to stand for Owls telling the rest of us how to live or who's snake chow at the end of winter. After that, you can answer to all your *people* and the Denizens you pretend to protect when you had a chance to end this, and you didn't. For the greater good."

Eli stood still enough that I thought I was talking to a marble likeness instead of a breathing human — though I wouldn't exaggerate and pretend he had a soul. My spirit eye couldn't penetrate him, his darkened visage, his chest. I doubt I'd gotten through to him, but . . . gods, at this point, I'd take what I could get.

"You know nothing!" he barked, wings fissuring wide with a thunderclap. "You choose now! Your friends or you. There's no middle ground!"

My ear twitched. I heard a whisper, familiar now as it was when I was submerged in the river, or when I stood in Natti's living room as she and Aunty murmured in that watery language. It was faint, a plea. Then a sharp wail sounded, distant enough to be mistaken for a sharp winter wind. Eli and the rest of the Owls collectively swivelled towards the noise, eyes widening as a black fume clouded the windows of the rotunda.

I smiled. "Cavalry's here."

The quarterpaned windows crunched inwards. River hunters, hundreds of them, poured in, landing on the marble with wet *splorps* like raining offal. Some landed on the unfortunate Owls and proceeded to grind through the ranks until they fell back into their own fights. Brother led the charge, ripped-open vertical mouth screeching a battle cry.

I heard shouts and bodies hitting the floor below, the shrieking of the hunters drowning out any doubt I had. Arnas cried, "Barton, now!" and the ground began to quake. Eli nearly dove through the pit after him, but I launched onto him, grabbing him by the wing and hurling him away from the opening. The anguish in his guttural yell fuelled me, and for a second I imagined that my hair was flames and I'd grown as large as a pyre.

Eli looked at me with something like shock, until his face contorted and he lunged for me.

❧

Now Barton is just showing off; he knows it, too, but he can't help the glee pulsing through him as the stone floor shatters underneath the Owl fighters gunning for them and reshapes into sharpened plinths to form a protective ring around the black star set into the floor. All from one slam of his fist into the ground, turning and tightening as he manipulates the very floor. The spikes leap up, slamming one man aside who'd nearly fallen on top of Phae.

She pivots and pins him with those big beautiful eyes, and he's suddenly sheepish but proud that this time it's him saving her. Phae smiles, dark eyes eclipsed by her power, hair braiding upwards as she raises a small shield around them. Barton knows this shield is temporary, though, as Phae scampers off through the melee to see if Natti or Roan need protecting.

"Are you ready for this?" Arnas asks from the opposite end

of the Star, on the other side of the stone barricade. There's nothing he can offer Barton now except encouragement.

Barton looks down at the black shapes under him, feels the rings sending shivers from the earth into his body as he imitates a lotus pose, hands hovering. He grounds himself in those vibrations with his palms, and looks up, barely nodding. This is his time.

He breathes, holding his hands out. "I present this spirit in the hall of the Star, under the gaze of Ancient, as it turns to us all by the grace given to the Five that came before us." His fingers twitch in the patterns he has memorized, has practised for hours, pulling the whispers of spirits from the crust to perform a dance older than the world. "I call to those loyal to this sphere, to rouse and place yourselves on my name. I command that the Earth be pulled in the four directions, and the Ring of Shadows be open to the living."

The glow of the golden circles intensifies, hotter than Barton had ever felt in his parents' summoning chamber, brighter than Arnas warned. His hands quiver, arms exploding into roots as they shoot hard into the star, and he wavers. Arnas reaches out as though he is trying to catch a tipping vase, but Barton grunts, trying to hold it together. There is a fist in his chest, tightening, but he can't stop now. The plates of the world are shifting.

"To the earth, the element that my house bears! Spirits of mountains, place your wills on my name, as is my right to ask! Open the heart of this Star and reveal the Bloodlands below!"

There is a crack like the bones of the world splitting apart, and the quaking becomes seismic.

❧

I heard Barton shouting, but my ears were ringing from the blow I'd just deflected off my ear. I staggered. Everything was chaos; the screams of both Owl and river hunter from the antechamber, the world shaking itself to dust all around us, and Eli Rathgar gunning for me again with death behind his snarled lips. I wheeled and ducked, his rage gradually changing him into the thing Sil called Therion that I'd first faced. I was losing energy, and I tasted blood. This seemed way too familiar. I was distracted — I knew I had it in me, knew I could be a pillar of light. I needed to get back into the fight.

I weaved and threw a fist like a flaming hammer at him, catching him in the gut. He lost loft for a second, but sank his talons into my shoulders and dragged me into the air. With a scream, he spun like a sadistic slingshot and threw me at the dome. I slammed into the shimmering barrier that I'd seen earlier, probably an illusion, but it could've been steel for the pain it shot through me. I crumpled, vision sparking, and fell.

Roan, someone whispered. *Ignite*.

I snapped awake and felt like a shooting star with a grudge. I curled inwards and blasted flames from my pores. They pushed me aloft like rocket fuel and I righted myself, careening meteoric towards Eli.

Crunch. I couldn't tell whether the sound was Eli's bones, or the stone we'd slammed into. There was a roar in my ears — not blood, but heat, and I only caught myself in his large, suddenly golden eyes; me, but not me at all. A Fox. A flame. A comet. A goddess.

A sonic boom and a crash of wind threw me aside, and Eli dragged his bloody wings from the stone, his clothes and feathers burnt and melting as he tried to compose himself.

He gripped the busted wall with his talons as I spun like a sparkler to the ground. He launched at me with a predator's cry, and I leapt backwards, blasting the floor with firepower until I was aloft again. I roared forward and wrapped myself around him.

Eli's faltering wings beat the air and his fists beat me. He howled, unable to keep his form. His owl-face was flickering in and out, until those golden eyes gave way to the desperate man underneath, burnt and beaten. "You can't win!" he screamed, wings beating furiously, wind doing nothing to extinguish my fire. "You can't kill me!"

I wrapped my legs around him and grabbed either side of his head. We'd been whirling around the rotunda like a dervish, but now we were above the Pool. Stricken, he looked into my eyes as the fire peeled away from me like petals.

"I'm not here to kill you," my fire whispered. "We're going down together."

Before he could snarl, I slammed my skull into his, and his wings folded. We tipped over, plummeting headfirst past the balustrade, black feathers exploding around our bodies as we careened into a net of golden strands, through the bones of the Earth, and into the Bloodlands.

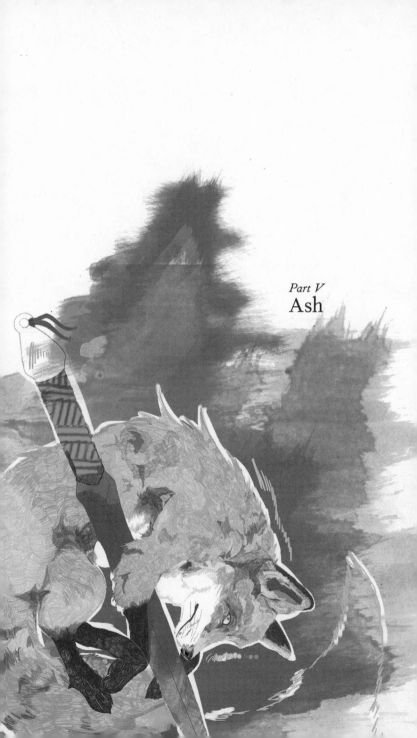

Part V
Ash

The GARDENER *and the* TARGE

Eli was a boy, once. His thoughts were his own. They were not partitioned from the hundred thousand thoughts of everyone around him. They were free to weave in and out with the whispers of the world. His mother taught him everything, despite her illness. Despite how sometimes she was not herself. He learned much, and he loved her for it. They only had each other to rely on, after all.

But the whispers of the minds among which he grew up were alien to him now, for all he'd heard for so long were the voices of his ancestors, beating raging wings against his better judgment. He'd lost himself to their bidding. He had known cruelty, swore never to give it, and yet he dealt it so easily now.

These strange, furious minds had been guiding him all this time, because of his willingness to obey and serve. Because he was told it would help save everyone from a terrible danger. In return, they'd given him a conduit for his incredible, frightening power that he barely understood, even now, at twenty-five. But he'd lost himself in the deluge of power. He had forgotten what it was to love or dream or desire.

Now he can't hear them at all.

For the first time in years, Eli feels relief. And he falls willingly into the arms of shadows, grateful for silence.

⋙⋘

I smelled burning. *Can't be the coffee, Deedee wouldn't leave it until it was done. Maybe breakfast? But I don't hear anyone downstairs . . .* I pressed my eyes hard into my skull to cease the pounding. I didn't want to wake up just yet. I'd been having weird dreams lately, which didn't exactly leave me feeling rested. And I couldn't remember if I had homework due today. Probably just essay prep. I could ask Phae when I got to school, though I know she'd make fun of me for being out of it. Lately I'd had a penchant for rereading *Game of Thrones* until the wee hours — my *fantasy dramas* Phae called them — and now my dreams were saturated with me in the hero-role, blood in my mouth and death on my heels at every turn.

Death . . .

My stomach churned, and I bolted up in time to vomit down my front.

My eyes opened. No coffee. No Deedee. Not Kansas anymore. Just the stench of burning, and an ashy haze blocking any discernible feature that could tell me where I was. Any life I had outside of here seemed as far away as a dream.

I spat and wiped my mouth, trying to stabilize as I shuddered through another impulse to heave, but thankfully nothing came. *Ugh, my head.* I massaged my scalp, trying to fight off each wave of nausea. Maybe I'd hit my head, and I was coming out of a concussion? I had no idea how I'd ended up unconscious, though. I kept having mental flickers that I was in my bed, and then not, the disorientation growing heavier the longer I thought about it. I tried to cup my skull in both hands, but when I pulled my left wrist up, I realized there was something heavy attached to it — another arm. Another person.

It was a boy — no, a man. Couldn't tell his age, but older than me. He was still out, but his face was relaxed, eyes completely still beneath their lids. He seemed serene enough, even though his face had been recently burned, and there was blood splattered across a cheek. He'd just been in a fight, then, which meant he might be dangerous. And I was tied to him.

I examined the rope binding us together. It looked and felt like a fine chain, golden and radiating in the ashy air. It was twined tight around us, and when I yanked it up, I heard the faint tinkling of another chain behind us. I squinted, trying to ascertain where it ended, but it seemed to curve up off the ground and disappear into the haze.

With my pal knocked out, I wasn't going anywhere to investigate, though. I brought my free hand around and touched his chest to make sure he was still breathing, but rather than warmth, I felt something hard under his tattered shirt. I pushed it aside and saw a rough, glinting stone embedded in the flesh of his sternum like a geode, white with flecks of black.

His hand shot up and crushed my wrist. Before I could feel relieved that he was awake, he had rolled on top of me and was trying to choke me.

"The hell!" I gargled, bucking until I managed to knee him in the gut and kick him aside. I didn't get far from him before the chain yanked my arm back.

He recovered quickly and attacked again. I caught his incoming hand and held ground. "Who are you?" he screamed.

"Calm down, okay?" I grunted. "I don't want to fight you. I have as little intel on what's going on as you do. You think I'd deliberately chain myself to some psycho?" I nodded to our bonded arms, and he seemed to relent, but barely.

"I'll ask you again: Who are you?" He hissed the words through his teeth, his inability to back off frustrating him more.

"I'm —" I caught myself, touching my head. I felt sick again and staggered forward to one knee, heaving up a mouthful of bile.

"What's the matter with you?" He pulled our arms up, which actually managed to get me to my feet again, except I bumped into him and had to rely on being steadied by the hands that had just tried to choke me.

"I don't . . . I don't know." I shuddered and pushed myself away from him. "I just . . . I tried to think of my name and —" I swallowed and gagged.

He was silent as I composed myself, surveying our surroundings. "I can't remember my name, either," he remarked absently, like losing his identity was a footnote. "Do you know where we are?"

"Yeah, I come here all the time, my kind of place," I

replied dryly. The air seemed to be growing hotter and thicker, and I coughed. "You?"

Rather than offering insight, I tripped as he started off to investigate, dragging me with him. "Hey!" I brought him up short by yanking on my arm. "A little warning before you go traipsing into the wilderness? We're not exactly independent units here."

Startled, he looked over our arms. "Fine. Try to keep up." But we soon found that the harder he pulled, the tighter the chain became, and we both winced. "What kind of sorcery is this?" he muttered, crossing our arms to grab the length trailing behind us, as we followed it awkwardly through the gloom.

"Sorcery?" I couldn't help but snort. "Like what? We fell into someone's D&D campaign in their parents' basement?"

"Is sarcasm your native language?" my cohort snapped. "What I'd give to be chained to someone *useful*."

I felt sheepish and bit the inside of my mouth. He had an educated brogue, full of condescension and entitlement. I knew I should be annoyed, but it just made me feel like a dumb Canadian nobody.

"Sorry. I get weird when I'm stressed. Besides, a little humour doesn't hurt in a situation like this."

He snorted, the chain sliding through his free hand as we trudged. "So you routinely find yourself in *situations like this*?"

I shrugged, no immediate recollections swimming to the surface to prove him wrong. "To be honest, I don't know. But I feel like I probably do."

I could hear the eye roll without looking at him. "Comforting."

We suddenly reached the end of the chain, which seemed to continue upwards and disappear into the fog. Our little quest had hit a wall. Literally.

I didn't have any clever quips this time, just chewed my mouth hard enough to break the skin. Because this meant we were trapped, and unarmed, and in a valley of some kind, with no clue as to what else could be down here with us. I tried to swallow my rising panic.

My fellow prisoner silently felt the rock face for climbable notches. Then he turned to me with what might have been an attempt at good-natured sarcasm. "We're in a pit."

My chest tightened. "Ugh."

He touched the wall again. "Look, there's no sense getting hysterical."

"I wasn't!" I shouted, but I was heading there.

He lifted his arm and shook it at me. "Well, if one of us goes down, the other is fairly screwed. We'll need to have our heads if we're going to get out of this."

He'd literally just tried to choke me, and now it was about teamwork? Even if he was trying to reassure me —

"Wait, shh," I hissed, wrapping my bound hand around his wrist and jerking him back. I flexed my feet, testing the ground beneath us. It was hard to tell in the gloom, and it had felt soft when we woke up — soft enough for me to mistake it for my bed — but . . .

"Did you feel the ground move just now?"

He cocked an eyebrow, bent down, and felt around with his free hand to humour me. "Ugh!" He jerked back upright with a glistening handful of mucus.

I screamed, trying to stagger away from him. I tripped over what felt like an upturned root and pulled the both of us down, dragging him on top of me as I rolled and pressed my face to the ground.

It was ribbed and warm and the slime gelatinous, but the ground was definitely not ground at all, which I discovered only as a huge grey worm pulled free of the tangle of bodies, and seemed to look me directly in the eye.

"Fuck!" I screamed, struggling to get out from under my partner-in-slime and hoist him back to his feet. "Worms! God! Why did it have to be worms?!"

"What the hell *is* this place?" he said through gritted teeth, suffering from as much a case of the heebs as I was.

Pain stabbed through my brain, and I tried to catch my head in my hands. The world was spinning.

"Get up!" he exclaimed, crouching to tear my hands away from my head and pull me back up. But he stopped. "Don't move," he hissed, his hands coming round to the back of my head. "You've . . . there's . . ."

I froze as he guided my free hand to the soft, throbbing thing planted at the base of my skull. I whimpered but stayed still as I tightened my fist around the offending globule, and yanked until it was free. I whined through my nose and saw the underside of the worm — rows of thistle-teeth with dollops of my blood still fresh on them, and a giant sucker-mouth in the middle of its terrible body, tasting the air as if my brain was just out of its reach. It convulsed and let out a shattering wail, which was answered in kind under our feet.

"Shit goddammit," I shuddered, throwing the thing away like a live grenade. My head thrummed, but the pain was gone. I felt clearer. "My name is Roan Harken," I choked, before the world toppled and the ground surged.

We were thrown aside and stopped only by the pit wall. The wailing got higher and louder, and all we could do was cover our ears and shout.

"You can remember?" my cohort screamed.

I dared to think about it and found no nausea fly up to meet it. I suspended reality (however much there was left) and guessed that the worm on my head had been feeding on my memories and making a damn fine feast of them. But some things were coming back: We weren't down here by accident, but by design — *my* design. I'd brought us here. I was still fuzzy on the why.

"Sort of," I admitted. "But I still have no idea what the hell we're going to do about *them*."

The worms had decided, apparently, that it'd be a better bet to join together and take us out at once. Their bodies wound into one massive, throbbing worm, pulling away from the ground and looming over us with a thousand aggravated squeals.

And the squeals formed a gut-piercing word: "HUNGRY!"

I was pulled roughly to my feet. "Get behind me!"

This was an awkward request, given the chained-up-ed-ness going on, and I was in no mood to let this random whackadoo be chivalrous. "Why?" I shouted. "What the hell can *you* do to get us out of this?"

His expression went from heroic to blank. The shrieking mass-worm pitched down and launched at us. It had a hundred piercing sucker-mouths and zero patience for us.

I pushed my prison-mate back and held my free hand up. I felt a slight tingle from my elbow to my fingertips, but I definitely wasn't expecting the air in my palm to catch fire and launch a comet's blaze at the hungry, writhing mass.

The heat was explosive, and my cohort reactionary —
he leapt to the side and dragged me down with him, so that
we were a bundle of limbs tumbling out of the way of slimy,
charred offal raining down on our heads.

"What the hell was *that*?" my buddy-in-arms shouted in
my face before being clocked in the side of the face with a
screaming wretch-worm detached from its hive. Half burnt,
the thing still had some kick left in it, and when I ripped it
off my cohort's head, it sizzled in my palms like a live steak.

"Agh!" I hurled it away from us, but I could see that the
worms that had survived my attack were regrouping. A
second layer of demon-slugs was churning up from under
our feet, too, respawning for the next wave.

My friend was blank again. "Is this really happening?
What's —"

"No time." I yanked us over, my hands feeling for the wall
of the pit. "I could probably barbecue these things all day,
but I have a feeling there's an infinite supply of them down
here." I felt around, but the rock was flat. "Dammit! Can't
climb out, can't see a foot in front of us, going to be eaten by
giant-ass worms . . . don't you have *anything* to contribute?"
I whirled on him, indignant. "What were you gonna do back
there with the big one, anyway? Stare vacantly at them until
they got bored?"

It was his turn to scowl. "I don't just stare at things! I got
that thing off your head, remember? Before that you were as
useful as a paperweight. Maybe if I —"

He stopped midsentence, and our chained-hands slapped
the back of his neck. Sure enough, dug deep in his black
hair . . .

Schplorp. The memory-eating slug pulled away with a

horrible sucking noise and a cry of dismay, cheated out of its meal. Luckily my hot-plate hands charred it to silence.

At first, he smiled with relief, then he clutched his chest, bringing me up short and so close to him that I was immediately uncomfortable. "Wha-what's going on?"

It was like a sea of ice was pressed between us — cold and harsh and powerful enough to capsize me. Whatever fire was inside of my body shrank from it, and I managed to push away his shirt to reveal the rough-cut stone I'd seen earlier.

It was pulsing in short bursts of white light, with a flicker of gold at the centre. When I looked back up into his eyes for an explanation, they were clear as the cold shard under my hand.

"My name is Eli Rathgar," he said. Then he put the other arm around me and held me tight. "And I think I have a way out of this."

"What the hell are you —" I blurted, but then he tilted his head upwards and closed his eyes as if I wasn't there.

I felt his body heave, and with a grunt two huge *somethings* crackled and burst out of the back of his already wrecked shirt. They were huge and black and heavy.

I gaped, resisting the urge to pump my fist. Instead, I swallowed and held on. With a slight bend in his knees, Eli launched upward, wings stirring the grey fumes to reveal the thousands of worms rearing up and shrieking at their meal's getaway.

My stomach flipped as we climbed, and I opted to look out and around for a sign of level ground. When we finally broke through the fog and the dark, I let myself get excited.

"I hope you know how to land this thing!" I shouted over the rushing air. He grinned at that, and in a swoop we banked, coming down like a diving swallow until he pulled up short, beat his enormous wings, and brought us to rights with a single step to the ground.

I let out the breath I was holding. "Wow. I take it back. You've definitely shot up the what-are-you-good-for pyramid." I disengaged from him gingerly because he hadn't yet let go. Before, his eyes had been human and affable. Now they were intense and unrelenting. They were weighing me as though he'd never seen me before.

I backed up as far as our short leash would allow. "Uh . . . what's up?"

He snapped his arm up and mine along with it, the golden chain glinting in the grey light. He wasn't studying the chain — he was studying me.

"Your eyes. They're different colours." His head tilted, like an animal's. I didn't contradict him.

"What else do you remember, before coming here?" he asked coolly — a demand more than a question — and he sounded accustomed to having those demands met.

I flinched, but he wouldn't put his arm down. "Like I said, not much. My name, my . . . family . . . I live with my aunt and uncle, but . . . we were staying with my grandmother. No. Not *with* her. In her . . . house." Then an image flashed over the vision in my left eye, and I jerked. Superimposed over Eli's face was an owl — the piercing golden glare of a prey animal about to clamp down with its powerful beak. His hand was an obsidian set of razor talons. And the feathers of his face concealed a hatred I recognized.

Then warmth and terror cascaded across my sight, a tidal wave that sent me reeling and trying to shut it out. I couldn't make sense of it — a woman who was also a fox made of towering flames, rabbits with severed limbs, and a girl with hair-antlers. An Inuit teen divided a river, a man with dark wings and a vendetta.

And an enormous snake-woman with her mouth open.

I swallowed my gorge before it came up again, and when the images finally dissolved, I focused again on Eli, who hadn't moved.

"I can't . . . make sense of my memories," I lied. Things were still blurry, but I knew that he and I were not allies.

He finally blinked — for a second I thought his eyes had changed. "Neither can I. But I have a feeling I want to kill you." He pulled a bit against the chain binding us together, testing it. "Which would be inconvenient, given our current state of . . . dependency."

I swallowed but couldn't help cocking an eyebrow. "Wouldn't want to cramp your style with my bloated corpse or anything."

His mouth twitched, but he fought the grin. I assumed showing any good humour was against his character; no wonder he wanted to kill me. "Look," I tried, "we are down here for a reason. And we're down here together. I don't think that was an accident, but because I planned it. And I don't think I would've put us together so *intimately* if I wanted us to fail or I was remotely suicidal. I'm guessing, anyway." I stepped closer, keeping eye contact and trying to assert myself, despite being a head shorter than him. "Like you said down in the pit. We have to work together if we're going to get out of this. So maybe put aside the homicidal yearnings for just a little while longer, and I promise we can get back to each other's throats once this is done. How's that sound?"

Eli's nostrils flared, but he didn't say anything. Then he winced again, clutching his chest. "Ugh . . . can't you hear that?"

"What?" I took a panicked look around; it was slightly brighter out here, and I could make out the dark shapes of twisted trees in the distance, tendrils of acrid smoke-fog still crept around our ankles. Though we'd been expertly pounced-upon earlier, it was quiet. I wondered how long that'd last.

Then Eli parted his shirt, chin down as he examined the stone in his chest. Seeing it up close now, it almost looked as though the stone was growing as a fungus would; there were smaller, glittering "spores" around the source stone, pushing the flesh away wherever it grew. It was still glowing, and I didn't dare touch it.

Instead, I took a chance while Eli was mesmerized. "What is it?"

He sighed for a moment, searching for the answer behind closed eyes. "The Tradewind Moonstone. I . . . earned it." When his eyes opened, they'd lost their intensity, and they seemed sad. "I can't remember why I wanted it. And I think it's . . . speaking to me now. There are many voices in my head. They told me how to get us out of that pit back there. And they're telling me that you need to die. But I'm able to resist their influence, and I don't think they're pleased. I . . . know how crazy this all sounds. A talking stone with a mind of its own."

I frowned, but didn't question him. I had a feeling all this stuff was legit, despite my immediate skepticism. I decided to meet him halfway.

"When I looked at you just now . . . you were an owl. I

could only see it through this eye." I pointed at my left. He nodded. "And I saw all kinds of other things, things that might seem crazy, too, but . . ." I looked down at my palms. "I can shoot fire out of my hands. We're on an even playing field."

He covered the stone with the tatters of his shirt. "You've got a point —"

An explosion rocked the air. I wheeled one arm, and we just caught ourselves in time for another horrible *boom* that sent us reeling again. The almost-thunder continued on with a steady beat. Then it stopped. My ears and knees rang with the reverberations, and I peered past Eli into the black knot of trees a hundred feet away, just in time to see a big one come crashing down. The fog and the dirt settled, but in the wake of the fallout, a peal of agonized screams followed, much worse and more pained than the worms. What the hell *was* this place? We looked at each other.

Eli squinted into the distance. "I have a feeling our time is limited, so we'd better get started doing . . . whatever it is."

I don't know how, but I suddenly felt he knew *exactly* where we were, and what would happen once we entered the dark bones of the woods. I wondered how long it'd take for the dazzling stone in his chest to convince him to cut the chain holding us together and leave me here to die.

I clenched my fists; they were warm, and that warmth tingled and spread throughout my limbs. He may have flight, but I could burn those wings off him if I needed to. I forced my face to become a blank slate, trying to prepare for whatever betrayal or pitfall I was about to face.

"Let's get a move on, then." I steeled myself as we set off at an even, cautious pace, the chain around our arms tightening as we headed for the trees.

Phae helps Natti up off the floor, making sure she hasn't sustained any injuries. The Owls around them seem lost now without their leader. Which means that Roan has succeeded — so far.

The doors of the legislative building crack open, and in come more men and women — older, less intimidating, yet purpled with rage all the same.

"What is the *meaning* of this?" shrieks the large man in the front.

Alien, horrible cries rise up to meet the challenge. The river hunters, led by Brother, slink from the shadows with their sideways teeth bared and throats chattering for more bloodshed.

Unsure, but tense for another round, Natti elbows Phae behind her. "Get back there and put up one of your fancy shields. Your other one is probably down by now."

Phae scampers away, leaving Natti to it. Although the sprinklers have run their course, there's still some errant puddles lying around, just enough to . . .

Another man, one with an ample steel-grey mane, strides forward and brings with him a storm-wind so fierce that Natti is lifted then dropped hard enough for her to lose her breath. She watches in dismay as the water dries up around her. The hunters shriek, skittering into shadows or heading for the broken windows from whence they'd come. Without water, their allegiance is broken.

But Brother lays his river-reeking body over Natti's and hisses venom as the powerful Owl approaches her. He stops. "This hunter is protecting you? How?"

Natti puts a hand on Brother's nearest claw, gently pushing him away. Though he obeys, he does not go far.

"He's protecting our *interests*, you could say." Natti wipes a hand past her lip to remove the blood there. Giving the man a once-over, Natti recognizes him. "You're *his* father, then. The nasty one that was after Roan."

The man's sharp eyes narrow. "Where is Eli?"

Natti straightens to her full height, standing tall despite barely exceeding five feet.

Natti snorts, making a decision. "This way," she turns, motioning for Brother to watch the man and his entourage as they make their way to the Pool of the Black Star. The other Owls, dumbstruck, come out of their shocked paralysis and follow.

Barton is still in the same spot, the marble tiles around his spirit-arms crumbling into finer and finer pieces as the roots penetrate for a stronger hold. Arnas is muttering reassurances, telling his pupil to *just hold on, just a little longer*, but Natti can see that keeping the gateway open is taking its toll. The golden rings set in the ground are fixed and strobing, and Barton shudders, eyes screwed shut, threads of light clinging to his shoulders.

As they get closer, Natti realizes that they aren't threads, but chains. They are knotted between Barton's limbs like a cat's cradle, and they culminate in one line, which feeds into the pit the newborn Rabbit is straining to keep open. The crumbled tile floats around the black cavern, tiny fingers of lightning bouncing off each shard. There is a foul grave stench coming from the pit.

"By all that is Ancient . . ." a woman with raven hair murmurs. "They've opened the Bloodgate."

Another man sputters, "Solomon, do something! Arrest them, close the portal! Who knows what could come out of that hole!"

Solomon stares into the pit, wordless. Phae and Natti exchange glances. They have nothing left to fight with now, fully surrounded and outnumbered, with maybe one river hunter to their name against dozens of Owls, and what appears to be their interim leader, now that Eli is gone. And if this *is* Eli's father, then surely he wants the same end for Roan that his son so desperately desires.

But Solomon does not look away from the open gateway, eyes fixed on the chain that vanishes down into it.

"My son is down there, isn't he." His voice is soft, and it isn't a question.

Natti nods. "They're down there together. They're going after the targe."

Solomon swallows. But the first man, wiry and furious, gnashes his teeth. "The *targe*!" he all but screams. "Stop this abomination now! The Fox-girl —"

"*My son*," Solomon bellows, and the chamber is silent — even he did not expect the words to rush out, but they are painful and necessary, another wound opening afresh.

Solomon turns to them all, Natti and Phae included. "The Narrative has changed. We were fools to believe it wouldn't. The time has come to realize we are custodians of a dead god, and our story is ours to shape." He turns back to the maw in the earth, expanding and shrinking, it seems, as the Rabbit beyond the edge strains to control it.

"And whatever the girl's fate or my son's crimes . . ." Solomon cannot bear to recall his nephew's broken body, barely clinging to life, but he forces himself to revisit the image, knowing it was the doing of his son and the thing he has become. ". . . they will be judged accordingly if they survive. The Narrative is in *their* hands, now."

～⚮～

The trees grew thicker the farther in we went. They were all dead, branches twisted and burnt yet stretched towards the misty light in a murky sky. I coughed, nostrils stinging from the bitter smoke.

"Wonder where the source of the fire is," I asked, less looking for an answer and more trying to fill the silence. We hadn't heard any more screams or booming for a while, and Eli had retreated into himself.

He made a face and grunted through his nose. "I think this entire *place* is just a landscape of ash. Hell's aftermath, or something like it."

That we'd stumbled into *some kind of* hell made sense, given how nightmare fodder was pretty much everywhere we looked.

I glanced behind us, the single chain that tethered us together dragging softly in our wake. Taking a longer look, I saw it extended way back past the horizon where we had begun. Seeing it reassured me there was a way out of this place, but the clock felt like it was ticking, and going back empty-handed didn't seem like an option. The truth hovered beyond the smoke around us.

"Wonder how much more of a leash we have," I muttered. Eli stared straight ahead, his eyes seeming to change colour from grey to gold. Maybe a trick of the nonlight. Or maybe he was fighting the urge to choke me to death with my sarcasm and stupid questions.

He looked my way and my cheeks burned, and not in a *human-torch* sort of way. Why the hell was I *blushing?* In the silence I'd remembered clearly that this guy wanted me dead, somewhere in his heart of hearts. Maybe we were dating? No, that sounded *way wrong.* Then I realized that I maybe wanted his respect, or at least his trust. Or maybe I was just embarrassed that he'd caught me looking, because I was a terrible sleuth . . . "You're not *terrible*, but you could work on the subtlety," he mused.

I flinched and went from embarrassment to wrath. "You can read *minds?*" I jeered, afraid to raise my voice and conjure more worms or worse. "Do me a favour and *stay the hell out of my head!*"

It was Eli's turn to be insulted. "I didn't do it on purpose!" he scowled. "I doubt you've got anything remarkable in there, anyway."

I prickled and brought us up short. "Listen, you high and mighty ding-dong. *I have value.* Or else I wouldn't be here. So unless you want full-body third-degree burns —"

"*Relax*," Eli sighed, pinching his nose. "I'm sorry. It just happened." He didn't seem like he wanted to make a concession, but he did so anyway: "There are so many things swirling around in my mind that I don't understand. So I just . . . reached out. To get out of my head. And yours was just so open and calm. I didn't . . . mean to intrude."

We walked on. Did his face just colour, or did he have total command over his blood vessels, too? I was about to crankily forgive him, but then, losing all empathy he'd just apologized for *not* having, he said, "And I'm sorry about your parents. I know what it's like. To be alone."

My throat thickened. "My . . ." *Yes, they're dead*, I realized distantly. They'd been dead a long time, too, though I'd only just recently discovered the truth of *how* they'd died, and what for. My breath hitched, and I narrowed my eyes at Eli. How far was I from joining them? And what game was he playing?

"My mother died, too," Eli admitted as we trudged. He touched his chest, where the Moonstone was. "She raised me alone. This used to belong to her, but it destroyed her."

I suddenly felt guilty for threatening him and the delicate common ground we shared. "I'm . . . sorry," I said, and I meant it, though I was still suspicious. "Is it going to destroy you, too?"

"Eventually," said a third voice, and we stiffened.

We had broken out of the knot of burnt death and into a clearing. A felled tree was just beyond, seeping black ooze into the cracked earth.

No, not ooze. *Blood*. The tree had been alive and pulsing with it. The screams had been the tree's, its roots now ripped clean of the ash they had once called home.

The source of the voice was a rock by the hole the tree had rent as it died. Suddenly the rock moved. A living creature straightening to its full, massive height. The creature's body was a muddle of spines and slate monoliths. It turned to face us, six topaz eyes arranged in an inverted triangle weighing every doubt we had as we stood before it. Its hands were shaped like axe blades and covered in the blood of the tree. A huge, tree-murdering mountain.

A crooked grin appeared in the crack of its stone face. "A stone-bearer and a firefox come to my garden," said the mouth. "You have come for the targe, at last."

Well, so much for subtlety. Eli and I exchanged an anxious glance. As I ogled the thing before us, memories snapped into place. "You're Urka. The Gardener."

Its hands were no longer axes, but separate fingers of knives. Instead of responding, it clinked the blades together as though it was scoring the air. Then its body was no longer shaped like a hulking stone but a spindly set of limbs that stretched. "Is that what they're calling me in the Uplands, these days?" Its arms morphed and twisted, knife-hands raking the ground and churning the earth. "I've had many names. But it is nice to know I am remembered by my favourites."

"What are you doing?" Eli asked, feigning curiosity even though he probably knew the answer. He was stroking Urka's ego, and we moved forward, apparently to show investigative courtesy.

The smile deepened. "Gardening."

One of its arms shot down into the hole left behind by the tree. It rooted around until it plucked something alive and throbbing. With all the tenderness of a mother, Urka brought the thing to its mouth, then gently placed it in the new hole. The blood of the felled tree seeped into it, and a spiny black shoot fingered its way through the soil.

"These are my Hope Trees. The damned reach towards the world they remember, to try to escape their misery. Just as they think they are close to breaking through the sky, I cut them down and replant them." Urka bared teeth that I could have sworn had teeth of their own. "Nothing tortures more than a hope."

My toes curled in my boots. I chanced a quick look to the trees surrounding the clearing, trying to ignore that the twisting of their bark suddenly looked like tortured faces and bodies, desperate to escape . . . a garden, indeed.

"Their roots go deep." Urka gestured to the felled tree. "Deep down to the Darkling Hold. Their hopes torment my remaining two masters, and I cannot have that. My masters grow restless waiting for their turn."

Darkling? The remaining two? This sounded like a story I'd heard before. My mind clicked again, and I tilted my head. "There were three down there once." I pointed down. "In the Hold, I mean."

Urka patted the soil one last time, with love. "Zabor has mighty work to complete. I admire her."

God, these nonanswers were driving me insane. "Look, let's skip to the part where you hand over the targe-thingy, and we let you get back to your super-sick hobby. We're kind of in a crunch." I held my hand out.

Suddenly Urka was huge and powerful again, arms heavy with their axe blades. The smile was gone, but there was still a mouth. It slammed an axe into its chest, shale shattering to reveal a disc of green crystal glinting around its neck.

"I am nothing if not a servant," spoke the mouth. "If you take this talisman from me, I will be dishonoured, and my mistress will detest me. Her love is worse than her scorn, but I would have the one over the other. And I would rather have your blood to keep our garden fresh. That is fair to me."

In one clean arc, the axe swung down on another tree, burying deep into its flesh. It screamed, begging for the chance to stay alive, to hope for freedom. I moved to cover my ears, but Eli yanked my hand back to my side.

"Would you make a trade for it, then?" Eli offered, as if there were no tortured wails echoing up and down the woods.

Urka pulled the blade free, staring at the fresh blood there. "Hmm. An exchange?" Urka held a blade to its mouth, smearing the dark ooze on its face with a strange delight. Then it huffed, and its skin rent apart, revealing coals glowing beneath the surface of the cracks rippling all over its body. A hole irised open in its belly, revealing a black furnace inside. It axed off the twisted branches of its newest tree-victim and fed it bleeding and screaming into the hungry, purple flames.

The smoke was foul and exhausted out of Urka's many eyes. I tried to force *mine* back into my head and keep a passive face, but I whirled on Eli. "And what kind of *trade* do you have in mind, boss?"

He turned to me, as though it were obvious. "I offer my prisoner, this lowly firefox who seeks to supplant your mistress," and he shoved me forward as far as the chain would allow. Naturally, I snapped back like a yo-yo, the warmth buried deep within me stoking higher.

"What —"

"Yes," Urka agreed, "*what* would I need with a firefox? My flame is darker and more beautiful than the children of the First Fox. It burns away the light. It lodges in the hearts of the brave. And Foxes are too common for my taste." The demon continued to hack away at the tree-flesh, which seemed to try to shrink away from each stroke. Urka fed its belly-furnace, stoking the black fire. "Whether it was Deon herself burning our glorious land into the ruin you see, or that upstart Ravenna who tried to take the targe from me once before, I grow tired of the red beasts."

My vision tunneled and my soul contracted. *Ravenna. Beautiful. Strong. Doomed.*

Mother.

"Ravenna was *my mother*," I seethed, the air around me shimmering as something inside me snapped into place. "Where is she?"

Urka laughed, laughed long and low and with so much intense pleasure that I could feel sparks coming off my eyelashes as the rage within me built.

"Why, I cannot recall if I incinerated her or planted her. Or if I offered her to my masters as benefaction. What I do remember is that there will be pieces of her scattered across the Bloodlands for millennia to come. And you will never find one." Urka was feeding itself frantically now, the tree it consumed silenced, each branch making the demon grow larger.

Not one to be forgotten, Eli cleared his throat. "This Fox is the daughter of your enemy. And seeks to undo Zabor's great work in the Uplands. Would you betray your masters by letting her go?"

Urka seized, the belly-furnace belching cinders and charred wood-flesh. "I exist to serve the damned. You question *my* loyalty?"

Eli grabbed a hold of my hand, wincing as he was clearly being burnt for doing so, but he held fast. His eyes were clear, and so was his intent. There was a smile there.

"I question your sense of *value*. What good is an old piece of glass to a creature of your standing when held up against a traitor to those you serve? The blood of your enemy would seed your trees well."

Urka's red eyes glinted with mania, and its enormous feet churned towards us. "*You mock me in my own garden.*" The black fire seeping from its mouth like a tongue. "Give me the Fox or perish!"

"But that is not *fair*." Eli held his free hand to his chest, bowing and refusing to retaliate the closer Urka came. "And you are bound by a law of equals. You must give in order to take." I jerked my head in surprise; I wasn't the only one with memories flooding back it seemed.

The axe hands became claws, and they held fast to the glinting targe around Urka's neck, hesitating. I saw only myself reflected in those six murderous eyes, and they were greedy. "Zabor's great work is nearly done," Urka salivated. "A fresh world is about to be born. And I must have my place in it, in the favour of the Three."

Urka was so close I could feel the roar of the belly-furnace. Eli still held tight to me, his flesh searing but face resolute. The great and terrible Gardener bent so that the targe was just out of reach, and when it was close enough to touch, Eli snapped out his mighty wings.

"*Now!*" he yelled, and with a kick from the ground, he yanked us, and the targe, backwards before Urka could swipe us back. I felt my body explode, the fear and the anger and the despair of my lost mother kicking through my skin in an inferno so calamitous that the wind of Eli's wings caught the flames, and made a hurricane of light.

I heard only howls and cries as Eli brought us up through the eye of our storm, the gleaming Moonstone in his chest cutting us a path as we navigated free of the woods. With one burning hand he held me, and in the other he held the targe.

A screech of anguish made us both look back, and we narrowly missed being crushed by the twisted trunk of a mighty, bleeding tree. Urka came barrelling out of the thicket with a crash, annihilating everything in its path, and emitting a scream so anguished that I knew I'd have nightmares about it later.

"We have to get higher!" I shouted, and Eli grunted as we turned over and shot upward. Then the afterthought struck me, and I immediately regretted my words.

"*Wait!*" I tried, but it was too late, because Urka had seen the glinting chain, had slammed its foot down on it, bringing us hurtling back down just as we cleared the treeline.

My vision spackled and my body tingled after the impact, but when I shook myself alert, I realized I couldn't move. I yanked hard on my left arm, and while it was still attached to Eli, he was stuck in a hollow made between two massive, bloody trunks, and he was unconscious.

"Dammit!" I snarled, trying to reach him with my free hand. "Eli! Eli, get up!" His wings were twisted and mangled, and he didn't respond as I tried to shake him.

Something shifted in my periphery. Urka wasn't nearby, but it was only a matter of time — trees were coming down like dominoes in the distance as the demon searched. Our golden lifeline-chain shimmered and shook with each quake and would eventually lead Urka directly to us.

Then I realized something worse and, glancing down into the hole Eli was wedged in, I threw myself down to join him.

"*Hurk!*" he spat as I landed on top of him. Well, at least he was awake now.

"Shh!" I plastered my sleeve over his mouth. "We're hiding."

Eli groaned, and I tried to ease up as much as possible to allow him to breathe. "Still not one for subtlety," he muttered.

"Not my style." I patted him down. "Pardon the familiarity. But where's the targe?"

"The — ?" Then he snapped, fully alert, searching himself madly and suffering for it.

As the crashing and the tremors grew closer, something tinkled nearby. The targe was caught on a crooked branch high above our heads. But with Eli lying broken under me, and the two of us stuck together, there was little we could do to get it.

He wheezed a laugh. "Looks like it's *my* bloated corpse holding you back. Plot twist."

"Just shut up and let me think for a second. Or you could, since you aren't doing much else." Falling trees and the footfalls of a super-pissed monster thrummed hard in my ribs. Not long, now.

"You know what you need to do." His eyes were clear. "I'd have done it. Though I'm strangely not proud to admit it." With what little strength he had left, Eli shook our linked arms. "Cut the chain. Get the targe. Escape."

I scrunched my nose. "I'm not leaving you here, you birdbrain. Besides, you're technically my ride out. There's gotta be another way."

Without thinking, I moved Eli's shirt aside, my palm still a glowing ember between us and the Moonstone sticking out of him like a weapon. "Maybe we can use this —"

He crushed my wrist in his grasp.

"Don't," he hissed, but this time it was less a demand and more a plea. I could see it in his eyes. He was afraid, but he was ready to die. "It'll be quieter soon. I can finally sleep. And you still have work to do." He didn't smile ironically this time. "I'm sorry I prevented you from doing this. It wasn't the best version of me, you could say."

My heart seized. "So it's safe to say both our memories are back."

Eli's face had nothing left to offer. "To think it only took trying to kill you three times to see the error of my ways."

I guessed that was as much of an apology as I was going to get.

"Just shut up," I snapped, and I wrapped the Moonstone in my hot grasp.

Traitor! Unworthy! Worthless! Sacrifice! To the snake!

A thousand voices shrieked and overlapped and took the form of one raging banshee. The words were blades and they cut my spirit down to its smallest part, but there was only so much they could damage — I was, after all, made of many tiny flames, that would incinerate the Moonstone.

The black forest faded into a whipping current. I was somewhere in the Veil, and I knew I had walked there with a warrior at my side — Sil. Cecelia. I felt her now even though she was a world away. I remembered her and the promise I had made her. I would do as she told me — respect the dead, even if they want your blood.

"I come to beg your help," my fire whispered. "To save your stonebearer."

To save yourself, the banshee wailed, the anger there creating a tornado so powerful I was afraid it might put me out. *To avert your fate. To doom all Denizens.*

"To preserve the fates of all," I assured. "Save him, and I will meet my fate. Too many have died. I give you my word."

The silence hurt worse than the words of all the Owls who had come before Eli, for they were surely locked inside this crystal, and all along had been torturing his mind with their influence. No wonder his mother had folded under it. No wonder his mind felt free without it. And for the man I'd seen in those fleeting moments of clarity at my side in Hell, I needed to make this gamble. I couldn't let anyone else die — even Eli, who had tried hardest of all to kill me.

Eli's words about value wove through my fire. What value did I have if I severed the chain binding us and made off with the targe, leaving him here to die alone? I'd be the villain then. And I'd be no better than him. Or Zabor.

Her heart is sure, the voices murmured. *There is no false-hood in it. She means to save the young Paramount and fulfill her destiny.*

My fire grew tight and peeled apart, the wind howling higher with an intensity that not only threw me out of the plane in the stone, but back into the Bloodlands awaiting our death.

My head throbbed and the world spun, even though I was still on top of Eli and trapped. Had I gotten through to his ancestors? I touched Eli's face, but it was cold and still.

The crashing suddenly stopped, and I sat up. Time to meet my unmaker.

Eli's eyes opened — glassy and gold and inhuman. His features started giving way to hundreds of feathers and a black beak.

Good.

I looked up at the dangling targe, only to see Urka's massive hand of knives closing around it before it stuffed the green glass into its mouth and swallowed it whole. With Eli slowly coming back into action, I'd have to take us the rest of the way as soon as possible.

I turned my spirit eye inward. I followed it down to the source of my fire. I needed it to climb high, needed it to *become* me. What I found down there was not anger anymore, even though it had made me strongest. It was the one thing that Urka fed on, and the one thing I could never let die in the bowels of the underworld.

It was hope. And the beautiful fire of it consumed me.

Tendrils of flame peeled off me and incinerated the trees that trapped us. Now unencumbered, and looming large and black, Eli's wings lifted and carried us free. We had grown in size, pulsing with the will to survive, and we were now face to face with our oppressor.

"You will give us the targe," I spat, crackling the flames that were my lips. "Or I will burn what is left of your precious garden."

The Gardener weighed us with its many eyes. "Your mother said the same. And the Bloodlands have not changed."

"But they will," I promised. "All worlds change. Some do not last long enough to see it happen." I felt my fire grow with each new hope tree it took in — not consuming, but setting them free, sparks of the imprisoned souls of this dark forest shooting like skylarks towards their heavens.

Sensing this, Urka backed away a step, hesitating.

"You cannot have it. *You cannot win.*"

I thrust my blazing arm into the open furnace of Urka's belly, and its terrified bellows with each wrench and twist of my hand only made me stronger. From the blackened sludge of its innards, I pulled the targe free and laid it in Eli's outstretched talon.

Urka howled, hands now the unforgiving axes once more, and with a swing it brought one down on top of me. I caught the axe and managed to throw the demon off, but as Urka fell, the blade came down on our precious lifeline, and severed it.

There was a rush of wings, and Eli shot outwards so fast that my great flames went back inside of me as we chased after the receding line. In between howls of pain came Urka's delighted laughter, but we abandoned the demon and its burning estate, chasing our only means of survival.

The line reeled faster and faster away from us like a broken rubber band. "Look!" I screamed, pointing ahead. Eli's powerful wings were peeling back the smoke the higher we climbed, and the way out was above us in a massive thunderhead.

The line was within reach, and Eli grasped it first. The shock of stopping it rippled through his powerful talons, forcing him to let go of me and hold on with both hands, leaving me hanging by the thin chain that bound our arms together.

We hung like that for a breath, the chain sliding apart.

His eyes met mine. But they were the eyes of the terrible Owl, not those of my temporary friend.

The arm-chain slid free of Eli's hand, and I fell.

⇜⇝

Barton grunts, arms and shoulders faltering. His face has changed — he is losing control.

"What is it?" Phae rushes as close to his side as possible, but there is nothing she can do; she cannot breach the rings while the ritual is in effect. She can only watch Barton suffer through the ordeal, and perhaps die from it.

"The chain's been cut!" Arnas shouts, frantic for a backup plan. The Owls in the gallery seem as distraught as he does. "That means . . ."

The lightning skittering through the floating broken tile shivers in a circle. The strobing golden rings are coming apart. The gate is closing.

"*No!*" Solomon screams, looking prepared to throw himself into the swirling chasm before Natti stops him.

"Wait!" she yells, as a different shape of black splits from the darkness. The gateway crackles with electric rage, and the great shadow smashes through it just as the hole closes. With that, the worlds are separate again.

The shadow has shot up through the Pool and to the second level of the antechamber. Phae pushes through the broken plinths of stone just in time to catch Barton and clutch him close. He is breathing, but barely, spirit arms smoking.

"Did I do the thing?" he mumbles, eyes shut tight against the pain and exhaustion.

Phae looks upward, fearing what has come out to meet them. "We'll see."

Natti and Solomon rush up the stairs flanked by the bronze bison.

"Eli!" Solomon cries out, relieved, but Natti brings him up short and holds him back. His relief shatters, and he is grateful that she has stopped him.

The creature is bigger than Eli could ever become. Its feathers are not just black, but blackened, burnt, his face hidden. The wings hang enormous, enclosing the figure like a cloak. Its talons cling to the balustrade over the Pool, compacting the stone like sand.

Natti's heart sinks, but she stands firm, holding Solomon up, even though the hope in her eyes is gone. There's only anger. "Where's Roan?" she screams. "What did you *do to her?*"

A light, faint enough to be missed, flickers between the black. The creature's head pulls up on a long, ponderous neck, revealing exhausted, blunted eyes buried in the feathers framing the face. The wings drop, and the feathers blow away with a great sigh, revealing the man and extinguishing the fire he has been clutching to his chest.

Roan's fire.

The two of them come apart and collapse onto the marble tile with a thud.

"No . . ." Solomon utters as Natti breaks away from him.

"Phae!" she yells. "Get up here now!"

The thundering of Phae's footsteps rushes in Natti's ear as she throws herself beside Roan; Solomon kneels on the other side to tend his son.

Roan and Eli look wrecked and beaten, but Roan suddenly opens her mismatched eyes, finding Natti's. She smiles. "Did we do the thing?"

Natti doesn't stop herself from gruffly hugging Roan tight, in spite of her friend's injuries. "You tell me, you stinkin' idiot."

Then Phae is there, her hands pulling Roan away from the edge of pain.

But Roan is frantic. "The targe!" She bolts up but sinks back as the dizziness takes over.

"Eli?" Solomon clutches Eli's hand. It's badly burned, and his broken son doesn't rouse. A white light glimmers at his chest, but subtly enough to look like a trick. Though he doesn't open his eyes, Eli speaks. "Here," he says, hand unfolding.

No one moves. Eli drags himself to a sitting position, struggling to find his feet. Solomon steadies him, but Eli pushes him aside. "Leave me be, old man. You'll hurt yourself . . ." By some superhuman trick, he's on his feet, clutching his side but standing. There's menace in his eyes.

Roan is still not fully composed, and Natti shields her with her body as she turns to Eli. "Nothin' changes, eh?" She juts her chin at him.

Eli scowls, raising the glinting green crystal flagstone. It contains three gold rings.

"A targe of Ancient," one of the council Owls murmurs, but no one moves to take it from Eli.

"Yes," Eli says, hypnotized by the green. Then he looks down at Roan. Natti and Phae block her, but the Fox-girl puts a hand up, stands, signals them aside.

His eyes narrow. "You should have let me die."

No smartass remarks this time. Roan simply rips off what's left of her sleeve, revealing a spiral scar, the imprint of a twisted chain.

"You could've done the same." She lets the arm drop to her side. "But you didn't."

The light at Eli's chest flickers. His breath hitches and he grabs his head. Solomon moves to him again. "Eli —"

"Enough . . ." he fumes from behind rigid hands. Voices, so many voices, fill the chamber. A wind picks up. And when his father touches him —

"*I SAID ENOUGH,*" Eli howls, and he throws the targe down like it's on fire. It skitters to Roan's feet.

Silence, again, but Roan doesn't pick it up. Instead, she steps forward.

"You could help us," she offers, hand out. "We need an Owl. It could be —"

Now Eli is laughing. "What? Redemption?" His eyes are still clear.

"I heard them, too. I know it's not you."

Eli is weighing her, measuring her, as he did when he first saw her image in the phone Arnas handed over. This young Paramount has done too much damage to bear, and he will have to answer for it, no matter the reason or motivations. What was him, and what was the stone?

"You're right." He glances down. "It's not me." And his wings are a thunderclap, snapping open, and in a torrent he is gone.

The silence is heavy. Roan picks up the targe, thumbing the incised markings.

"That sounded *really dramatic*," Barton squawks from the Pool.

Roans sighs, looking up to Solomon. "Now what?"

He turns to her. "I'll help you. I'll be the last link you need. To finish this."

She nods.

"The cunning of the Fox at work." The voice carries through the building of statues and secrets, followed by a set of soft footfalls. The crowd parts. Sil.

"Oh, look who shows up," Roan grunts. Sil turns away from her, casting her golden eyes at all assembled. Whatever relief there may have been in finding the targe is underscored by a frightened heaviness.

"The ice is broken." Sil's words rocket through the chamber. "Zabor is awake."

RED RIVER RISING

"*The water levels are rising at an alarming rate, unprecedented for the Red River Valley in the history of our flood recordings. While precipitation and heavy snowfall from this past season are major contributors, coupled with frozen ground layers unable to take on the extra water, there is very little evidence for why the Red River has risen so quickly and so early in the season. Heavy rains are expected to continue over the week, making the building of sandbag dikes and the opening of Duff's Ditch a futile effort to save the city of Winnipeg. The river is expected to crest above the levels of the 1997 calamity. The damage is already mounting, and will end up being catastrophic — not just for the city, but any other municipalities throughout the valley.*

"*Therefore, we are declaring a state of emergency. The red line has been reached and the city is in jeopardy. Residents of the core and surrounding communities are urged to evacuate. Relief efforts are mobilizing, and we are doing everything humanly possible to maintain calm in the eye of this storm.*

"Nature seems to have her own agenda, and we must work around it."

The premier's words echo in everyone's minds for weeks after, as people's lives are consumed by water, and higher ground never seems high enough.

The rain comes down in sheets. The waterfront that has only ever been a picturesque caution of destruction is eating away the land on all sides. *Should've known something was up when the animals started booking it*, people concede too late. *Should've moved to our time-share when we had a chance*, others groan.

But the uneasiness in the hearts of humans and Denizens alike lay in the dream they all seem to be having. Some details are different, some exaggerated or under-admitted, depending on who you speak to.

But the dream is the same.

There's a massive woman, angry and hungry and beautiful. Tadpoles are sloughing off her like old scales, and they have teeth and claws and are made of tar. All this monster wants is to devour. Thousands flee her, but she is everywhere.

In the waking world, the rain comes down harder. The river gets higher.

~ঞ্জ~

I stood in the middle of Cecelia's living room, the broken furniture and fixtures cleared away now, the door repaired and cordoned off. Arnas and Deedee were over at my parents' old place in Wolseley, on the other side of the river, helping the tenants save what they could. On Wellington Crescent, the water was over the street and nearly knocking on doors, Cecelia's door an exception. The rain was still going strong, and the storm drains bubbled and gasped into roads and parks.

I took a long look down the hall to the basement door. "What happens if the water gets into the summoning chamber?" Water and fire rarely mixed, and after seeing what happened to Sil after being "snuffed out," I was anxious.

Sil, at my ankles, said nothing for a bit. Then she sighed. "The hearth is empty. If it floods, it floods. Another chamber can be built." She padded towards the basement door, completely avoiding my question, and that made me feel worse than I already did.

I followed her to the chamber, past the debris of the destroyed basement, and down into the place where I'd agreed to this stupid enterprise in the first place.

Cecelia's body was laid out in the centre of the golden rings. They pulsed gently, as if singing a lullaby in melodies of light. Her breathing was shallow, no IVs connected. Just the cradle of the chamber to protect her now, with her head resting in Aunty's lap. Sil had said this was the safest place for her "shell" — safer than the hospital, anyway. It still made me nervous, seeing her there, so vulnerable.

"I'll keep the water at bay as long as I can." Aunty winked, though her brown, weathered face looked much older than when I'd last seen her in Natti's living room. The flood was eroding us all. "You just take care of Natti, you hear?"

I rubbed my foot against the shining granite floor. "More like she'll be taking care of *me*."

And I needed all the help I could get. The others were

downtown now. A Grand Council had been called, meaning every head or representative of the Families in this district were gathering. And I had to speak my piece to them all.

"Roan." Sil sat at the feet of her human body. She'd said little to me over the last week as the flood waters rose and panic rocked the lives of both humans and Denizens. There was nothing to say, and so much unsaid. We were trapped in separate cages of pride and grief, but time ticked, and we were nearly run out of it.

Then she looked at me, eyes shining and ears flattened.

"This battle is yours. And mine. And your mother's. You are the scion of this family. I would not trust our fate to anyone else. I would bite the head off Death herself to save you again. But I can only do so much, and so can your friends."

I stiffened and tried to swallow around the huge lump in my throat. I glanced at Aunty, but her eyes were closed, and she was humming low, lost in her own world.

I tried to smile, to laugh it off. "Ah, don't worry about me, Gram. I've come close to snuffing out too many times to be concerned." But I was. Phae was a gifted healer, but it was taking its toll. She'd helped Seneca recently, and Barton and me too many times to count. Solomon Rathgar told me that she may have the power to heal, but not to bring anyone back from the dead. And if she did it too many times . . .

"You've come far. Your power is great. And you are *all* worthy of the targe," Sil continued. "But each one of you can still die. We all can. And we all may, when this is done. But when it is . . ." Sil stared long and hard at her shrunken, empty body. Then she looked away for the last time. "I want us to be the family we ought to have been. There is still so much you must know, that I have to tell you. I need to do it before my body gives out. I will hold on as long as I can, and I will fight alongside you. I won't let you down again."

I felt my knuckles go white without looking at them. I badly wanted to shrug off this promise of hers, to protect myself from the disappointment that loomed familiar.

But my heart opened willingly as Sil did her classic vertical leap into my arms, fur warm in my open hands. My spirit felt heavy with possibility, and I smiled back the tears.

"Okay," I nodded. *A family*.

The Grand Council was held in the hidden chamber above the legislative building. Before all of this happened, I'd read *The Hermetic Code*, an official coffee table book on the elaborate mythology of the building, and I had pretended secret cultish meetings were taking place in the dome. Now I felt vindicated; too bad I couldn't tell anyone about it . . .

At the head of the gathering, on a raised dais in an extremely over-the-top Owl throne sat Solomon, flanked by the other Owl council members I'd met when the Bloodgate swung shut. Solomon was silent, but his features were arranged carefully, like those of his son — who hadn't been seen since he'd come out of the Bloodlands with me. Everyone told me he could still be a threat, that the Moonstone would try hard to regain control of his incredible powers, but I didn't feel worried. I looked down at the chain scar on my arm often. His spirit was stronger than any of them knew, strong enough to hold that rock at bay.

And though it seemed like eons ago, the demon Urka's answer still echoed in my mind:

Is it going to it destroy you, too?

Eventually.

I glanced down at Sil. I hadn't seen any kind of fancy stone in Cecelia's chest, yet she was the Paramount — did every house have one? I knew little about these stones, in general, except what Eli had revealed, and what I'd seen when I touched it. They were shards of Ancient itself and contained within them were the spirits of every Paramount that had borne it before. The only stone I'd come across was the green gem hidden in a busted fox statue. But that was as good as gone, lost to that shadow. After that everything had changed, and I hadn't thought of, or seen the thing since. Maybe that was a good thing.

But the stones, like the one Eli had . . . they were not to be used lightly or trifled with. Doing so came with a certain madness. *I wasn't the best version of myself*, he'd said. Maybe I'd shorted out the big shiny shard, maybe nothing was different. Maybe I'd partly forgiven him, but I didn't admit it — even to myself.

Sil, Barton, Phae, Natti, and I were standing at the front of the assembly, near Solomon, completing our band of misfits that could activate the crystal targe hanging around my neck, inside my jacket. Seneca (his first name was Jordan, but it seemed no one called him that) was still recuperating from his cousin's attack, but he sat in the front row, face relaxed, almost hopeful.

I examined the room, which was made up of representatives from the Families living in Winnipeg, Brandon, and the surrounding towns, all of which stood to be completely destroyed in the next few days, and which were the only line of defense if Zabor went further with her vendetta. She could go only so far as the river allowed, but she could cut new byways to the sea, and the world would be in the palm of her scaly claw if that happened.

The crowd was mostly made up of Rabbits, Owls, and — my heart caught — Foxes, of which I'd seen few. There were no Seals present, save for Natti and her brother, Aivik, who slouched nearby. There weren't many Seals this far south, since most preferred colder climes closer to the ocean, and Aunty was busy protecting Cecelia. As for the Deer, there were none around that were still human except Phae. Many had already taken on their animal forms for good and fled. I didn't blame them.

All in all, there weren't very many of us. Denizens were thin on the ground in a town that fed their kids to the monster now threatening them all. There was as much animosity here as there was terror. And whatever happened, I was both the cause and solution.

Phae squeezed my hand, and I snapped out of surveying — the proceedings were starting.

Solomon had stood. "Denizens, by Ancient and the Five we serve, I welcome you here in this time of grave emergency. I have asked you all to convene here, as the Narrative demands."

"The Narrative demanded my *son*, too," said a Fox in the back. "And now you're telling us you were *wrong*?"

I suddenly felt bad for the Owls, in spite of everything. Solomon's face didn't change. "Yes. We were wrong."

The murmurs in the chamber bounced off the wall until their volume rose and the anger grew with it.

"Murderers!" someone yelled and had to be restrained. My pulse climbed. The last thing we needed right now was an angry mob.

"Please," Solomon tried, his mouth a hard line. "Please. Yes, I will say it again. We were wrong. We felt we had no other choice. For the sake of Ancient. For everyone." He looked at me then. "It was wrong. We did not feel we could defeat Zabor, and that trying and failing would only put the rest of this tenuous world in harm's way. Letting her loose would have been catastrophic at any stage. We should have trusted that there was another way. And there is." This time, he was speaking directly to me. I tried to control my face, but in the end my mouth just twitched.

"You're up, chief." Barton nudged me in the ribs. I forced myself to climb the dais and stand beside Solomon. Everyone said he should've been Paramount, but he was old, and for a while I wondered if he could handle this. Standing near him now, I felt his wisdom and experience, and above all his trust in me, and that was enough.

I turned to the furious crowd, barely containing themselves, and felt my face scorch.

I swallowed. When was the last time I'd done any public speaking? Maybe a presentation on *The Great Gatsby* in November . . . but that was a lifetime ago.

I saw Sil shift at Phae's feet, but her eyes never left me.

"I'm. Uh . . ." I immediately lost my train of thought, my throat thickening. I coughed. "I'm . . . terrible" — *Yeah, great start* — "at these sort of things. I mean."

I scratched the back of my neck, remembering the bloated worm I'd ripped from there. I thought of Eli, faltered, dropped my hand, and tried again.

"Err. Okay. Look. Here's the thing." I made an effort to keep my hands busy and opened them out in front of me. "This is a horrible thing to talk about. Because . . . because so many of you have lived in fear for so long. And because some of you had to literally sacrifice everything because you figured, *Hey, I'm doing my part*, right?" It didn't seem like people were reacting, but I caught a nod somewhere in the crowd, and I realized it was Barton's dad. So I went on.

"And no one should ever be asked to do what you did. But you did it. And . . . and I think you remember *why*. Because you believed it was the right thing. Thought that it really *was* for the best, 'cause you trusted Ancient to know what it was doing. Now, it's like, *Well, we're all going to get eaten anyway, so what was it all for?*"

Silence. Stillness. *Shit*. I could feel my face going from red to purple, and my super-heightened pulse wasn't helping any. *Wrap it up, Harken!*

"But!" I accidentally shouted. Some people jumped — *Good, they're paying attention*. "But . . . look." I pulled the targe over my bushy haircut and raised the glistening gem. "I didn't get this on my own. If it wasn't for Eli, for the Owls, I would have never come out of the Bloodlands alive. He could've left me down there, could've destroyed the targe. But he didn't. Because when it came down to it, even he believed we could do this."

I heard Solomon make a choked noise, but I doubt anyone else did. I plowed on.

"And I know it's a big ask. But I need you to trust, again." I pressed the targe to my chest, suddenly afraid I was going to drop it my hands were shaking so badly. "Before any of this, I wasn't really anyone. The only person relying on me was *me*, which was enough. Then it turned out I was even *less* of anyone. I was a toll to be paid for some demon and all for a crazy-ass mythological world that I had no idea even *existed*. I could've run off, or let Death have her way. But . . . but I *trusted*."

This time I spoke to Sil, and I couldn't help but imagine that her fur was sparking with involuntary pride. "It wasn't easy. And it didn't *get* easier. Not really my fault." I slid the targe back around my neck. "But I *trust* we can do this. And I say *we* because I never imagined in my wildest nightmares that I could take on Zabor alone."

I walked down the steps to everyone's level. I made sure to study every face turned up at me, to imagine their fear, their hopelessness. I wanted them to *see*. "I trust. I trust that if Ancient is listening, it'd want us to stand up and fight. If we can. We've all got this Grace inside of us, and we can't let it disappear because we've given up. If this is all about some story we've got to fulfill, some kind of order that has to be maintained — then we need to start writing the story ourselves before Zabor washes away what ink we've got left."

There was a low murmur, but no one interjected or really responded. My words buzzed in my head over and over again until I was certain they sounded extremely stupid.

Then: "So . . . who are you, again?"

My eyes throbbed with my heartbeat. *Wow, that's what they got out of all that?*

"Roan Harken," said Barton, as he moved into full view next to me and put a hand on my forearm. His other hand was holding Phae's, who was followed by Natti, who joined me on my other side, between Solomon and me. "Roan Harken's parents were Ravenna and Aaron. The two of them died trying to get half as far as Roan has, and her grandma gave up her *body* to help her get there." Barton nodded at Sil, whose ears flattened and golden eyes flashed.

I don't think she was pleased about being outed in the middle of a crisis.

"She's the Fox *Paramount's* granddaughter?" someone objected.

"Her family gave up everything. And so has Roan," Phae continued, eyes rolling white, and her great black mane knitting its blue, sparking antlers. "She brought us together. She made us believe. She and her family trusted that this could be done."

Thunder rumbled and lightning cracked behind us, but Natti wasn't about to let it distract anyone. "The targe needs a member of each of the Five to activate it, to send Zabor back down where she belongs. And we're willing to do it. But we can't do it without help. And we can't let her destroy our home. No matter what part of this city we came from, or what Family we trace our blood to, this city is ours. If we can't come together now, then we might as well abandon Winnipeg and let Zabor have her way with the rest of the world."

Solomon nodded, grave but determined, and the other council members, for once, stayed quiet.

A Fox, a Rabbit, a Deer, a Seal. And an Owl. I touched the targe. As one, we stared out into the crowd to await their judgment.

Another wave of thunder, and in its wake, Sil rose, flames consuming her as her limbs stretched out and she became the Fox-woman, nine tails blazing, mantle rustling in the breeze of her holy heat. Her massive Fox head seemed to smile as she stood before the gathering, and she half turned, the snout melting back into flaming tongues, until the face of a woman with raven hair smiled out from behind it.

Cecelia, her true spirit, Paramount of all Foxes. From her back she pulled a flaming garnet blade.

And she clanged it into the dais before us like the warrior queen she was. An oath.

Soon, others came forward, too. Foxes first, following the example of their Paramount. Then Rabbits, Owls. Even Aivik pumped his fist in the back, releasing a firework of the water that everyone had dragged in and scaring those who were standing near him.

I smiled, but the lightning was getting closer now, the sheets of rain heavier above our heads.

"For Ancient!" someone cried out, and a cheer followed. My friends and I looked at each other, unable to join in the battle cry.

"For our families," I said. And they nodded.

It was time.

※

The water had reached the legislative grounds. Louis Riel himself was drowning, but he faced the river head-on, rooted in place. The rain came down so hard and heavy that it was nearly a whiteout, and the chill in the air hadn't improved with the storm front.

A single black shadow clung to Louis's arm, rocking in the fierce winds and unwilling to leave its post.

"Brother," Natti muttered. Aivik didn't bat an eye — he knew she wasn't talking to him. He adjusted his skater-hat, looking grave. Brother wasn't moving, seemed a part of the statue, now. He'd heard his mother's call and, though his loyalties were now divided, he whimpered and listened.

Natti and Aivik took the head of the pack and seemed to move together. I had to hand it to Aivik — he was all ponderous largeness, as tall as he was wide (like Aunty), but he had as much power and control as his sister. They raised their arms to move the deluge aside, allowing Solomon, Barton, Phae, and me to advance. Sil was at my side, still in her Foxwoman form, but the rain merely hissed as it struck her. We stood on the brink together. Waiting for the wave.

As Natti and Aivik pulled the rain apart like a heavy curtain, the lightning cut through, sharp, glinting fingers striking closer and closer to us. I counted — one one-thousand, two one-thousand . . . Another finger sliced directly in front of us, seeming to divide the river in half like a cracking bone.

We recoiled, and when I turned I saw Natti and Aivik standing next to us, faces turned up and afraid.

I did a double take from them to the river, which was still pulling back into its banks, forming an enormous wall of water.

Thinking it was them doing it, I shouted, "Hey, are you guys —"

Aivik shook his head, suddenly preoccupied by his hat being ripped off his head and carried away by the storm.

"It's not us," Natti said. "It's her."

Every bit of the river that had climbed over its limits and washed the city into despair pulled away from its holding grounds. Creeks, ditches, neighbourhoods, water mains — the water retracted, pulled inward like an embrace, coming back to the river like children flocking to their mother. From the air, this may have looked like a relief. From the ground, it was madness and catastrophe.

But I knew it was the beginning of something worse.

The river, penned in by an invisible fence, raised higher. The rain ceased but the sky stayed black, a bruise turning red and purple. The wind died.

And when things cleared, when the river finally pulled every last thread to it, we could see what the watery coffin contained behind the glass.

She was bigger than I'd ever had space in my mind to imagine. And more beautiful, too.

Her hair stretched and eddied behind her, a tangle of darkness. I couldn't tell if it was all hers, or if it was the bodies of her hunters dancing around her head. Her arms covered her chest like a sleeping princess in a fairy tale, and there were no legs to mention, just a massive spiked tail that extended out of her ribbed, scaly belly. The tail went on forever.

And suddenly the water contracted, made her grow even more and, with a screeching inhale, Zabor's eyes opened and we were blasted backwards by the force of the river that was hers.

Natti tried to stop the wall, which gave us a grace period of about a second before we were all airborne and smashing into each other or anything solid enough to stop us. When I shook the ringing out of my head, I got to my feet as quickly as possible, fast enough only to cry "*Get down!*" before the enormous tail swung out towards the Osborne bridge, and took it out like a dandelion.

Cars, concrete, and a bus took flight before crashing into nearby buildings or coming to rest in the water. The tail swept anything that might hinder the progress of the water as it rose and smashed down into the city that had grown around it.

Then a scaled claw as large as a tractor-trailer dug into

the great staircase under Louis's vigilant, doomed watch. The other found the opposite bank and, like an Ophelia rising from the dead, Zabor lifted herself free of her watery prison.

She opened her mouth and screamed.

"Jesus, she's been sleeping for decades, you'd think she'd be in a better mood," I yelled, though to no one in particular and for no other reason other than to crack the nightmare we were in. No going back this time.

The snake-woman stilled, her enormous breasts quivering as she turned towards the sound of my voice and rose on the tight coil of her tail.

"*You*," shuddered Zabor's toxic voice at about a hundred decibels above what my ears could handle. She pointed at me, rows of sharp, soul-rending teeth exposed in a mouth open enough to show her forked tongue.

Her hunters slithered by the hundreds onto dry land, but they didn't advance far, clinging close to the shadow of their fearsome mother. Brother clung to the Louis Riel statue, burying its head in the stone, weeping.

"I demand the blood I was promised." The screech tore a hole in my head and the words tried to stretch it wider. *"I will not be disobeyed. I will be honoured! Or the world will pay!"*

I felt paralyzed in place, felt like my bones were drying out and soon I'd blow away in the wind of Zabor's fury. But my spirit eye opened wider, and in those razor teeth of hers I saw every person who she had churned up and destroyed. Every drop of Denizen blood at the back of her throat.

"The world *has* paid!" I screamed, igniting from head to toe. "And now it's your turn!"

Her expression of grim hatred sharpened into a glee I'd recognized in Urka's face in the Bloodlands. Zabor's peals of laughter set off car alarms and, I'm sure, shattered glass in nearby apartment complexes.

"I am the river! I am the ending of the Great Narrative! Your forebears could not quell me, and neither will a morsel!" Her tail lifted and cracked like a whip, throwing me off my feet and slamming an instant trench through the sidewalks and statues flanking the legislature.

The river hunters leapt up, and their clattering assured us we'd be dead before we could reach their maker.

I scrambled to my feet, unsure what the first move would be. This wasn't a video game, there was no team-turn system. This was an all-out melee with no controls, no special moves, no second lives, or reset buttons. We each had one life to give, and when it was gone, it was gone.

The ground quaked, pulling Zabor up short. I twisted to see that the statues of the legislature, scattered on the grounds, toppled on their sides or carved within the building itself . . . *were moving*. With each pulse of the ground their bodies rippled and animated, pulling free of plinths and reliefs. And they were marching for the river.

Louis Riel himself lowered his hand, still wielding a proclamation. Then he pulled it back and smashed into three advancing river hunters, the force of the blow cleaving one in two.

"What the actual f—" I muttered, before realizing that all the Rabbits, including Barton, had come forward to form a line with him at the front, arms buried in the ground.

The other Rabbits' fingers twitched, as though they were playing delicate, invisible instruments. Or, more likely, commanding marionette strings on their new Tyndall stone and bronze soldiers.

With the first blow delivered, the battle was on, and the promenade erupted into chaos.

Our side seemed to collectively cry out, and I ran into the breach, losing sight of my friends as they branched out to stop the incoming onslaught. I felt, for a split second, as though I was back at Omand's Creek all those weeks ago, when the snow still ruled and the idea of having any power over myself was laughable. This time, I let the fire take me up in its embrace, and I spun into the fray like a flaming hurricane. I tore hunters aside, I grew as large and wild as a Fox on the run, and as they burnt away under my fists I thought that I could do this.

I was smashed aside by a river hunter that was twice my size, flying headlong into a statue of Queen Victoria. I say headlong, because the impact knocked her head clean off. She staggered, but reeled back and swung with her sceptre to clear a path.

I rolled on the soggy ground and righted myself, trying to refill again with the inferno I needed to keep going. Instead, I found myself whipped from the ground by a huge wind and thrown into a nearby shrubbery while a lamppost, lately of the Osborne Bridge, scythed through the place I'd been formerly collecting myself.

I looked up to see Solomon standing over me before he hauled me back to my feet.

"Thanks," my flames hissed, but the gratitude was short-lived; an explosion rocked the air as Zabor's tail cut through the apartment towers on the other side of Osborne. We heard screams over the din as they crumpled into themselves in a mass of smoke and destruction. Some of these buildings weren't empty, and Zabor knew that. She laughed as the towers came down, swinging again to take out anything near her.

From the sidelines, we caught our startled breath. Solomon was covered in black muck, his face tight. Some of the statues were falling as the Rabbits that controlled them were overtaken by black, devouring shadows. A group of Foxes had banded together with some Owls to create a fireball tornado to cut through an advancing group, but no matter how many river hunters they sheared down, more rippled up from the riverbanks like slimy salamanders, shaking free of the mother who had no shortage of them. Natti and Aivik were trying to use whatever water was available to them for direct offense, freezing hunters and debris before it could crush someone, but Aivik sent a frozen hunter flying directly into Zabor's chest, which made her twist around, angrier than she'd yet been.

Tail still submerged, Zabor struck down with the power of her mighty coils for the Seal that had *dared* use one of her children against her, but something threw him out of the way. Something black and screeching.

Brother.

Zabor pulled up short as Brother rattled out a cry that made the flames coming off me gutter. For a moment, the great snake looked pained, even moved back a little.

Then her face rearranged into a sneer and, with one swing of her hand, she smashed Brother down, killing him instantly.

Natti's guttural cry rose up and diverted Zabor's attention just enough — huge spikes of ice flew into her face, glancing off her powerful scales . . . but one shard struck an eye, and she bellowed as she staggered back, tail flailing and pulling trees up by the roots.

"The targe!" Solomon grabbed a hold of my shoulder with a claw, shaking me out of my daze. "Before she takes out the entire downtown core!"

I swallowed and leapt forward, but I brought myself up short. One of Zabor's hands, finally tired of the pest Natti was making of herself, struck out and broadsided her, throwing her into a knot of screeching hunters. Phae broke away from a group of Rabbits and encased Natti in an orb of light. Natti smashed through the hunters like a bowling ball, and came to rest with Phae, who looked more fierce than I'd ever seen her. She spun out, her fist filling with blue lightning and sent the hunters retaliating to the riverbank, blinded.

She turned to me, face triumphant, but then it fell. "Roan!"

A hunter screeched from behind us, and Solomon's scream punched a hole in me as I lunged, wrenching the hunter's jaws from his leg — or what was left of it.

I threw myself down by his side. He was down, not dead. But how could we activate the targe now? Another Owl found us, the sharp-faced councilwoman. She looked to me, and I nodded, and she whisked him from the battlefield with a gust.

I turned back to the river. Zabor clutched her damaged eye, but pulled her hand away so she could fully take in the new adversary beneath her.

"Shit," I hissed.

Sil, bright blade flashing, crackled like a living bolt of lightning, growing in height, though still miniscule compared to the river serpent. Zabor's cackles saturated the dark air, her arms outstretched in supplication as she tilted her head up.

"*What a boon that has been delivered me,*" she cackled. "*The Fox Paramount herself! A fine tribute. An enemy worthy of my wrath.*"

The river hunters chittered with her, and as I looked around at our small contingent falling back, pulling injured comrades to the side for protection, I realized the demon and the warrior were going to have it out, one-on-one. Sil raised her blade.

"For my daughter, for my granddaughter, *and for me*!" And with that, she leapt and smashed her fire headlong into Zabor's face. The skyscraper-huge tyrant recoiled, throwing every bit of her petulant rage forward as she chased after the Fox warrior, who gracefully danced out of the way.

Sil vaulted and wove — and brought Zabor farther and farther out of the river, closer to the legislature. I knew the drums I heard pounding in my blood made the beat she followed. She spun, a wild streak of joy and rage. And Zabor chased still.

I caught Sil's eye and her smirk. This was a distraction. This was our chance to put her away. But with Solomon gone . . .

Another river hunter — quick and sleek — fell on me, snatching the targe from around my neck. The hunter nearly slipped my grasp, but I got a hold of its leg, hurling it into the front of the building.

It let go of the targe, which flew skyward and was hurtled by the gale-force winds to the top of the dome.

"Dammit!" I yelled, and in a fiery surge, I spun upwards to the first frieze of the building. I kicked off to the next level, cutting through the cold. I was getting close, but the higher I went, the harder it was to stay lit. I reached, but missed the edge of the temple-top.

Talons sank into my flesh and threw me so high I had to reach for the Golden Boy statue's outstretched wheat sheaf.

I swung over it and landed beside the statue, nearly slipping to my death.

Eli landed next to me, and steadied me on the wet dome before I could tumble back down. I clung to the Golden Boy with one arm, my other hand firmly around the targe dangling there. I slipped it back over my head. The way down was blocked by the curve of the roof, and I couldn't see the full extent of the distance. I squeezed my eyes shut hard and swallowed.

"And where have you been!" I screamed, surprised and happy to see Eli, despite it all.

He didn't say anything, face drawn and tight. I tilted myself as far out as I could to see Zabor and Sil coming closer to the building. From here, I could see the extent of the great snake's destruction, and how far her tail stretched. She was half free of the water, but a massive amount of her tail still remained there. I searched the crowd for Natti, Barton, and Phae. They were rushing to three points around the colossal skirmish, preparing themselves.

I suddenly realized what Sil was doing, before she darted out from under Zabor's grasp, landing on her tail in a dervish of fire, her blade rising above her head in her mighty, powerful arms.

The blade sank home, and Zabor convulsed hard enough to throw Sil aside. The garnet sword had cut deep, but not deep enough.

Something was spurting out of the wound — hissing and burbling and alive. It shot out for Sil and hit her directly in the eyes just as she'd risen back to her feet. She staggered, blinded, dropping her blade and clawing at her face.

This was enough of a stall for the giant tail to rear up,

showing its terrible spikes as it pulled free of the mud bank.

"No!" I heard Eli screech, just as I let go of the Golden Boy and skittered down, a flaming bullet as I threw myself headlong for my grandmother. I flew faster and faster, the Canadian comet, any fear of heights or dying lost in the embers of my heart. *I can make it, I can make it, I'm going to make* —

The spike pierced Sil's body like a spear. I landed short of her by a few feet, pulling myself up just in time to avoid merging with the pavement. But I couldn't reach Sil, couldn't do anything as she was thrown up like a newly caught trout on the end of a barb. Then the spike slipped free of her, and the tail smashed her aside.

Ragdoll limp, she came to a stop on an upturned tree. My fire went out as I scrambled to her side.

"No, no," I said, the words sounding terribly calm in my ears. "Nope, no. It's okay, you're okay. Phae! *Phae!*"

I looked around for her once, but I didn't move from my place beside Sil. My hands were on either side of the wound gaping in her chest. Her eyelids were stuck together with the black muck of Zabor's toxic blood and, with an exhale, the warrior body dissolved into ashes, leaving only the fox behind.

I pulled her up in my lap, careful not to jostle her, afraid that it might . . . that she . . .

"It's just a body." I was suddenly blubbering, breath heaving in and out of my lungs. "You're fine. You've got a backup. Just go to it, okay? I'll see you — I'll see you back at home." My fantasyland logic couldn't be flawed. I wouldn't allow it to be.

Sil laughed around her pain. "It doesn't work that way, you silly pup." The fur under my hands seemed to be cooling.

"Now stop whining. Finish . . . finish the job." Her fire was going out; I could feel it turning low. I held her tighter, closer.

"Not without you," I seethed through gritted teeth. "Not without you."

She pulled her black lips over her bleeding gums. "Never," she sighed, and the fire she had left passed through my flesh and into me.

I erupted.

My body suddenly felt *crowded*. My bones argued against accommodating so much in such a small space. But any protest only sizzled away. I was the Fox warrior goddess. I saw the beginning and a glimpse of the end.

And I knew that end was not today.

I stood again, the storm whipping up anew, the river hunters a dim razor in the back of a mind too busy to acknowledge the sound. I moved towards the sword that had been abandoned and, though shadows in my periphery moved to stop me, I only turned them aside with a whisper of fire, and they burned.

I picked up the blade and soared towards the spurting black limb. More screaming and flailing. I moved with the curve of the Earth as it spun under Zabor's rage. I wove through her aggravated attacks and smashed the blade down again and again. I cut and cauterized as I went, and finally the bone was cleaved apart, the snake and its tail separate at last.

I came back into myself for a moment, saw the tail lift itself up and smash to land, flipping and tossing and sending Denizens scattering. It sprayed black acid in a terrible pinwheel, and I saw Natti rear up and freeze it before it struck anyone. Rabbits, on Barton's command, dashed in around her, bringing the ground up in plinths of rocks to pierce the tail and nail it in one place.

But the owner of the tail still had her wits, and she came down on me with all her body. I flew to the side, and the targe ripped free of the cord around my neck and, before I could grab it, it fell and smashed apart on the pavement.

I didn't have the chance to gather the pieces of the targe. Zabor's arm smashed into Natti and Barton. The next moment saw river hunters overtaking Phae, teeth coming down on her leg. Her scream nearly knocked me out.

Whatever power Sil had passed on to me overwhelmed every sense, until fear took them all. Zabor's huge hand pinned me in a bed of my — Sil's — nine tails.

"*You think you can part me from my river?*" Her horrible voice cut through my ears and my fire. "*You think you can cut me from my tail and I will lose my terrible power? I will rip a hole so great in this world that my brothers will surge out, and we will blacken Ancient's great creation as we were meant to. Your grave will pave the way for millions.*"

I heard the beating of wings, and my spirit eye showed me only moths and the end their Great Queen had promised. I conceded that I had come as far as I could allow. That my parents would be proud, that what was left of my grandmother fluttering inside of me was satisfied.

But they were not moth wings. They were Owl wings. And I saw those unforgiving claws sink into demon-flesh, pulling the serpent's head back with a howl as she batted Eli away.

But that's what he wanted, her face turned to him and exposed, as he raised a shard of the glittering green targe and smashed it into her skull.

The sky opened and the river rumbled. Zabor reeled back, clawing at her face, but there was no removing the splinter. It burned like an oil flash, turning black, and there it stayed. I rolled to my haunches and managed to spot three pieces scattered near me. I ripped apart a river hunter who was making off with the fourth one. I turned and found Phae in Barton's exhausted root arms, what was left of her power trying to reset the wound in her leg. Natti, eye blackened and hands bloodied, supported the weight of her injured brother nearby. Eli helped her rest Aivik against a downed tree.

We all turned to face the raging demon as she stumbled on the bloody stump of her tail, making for the confines of the river. She swatted away her faithful children as they swarmed her, despairing.

Sil's and my words overlapped. "The pieces of the targe must be put into place." I looked down at my scorched claw-hands, offering the glittering green shards to my friends. They each grasped one close, faces drawn.

"Okay, fly boy," Barton said, holding out his piece. "Here, stick this one in her for me, would ya? Don't think I can reach."

Eli scowled and didn't move. "I've done my part. Now you all must do the same."

Barton tensed. "You want Phae and Natti to grow wings, too, and risk dying in the process? We all can't be animal gods, for fuck's sake." He spat blood.

"Stop it," Phae wheezed. "He's right. We've come this far. We need to do what we came here for."

"Then what? We're fresh out of Bloodgates," Barton persisted, clutching Phae to keep her steady as her healing did its work.

Eli's eyes tensed in the cold dark, but he still didn't move. "The targe will rend the two worlds apart for us and chain her to the Bloodlands in the process. But we'd better act fast, before she pulls the river back up and floods us all."

The ground heaved beneath us, but the two of us stood firm. Unable to consolidate whatever was going on inside me, I turned my gaze outward instead, following Eli's example. Zabor scrabbled and screamed at the shard in her head, but her thrashing, stump of a tail had a nubbin of new flesh where I'd cut it free. Her tail was growing back.

Phae was finally able to get to her feet, helping Barton into his overturned wheelchair. Part of me longed to hold her and reassure her. The dominating part, however, only acknowledged my best friend as nothing more than a passing shade; I was too high to feel anything.

"Roan —" she reached for me, but Natti pulled her back. They were afraid of me, but I felt that they ought to be.

Phae broke from her, mouth set, hair a sopping, tangled mess around her throat. Her dark eyes slid away, and her mighty antlers climbed slick and high.

"For Sil," she whispered, blue lightning crackling. She turned to Barton and Natti, pressing her shard to her lips. "Once and for all."

They nodded as one and left the cover of the fountain to meet their fate.

The river hunters, howling and furious, rushed forward like berserkers. A refreshed contingent of Denizens saw the approaching three and afforded them a defense, cobbled together as it was. Even still, Barton had to intervene, punching a fist into a piece of rocky debris, rippling the pavement under it. Phae, beside him, encased him in a solid ball of white light, and sent him tumbling like a pinball into the rocky outcrops he'd made. On her other side, Natti had swirled up armfuls of the river, freezing it behind her with such a force that she skated up it like a giant frozen geyser. She took Phae with her and, as they rose higher, Phae fixed her shard into her mighty antlers, goring the piece home into Zabor's head as she swerved to meet them.

With the shard planted and smoking black, Phae fell free and into Eli's talons. He jerked her smoothly out of Zabor's path, and while she dove after them, Barton punched a plinth out of the ground, rising on the rock column until he could jam his shard into her jaw.

This time, the great snake queen struck. Barton soared, but Natti slid under him, her hailstorm still massive and growing behind her. She deposited him safely with a group of Rabbits who had seen him fall and turned again for Zabor.

It may have been *her* river all this time, but now it was Natti's. With her fist held high, the Seal pulled the river to her and wrapped Zabor's flailing, severed body in a coil of ice. Another fist of water shot Natti's piece home.

Zabor's rage reached a new volume. It was time to add my piece.

Beneath my feet, I felt the five gold rings rise and flash. Each one found my comrades, tethering our spirits to the Families that gave us power. We'd need to come together one last time.

The rings were alive. The voices on the other side called us, and Eli, Barton, Natti, and Phae each closed their eyes and I felt their spirits pray.

My shard winked with the light from my shining fire. Cecelia's fire. I did as Phae had and pressed the shard to my lips in benefaction. Then my mouth moved again on its own. "To the power that gives our spirits light. To the Ancient force that guides us in its silence. From the Warren of the Rabbits. From the Den of the Foxes. From the Roost of the Owls. From the Glen of the Deer. From the Abyss of the Seals!" My voice rose louder and louder, and it wasn't just mine, but Cecelia's, too. "Place your Grace on us, and upon this targe!" This time I had control, and I walked steadily towards the snake.

Zabor struggled mightily, face fierce and pupils so small as to be invisible. Her icy bonds were cracking, melting, but not leaving her. She was calling the river to her in one last bid to annihilate. The water rose, and she with it, frantic and screaming so brutally that her children fled, but seemed to die as soon as they reached land, turning into river mud as they scattered. The remaining Denizens and the injured took cover behind me. But I stopped, at a standstill beneath her. Then I rose high on a twisting inferno churned up by my mighty tails, and we were face to face.

The voices of my friends became one. "We stand before you with willing hearts and spirits. We command our power to be united."

Golden chains shot from the edges of the broken targe, and I pressed the last piece in the centre of Zabor's head. The chains cut into her flesh as the ice hadn't, binding the thrashing demon's arms to her torso, and closing around her squealing throat. The world seemed to be shifting apart, and the water that Zabor had been trying to unleash swirled around her in a maelstrom that only grew as the storm above spun parallel.

The great black wheel of the sky crackled, and above and below a terrifying column of red light opened. We were no longer standing on the bank of the legislature grounds. We were no longer separate. The small space inside me became more crowded, filled with thoughts and fears and desires that weren't mine. The rings bound us together, and everything that made us unique fed into the targe and gave it power.

The world split, just as Eli said it would. The howling of the elements shut off all perception, kept us from our bodies. We were one spirit in that moment, unable to untangle, unwilling to let go. But we knew we were going too far, that the power was enough to send us through the gateway we had made. We needed to detach or else perish.

A great, terrible light enveloped the world.

Then, darkness.

The DRAGON OPAL

Phae thinks of her parents. She regrets not introducing them to Barton. She knows he and her father would have gotten along, maybe.

Natti reaches out a tired tendril of her soul into the world, and realizes, with relief, that her missing mother is still out there, somewhere. And that someday, she will find her.

Barton is running on carbon-fibre blades. His son is cheering from the sidelines of the running track.

Eli revels in silence. He wonders if it will last, and if he will someday share it with someone else.

Roan sees her mother. No, her grandmother. No, someone else entirely. Someone who is older than both of her matriarchs, older than time, but so familiar. The first mother of all. And the last.

The woman puts two hands on Roan's face and smiles. Her triangular moth wings flex.

"Not yet," she says.

※

Eli wakes first. The ground beneath him is wet but not drowned. He sits up, bones stiff enough to make him feel as though he's been torn apart and very hastily put back together.

The sun has broken, only just, through the scattered clouds. Buildings are down, bridges ruined, the grounds of Manitoba's grand parliamentary building rent asunder. Statues have toppled or else are ripped of their moorings. A giant trench is stained with sizzling black muck, but whatever occupied it has gone.

The river is calm, flowing as a river does, powerful and pushing the debris that now fills it but doesn't stop it. It has receded to where it should be. It is quiet once more.

Eli catches movement on the deserted battlefield. The Denizens that had fought alongside them stare in disbelief at the destruction, taking the moment to accept exhausted paralysis.

Nearby, Barton, the root-armed Rabbit, stirs. He is held tight in the arms of the Deer. Eli recalls something from a dream he heard, about Phae's parents, and . . . he clutches his head. They must have occupied the same mind, for a moment. And it had been painful, intrusive, too much. For a moment, he'd felt close to death. All of them had. But someone pulled them away . . .

Natti is the only one sitting up, her brother lying next to

her, calm and unconscious as he seemingly naps off the stress of the fight. She has one hand on his round head. The wind stirs the Seal's soaked, black hair. She is staring at the river, and the figure on the bank.

Roan seems so much smaller since Eli saw her last. Then, her soul had been eclipsed by the power of the Paramount, a creature that walked the world as the avatar for the First Fox. A warrior. A connection from this world to the next.

But now she is merely a girl, awkward shoulders hunched, hair mussed and clinging to her fragile skull.

She cradles the fox in her arms, the body small and delicate. Roan's tattered clothes shift in the breeze, and when her eyes meet Eli's, she erupts into a clutch of sparks.

And she is gone.

⁕

I was walking in a dream. Had to be. I'd only just come back into my abandoned body, but now it was in a million pieces, each a separate match-light in the dark. I was gathering them close again as I wove through the shadows.

Another light, separate from mine, guided me. "I'm coming," I said in my mind, the little candle lights fusing into me like droplets of bright mercury. "I'm coming."

Then we were falling, slowly. We passed through a membrane in the bottom of the darkness, and I crumpled to the floor of the summoning chamber, hands still clasped protectively over the light I'd been chasing in my dream.

"There you are," said a sad voice. I opened my eyes, and a figure swam before me. Then it was two figures.

Aunty. And Cecelia.

"I brought her back," I whispered, eyes heavy like I'd been staring into a bonfire for hours. "I had to."

"Good girl," Aunty said, and I sat up. Everything hurt. I don't think I'd ever nail the spirit-to-body landing.

I unclasped my stiff fingers. A tiny, blue flame beat in the centre, like a heart.

It floated free of my palm like a flake of ash. I hadn't the strength to try to get it back. I knew that I couldn't keep it alive for long.

The flame slipped into Cecelia's chest. Aunty slid back out from under her head and let it come to rest on the obsidian floor. She scooted out from the pulsing, golden circles, shut her eyes, and hummed.

Cecelia lit up like a funeral pyre, and in the heart of the flames she rose to her feet, levitating inches above the ground. The circles began to revolve, catching her fire and burning low. The flames hummed along with Aunty.

Cecelia opened her eyes, as bright and gold as her fox eyes had been. They smiled down at me. "Silly pup," she said. Her voice was honeyed and warm.

I couldn't move. "You're leaving, aren't you?"

Her eyes fell. She looked at her hands. "This body has nothing left. My spirit has been trapped inside and outside of it for too long. I'm sorry."

You promised, I wanted to scream, to pound my fist on the floor. *A family, a family! You said!*

"Well." I swallowed. Cecelia held out her hand. I clasped it and stood. The fire was cool to the touch, and her words were a diminishing heat. "You are my granddaughter. You are my blood." Her eyes were suddenly hard. "Zabor may be silenced now. But something else is rising. It is something you must face."

I was suddenly angry, pulling away from her. "Stop! I can only do so much! I can't. I just . . . don't make me do this again. Don't . . ." I lost my breath, shaking, weak. "Please don't go," I begged. "Please don't leave me alone again."

Cecelia's hands came back to mine, and her face was inches away. She planted a kiss on my forehead, full of all the love she had left. I felt a great warm gust — a final exhalation — envelop us.

"Never," she said, before the sound of wings took her, and I was alone with Aunty in the summoning chamber of my dead grandmother.

Cecelia was gone, body and all consumed. The fire broke from the circles incised in the floor, and cut a zigzagging diagonal across the room. The black marble shook, the veins of it pulsing red as if something burned under the floor. In a rush, the fire came to rest in the great, empty hearth at the back of the chamber, the walls climbing with veins of flame.

Then the fire went out, and the great black floor opened, revealing something glassy, sharp, and glowing. A geode wrenched free of its hiding place, the jet granite sliding back into place. The chamber was dark. The chamber was silent.

The stone glittered with too many colours to name — a conflagration of green kept inside glass. I knew this stone. It whispered and murmured, and I knew immediately that it was just like the stone Eli had. The stone that had nearly ruined him.

It dropped heavily into my shaking hands from the air.

"The Dragon Opal." Aunty nodded. "It's chosen you. It's yours now."

I gazed up at her, as though I'd forgotten she was there. The voices were mounting, desperate. "Mine?"

Aunty let her eyes fall. "I'm sorry."

I was outside of myself again. The stone was so warm. It reminded me of Cecelia. I wanted her back. I wanted her close. I was completely alone now. I was the last of my family, no one left. I was desperate. Angry. Afraid. The voices promised to make those feelings go away.

I wanted them all back. My mother, my stepfather, my grandmother. I wanted to hear them. Whatever it took.

I smashed the stone into my chest.

FLIGHT

Eli stands at the back of the lawn, though he doesn't deign to hide himself. He's come for . . . support. He didn't imagine he would, but he's found himself here, outside the high school. All his studies were conducted in an unorthodox way, but observing this ritual won't do him any harm.

Grad caps fill the air like confetti. He looks up and catches one in his hands. A startled blond reclaims it from him, sheepish and grateful as she scurries off to join her friends.

Eli had hoped that Roan . . .

The Deer — Phae — sees him. He doesn't bother probing her mind. She just shakes her head.

❧

It takes Eli more time than usual to find her. It seems she has been trying to keep herself hidden. Annoyed, he banks low over Sargent Avenue.

And there she is, weaving in and out of traffic on that blasted bike, body pressed low to the handlebars. Roan is heading for the airport, a small bag on her back. A short trip? He probes her mind cautiously, a cold finger. But he recoils, climbing higher as she whips her head around, searching for the pinprick she most definitely felt.

Eli frowns, teeth grinding as he flies ahead and out of sight. She's pushed him out of her mind. Something her grandmother taught her, no doubt.

He'd have to do this the old-fashioned way.

Out of her sight, he observes, curious. Roan parks her bike by a railing, but doesn't lock it up. Her hand lingers over it until she adjusts her pack and strides purposefully to the pneumatic doors leading to the main terminal of James Armstrong Richardson Airport.

He follows at a leisurely pace behind her, and for once, removes his invisibility. He wants her to see him, eventually, and also doesn't want to come off as a *mega creep*, as she'd probably say.

She doesn't have a bag to check, so she moves swiftly through security. Eli goes around the officers checking carry-on, and no one notices him, because he wills them not to. He allows Roan her space to find her gate and settle in. She sits down and turns her face to the tarmac beyond the windows.

It's the first time Eli has seen her since . . . he closes his eyes, and there she is on the riverbank. A faded star. Her light is even more diminished now, but it glows beneath the surface of her uneven skin like sleepy coals. Her hair has grown, sweeping her shoulders in choppy lengths.

There is something different about her. The weight in his chest grows heavy.

Roan finally turns her head away from profile, and the moment is gone. Eli suddenly recognizes that he's been clutching the blue plastic folder so tightly that the edge is cutting his palms. He relaxes. *Why are you letting a yippy little thing like her get the better of you?* he chides himself, striding out of anonymity and sitting directly behind her on the opposite bank of seats.

Eli abandons preamble. "So."

Roan leaps up, whirling to face the back of his head. Eli doesn't turn, savouring the slight triumph.

"Ugh," she groans, slouching back to back in her seat. "I knew it."

He scratches the place under his eye where she'd given him a burn scar, carefully arranging his face. "Hail the conquering graduate, off to see the world." He offers her the diploma over his shoulder.

After a moment, Roan takes it. "Where'd you get this?" He hears her opening it and shutting it just as quickly. She puts it down on the seat next to her but doesn't touch it again.

"Your friends wanted you to have it. Or something."

"Thanks," she says, ungrateful.

Eli snorts. "Right."

A swift backhand connects to Eli's head. He spins around, Roan's eyes blazing as he meets them.

"Who do you think you are, coming here? Can't you see I want to be alone?" She barks this through rigid teeth, hair and hackles up.

Eli doesn't bother addressing her directly. "What are you doing here, anyway? Running off somewhere?" He suddenly forgets why he's come here. She thinks it's out of concern, but he needed to see her because something was —

"Look, I'm . . ." Roan searches the floor. "I'm not in any state to be around anyone. It's —"

"Your grandmother. I know —"

She slides from apology to aggravation in a beat. "Stop doing that!"

Eli looks away and sits back down, body angled half towards her. "I'm sorry," he's surprised to admit. This apology is about Cecelia, since a word won't umbrella all his misdeeds.

She shrugs, eyes back on the tarmac. "Yeah. Well. Stuff and life and things, et cetera."

Another beat of silence pulses past them. Roan's fingernail flicks the diploma open, tapping it. "Someone else's life, that's for sure," she mutters to herself.

The boarding call dings over the intercom. Eli's looks up, and he reads the departure screen. *Toronto: Pre-boarding*.

Toronto. Either that's her final destination, or she's transferring to an international route. It could be a trip to anywhere. But something hums again in his chest — he knows what it is, allows it access to his mind just this once — and it warns him that he shouldn't probe her further for information. That her secrecy is as much to protect her as it is him.

But Eli ignores the wisp. "Where will you go?"

Roan is on her feet, backpack slung over both shoulders. Her eyes are for the advancing plane and nothing else. "Things have changed for me. I can't . . ." Her voice drops, and she looks at him frankly. "It's not safe for anyone to be around me anymore."

Whoever she means, she doesn't elaborate. Eli just nods and stands, coming round closer to her. They both consider some point or another in the distance.

"You're an idiot," Eli says.

Her face doesn't change. She shakes her head. "Ain't that the truth."

The whisper behind his controlled mind prods again, this time more insistent.

"What is it? What's changed?" he asks.

Her gaze is distant, unfocused. A baggage cart is leaving the docked plane, exchanged for another full one. The crew of the previous flight bleeds out of the aircraft, and Roan's breath catches, like that spirit eye of hers is showing her something unspeakable.

Then she touches her chest with her bitten-to-the-quick fingers. And Eli knows.

He grabs her roughly, startling her out of her reverie. She yanks away from him.

"You can't —" He looks blatantly at the space over her sternum, pulls back from the rising heat there. "You have to get rid of it. It'll *ruin you*."

At this she only smiles, faint and tired and utterly spent. But she doesn't acknowledge his words. She knows, as he does, that you can't simply *get rid of* the burdens they now share.

"Thanks for seeing me off. Sorry for being a grouch. I guess I'm still sore from all those times you tried to kill me."

Her hand twitches as though it might reach for his. But it doesn't. It stays at her side, then clutches her backpack strap as people begin boarding.

Suddenly her eyes are fierce. "Don't you dare come after me. And tell Phae and Barton and Natti that . . . that it's going to be fine."

Eli watches her go, rooted in place and only able to do as she's asked him, which is nothing. He saw the same thing behind her eyes that continues to plague him, though the trace of it is faint for now. But it will only get worse. For whom was she taking this risk? Where was she going? Why? *Why* had she accepted the stone?

Eli throws his mind into hers, but something pushes him back with as much force. He rebounds back to himself, the only fleeting image he is able to grasp being a crater of fire, and the world disappearing into it.

He blinks, and Roan Harken is lost in the crowd. Her high school diploma remains abandoned on the waiting seats of Gate 5.

EPILOGUE

The Bloodlands echo with the screams and anguish of its inhabitants. They feel the reverberations of one of their great masters in the depths of the Darkling Hold. Her brothers are often silent, but she has always made the worst protests.

She had tasted freedom. She had tasted Ancient blood. And now, that has been undone.

But her noise is not for pain.

The Gardener Urka cleaves its way through the hard-packed ash that is the ground, tunnelling until it slides into the hollow cavern, here, on the dark side of the universe.

Zabor's golden chains flash as she writhes, her tail blood-ied but coiled tight around her, pulsing, throbbing, aching.

"My mistress," Urka heaves, unable to withstand her misery any longer.

Zabor is suddenly still, her tail's coils coming undone

behind her mighty chains. She is gleaming with exertion and short of breath, but she is smiling. Urka's belly contracts with pride.

"*Obedient Gardener,*" Zabor sighs, content, "*you gave the Fox and the Owl the targe. You brought me home.*"

Urka bows low, filled with pleasure. "As you commanded, my mistress."

Zabor pulls something free from under her massive tail. Rounded and shining and heavy.

A black egg.

"*They gave me their children for hundreds of years. They gave me their power. All of the Five poured their blood into my greatest creation. And they manufactured their own ruin.*" She strokes the egg, rubbing it against her scales. "*Now we may begin.*"

Zabor tightens her tail around the egg, laying it at Urka's feet.

"*Bring it to your garden, above the holds of my brothers. It must hear them. And you must go with this child, Gardener. You must help it pave the way.*"

Urka feels blessed with this task. Were it able to weep, it would weep blood and ash and tenderness. It clutches the egg to its body and slithers back to its home above the Hold.

The Hope Trees growing above the Hold have been cut down and not replanted. From the warm remains of bark-flesh and ash, Urka builds a nest. The black egg responds to the Gardener's devotion. Urka feels something beating inside it.

Urka stands aside, and the darklings begin to sing.

The Bloodlands are quiet, reverent. Thankful. Their time has come.

Red lines seep upward around the stumps of the great trees Urka has felled. They intersect and in the ground make a fractal of bright circles.

The egg quivers with the song, with the pulsing ritual that it powers. The top of the egg cracks, and a red beam slices between this world and the next.

On Earth, in a subway station in Edinburgh, a man thought derelict, but who is consumed with devotion, receives the red signal of light, and allows it to consume him. Two trains thunder by on opposing tracks, whipping up garbage in the prickling air as the man offers his body to be made into the Great Hammer the darklings have been waiting for.

He inhales, eyes black and unforgiving.

Acknowledgements

In the intervening years since I first published a book, I've learned some things. Writing books — for me — is a fairly straightforward thing. One word in front of the other and four hundred pages later there it is. I said in the last book that it's a solitary activity, and it's still true. But staring at a wall doesn't make a good book, and it won't make you finish it. It takes a village. Lots of villages and different kinds. They influence you and inspire you to keep going. Without them, what's it all for?

So here are my villages:

Thanks to my publisher, ECW Press, who put this book out into the world and whose team has thrown themselves tirelessly into making it the best it can be. Special thanks goes to my editor, Jen Hale, whose continued unflagging support and enthusiasm keeps imposter syndrome at bay.

To my friends, colleagues, and companions who bolstered me the entire way: Clare Marshall, the bestest best friend anyone could ask for (who is more a sister, really); Sandra Kasturi and Brett Savory, my fake-parents no matter how far I roam; Chadwick Ginther, whose insights on writing a Manitoban fantasy series never steered me wrong; and everyone else — too numerous to name — from the epic Canadian spec-fic community at large that I am humbled to be a member of: you all inspire me daily. Thank you for taking me into the fold.

To my parents, who expected nothing less when I told them I was "working on a magic animal book with lots of action and violence" because they raised me on a strict diet of fantasy books, Star Trek, and Sailor Moon.

And to my husband, Peter — mostly known as Bear and sometimes referred to as "Dr. Hubs." You're the soul of patience when I'm up 'til three a.m. chewing my nails down in the word mines, or when I'm travelling nearly every weekend for work. Thank you for cleaning the kitchen and watering the plants when I forget to (which is often). You take me (and Sophie) on long walks to ease my manic writer heart and listen calmly to every idea, dream, complaint, or anxiety with the brevity of a sage, demanding I stay true to myself and keeping me from flying off the deep end. We've got more adventures ahead, you and I. Thanks for keeping me kind.

This is a different book. And the biggest chunk of thanks goes to the city that inspired it — Winnipeg, haunted and distressing and marvellous and magical city of rivers, home now to demons and teens who seem pretty bent on destroying it. If it wasn't for a fox crossing my path on Wellington Crescent in the winter of 2012, this book wouldn't exist.

And hi there again, reader. Thank you, most of all. It's nice to see you after such a long while apart. Please drop me a line whenever you want. It's you I do this for. And without you I'd be nothing.

❧ Coming Fall 2018 ❧

CHILDREN
OF THE
BLOODLANDS

THE REALMS OF ANCIENT, BOOK 2

❧ Sneak Peek ❧

The ONE TRUE CHILD

Northern Scotland

S top crying and be braver, Albert had said. He had said a lot of things. But now his mouth wasn't moving. The skin of his forehead was as split as the crack in the world they had found, but his forehead was leaking red, leaking too quickly and too much. Saskia had been crouched stiff and numb, more than an hour, pressing her whole body behind her hands into the wound to make the red stop.

Stop crying!

But she couldn't. Not in the dark, in the cold, as she made slow progress through the woods. She thought about all the things Albert had said, the things that led to this.

She swallowed, dragging the heavy sack through the crunchy leaves. The rope burned her small hands. Albert wouldn't say a thing anymore.

It had been their secret — his and Saskia's. What they'd found down in the woods at the bottom of the scrabby glen that day, months ago, just after Saskia had turned eight. Papa had been home, rare occasion that it was. She understood that they needed money to pay the bills, and that Papa needed to work as much as he did, but sometimes she resented the long road that kept him from them for weeks and weeks. And there was also the invisible road inside of them that divided their hearts. The road paved black when Mum had died.

On that brighter day, the day after her birthday, Papa took them for a walk. He wasn't as strong as she remembered him. He seemed bowed as a croggled tree. His knees weren't in good shape, and he was not young. Albert was fifteen, but their parents had had them late in life. Saskia didn't mind; this is how she thought all parents were. Old and grown and wiser than she ever could be.

But she could see age in Papa's stiff walk, the hours and days of driving taking its toll. It made her feel sick. "Go on ahead, ye wee gommerel," he'd said, sitting on the crest of a hill. "I can see ye from here."

But they'd gone too far into the woods, and Saskia knew Papa couldn't see them anymore. Albert always had to go far, as far as he could, to make it count. Saskia only ever wanted to be near him. She wanted his protection, and she wanted to protect him, too. But above all, she wanted to show she could be brave.

Albert stopped at a massive split in the rock of the munro, as if a big axe had cut it in half. The sun shone into it, revealing the barest crack in the world.

Albert climbed down first to investigate. Saskia didn't protest, but she wanted to.

"There's something down here," he said, frowning into the small crater. "You've got small hands. C'mon."

Saskia twisted her shirt in those small hands, swallowed, and picked her way down. She and Albert bent, heads touching, and she put her hand in—

"Ss!" Saskia pulled her hand back, shaking it.

"What?" Albert grabbed her hand, alarmed, and they both stared at the cut, the blood trickling around Saskia's wrist and dripping into the crack.

The ground shook, and Saskia screamed. Albert grabbed her hand, pulled her up the hill, and they took off in a blur back the way they'd come.

Papa was close to laying an egg because of how long they'd been gone. Albert was too breathless to explain the cut on Saskia's hand, to waylay Papa's anger as he wrapped it up too tightly in his handkerchief, making Saskia wince as he dragged them both home in furious silence. "Where did you get a knife?" Papa asked gruffly, not believing either of them when they said there was no knife. Just a crack in the ground whose darkness haunted them all the way home.

Albert stayed up all night thinking about that crack. "I had a dream about it," he said. "We have to go back." It didn't matter what Saskia felt about it — she would go where Albert went, and that he'd said *we*, said he wanted her there, meant she had to. They rushed out when Aunt Mildred had fallen asleep in her chair in front of the telly. They knew they'd have more than a chance the minute the whisky bottle clattered onto the sideboard. It was summer — what little they have of it in the north — and out here, children could do as they pleased. They could chase the massive herds of deer, they could scrabble up and down rocks. They could get into trouble. It wasn't like in the cities or bigger towns like Durness or Thurso. So much desolate freedom here. Saskia knew it'd have to end sometime, but she didn't suspect it would be this soon.

They went back to the crack, and it was so much wider. The ground around it was black. "Probably that earthquake," Albert guessed, but Saskia didn't remember there being earthquakes in the Highlands.

Then there was a bang, loud like thunder, and Saskia jumped and ran, ran fast and far without looking back until she realized she was running alone. She twisted and screamed, "Albie!" But he hadn't followed. She couldn't leave him behind, knew he'd never do such a thing to her, so she turned around, and he was just as she'd left him, standing there above the crack, mouth open, frozen in awe.

The grey amorphous thing crawled out of the world and into the air. A column of ash. A straight cloud of smoke. It opened a mouth and words came out. "I am the gardener," it said. "Thank you for raising me."

The voice was soothing, calm and clear. Saskia was shaking all over, but she wouldn't leave Albert. And she looked down at her hand, with the big scratchy bandage, and knew this was all her fault.

❧

There was no road in the woods. Saskia was following the brook, which crept along an impassable munro. *What's inside the mountains?* Albert had asked whenever Aunt Mildred took them driving for a change of scenery. *The sharp, dead peaks have many secrets*, she'd say, but Aunt Mildred wasn't prone to fairy stories. Or tales of monsters.

But they'd found themselves in a monster story anyway.

Saskia stumbled, pitched, and slid on her knees. She'd dropped the rope, but when she whirled around, the sack was still there. She'd wrapped Albert in his Ninja Turtles bedsheet, but it was faded from years of washing. It seemed to glow in the dark.

She whimpered when she noticed the dark patches showing through. She clenched her bloody hands and stood on shaking feet.

Her hands stung even worse now, as if the cut were still fresh. Picking the rope back up and continuing on was so much harder than starting out. Why did she have to be such a crybaby? Why couldn't she be like Albert? Why did she have to do this alone? There wasn't much she really understood — not in the way grown-ups did — but she knew that if she didn't do this, she'd lose her brother forever. She would be in the biggest trouble of her life. And not with Papa or Aunt Mildred. What waited for her in the dark woods scared her most.

She could tell she was getting close, though. The humming in the ground thrummed through her tired legs into her bones. So she kept going.

❧

Urka told Albert and Saskia that they were special. That it had come from a land plagued with ruin, and that she and Albert were the key to saving the three rulers of this faraway place who were imprisoned there forever.

These three rulers, according to Urka, had a precious child, and it had been sent to the Uplands — that's what it called Earth — to get help. To find a family. And Saskia and Albert were the family they were waiting for.

Every day that they sneaked out to visit it, Urka got bigger and the forest around it got smaller. It said that eating the trees was the only way to get its strength up after the long journey, and that the trees here weren't like the trees back in its home. "But soon that will change," Urka promised. "Soon this world will be covered in the trees I know."

Saskia tried to look Urka in its eyes, all six of them, to try to see if it was telling the truth, the way she did when Albert told her a fib to get a rise out of her. But it hurt to look into those eyes — like looking too long at the sun. She should have known then.

Albert asked, right at the start, if Urka could grant wishes. Urka was quiet a long time as its ash body hardened to stone, grew huge in the shadow of the mountain that hid it. It said *yes*, a horrible bone-grating affirmation, then praised Albert for his cleverness. Saskia scrunched her nose and questioned *how*, especially because Urka could barely move a few feet from the crack it had crawled out of and seemed weak despite how many trees and dead things it had shoved into the big mouth in its growing belly. That was when the eyes fell on Saskia, and she turned away. That was when Urka saw she doubted. That was her second mistake.

❧

In the deep, dark woods, she finally collapsed. The moon shone through the cleft in the rock, shone onto the place where the crack had opened into a valley and devoured the light. Her head pounded and she was impossibly hungry.

"Child," came the voice, like the metal hangers in her closet grating on the rusty bar Papa said he'd replace but never did. Saskia shrank and instinctively twisted, covering the sheet-covered lump of Albert with her body. "Child," it said again. "At long last."

～≈

Albert became loyal to Urka the minute its smoke-column head came out of the ground. Albert trusted it and everything it said. "It's a proper quest," he said, almost to himself, nodding and walking with a determined spring all the way home. "I knew I was destined for it. I knew it."

Papa had always given Albert a hard time for not being more into sports, for not getting better grades. Papa was a hard person with high expectations. But Saskia always saw that it hurt Albert, even when he pressed his mouth closed and said "Right," after each critical blow. Saskia thought if she did her best, it would be good enough for both of them, but it never was.

And Urka bestowed easy praise. It was grateful that Albert tended to it. The bigger its body got, the bigger its promises became. Promises of great power, of rewards, of wishes granted. They gathered bigger and bigger bundles of wood, stole the axe from the garden shed. "I don't think we're supposed to do this," Saskia had warned. Cutting down the trees here seemed like a crime, but Albert told her to stop whining. That this didn't happen to every kid, and they should be grateful.

Then Urka spoke of their mother.

"Do you miss her?" it asked. Albert flushed in the way he always did when he was about to cry, but his jaw compressed and he nodded. Urka seemed only to speak to Albert now, almost wary of Saskia. She missed their mother, too, though she barely remembered her.

"My masters can bring her back." Urka's biggest promise of all. "They can bring back anyone you have ever lost."

"How?" Saskia asked. Her doubt was sharp still, and her words echoed loud off the split mountain.

Urka smiled, feeding a massive tree trunk into its belly. That was the first time Saskia had noticed the dark flames there. "With a power I can give to you. A power you have earned."

Albert was desperate. He demanded that power, like it was Christmas and he wanted lordship over Saskia's new toys. She thought he'd been changing more into a grown-up before this, but when they'd met Urka, Albert's eyes shone with a petulance she'd never seen. A willingness to do anything blindly for what he was owed. "Give it to me!" he barked. Urka was more than happy to deliver.

Something black and cobweb-wispy floated out from the horrible furnace inside Urka's belly into the daylight. Saskia screamed when it touched Albert. To her shame, she went totally numb, unable to stop it, because she knew it was bad, knew she could never abide it on her skin, knew she wasn't brave enough. But moments after it touched Albert's hand, it vanished.

Albert jerked. "What did you do? It's gone! I don't feel any different!"

Urka bowed its head. "Patience," it said, and Albert

looked insulted. "Soon all our family's dreams will come true."

Albert got reckless after that. He pushed his mates too hard. He didn't play fair. He hit his best mate Roger right across the mouth and broke the skin, all because Roger said Albert was acting funny. No one said anything after that. No one said much to Albert in the days before Aunt Mildred said the same, reaming him out for hitting Roger. Albert was scratching his neck, the place where the black splotch had appeared the night before.

"What's happened to Ava's sweet boy?" Millie muttered, resurrecting their dead mother — her own sister of whom she'd always been jealous. "Imagine what she'd think to see ye now."

Saskia yelled, tried hard to wrench Albert's hands away from Aunt Millie's throat the minute they shot there. Saskia clawed and scraped at him like an animal, but he swept his sister aside like tissue paper, and she crashed over the table, taking a lamp with her. She looked over her scabby knees to see Albert pull away from Aunt Millie gently, like he'd planted a kiss on her neck with his hands, and Saskia saw that she was still breathing, clutching the arms of her chair like the room was spinning.

A collar of black webbing spread over her pasty neck. Her feet hammered against the chair like she was trying to run away but couldn't get up. Then her shoes burst, and horrible black tendrils — roots — stabbed through the carpet and the hardwood, and as Albert slipped out smiling, Saskia screamed and screamed.

"Come closer, child," Urka spoke to Saskia now, out of shadow, reaching her with smoke tendrils. "The time has come to reclaim what has been lost. Do not be afraid." But Saskia knew better.

"The time has come," Urka said again. "Bring the boy to the gardener. Urka will make it better. My masters will be your new fathers and mother. They will heal all."

"How?" asked Saskia. "What will you do with him?" She hadn't realized she was crying so hard, tears and snot mixing, drowning her, falling onto the blackening face of her brother, who could have been sleeping but for the blood. She dared not ask "Can you really bring him back?" in case Urka changed its mind.

"Oh my sweet child of earth and ash," Urka said, and Saskia felt something in her hair — something hard and sharp; that must have been Urka's hand trying to soothe her. It clenched her scalp. "Give the boy to me, and I will show you."

⌇⌇

When Saskia had stopped screaming and retching in the living room, she was afraid to move. She stared at Aunt Millie, who had become some kind of horrible tree, her feet roots throbbing and churning the floor, her hands and arms stretched above her head, branches reaching into the ceiling, searching for a way out through the cracking drywall.

Albert had killed Aunt Millie. Or had turned her into a monster. Either way, he had done this. Air still rasped out of the place Millie's mouth had been. Her eyes were covered in hard black bark. She looked like she was trapped in a nightmare.

Albert had not returned, and Saskia was afraid to go after him, afraid to move and wake up the thing occupying Aunt Millie's chair. But she wanted to be brave, even now, so she went outside shakily. It was morning, grey and overcast. Looking out onto the glen, there weren't many places Albert could be, but Saskia zeroed in on the middle distance where the woods dipped down towards the brook and the cradle of hills. She knew Albert was there, but she wasn't about to go. She would wait. She would scream and cry and beg and she would get Albert far away from here, from the monster they'd woken in the woods, and to a hospital in a city. Because surely he was sick. Surely a doctor could help.

Saskia sat on the wooden step, knees drawn up, head buried in her arms, until it was dark. She heard a stick break and whipped her head up. Albert stood very close by. He looked much older, and grave. But more than that — even in the darkness, Saskia could see the black creeping up the collar of his T-shirt, the tips of his fingers. He stared at her like he couldn't believe she was there.

"Urka said it could bring Mum back," he said. His voice was distant, and more childlike than ever. It was a reason, but even Albert didn't sound like he believed it.

"Aunt Millie . . ." Saskia started. But she was so tired. She wanted her mum, too, wanted Papa more than anything, but she and Albert were alone now. The roots of the tree that had once been Aunt Millie had ripped out the phone line. The nearest neighbour was a car ride away. They were trapped.

"Roger is a believer now, too," Albert said quietly. "It's starting. Soon all our dreams will come true. We will be a proper family. You'll see."

He reached for Saskia, but she was lightning fast, on her feet, off the stairs, and away from him, a bit down the hill. Albert didn't reach for her again. "You're so selfish," he said. "Stop crying." And then he went into the house for the last time.

Saskia shouldn't have followed. But she was too young to stop and think. "A-Albie," she sobbed. "We have to . . . to call someone. We can't—"

He twisted and lunged so suddenly Saskia barely had a breath to get out of the way. Albert smashed into the sideboard, glass and wood exploding with strength that had never been his. Saskia stumbled deeper into the house, towards their shared bedroom, not thinking, blinded by tears and terror. But when Albert struck out again, like a venomous snake, something turned to rock in Saskia's stomach. "Stop it!" she shouted, as if it were just a game and she'd had enough.

And she met the blow of her brother's whole body, turning him aside with a powerful shove. Slowly, as if underwater, Albert's shoe caught the carpet, his eyes his own, only for a second, before his head struck the bedpost, and the light left those frightened eyes forever.

❧

Be brave, Saskia thought again. She unwrapped Albert all the way and did so gingerly, afraid that she would catch the black sickness that had twisted her golden-haired brother so. But she would do anything Urka said if it meant bringing him back. If it meant untangling the thing that had wrapped itself so firmly around his heart. Or erasing her own horrible mistake.

She stood back and turned. Urka had grown enormous, like it was carved from the munro it had split in half. It spread its arms, and at the end of them, the two axes it had for hands twisted and changed into claws. It gathered Albert up and fed him into its belly furnace. Albert did not burn, but glowed like a coal. Saskia held onto herself in a tight hug, because there was no one else to hold her, to tell her it would be okay. Because she knew she could never go home again.

"You must believe," Urka said, straining its horrible hands to the sky and then to the ground, its rocky body growing and humming and glowing ever brighter. "Will you help my masters rise to their rightful place? Will you devote yourself to your fathers? Your mother?" A flicker in the furnace. "*To their one true child?*"

Saskia was not stupid, no matter how many times Albert had told her she was. Saskia was bright and selfless and knew deep down she was a good person. But she would have done every terrible thing she was afraid of to bring Albert back. So she took that goodness and locked it tightly away, hoping maybe one day it might save her.

"Yes," she said. "Yes."

Deep within Urka's furnace, she saw Albert's eyes open, and a black tendril from her brother reached for her and made her part of it.

GET THE EBOOK FREE!

At ECW Press, we want you to enjoy this book in whatever format you like, whenever you like. Leave your print book at home and take the ebook to go! Purchase the print edition and receive the ebook free. Just send an e-mail to ebook@ecwpress.com and include:

- the book title
- the name of the store where you purchased it
- your receipt number
- your preference of file type: PDF or ePub?

A real person will respond to your e-mail with your ebook attached. Thank you for supporting an independently owned Canadian publisher with your purchase!